THE SORCERESS AND THE BARBARIAN

"Is this supposed to be someone's idea of a joke?" Deanne demanded, putting angry fists to her hips.

"I believe you already know who I am," Tarren answered, his own anger and annoyance rekindled by hers. "I have come to demand that you stop dreaming about me."

"What are you talking about? I don't dream about Tarren the Barbarian, I write about him," she growled back. "I don't know what sort of game this is, but I don't give a damn. My final response to you is a one-key answer named 'return.'"

This time she reached out to touch something below a demon-lit box sitting atop another gray box. On the instant, a sound began and the woman turned back to show him an annoyingly pleased smile.

Tarren felt a bodiless tugging through the magical doorway behind him. He was about to be drawn back into another bit of madness. Tarren had never been so furious in his life and with one step forward, he reached out and pulled the sorceress to him and allowed the two of them to be swept back through the doorway together.

PUT SOME FANTASY IN YOUR LIFE—
FANTASTIC ROMANCES FROM PINNACLE

TIME STORM   (728, $4.99)
by Rosalyn Alsobrook
Modern-day Pennsylvanian physician JoAnn Griffin only believed
what she could feel with her five senses. But when, during a freak
storm, a blinding flash of lightning sent her back in time to 1889,
JoAnn realized she had somehow crossed the threshold into another century and was now gazing into the smoldering eyes of a
startlingly handsome stranger. JoAnn had stumbled through a rip
in time . . . and into a love affair so intense, it carried her to a point
of no return!

SEA TREASURE   (790, $4.50)
by Johanna Hailey
When Michael, a dashing sea captain, is rescued from drowning by
a beautiful sea siren—he does not know yet that she's actually a
mermaid. But her breathtaking beauty stirred irresistible yearnings
in Michael. And soon fate would drive them across the treacherous
Caribbean, tossing them on surging tides of passion that tran-
scended two worlds!

ONCE UPON FOREVER   (883, $4.99)
by Becky Lee Weyrich
A moonstone necklace and a mysterious diary written over a century ago were Clair Summerland's only clues to her true identity.
Two men loved her—one, a dashing civil war hero . . . the other, a
daring jet pilot. Now Clair must risk her past and future for a passion that spans two worlds—and a love that is stronger than time
itself.

SHADOWS IN TIME   (892, $4.50)
by Cherlyn Jac
Driving through the sultry New Orleans night, one moment Tori's
car spins out of control; the next she is in a horse-drawn carriage
with the handsomest man she has ever seen—who calls her wife—-
but whose eyes blaze with fury. Sent back in time one hundred
years, Tori is falling in love with the man she is apparently trying to
kill. Now she must race against time to change the tragic past and
claim her future with the man she will love through all eternity!

Available wherever paperbacks are sold, or order direct from the
Publisher. Send cover price plus 50¢ per copy for mailing and han-
dling to Penguin USA, P.O. Box 999, c/o Dept. 17109, Bergen-
field, NJ 07621. Residents of New York and Tennessee must
include sales tax. DO NOT SEND CASH.

ENCHANTING

SHARON GREEN

PINNACLE BOOKS
WINDSOR PUBLISHING CORP.

For Nina Romberg and Jane Archer, two of the best friends it's possible to have. If not for you, this book would never have been written.

And for Kerry Gilley, who is sometimes silly enough to ask for things.

PINNACLE BOOKS are published by

Windsor Publishing Corp.
850 Third Avenue
New York, NY 10022

First Printing: December, 1994

Printed in the United States of America

Prologue

The cavern he had come through was pitch black, and nothing but the torch he carried kept him from any number of hidden ways to die. But now he stood at the rear of the cave, and a pearly light made the torch unnecessary. Where that light came from was a question he could not specifically answer, but in general he knew its source: magic . . . the same magic that had brought him there . . . the magic he would have to overcome if he was to triumph. And he *had* to triumph . . .

For Tarren the Barbarian, there was no other thought than victory. He stood more than six and a half feet tall, with long, bright red hair, eyes the blue of winter ice, shoulders wide enough for two men, arms thick with corded muscle. He wore his mighty broadsword scabbarded across his broad back, a long dagger strapped to his otherwise bare thigh. There were few beings, mortal or otherwise, who would challenge him. To do so would be very unwise. Tarren the Barbarian refused to acknowledge the possibility of defeat, and for that reason he had never made its acquaintance.

He set his torch into an empty sconce on the wall,

then wiped his moist palm on the blue breechcloth that was his only clothing. He had found the lair of the serpent, and somewhere behind it was the fabled treasure room he sought. There was more in that room than gold and jewels. If the fates allowed him to walk in without opposition, he would take the magic crystal and no more. Treasure he already had in plenty; the rest the serpent could keep.

A slithering sound from behind him made him whirl around as he reached for his sword, and not a moment too soon. The guardian of the treasure had appeared from wherever it slept, and now rose up in preparation for battle. Tarren had known it would be big, but even the word *giant* failed to describe the creature's dimensions. Tarren was used to looking down at his opponents; this time he looked up—*way* up. The snake was hooded like a cobra, and coiled at least seven feet above the human it meant to kill.

Had shock frozen Tarren in place he would have been dead, but this was hardly the first time he had found himself pitted against a seemingly invincible opponent. The snake hissed and weaved back and forth, getting ready to strike, but the man anticipated the attack and struck first. Swinging the famous sword that almost had a life of its own, Tarren's muscles drove the weapon in a sweep meant to cut the serpent in half. That would be the end of the fight, and then he could—

But his blade merely bounced off the serpent's skin, slicing it open only shallowly. Instead of blood, green slime oozed from the wound, which had in no way incapacitated the creature. The snake's hissing increased in volume and it struck in turn, making it necessary for Tarren to jump back as fast as he could. The fight was on, and the quick victory the barbarian had been expecting was now hiding somewhere in the shadows.

The pearly light glinted off Tarren's blade as he settled down to swinging and jumping, swinging and jumping. Rather than retreating, the serpent struck for him repeatedly in an effort to put an end to the cutting wounds its opponent delivered, and it was not entirely unsuccessful. After a short while Tarren also bled, and red mixed in with green on the cavern walls and floor. The creature's fangs were filled with poison, and if not for the charm Tarren had found in an ogre's cave, he would have already been dead.

But he *did* have the charm, and despite the pain and growing exhaustion that filled him, he continued to fight. He had to keep going until Fael and the other men arrived, and prayed they brought with them what Tarren now realized was his only hope against the serpent. He had won *that* magical device during a different battle. If only he had realized sooner how much he would need it . . .

Fael, second in command to Tarren the Barbarian, led the small group of men toward the only source of light in the cavern. He had felt strongly that his help would be needed, and now, thanks to whatever kind fate watched over his giant leader, Fael knew what would surely be required.

He and the men heard the battle before they saw it,

and once they got close enough they were sorry they *could* see it. The serpent was bigger than any of them had expected, and Tarren looked like a child beside it. But Tarren was a deadly child with a deadly weapon, two things the creature was clearly learning. While it bled an oozing green substance from countless wounds and its swaying movements looked unsteady, it was, however, far from defeated.

Tarren, unfortunately, was another story. The man had shoulders like an ox and the chest of a stallion, bulging muscles and an uncanny skill with a sword, but one look at him said his previously limitless strength was threatening to fail him. His body was covered with the snake's green slime and the red of his own blood, and his mighty sword, Fael determined, would soon be too heavy for him to lift.

But that was why Fael had brought the magical arrow Tarren had won during their last adventure. The legend on its box said it was meant for the slaying of the undying, and *something* had told Fael to dig it out and bring it along. He did not entirely trust that strange inner voice, but it was hardly the first time he had been possessed of the alien conviction, and it always turned out to be working for Tarren's benefit.

Taking the arrow carefully from his quiver, Fael nocked it. For someone who made his living selling his skill with a sword, Fael was incredibly good with a bow. Right now he would need every bit of that ability, for that voice was back and whispering in his ear again.

The small diamond-shaped marking, just below the jaws of the snake. *That* was the target he would have to hit, the voice in his head insisted on it. It made no matter that the huge serpent was swaying back and forth like a reed in a gale. Hit that diamond, or Tarren would die.

Fael took a deep breath, then raised his bow and drew back the nock. Even as he did, his eye had seen a pattern in the agitated swaying and his fingers released the string without further thought. The arrow sang on its lightning-fast flight—and sank deep into the center of the diamond.

The serpent screamed as if it were a woman in agony, a sound that made every man there clap his hands to his ears. The sole exception was Tarren, who looked as if he were in nearly as much pain. With what must have been his last ounce of strength, he swung his sword, and the giant blade cut the serpent in half. The screaming stopped as the serpent collapsed, and once it was down Tarren fell to his knees.

One

It was a pretty enough day for almost anything, and I wasn't the only one who had decided to take a run. The only difference was that I ran three miles every day, and most of the others out were Sunday runners. If you think there's a correlation between Sunday runners and Sunday drivers, you're absolutely right. But where the Sunday driver can kill you with a couple of tons of mishandled automobile, the Sunday runner can only annoy the hell out of you while in the process of killing *himself*. They think a pair of jogging shorts and a tank top worn by a female are open invitations, and if the female is attractive enough, they half kill themselves catching up and trying to *keep* up.

"Well, hi there," the specimen I'd noticed a few minutes earlier panted as he finally reached my side. "Great day for a run, isn't it?"

I gave him no more than a glance and a nod, but couldn't help smiling at the line he'd come up with. I would have preferred laughing in his face as a comment on his originality, but I didn't want to encourage him.

"Isn't this a great neighborhood for running?" he

tried next, the words as uneven as his breathing. "Imagine, putting a running track in the grass median—now that's town planning. I always say it pays to live among folks who demand as much as you do. Have you lived around here long?"

"About two years," I supplied in a murmur, paying more attention to the beautiful houses on either side of the street than to him. He had light brown hair and blue eyes, and was a bit over six feet, only a little taller than me. He was wearing sweats rather than spandex and a tank top, which probably meant he was out of shape. But I'd no doubt he owned the latter. He struck me as the sort who flaunted what he had, even when what he had wasn't much.

"Two years!" he echoed, making himself sound surprised. "You've lived here two years, and this is the first time we've met? I really must be slacking off in getting to know my neighbors, and that can't be allowed to continue. We'll just have to have dinner tonight to make up for it. What time should I pick you up?"

I felt tempted to point out that he obviously thought he'd already picked me up, but that just would have prolonged my annoyance. I needed something—short of breaking his arm—to make him go away, and a moment's thought gave me an idea.

"Gee," I said with an empty-headed glance in his direction, which underscored the blondness of my hair. "I guess dinner would be okay; but my doctor said I better not do anything else, at least until I'm not *contagious* anymore. But all the penicillin must have done *something* by now, so if you want to try anyway—"

"Uh—thanks, that's really nice of you," he said as fast as possible, a trapped look suddenly replacing the interest in his eyes. "I'd take you up on that, but—I just remembered an appointment I forgot all about. We'll have that dinner some other time—and how about that? This is my street."

He actually put on a burst of speed to reach the corner we were approaching, then turned left and jogged away without looking back. I couldn't help laughing. Every now and then it's fun to play dumb blonde, and thinking up outrageous stories to go with the pose is the easiest part. After all, if a writer can't do it right, who can? It was just—

I took a deep breath to push away the agitation, trying for the millionth time to handle the dilemma I was in as easily as I handled everything else. But "everything else" didn't involve my family, not to mention a problem with them that everyone else in the world thought I should be able to laugh off. It wasn't even slightly important, so why couldn't I simply ignore it? Sure, right, ignore it, along with the fact that I'd have to be *with* my family in another few days.

I was momentarily distracted by a red convertible with its top down cruising up the street to my left. If it had been moving any slower, it would have been parked. The two men inside just kept staring and grinning until we'd passed each other, looking as if they were considering the idea of buying me. I know there are women who are bothered by things like that, but being stared at isn't hard to tune out, especially if you know how to take care of yourself.

Oddly enough, it was my family problem that had freed me from worrying about what strange men might have in mind, but that didn't make the problem any easier to live with.

The headphones attached to my belt brushed my arm, almost as if they were reminding me they were there, but today I was in no mood to listen to music. I'd intended to use my three-mile run to decide whether or not to attend the family barbecue that was coming up, but the run was almost over and I still hadn't made up my mind. My father and brothers were expecting me to be there, of course, since from *their* point of view there *was* no problem. It had been the same all the years I'd been growing up. Maybe if Mom hadn't died when I was still so young . . .

But she *had* died, so it was just Dad and my four brothers and me, the only girl and the baby. Being the baby usually means being spoiled rotten, and being the only girl means more of the same, but if you happen to have a mind, the day comes when you stop wanting to be spoiled and start to look around for what all that spoiling has made you miss.

And what it had made *me* miss was being a full member of the family. Dad and my brothers had gotten into bodybuilding together. Talk about bonding! They always went to the gym together, a practice they continued even when two of my brothers married and moved into homes of their own. When I first realized I was excluded from an important part of their lives, I pointed out that I wasn't that much smaller than they, and that I wanted to go too.

Once all the laughter died down, I was told that bodybuilding wasn't for the "baby," and certainly not for a girl. I was welcome to come along and watch, but as for joining them—uh-uh, no way. Stubbornness is an integral part of my character, so I pestered my father until he got me a membership, then set about trying to do as the rest of my family did. The only problem was, no matter how well I did, my brothers were able to do better. The male body is made to be stronger than the female body, and I had no real desire to look like some of those lady bodybuilders, all ropy slabs of muscle.

I broke out of my musing momentarily to notice that two women were trotting toward me from the far end of the block; it wouldn't be long before we reached one another. Since they ran side by side rather than single file, I wondered if they'd separate to let me by, or if they would try to force me to go around them. Knowing the people in that neighborhood, it could be either, forcing me into the position of needing to *show* them . . .

The way I'd felt I had to *show* my father and brothers. I'd been forced to accept the fact that I couldn't do what they did even when I was given the chance, so I decided to do *better* than they. All they did was work out with weights, so I branched out in every direction I could think of. I learned to fence and use a bow and ride a horse, I learned to shoot pistols and rifles, and even learned karate. If it was considered physical and rough, I learned how to do it, but somehow none of it ever gave me what I really wanted.

So I began to write, and the character I created put my father and brothers to shame. My character was a giant barbarian who was not only an expert with weapons, but was also stronger than the male members of my family could ever be. He was better than all of them put together, and the adventures he had were ones that would have made my father and brothers faint. The books turned out to be immensely popular, so much so that I'd been able to buy the house I now lived in, but—

"Excuse me, but aren't you Deanne Lane?" A voice interrupted my thoughts, and I came back to the world to realize I'd reached the two women. They now ran to either side of me and a little ahead, going back the way they'd just come.

"Yes, I'm Deanne Lane," I agreed, speaking to the woman on my left, who had asked the question. She and her friend were both of average height with brown hair and eyes, and they seemed to be in better shape than my previous company. They not only wore shorts and tank tops, they weren't breathing any harder than I was.

"Oh, Ms. Lane, we were hoping it was you," the woman enthused, her friend grinning silently to my right. "We don't mean to bother you, but we're both really big fans of yours. We *love* your barbarian, and we've even gotten our husbands hooked on your books. How ever do you manage to write so *realistically?*"

"To be honest, I have no idea," I admitted with a wry smile. "My editor claims I use black magic, but that's not to say she's complaining. She and I agree that wherever the stories are coming from, we hope they just keep on coming."

"So do the rest of us," the woman on my right contributed with a laugh. "Would you mind if we bring out a couple of books for you to autograph the next time we see you coming by? We live just over there, and we know you go by here almost every day."

She waved toward the houses on the right; the women were fairly close neighbors of mine. But even if they weren't, I have certain beliefs concerning autographing.

"Not only wouldn't I mind, I'd consider it a pleasure," I told them both as firmly as I could. "If not for the people who buy my books, I'd be doing my running in a much less charming neighborhood. You bring out the books and just *try* to keep me from autographing them."

"No thanks," the one on my left said with a laugh, holding her hands up. "Not only don't I *want* to stop you, I'd hate having to try. Can you *really* do all the things it says you can in the back of your books?"

"Yes, but that means I *can't* do the much larger number of things that *weren't* mentioned," I pointed out with a grin.

The women laughed, and then said goodbye and went back to running in their original direction. The encounter made me feel good—until I remembered what I'd been thinking about before being interrupted. My barbarian novels were immensely popular, but they still didn't change my family standing. Dad and the boys were as proud as possible of me, but they continued to treat me differently.

Each of them was allowed to live his own life without interference from any of the others, but *all* of them felt free to get on *my* case. The five of them were equals, but the baby girl of the family needed to be looked after and guided into doing the right thing. For the last year they had been guiding me toward marriage, despite the fact that two of my brothers were still single. *I* was a girl, and girls needed to settle down and have families of their own. When they found out eight months ago that the man I was dating slept at my place more often than his own, the fat really hit the fire.

"Which started a fight that almost ended up with physical casualties," I muttered out loud, almost as annoyed now as I'd been then. My unmarried brothers were as far from being virgins as it's possible to get, but *I* was supposed to be different because *I* was a girl. Telling them where they could put their narrow-mindedness had caused something of a scene, and if Dad hadn't shouted the boys down I probably would have had to hurt one of them.

But then Dad had turned on *me,* and the lecture had lasted three times longer than any previous ones. It ended with the ultimatum that I'd better find someone to marry before they found someone *for* me, and contained a warning: If they ever came visiting unexpectedly and caught me with a man I'd been sleeping with but wasn't married to, they'd make sure it was a long while before he slept with *any* woman ever again. When I told them they'd have to go through *me* to do anything like that, they shrugged and ignored the threat. After all, what could a baby girl do?

It took me a couple of minutes to calm down, and by then my house was in sight. Three miles of running was behind me, and I still hadn't decided whether or not to go to the barbecue. It had been four months since the latest explosion, and by now they might have mellowed out and forgotten about the whole thing. But the moon might also be made of green cheese in the places no astronauts had landed. If I went to the barbecue without a prospective husband but still insisting on my right to conduct my personal life the way I saw fit, there would almost certainly be another fight. And yet I missed my father and brothers and wanted to see them . . .

"Damn fool," I growled at myself as I reached the driveway and slowed to a walk, at the same time pulling off my sweatband. "You're like the mule who starved to death between two haystacks because he couldn't make up his mind which one to eat. Maybe you'll get lucky and have a building fall on you, or you'll get hit by a car. Then you won't *have* to decide."

I was really disgusted with myself, and what made it even worse was that I *liked* the idea of having a building fall on me or being hit by a car. When you find two fates like that preferable to making a decision, it's safe to say you have a problem. I felt the urge to mutter some more, but as I approached the front door it opened, and Jessie, my housekeeper and all-around helper, stuck her head out.

"Great timing, Dee," she said, waving the cordless phone. "Your editor wants to talk to you."

"She could have at least waited until after I showered," I muttered, but not with any real annoyance. Erin Wayse was a friend as well as my editor, and wouldn't have minded waiting if I asked her to. I took the phone as I walked through the door and said to Erin, "What do you want *now,* Simon Legree? I told you I'd have the new book finished by last night. It's finished. If you want to know if I've started the next one yet, the answer is no and get off my back."

"I see you haven't made up your mind about the barbecue yet," Erin commented evenly. "If it takes much longer, I'll forget what you're like when you aren't in a foul mood. How did the book turn out? Did my suggestions work?"

"Suggestions?" I echoed, carrying the phone into my office and sitting in a chair Jessie had covered with a towel, to prevent me from staining it with sweat. It was little things like that that made her an absolute jewel and a lifesaver, and I wondered what my father and brothers would say if I announced I was marrying *her.*

"Those weren't suggestions, they were orders," I replied, enjoying the house's air conditioning after the heat outside. "If they hadn't been I probably would have ignored them. Okay, so here it is: The barbarian inadvertently insults a magician, and because of that he has a series of amusing 'accidents.' Or maybe I should say the readers will find the accidents amusing. *He* finds them embarrassing and infuriating."

"It's about time he misses getting his own way with everything," Erin said. "The experience will do him good, even if it doesn't happen to teach him humility. What about the love interest?"

"Yes, she's in there too," I sighed, noticing that my office needed straightening again. Jessie wasn't allowed to touch that room, so it only got cleaned when the debris and dead bodies were piled too high for me to climb over. It was almost that time, maybe in another month or two . . .

"You still don't sound happy about giving the barbarian a woman of his own," Erin commented. "Doesn't she work well in the plot?"

"As a matter of fact, she doesn't," I admitted with another sigh. "If you want the truth, I can't see how *any* woman can find the barbarian attractive, especially a competent woman. If it were me and he started to order me around, I'd tell him what to do with himself in one-syllable words."

"And then the sparks would fly," Erin said with a laugh. "He definitely isn't the kind of man to take backtalk. But the woman he pairs up with can't be a dishrag or doormat, she has to be almost as strong as he is. So what did you do?"

"I used magical 'accidents' to make him unbend a little," I told her. "He doesn't develop humility, but he does learn to have more of a sense of humor. Considering what his lady-fair is like, he tends to need it . . . Erin, why are you so interested in this woman? If I didn't know you better, I'd say you wanted the love interest to be there so you could identify with her."

"That's ridiculous, Dee," she answered much too quickly. "It just happens to be time for a woman to be introduced, and I wanted to be sure it was done right. But what did you mean, considering what his lady is like, he'll need his sense of humor? Just what exactly is she like?"

"She's tough, mean, and nasty, and she loves to give him a hard time," I said, curious about the reaction I'd get. "She keeps him in a perpetual rage, and his happiest thoughts are ones about murdering her with his bare hands."

"Dee, you didn't!" she almost wailed. "Tell me you didn't give him a woman he can't even make love to!"

"All right, I didn't," I obliged, enjoying her distress. "He starts out distrusting her and ends up wanting her more than that throne he'll eventually be fighting for. He does get her, but the book ends before he decides whether or not to stay with her. Or, to be more precise, whether or not *she* decides to stay with *him*. Not an easy decision."

"You know, sometimes I really don't understand you," Erin huffed. "You sound as if you don't find the barbarian the least bit attractive, or even particularly interesting. Considering how the rest of us feel, why are you the only exception?"

"Maybe I'm the only sane person in a very large madhouse," I replied wryly. "I told you before what would happen if the barbarian and I ever came face to face, and it would probably happen in about five minutes or less. You seem to forget that I *can't* have a crush on him the way the rest of you do. If I did, I'd never be able to put him through what he *has* to go through. I suppose I'd think twice about kicking him out of my bed if I ever found him there, but only for as long as he kept quiet."

"Dee, you're impossible," Erin pronounced. "Any other woman would kill to be in bed with that hunk you created, but you don't give a damn. You're a pain and you make me sick, and I want a copy of the manuscript by tonight."

"After you asked so nicely, how can I refuse?" I said. "Do you want it printed on scented tissue paper, tied with a passion-red ribbon, and hand-delivered to your door by a bard strumming a lute?"

"The usual twenty-weight bond will do," she said lightly, "with or without the scent and ribbon. And tell the bard he can stay home with his feet up. I'll only be about twenty-five miles away from you today, attending my aunt's birthday party, so I'll swing by. But seriously, if you didn't plan to print it out today . . ." Her voice trailed off; she didn't want to appear too eager, poor thing.

"I do have plans to go out, but that shouldn't make much difference," I soothed, trying to make up for the way I'd teased her. "I'll start the printing now. It ought to be all done by the time you get here even if I'm not back."

"Since you haven't mentioned where you're going, I won't ask," Erin said. "I'll just say thanks for accommodating me on this, and I'll call you the instant I finish reading—if it isn't some ungodly hour like eight or nine in the morning. I know you night people need your beauty sleep."

"And don't think I don't appreciate it," I said with

a laugh. "Not all of us are in bed by ten o'clock. If I do happen to get back early enough to see you tonight, I intend to force you to sit down to a cup of coffee. If that happens, promise you won't cry because you can't start reading the book immediately."

"Oh, all right, I promise," she pretended to grumble, then she laughed. "As a matter of fact I'm hoping I see you, so if it's possible try to be there."

I told her I would try and then we both hung up, and I went looking for Jessie. I needed to give her instructions about finishing the printing before she left, but I'd stayed on the phone too long. Jessie and her car were both already gone, which meant I'd have to leave a note. It was too bad I hadn't gotten around to putting up that message board she and I had talked about, but that was life. I made do with putting a note on the kitchen counter next to the fridge, where she'd certainly see it when she got back from food shopping.

I stretched my back a little on the return walk to my office, having decided to start the printing before going in to shower. Once I was clean and dressed, I intended to drive to where my mom was buried and spend the day near her grave. I'd done that only a few times over the years, but when I'd had a problem I'd discovered that thinking about it there had made solving it easier. This was one problem I really needed to solve, and I wanted it to happen fast enough to let me get home in time to visit a while with Erin. Maybe she'd met some new men, and one of them would be perfect to drag to the barbecue and parade in front of my family. Afterward I could tell my brothers that the perfect man had run away, frightened off by *them*. That would teach them a thing or two, and get to the heart of the *real* problem . . .

Two

"Fael, you have been successful!" Jord, one of the barbarian's men, shouted in delight, then he danced forward toward his fallen leader. "And you have prevailed once again, Tarren! Now we may search for the treasure!"

The others took up the shout of "treasure!" and began to spread out in search of it. Fael walked over to Tarren and crouched down beside him.

"Here, I brought a small skin of water," Fael said, untying it from his belt and offering it to the man, who knelt with his head hanging low. "If it had been *my* choice, I would have brought wine, but I could not fight the voice that told me otherwise. Do you need me to hold it for you?"

Tarren shook his head and reached shakily for the water, and after taking a very long swallow he poured the rest over his head. His broad hand moved over his face, and then his ice-blue eyes stared at Fael.

"That was the last of it I will accept," Tarren said in a deep rumble. "That abominable snake nearly had my life, and that despite the fact that it was no idea of mine to come here. I say again, Fael, I have passed the limit of my patience and understanding. I refuse to endure anything of this sort ever again."

"But Tarren, how will you find it possible to stop it?" Fael protested as he helped the bigger man to a sitting position on the marble floor. "We have both been trying since this first began, but each time we believe our lives are our own again, another . . . episode occurs. We must surely have offended a wizard without being aware of it."

"I have never even *met* a wizard," Tarren denied, his hand pushing back long strands of sopping wet red hair. "But now that must change. Massaelae is known as the most powerful mage of our time, and if *he* cannot tell us what causes the madness, no one will be able to."

"You expect the men to follow you while you go chasing after a wizard?" Fael demanded. "For that matter, you expect me to? Those who involve themselves with High Magic always regret it."

"You are of the opinion that we have no regrets as it is?" Tarren demanded in turn. "If you and the men prefer not to accompany me, you may make camp wherever you wish and await my return. As soon as these wounds heal enough to let me move freely again, I mean to travel to the house of Massaelae."

The determination in his leader's eyes told Fael that arguing would be a waste of breath. And it might even turn out that Tarren was correct. If it *was* magic causing all these strange things to be done to them, who better to consult than a powerful sorcerer?

"Very well, I will convince the men to ride with you," he grudged. "But you may expect none of us to accompany you closer than five miles from the wizard's house. No man of sense voluntarily involves himself with High Magic."

"No man with a choice, you mean," Tarren muttered. Now that the fighting was done and the decision had been made, his wounds were beginning to make themselves felt. He was weakening . . . Fael leaned forward fast to support him when he slumped over, then lowered him gently to the marble floor. It would take at least four of the men to carry Tarren out of the cavern; the men had better not be gathering too much treasure.

Too much treasure. At one time Fael would never have believed there *was* such a thing, but he had unfortunately learned differently. He and Tarren had enough gold and jewels hidden away to buy them their own kingdom—if they had been allowed to direct their lives long enough to do the buying. Perhaps that wizard *would* be able to help . . . if he failed to turn them all into orange frogs even from five miles away.

Brooding, Tarren thought as he looked up at the big, dark house. *Brooding would be the best word to describe the place, but it also looks cold and hostile. If it were a man, I would already have my sword loosened in its scabbard. Fael and the others may well have been wise to keep their distance.*

But he had made up his mind to go through with it, and after three months worth of healing and traveling, merely standing and staring was no more than a waste of time. The big man shifted his shoulders to settle the sword more comfortably across his back, then left his horse and headed for the heavy wooden front door. Set into the dark gray stone and slate of the house, the door was nearly as dark.

An imposing iron knocker in the shape of a closed and gauntleted fist hung on the door. Tarren used it, hearing a reverberating *boom-boom-boom* inside as he did. For some reason it brought to mind a summons for the dead, which made Tarren glad he was so determined. A wise man would certainly be well on his way back to camp.

He found it necessary to knock a second time, but a moment or two after that the door began to open. A man stepped into the narrow opening, a perfectly ordinary man who looked up at him without expression. Of average height and build, the man had sandy brown hair and soft brown eyes, and he wore the leather trousers, blue cotton shirt, and comfortable boots of a common villager.

"Yes?" he said in a neutral tone. "Is there something you wish?"

"I have come to see the wizard Massaelae," Tarren answered, very nearly amused. People usually expressed awe, sometimes fear, on meeting him, because of his formidable size and bearing. Never, though, had he been treated like an itinerant peddler.

"Come in," the man said, stepping back to open the door widely. "If you have gotten this far, your business must be truly urgent."

"It is," Tarren confirmed as he followed, then

looked at the man curiously. "What did you mean, if I have gotten 'this far'?"

"Through all the illusions," the man said, waving a hand as he closed the door. "Come into my study and tell me what the trouble is."

Tarren glanced around at the interior of the house. Pleasant reds, browns, and tans gave the place a cheerful look, in stark contrast to the grim exterior. The man took him down a corridor, to a room any burgher would have been pleased to own. Bookshelves held many texts, all neatly in their places, and a desk stood to one side, on top of which was an inkwell, pen and paper, and an unlit lamp. To the right of the door was a fireplace with two black leather chairs in front of it, and it was to these chairs that Tarren was led.

"Please seat yourself and tell me what troubles you," the man invited, taking one of the chairs for himself. "Would you care for some refreshment?"

"You *are* Massaelae?" Tarren said as he began to lower himself into the chair. At the last moment he remembered the scabbarded sword across his back, and removed it before sitting.

"Yes, I am Massaelae," the man said, now looking at Tarren curiously. "Why do you wear your sword in such an . . . unusual and awkward position?"

"It is all part of the story I have to tell," Tarren answered with a sigh. "And yes, I would appreciate some wine."

"Then I shall join you," Massaelae said with a smile, but instead of waving his hands and conjuring the items, as Tarren had expected, he got up and went to a nearby sideboard holding decanters. He poured wine into two goblets of still-rare glass, carried them back, then gave one to Tarren before reseating himself.

"This goblet is lovely," Tarren said, admiring the delicately intricate etching in the glass. "My father bought one of the first sets of etched glass goblets when I was a boy, but the workmanship was not quite as fine as this."

"Thank you," Massalae said, studying his guest rather than tasting his wine. "And you must forgive me for forming the wrong first impression of you. From your appearance I took you for a barbarian, but it is evident that you are a man of family and breeding. Why do you dress in such an . . . unusual manner?"

"I believe you were about to call my attire 'outlandish,'" Tarren suggested with a humorless smile. "My manner of dress pertains to why I came here to speak to you. But if you are to understand any of this, I had better begin from the beginning."

When the wizard nodded in agreement, Tarren took a fortifying swallow of wine and began.

"I am a younger son of lower nobility from a kingdom a good distance from here. When I became a man, I left home to find my own way in life as most younger sons do, and after a while began to make a success of it. Being well trained in arms, I was able to form a fighting company, and we grew to have something of a reputation in the field. Just as offers of hire began to come in on a regular basis . . . *it* happened. Every occasion was unpleasant, not to mention perilous and disorienting, but that first time—!"

"Try to remain calm," Massaelae soothed, seeing the way the man agitatedly gulped down a second swallow of wine. "Obviously even thinking about your trouble disturbs you, but try to explain to me what ails you in words I can understand."

"That is easily done," Tarren said, finally composing himself. "One morning I awoke to feel a strange tingling all over my body, and after that the only piece of clothing I was able to tolerate wearing was my breechcloth, just as I now appear. I also felt compelled to go barefoot and to sling my sword across my back instead of wearing it hanging to my side. I had no control over these things.

"And that was merely the beginning. *Something* compelled me to ride to the mountains, and once there I was required to fight an ogre whose nest was in a cave. The ogre had taken a captive, a pretty girl who turned out to be the daughter of a king whose throne had been stolen from him. Once I freed the girl, I helped her father to reclaim his throne."

"But ogres never *take* captives," Massaelae pointed out with a frown. "They kill whatever or whoever comes near them at once, then let the carcass rot until they consider it edible. And any king so incompetent as to let his throne be stolen from him has little or no right to reclaim it through the efforts of another. And what became of the girl?"

"That was the only part of the madness that had an agreeable outcome," Tarren said, remembering the time far too well. "The girl was offered to me in marriage, but happily, that force that took control of me at such times made me refuse the offer. She was the sweet, delicate sort, never raising her voice, never complaining. She also fainted on a regular basis, usually at the worst possible times, when anyone with sense would be running for his or her life. Of course, that meant I was required to stand and fight alone against more men or creatures than is typically healthy for a man. And her idea of a proper reward for having her life saved was the bestowal of a kiss. She seemed unknowing of the fact that a kiss is meant to be the beginning of matters, not the end of them."

"It sounds as though you were fortunate to get away with your freedom," Massaelae agreed, his brows high. "That sort of woman tends to bore a man to tears, particularly when he takes her to bed. What happened then?"

"I was given a reward in gold instead, and they waved farewell as I rode off," Tarren said. "By then I was very nearly too confused to walk straight, as well as badly wounded from all the calamities I had undergone. Once my men and I were away from the king's city, I collapsed the way I should have done a good deal earlier. I had no idea at the time, but that was the end of it—of the madness—at least for the moment."

"But there were other incidents of the same sort?" Massaelae asked, intrigued. "How many altogether?"

"To date there have been five such occurrences," Tarren responded. "On occasion the thing took only a matter of weeks to run its course, but once six months passed before it released me. I find it impossible to list how many times and in how many ways I have nearly been killed, the last instance taking place only a bit more than three months ago. I decided then that I had to know what was behind it all, since it may prove possible that knowing will allow me to find a way to make an end to it."

The wizard nodded, his mind busy behind distracted brown eyes. "It may be possible for me to aid you, but first I would hear a bit more. What of the people about you? Are they affected as well?"

"Only at times," Tarren answered. "My men usually follow where I go, and although the madness centers on me, they are sometimes drawn into it. This last time my second in command, Fael, followed me into a cavern, where I fought a giant serpent guarding an incredible treasure. He was compelled—and I am certain it was by the same force I am subjected to—to bring a magic arrow with him, and used it to wound the serpent enough that I could finish the job. He also brought a skin of water, which he apologized for. If it had been up to him, he would have brought wine or brew."

"Which you certainly would have appreciated more than the water," Massaelae said with a nod. "Aside from its uses as a depressant, alcohol is helpful in cleansing wounds. Either your tormentor is unaware of that, or for some reason wished to keep the assistance from you. Do you have any idea who might be responsible for your plight?"

"If I had, I would likely commit the first pleasure-killing of my life," Tarren answered, unable to keep the growl from his voice. "Do you believe you might aid me? Fael feels we may have offended a wizard at some time, but I find it impossible to imagine that such a thing could occur without my knowledge. If somehow it did, I am perfectly willing to apologize— but if the apology is refused, I am also perfectly willing to fight. Should I not be strong enough or fast enough the next time the madness comes, I may well fail to survive. To me that means I have very little to risk."

"If there *is* a wizard responsible for this . . . madness, as you call it, I pity him," Massaelae said after clearing his throat. "The illusions around my house have all my strength behind them, and they have been designed to discourage all but the most determined from finding their way here. Most who make it to the front door are unable to knock; you, however, knocked not once but twice. Come with me to my workshop, and we shall see if we can get to the bottom of this."

The wizard stood and led the way out of the room. Tarren hesitated a full three heartbeats before getting up to follow. He really did want to find out who was responsible for the madness, but the idea of entering a wizard's workshop—! Most men would have run the other way. But Tarren was desperate—to the point of unsound reasoning. But determined, that could not be denied . . .

Massaelae led his guest upstairs to the third floor of the house, which comprised one very large room. Four high and heavy wooden tables stood in various places across the floor, one of them topped with

what looked to be polished slate. Each of them had
different items standing on them: jars both empty
and full, candles in holders both lit and unlit, tools,
instruments, yardsticks—a sampling of the much
larger variety to be found on the multitude of shelves
lining the walls. But all of it was neat, as though a
house girl had just been through. Was it untrue, then,
that wizards lived in the midst of chaos? Tarren wondered.

"Ignore the chaos and sit there," Massaelae said,
pointing to a stool positioned in the middle of a pentacle. "I may not need the circuit diagram, but should
the need arise, it should be close at hand."

"Surkut digram?" Tarren echoed. "What might that
be?"

"Merely wizard jargon," Massaelae said with a
brief smile and a shake of his head. "It is of no importance. Sit on the stool and we will begin."

After everything Tarren had been through, walking
into the pentacle and sitting down was not very difficult. Or so he told himself as he watched the wizard
taking jars containing powders, liquids, and solids, as
well as two heavy, dust-covered books from the neat
shelves to the nearest table.

The first thing brought near him was a powder,
light green in color with bright bronze flecks. Massaelae took a pinch of the mixture, uttered some
strange words, then sprinkled Tarren with the substance. The powder drifted down toward his arm ever
so slowly, but just before it touched his skin it disappeared!

"Hmm," the wizard murmured. "How interesting. I wonder . . ."

He returned to the table, then came back with a jar of blue liquid with red swirls in it. The handle of a small, narrow brush stuck out of the jar, and after speaking a few more incomprehensible words, the wizard spattered Tarren with the brush. Again, the droplets descended slowly but disappeared before touching him.

"Fascinating!" the wizard enthused, apparently to himself. "There is definitely a link there, but not to here. Where could it be, I wonder?"

He turned back to the table again, but this time to consult one of the heavy books. Tarren considered asking the wizard what he had learned, then decided against it. It was fairly obvious the mage had no answers yet. Time enough to ask questions once he had reached some conclusion . . .

A circumstance which took a considerable time in coming. Massaelae divided his time between searching through his books, reading passages here and there, and occasionally approaching Tarren to sprinkle some substance on him. None of the powders or liquids managed to touch him—except for one.

"Ha!" Massaelae exclaimed in triumph. "I have you! Now we know where, so what remains is who."

"Does that mean you have part of the answer?" Tarren asked as he tried to brush away the reddish-brown mold he had been sprinkled with. The powder looked very much like dried blood, and he found himself wondering *whose* blood it was.

"Yes, I now know *where* the interference with your

life is coming from," the wizard answered while thumbing through his second book. "It originates in a world other than ours, of course, else I would have found it an hour ago. I was looking for an actual spell, but that is not what has been affecting you. It seems more like a . . . a dream, I think, yes, that would be a very close description. A dream."

"Someone in another world is dreaming of me?" Tarren asked, struggling to understand what he was being told. "I was unaware there *were* other worlds; and how is it possible for someone in one of them to dream of me? And if it is, why would they dream the madness? Are they deliberately trying to kill me?"

"Actually, your death seems to be the last thing they want," Massaelae said, glancing up at him. "The currents I have been testing tell me the dreamer has actually protected you in certain ways. They seem rather strange ways, and some I fail to understand at all. For example, I will wager you have rarely suffered colds, or upset stomachs, or headaches during any of your adventures. Am I wrong?"

"No-o-o, you have the truth of it," Tarren said slowly, thinking about the matter. "I had failed to notice that in the midst of everything else, but even riding around almost naked in the cold has never sent me to my furs with illness. But what kind of person would protect me from things like that, while at the same time sending me up against an ogre, a giant serpent, and six swordsmen at a time?"

"I fear you will need to ask *her* that," Massaelae replied, then saw Tarren's expression. "Oh, have I failed to mention that the culprit is a woman? Probably a very minor sorceress. And, if I had to speculate, totally untrained. No one with even the smallest amount of training would use dreams when there are so many better— Ah, here we are. Now we should be able to get a line on her."

The wizard chuckled as though he had said something amusing, but Tarren was missing the jest. A *woman* had caused him all that trouble? By dreaming about him? He liked women as well as the next man, but—Hellfire and Ogre's teeth! Had the bubbleheaded female no sense at all . . . ?

"This end is yours," Massaclae said, this time sprinkling Tarren with yellow and white powder. The wizard had spoken words again, so the powder fell on him and stuck. Luckily the other powder seemed to have disappeared, otherwise he would surely look like some sort of plague carrier. "And this end will find *her.*"

The wizard spoke what sounded like different words, then threw a second pinch of yellow and white powder into the air. Rather than seeing it hit the floor, Tarren watched the powder expand into a roiling cloud. The cloud billowed as it widened, a hissing sound accompanying the growth, and after a moment both hissing and billowing stopped. The cloud now formed what looked like a doorway, and a faintly glittering line shimmered through the air from Tarren all the way into the opening.

"The woman you seek will be at the other end," Massaelae said, gently brushing his hands clean. "The currents tell me she knows you but does *not* know you, therefore you will need to explain your problem.

She will be unable to cast any spells on you, at least, so you need not let that cause you worry."

"You mean I must—walk through—*that?*" Tarren asked as he rose. He had replaced his sword across his back, but he still felt strangely naked and weaponless. "What will occur if it closes up and I find it impossible to return? Where will I be?"

"I do not know," the wizard responded lightly. "But calm your fears on the matter of being trapped there. If you have failed to return by noon, my spell will draw you back. Not to this room, however, as I will be elsewhere. When you cross back into this world, you will emerge at the place where your men are camped, down near the river. Is that acceptable?"

"Yes, certainly," Tarren said after taking a deep breath. The wizard had located his tormentor—how could Tarren now complain? "Do I simply walk through?" he added.

"I would recommend stooping just a little," the wizard suggested, a twinkle in his mild brown eyes. "That doorway was designed for someone of *my* size, and it may not be adjustable. Why take unnecessary risks?"

Tarren felt the urge to laugh at that. He was about to step through a smoke cloud into another world, and the wizard spoke of not taking risks? Well, all laughter aside, he *was* going to attempt it. It might be his only chance to make the madness end.

Moving forward slowly but with resolve, Tarren approached the insubstantial doorway. Through the mists he thought he could see a room, but one unlike any he had seen before. And there was a figure in the room, someone to whom the thread of light seemed to lead. He took a deep breath, and followed that thread of light . . .

Three

It didn't take me long to turn on the computer and load the print program for the laser printer; it was such a familiar activity, I could do it in my sleep. Which was a good thing, because my thoughts were elsewhere. All I had to do was hit the return key and the computer would take care of the rest. I reached out to the keyboard, and—

—And came up fast out of my chair to turn at the sound of metal striking metal, ready to defend myself. That sound was one that definitely did not belong in my house, especially since I was alone in my office, and had closed the door behind me to keep the cat out while I was printing. The door remained closed, but standing in front of it was something else that didn't belong in my house . . .

I stared, dumbstruck. I remembered how I'd felt when I saw the cover of my first book, the shock of actually seeing the characters who had been only a vision in my head up till then. But that was nothing to what I felt now, staring at the man no more than five feet away. Men taller than six and a half feet tend to fill a room, especially when their shoulders are wide enough for two men. And when their chests are great flat slabs of muscle, lightly covered with reddish hair. His waist and hips tapered to powerful, thickly muscled legs . . .

I felt the urge to close my eyes and shake my head, but somehow I knew that that would *not* get rid of him. Long red hair, cold blue eyes, a handsome, masculine face—it was my barbarian in the loincloth-wrapped flesh, complete with sword strapped across his back. He was *right there,* emerging from a strange, mistlike doorway. For an instant I thought I'd finally snapped from the pressure of that stupid decision I'd been trying to make, but—

But damn it, he was right there!

Tarren stepped through the doorway of mist. One glance at his surroundings told him he was definitely in the workshop of a sorceress, and one who was a good deal more typical of the breed than Massaelae. Books and papers were stacked everywhere, some lying on the floor near a receptacle that seemed to be meant for refuse. The thread of light he followed led directly to a woman who was seated before some outlandish contraption, one that appeared to be partially alive, to judge by the light and flash and hum of it. That she communed with the thing disturbed his peace of mind, but the wizard had assured him she would be unable to cast a spell against him . . .

He took another step forward, and as he did the sword hilt that jutted up above his right shoulder came in contact with the doorway of mist, and the resulting clank was more like metal on metal than metal on mist. It was hardly the first time an inadvertent sound had betrayed him, but this time it was a sorceress who jumped up and whirled around.

She stood openmouthed and stared at him. For his part Tarren was not displeased to return the stare, although he felt the urge to raise his brows. The woman was golden-haired and green-eyed with a beautiful face, although with the sheen of sweat on her skin, she appeared to have undergone some recent labor. But what really took Tarren's attention was the manner in which she stood clad in almost nothing, long, beautifully shaped legs entirely bare, full breasts thrusting hard against a thin, low-cut blue covering, flat middle and small waist above sweetly flaring hips well outlined by a thin white cloth. She was also of a good size in height, a preference of Tarren's that he rarely found the opportunity to indulge. Not that he was likely to indulge it now, he reminded himself wryly. The sorceress had looked stunned at his sudden appearance, but now her expression turned indignant.

"Is this supposed to be someone's idea of a joke?" she demanded with an odd accent, putting angry fists to those nicely rounded hips. "Who are you, and how did you get in here?"

"I believe you already know who I am," Tarren answered, his own anger and annoyance rekindled by hers. "As to how I entered your lair, it was by means of that doorway behind me. I have come to demand that you cease dreaming of me."

"Lair?" she echoed, even more indignant as she straightened in an attempt to match his size. Tarren found the attempt vaguely amusing, but all amusement disappeared as she continued. "What in hell are you talking about? I don't dream about you, or even about the one you're obviously trying to impersonate. Why don't you just go back to whatever perverted idiot sent you as a gag. That has to be what this is about, and I don't need some overgrown fool wasting my time."

"Overgrown fool?" Tarren echoed in turn, the growl his voice had become stopping the woman from turning completely away from him. "No one speaks to me that way, and certainly not a dagger-tongued hellion who fairly begs to be taught her proper place! You *do* dream of me, and that doing puts me through madness I refuse to endure again. I will have your word *this minute* that the dreaming will stop, else will there be a great deal of unpleasantness between us."

"Look, stupid, I don't dream about Tarren the Barbarian, I write about him," the woman growled back, almost taking Tarren's attention from the way she had insulted him. *No* one ever growled at *him*, especially not a female. "Writing is what I *do*, so take my word that whoever came up with this elaborate gag did a bad job on your dialogue. I also can't see the point to it, but that doesn't matter. Whatever way they snuck you in here, let's see if you're bright enough to take your special effects and leave the same way."

Tarren found himself straightening in anger just as she had done, and it annoyed him even more when the woman seemed completely unimpressed. She stared up at him in a way that made it appear that she looked *down* instead, almost as though she were deliberately attempting to provoke him.

Had a man insulted Tarren the way this sorceress

had, there would have been very little left of the fool even without the use of weapons. From time to time there *had* been men rash enough to try it, although none had tried more than once. But with women Tarren was at a great disadvantage, as he found it impossible to do to them what he would to another man. There had once been that girl who had fancied herself a warrior, but she had done the attacking herself. After disarming her he had warmed her seat properly, and then had sent her home weeping . . .

But this woman before him seemed ready to fend off attack, not begin one herself. It still would have been pleasant to put her over his knee and teach her the hazards of giving insult, but his mind had been distracted by her declaration. Writing rather than dreaming? The wizard had specified dreams, but with writing the matter made more sense. Tarren had read any number of books, and some few of them had contained happenings that would be considered madness by any man *forced* to do the same. Adventures, such books were called.

And yet the point remained—dreaming or writing, his life would not be his alone until the woman ceased her efforts. She continued to stare up at him belligerently, the gaze of those green eyes calm yet alert, and Tarren nearly grinned. Women of fire had been rare in his life, and this one would have fit rather well in his bed. A pity he had other business with her, business which contained little in the way of pleasure.

"Perhaps we do speak of writing rather than dreaming," he granted her sourly, folding his arms across his chest. "Nevertheless, the problem remains the same. Your—*writing*—disrupts my life, and I will have no more of it. You may now consider what you *do* as already done and over with. Best if you distract yourself from now on with a man and what children he gives you, as women were meant to do."

"Is that so?" she returned immediately and much too softly, her eyes narrowing. "Why am I not surprised that you'd side with *them?* You're just as bad as they are, and maybe that's who sent you. I still don't know what sort of game this is, but I also don't give a damn. My final response to you is a one-key answer named 'return.' "

This time she completed her turn away from him and reached out to touch something below the demon-lit box. A sound ushered from a third contrivance beyond the first two, and the woman turned back to show him an annoyingly pleased smile.

"It may only be doing the title page and chapter index right now, but that, my friend, is my newest *writing,*" she purred. "If you don't like it, don't buy a copy when it comes out. In fact, for all I care you can picket my publishers, but whatever you do I want you doing it away from me. Get out of my house, and I mean *right now.*"

The purring had turned to steel-hard command, but Tarren could not take the time to respond. As soon as the demon-device had begun to make noise, Tarren felt a bodiless tugging through the doorway behind him. He was about to be drawn back, and even worse, the tingling in his body heralded a new bout of the madness, just as it had done too many times before.

The sorceress had not only refused him, she also meant to punish him.

Tarren had never been so furious in his life, and it was that fury which moved him without conscious decision. As the unseen forces dragging at him became too strong to resist, he took one step forward and pulled the sorceress to him, and then he allowed the two of them to be swept back through the doorway together.

Four

If I ever actually wondered what it would be like to get hit by a car while a roof fell on my head, the next few minutes gave me some idea. The giant with the uncanny resemblance to my barbarian moved so fast I thought for sure he came equipped with over-drive and cruise control. Before I was able to realize what was happening, he had those arms wrapped around me, and then we were going through that weird misty doorway. I had just enough time to begin to struggle, and then something heavy and hard just seemed to hit me from all directions . . .

Which is not to say I blacked out. It felt more like I'd had the breath knocked out of me. When I was put back on my feet, my head whirled as if I'd been spun around a dozen times, but at no time had there been any actual pain. Just a momentary constriction, as if I'd been squeezed through an impossibly small hole. And then I looked around.

"This . . . isn't . . . possible," I muttered, the sense of shock growing stronger as my surroundings began to register. A moment ago we'd been standing in my air-conditioned office, but now there was grass under my feet, the sun was blinding and the air humid. Not far away were the tents of a middling large camp, with men moving around among them. Beyond the tents were trees and a river; everywhere else was open meadow with occasional stands of trees.

But it was the air that bothered me most, the kind of air I'd breathed only once before. City people usually talk about how fresh the air is out in the country, but that's only in comparison with city air. I'd once been invited to a private island that had had *nothing* in the way of machinery, not even a generator for electricity. We'd been taken to the island on a sailboat, and there hadn't been a single pollutant to affect what went into our lungs. Most of us had wondered what the funny smell was, having no idea that that was the way air was *supposed* to smell.

And now that funny smell was back, touched lightly with the scent of green grass, burning wood from a cooking fire, some horse droppings, and a number of unwashed bodies, including mine. Anyone playing an elaborate practical joke would be able to fake everything else, but not that special-air smell. I looked around for the doorway of mist but it was nowhere in sight. "This isn't possible," I repeated in a whisper.

"It seems the wizard is a man of his word," the redheaded giant commented, reminding me he was there. "I have been returned to the place my men made camp. Now that I no longer find myself surrounded by strangeness, we may turn to the reason I brought you with me. The madness may be about to begin again, but this time I will know what I face *before* I face it. Tell me how and when your newest writing begins."

"This just isn't possible," I said for the third time, starting to be really angry with myself. Something inside me wanted to believe that everything I saw and felt was real, but that was ridiculous. It *couldn't* be real, even though everything now seemed familiar from my books. So what if theoreticians talked about an endless number of alternate worlds where every possibility in the universe could be found? *This* was *not* possible, especially not when it would mean that the barbarian standing behind me was really *my* barbarian . . .

"Answer me, woman," that deep voice came again, now tinged with annoyance. "Tell me how your writing begins, so that for once I can prepare for it, rather than be at its mercy. Do not think you may refuse to speak, for that will not be allowed."

"You mentioned something about a wizard," I said, turning to face him. He stood with arms folded as he looked down at me, a hardness in those ice-blue eyes. "I know magic is supposed to work in this world, but the idea of a wizard is ridiculous. And what happened to that doorway of mist?"

"The doorway of mist was created by that wizard you find so ridiculous," he answered dryly. "It enabled me to reach the place where you were, and also brought us both to *my* world. Now—"

"Then ridiculous or not, it has to be the answer," I said, my mind only just beginning to work again. "Whether or not this is real, I'm *seeing* it as real. That means I have to find your wizard and have him conjure up another doorway, and then I can go home. So what's his name, and where can I find him?"

He stared down at me in silence for a moment, then shook his head. "It amazes me that there are those about who consider *me* arrogant and overbearing. Undoubtedly those who do have never made *your* acquaintance, else I would not even have taken their notice. Your question will be answered when *I* have been satisfied. How and when does your newest writing begin?"

"You consider the demand to be answered first as nothing more than reasonable?" I countered with a sound of ridicule, swallowing the urge to throw something heavy at him. "Since my being here at all is *your* fault, the least you can do is tell me how to get home."

He continued to stare at me, his eyes narrowing. I glanced at his camp. It was unlikely I'd get any information out of his men, since he was obviously their leader. If I wanted to go home, I'd have to do it his way.

"All right, all right," I said grudgingly after a moment. "This is insane, but I'll tell you what you want to know, and then *you* can tell *me* how to get out of here. My new book starts with an attack against your camp at midnight, when everyone is asleep. Someone who you don't realize is an enemy wants you assassinated, and you learn all about it from the prisoner you take. Now, who is that wizard, and where can I find him?"

"That will be told you once your words prove themselves true," he said. "Now I must arrange a reception for those who come in the night, to be certain they do as little damage as possible. Follow me, and I will show you where you will sleep. We must also find decent clothing for you, after you have made use of the river. A woman's presence should not be as noticeable as that of a hard-run horse."

He brushed past me on his way toward the tents, obviously expecting me to do exactly as I'd been told and follow him. Not only was he giving me orders, he'd reneged on his promise to tell me about the wizard, he'd decided he hated my clothes, and he'd said I smelled as bad as a sweaty horse! I couldn't argue with the sweaty part, but the rest of it was something I was not about to put up with. Whether or not this world was real, I wanted out of it as fast as I could. Since I wasn't likely to find the answers I needed from anyone around *there,* I'd just have to go somewhere else.

I turned around abruptly and walked in the opposite direction from the redhead, and tried not to let the sight of endless meadow discourage me. I seemed to be experiencing a very strong affinity for the place, as though it were an area I was familiar with but simply hadn't visited for a long while. I was sure there was a road somewhere ahead, one that would lead to a town if I turned left when I reached it. The whole thing was really weird, but I'd have time to wonder just how crazy I'd gone once I found that wizard and had him send me home.

"My tent lies in the other direction," a deep voice said, and suddenly the redhead was there in front of me like a living brick wall. His voice was as steely as the look in his eyes, but I wasn't impressed.

"I don't give a damn where your tent lies," I told

him bluntly. "I don't associate with liars, and since you're too busy to tell me what I need to know I'll find someone else to ask. Now get out of my way."

"There are times when deception is necessary," he said, looking uncomfortable but still not moving. "My need to know what lies before me is great, therefore did I use the deception. And yet I have not lied. When once this madness is behind me, I will take you myself to the house of the wizard. For now, however, you must remain with me."

"The hell I will," I said as flatly as possible, just to make sure he understood I wasn't joking. "I may not believe any of this, but that doesn't mean I intend to stand around waiting to wake up or stop hallucinating. When I get home I'll print out another copy of my book and leave it for you in a ring of toadstools along with some cookies and milk. Just have your wizard friend retrieve it, and you'll know exactly what's ahead of you."

I tried to step around him then, but he moved directly into my path again. I looked up into those ice-blue eyes to let him know I wasn't amused, and damned if he wasn't grinning.

"How interesting to learn that anger makes green eyes even more attractive," he commented, almost in a murmur. "Had someone spoken of the matter, I would not have considered it possible. Woman, I am unable to ask the wizard to do as you suggest, for the same reason that you cannot ask him to return you to your world. He has left his house and the time of his return is uncertain. It was for that reason we returned to my camp rather than to his workshop from where

I departed. What gain in learning the wizard's name and the place of his residence when he is not about?"

"You expect me to take your word for that?" I asked with a snort. "I can't possibly look *that* gullible, but even if it's the truth it doesn't matter. If the wizard isn't home when I get there, I'll wait."

"Without knowing how long a wait you must face?" he countered, one reddish brow raised high. "Without shelter, food, or clothing adequate to keep the night's chill at bay? Surely you would do no such foolish and unreasonable a thing. Walk with me now, and tell me by what name you are called."

"I can tell you by what name I'm *not* called," I returned as I knocked his arm away. He'd been about to put a coaxing arm around my shoulders to get me turned back in the direction of the tents. "I'm not called 'doormat' or 'pushover' or 'mindless female who can be soft-talked into anything.' I *will* find your wizard's house and I *will* wait for him there, and if you consider that foolish and unreasonable, hey, that's life. You may be the one who forced me to come to this world, but I'm not *about* to let you keep me here. For the last time: Get out of my way."

"Why do I constantly feel as though you see nothing of a difference between us?" he demanded, now thoroughly annoyed. "No *man* of this world, or of any other, for that matter, would dismiss my size and prowess, and yet you, a woman, behave as though I were small and cowering and weakly. I have said you will remain with me for the time, and willingly or otherwise you will do just that. My tent is this way."

His right hand reached for my left arm in an effort

to turn me around and head me back in the direction of his camp. The maneuver came as something of a surprise to me, since *my* Tarren the Barbarian would never have been that foolish. But the big redhead hadn't been acting much like my Tarren right from the beginning.

I used a very basic hold-breaker to force my left arm out of his grip, turning to my right as I did so. I then brought my left elbow back hard into his abdomen, pivoted, then did the same with my right elbow. He grunted from the force of the blows and bent forward, allowing me to reach over my right shoulder with both hands, get a grip on his hair, drop to one knee, and pull. He shouted as he flew past me and landed flat on his back—and his sword—with a thud. And that was that. He was now out of my way, and had no one but himself to blame for his present condition.

I got a glimpse of his men in their camp as I stood and turned toward that unseen road again. I didn't think any of them would come after me after seeing what had just happened. Their leader had had the breath knocked out of him, but it would have taken a lot more than what *I'd* done to do lasting damage to a man his size, and I probably wouldn't have done even that much if he hadn't gotten me mad. And maybe even a little desperate. I *had* to get out of that place before I really did go mad, from fright if nothing else. If I ever stopped to think about the fact that I was trapped in another world . . .

I cut that thought off fast as I wiped the sweat off my forehead with the back of my hand. The humidity was starting to get to me. I was thankful for my shorts and tank top, but would have given anything to be home, standing under a nice cool shower. It was a bad moment to indulge such a thought, however. Bare feet make no sound in grass unless their owner tends to stomp, and the owner of those particular bare feet moved too lightly for that. He caught up to me before I knew it, and threw those muscular arms around me. The next instant we were both falling, and although he hit the ground and I hit him, his body wasn't noticeably softer than the ground. And then he rolled over and pinned me down, ruining my last chance to fight my way free.

"I believe I see now why you took no notice of the difference in size between us," he murmured as those oversized hands closed on my wrists. "Your magic is a potent thing to allow you to fight in such a manner. That will have to be dealt with. You *will* remain with me for the time, yet you need have no fear. When the time is done, I will see you returned to your own world."

I was too busy struggling to answer him. His hands held my wrists and his body held my legs, and his face was too far away to throw my head back into it. He had me good, but since he'd have to release me at *some* point, the situation wasn't entirely hopeless. But then I heard the sound of running feet, and had the sinking feeling the situation was about to change.

"Here is the length of leather you gestured for, Tarren," a young male said breathlessly. "Do you truly mean to keep a female such as that? Perhaps it would be best if you knocked her senseless."

"Any man who finds it necessary to knock a woman senseless is no man at all, Lamor," my captor answered calmly. "As you continue to learn the art of a fighter, boy, you must also learn that caution is a beneficial use of fear. There is no shame in fearing a thing; shame enters only when that fear causes you to lose your head. Also are there certain things in this world that a man finds worth a bit of risk."

He was chuckling by then, but that didn't stop him from tying my wrists behind me with the leather the boy had brought. The softness of it said it was old and well-used leather, but not old enough to pull apart, something my actions proved.

"And now you will be shown the place where you will take your rest," the redhead said, beginning to get up. I waited for the chance to kick him, but it didn't come. His big right arm went around my waist, and when he stood I was slung under his arm like a bundle of dirty clothes. Kicking the empty air didn't even so much as throw him off balance, but I continued to struggle even after I was carried into a tent and put down flat on the rug-covered ground. The big redhead knelt across my legs, there was a clanking sound, and then the soft leather on my right wrist was replaced with something smooth and cold. Right after that the leather was taken away entirely along with the big body across my legs, and I was finally able to sit up.

"This shackle has proven useful before," the redhead told me, holding up his left wrist to show that he wore a smooth steel bracelet like the one on my right wrist. From the clanking I'd heard I'd expected to see chain linking the two bracelets, but nothing but empty air appeared between us. I immediately aimed to head out of the tent. Halfway to my feet I was yanked back hard by *something* attached to my wrist, and ended up sprawled on the rugs where I'd been sitting.

"A shackle produced by magic may be ignored even less than one produced by a blacksmith," the giant told me, mildly amused. "This one will keep you as near or as far as I wish you, a truth you have just learned. Wisdom now dictates that you accept your defeat gracefully."

"I don't think wisdom's doing the dictating here," I countered, staring at my wrist. It *couldn't* be magic, there wasn't any such thing except in books . . . "What happens if I kill you? Will I have to drag your body with me all the way to the wizard's house?"

"Should you manage to slay me, everyone about, *including* the wizard, will be senseless with shock," he returned with a roguish grin. "Clearly it has escaped your notice that I am not so easily done away with. Tell me now what name you are called by."

"Let me see if I can make my position clear enough for even *you* to understand," I said exasperatedly as I ran both hands through my hair. "I do *not* want to stay in your world, I want to go home. Thinking you were a man of your word, I answered the question you asked about what happens first in my new book. When you chose not to honor our deal I didn't argue, I just tried to walk away. Now you're keeping me from doing that as well, thinking that you'll gain something from holding me prisoner, but you're wrong. Since I've already answered the last question I ever will for you, keeping me here is a waste of time. Now take this stupid thing off my wrist so I can go *home!"*

I came close to losing it at the end of that speech, but nothing I said seemed to have an effect on the man. Or much of an effect. When the word "honor" came up he'd looked pained, but by the time I finished he simply seemed wryly uncomfortable.

"As I said, you will be allowed to return to your world when this current madness is over and done with," he repeated softly. "Until then you may consider yourself my guest, however reluctant a guest you may be. And now I feel a need to visit the river, to refresh myself after my exertions in the heat. You will find accompanying me willingly far superior to being dragged."

He then got to his feet and started for the tent entrance. He hadn't gone more than two steps before I was pulled after him by the wrist, just as if there was about four or five feet of chain between his bracelet and mine. He paused then to look back at me, and his expression also made it clear that if I didn't walk I *would* be dragged. I got to my feet fast with the intention of seeing just how hard killing him really was, and he quickly held up a hand.

"Do *not* come at me again in attack," he said, his voice and gaze having turned very hard. "I appreciate your distress and great unhappiness, yet do I refuse to take the entire blame for your predicament. Had you not created your writings and forced me through constant madness, I would not have gone seeking you nor carried you back here. Patience is a virtue I find well worth cultivating, yet mine now runs swiftly upon an ending. Follow me to the river, and do nothing which will cause me to punish you."

When he finished his speech he turned and continued on his way, and the bracelet on my wrist pulled me right after him. Outside, there were still a large number of men milling about; they continued to regard me with a mixture of suspicion and interest. But *they* weren't my problem. Staying sane in that madhouse was, something I didn't know if I could do. I *had* to get out of there, but the head madman refused to let me go. But somehow I felt more annoyed than desperate, more angry than terrified. Maybe I already *had* gone crazy . . .

Five

"Should those of you who stand about here have no tasks to see to, I will find tasks *for* you," the giant said, pausing to glance around at our audience. They all seemed to come out of the fog then, and a moment later most of them had disbursed. The boy Lamor remained, as did another man who caught my attention. He wasn't the size of his red-haired leader but he was still big and broad-shouldered, wearing tight black leather pants and a blue shirt that looked to be silk. With long black hair and gray eyes, he seemed to be familiar, but when the giant addressed him by name I immediately refused to believe it. This whole thing had to be a very elaborate practical joke, and in just a little while I'd figure out exactly how they were doing it.

"Fael, I would have you see to a thing for me," he said, and the black-haired man immediately joined him. "The wench and I go now to wash in the river, and when we return she will need decent clothing to cover herself with. I would not care to tempt the men into behavior that would cause difficulty. Best to cover her properly and lessen the chance of misunderstandings."

"A pity, but I agree completely," the one called Fael

answered, turning to look me over with a grin. "And should you decide you want nothing of the capture rights, gladly will I exercise them in your stead. She would be well worth the scuffle."

"Best you and the others understand it would be more than a simple scuffle," the redhead returned, looking faintly amused. "This female is the author of our constant difficulties, found for me by the wizard I visited. I was told she is incapable of casting any spells upon us, and yet you saw how easily she threw me about. Could such an action be anything other than magic?"

"By all the gods, it could not," Fael said, his grin fading. "I had not realized . . . Tarren, how wise is it for you to toy with one such as she?"

"The wisdom of a man's doings—or lack thereof—comes clear only after the doings are completed," the giant said. "Have the men prepare themselves, for we will be attacked this night when our enemies believe us to be asleep. Half of them should take to their furs now, the rest at dark, after the first group is roused. When I return from the river, we will discuss the matter in greater detail."

The black-haired Fael nodded as he moved off, and a crook of the giant's finger brought the boy Lamor to his side. Lamor looked to be about fifteen, with light brown hair and dark brown eyes, a tall, gawky teenager who still had a lot of filling out to do. He wore cloth pants of faded black and a faded gray shirt, with worn brown boots.

"Boy, go and fetch two generous lengths of that thick cotton cloth we were given as partial payment for our last employment," the giant told him. "Bring them to the provisions wagon, where I will be gathering a meal for the woman and myself."

The boy gave me a nervous glance before nodding and running off, and that seemed to be all the preparation the redheaded giant intended to make. A movement of his wrist tugged at me to get my attention, and then he started off again through the camp. I didn't follow him willingly, but I followed him—while my mind continued to rage in inner argument.

I'd been debating the main point since just before we'd left the tent, and still had no easy answer. I'd really wanted to do some damage to the big fool for chaining me up, but I kept being reminded that it was *him* I was chained to, and if I didn't kill him I'd better be prepared for his retaliation.

I pushed the hair back out of my eyes, only partially aware of the tents and people I passed. I'd never realized how tempting the thought of cold-blooded murder could be while at the same time finding it absolutely appalling. I'd never killed anything in my life, hadn't even considered it, and not simply because the law frowned on the practice. In that place there didn't seem to *be* any law, not the sort with police immediately available at the other end of the telephone line. It was just that I considered it wrong to kill someone simply because they got you mad as hell, even if you wouldn't have minded denting them a little . . .

But self-defense was a different matter. I mean, he *was* a madman, believing he had to live out the books I wrote. He'd even found himself a second-in-command named Fael, who looked as much like the man of the same name in my books as the giant looked like Tarren. But neither of them could really *be* those two, so it was *all* madness and the sooner I got out of there the happier I'd be.

Which meant that, in the absence of killing him, I had to stick to my promise not to answer any more questions. Once the giant understood I meant what I'd said he'd let me go, and then I could look up that wizard. But if none of that was real, how would a wizard help me . . . ?

"Do you sleep on your feet, woman?" the giant's voice interrupted my thoughts, and I looked around to see that we'd stopped near a large wagon. "I asked if you preferred red wine or blue."

"If I were answering questions, I'd say I don't want either," I told him, deliberately looking everywhere but at him. "Since I'm not answering questions . . ."

I just let the sentence trail off as I toyed with that bracelet, examining it more closely. It showed nothing of a keyhole or a seam, and was just a little too small to force off over my hand. How he'd gotten it on me in the first place was something else I couldn't let myself think about, not if I hoped to keep what little sanity I had left.

"Perhaps you *are* too young yet to be allowed wine," he drawled in answer, and I glanced up to see his renewed amusement. "What a good wench you are, to behave in so proper a manner. Should you continue on so, I will find you a sweet as reward."

"I'm not *any* sort of 'wench,' and you know what you can do with your rewards," I came back, fighting to hold my temper. "If you *don't* know what to do with it, just ask me. That's one question I won't mind answering."

"It's said a woman of high temper is also a woman of high passion," he commented, leaning on the wagon with one arm as his eyes moved over me slowly and deliberately. "When we return to my tent from the river, we must certainly discuss the contention."

"You can discuss anything you please," I returned as I folded my arms obstinately. "What you'll have to live with is the fact that in my case, you, personally, will never find out for sure. In case you hadn't noticed, I don't happen to like you. I've always made it a practice to save my passion for men I do like."

"What was true up until now has no bearing on what your situation has become," he said, the faintest surprise now in his expression. "Do you fail to realize that your actions forced me to take you captive? A man who takes a woman captive may do as he wishes with her, and she must obey him. In most instances the man must first face one or more of her male kin— or a guardian she has the right to designate—but if he succeeds in besting his opponent, the woman is then his. It seems certain you have no male kin in this world, and although you stood guardian for yourself, I was still able to prevail. You now belong to me for as long as I care to keep you, and capture rights are also mine."

"Do you really think I'm stupid enough to believe that?" I demanded, more shocked than I had any intention of showing. "You started out by claiming that this is the world I created in my books, but that captive thing isn't any part of them. So, if I ever find one of your hands on me, I'll break that hand off at the shoulder."

"It seems we speak at cross purposes yet again," he said with something of a sigh. "What you were told was that your writings force me to what I consider madness; nothing was said concerning this world being of your creation. As I have never seen your writings I cannot be certain, yet do I feel that what occurs during a time of madness has only a little to do with the realities of my world. *Your* world at times exists *within* my world, but leaves no lasting mark upon it. And should you doubt my word concerning capture rights, you may question any man in this camp. They will say what I have."

I wanted to point out that that was no guarantee I'd be told the truth, but that was beside the point. What seemed to be bothering me most was the contention that I *hadn't* created that world, I'd only somehow been *using* a part of it. That meant there was a lot to it I didn't know anything about, and unfamiliar primitive worlds tended to be more than a little dangerous. If I wanted to keep breathing I'd have to get out of there as fast as possible.

"I don't care if every living being in the entire universe agrees with you," I stated, forcing myself to meet his gaze. For some reason the giant suddenly looked a *lot* bigger than he had before. "Capture rights or no capture rights, I won't be cooperating with *anything* you have in mind. If you don't like that idea, find another woman to chain up."

"For what reason would I seek another woman when the one I have is the one I desire?" he countered mildly, that damned amusement back again. "After we have eaten and bathed in the river, we will return to my tent and discuss this matter further."

He turned then and climbed into the wagon, leaving me to stand there staring after him. The way he refused to be rattled by anything I said was really getting to me, making me feel as if I'd been smiling and batting my eyelashes at him instead of threatening mayhem. I tried to move off back the way we'd come, but one step was as far as that bracelet would let me go. It wasn't dragging me after him into the wagon, but it *was* keeping me where he'd left me. I thought about grinding my teeth in frustration, but gestures seemed kind of pitiful just now. I'd be much better off trying to come up with something besides threats to discourage him.

By the time the giant climbed out of the wagon, the boy Lamor had returned. He edged around me tentatively and stopped in front of his leader.

"Here are the lengths of cotton cloth you requested, Tarren," he said, holding up a dark blue pile. "Shall I carry your sack as well?"

"Lamor, you have more need of sword practice than I have need of assistance," the giant said gently, taking the cloth from the boy with a smile. "I also have no need of one to stand my protection; you needn't be concerned. Go now, and spend your time learning the skill that will help you to retain your life."

Despite the nervous glance the boy sent me, there was a great deal of reluctance in the way he left. It was obvious he *had* been thinking about protecting the giant, and considering the way he kept looking at me he'd been trying to do a very brave thing. There had to be more than simple admiration in his feelings for the leader of his company to account for that.

"My men and I freed the boy from a painful, difficult capture some months ago," the giant murmured as we watched Lamor slowly disappear, almost reading my mind. "Brigands often take children to serve them in their home camp, using them badly. The one who had constantly savaged Lamor would have escaped dragging the boy with him had I not intervened, and now the boy feels that his life is mine. I see to his training with weapons, yet is it unlikely that I will permit him to take part in serious combat. Those who are not warriors born should never have to stand in the midst of battle."

I happened to feel exactly the same way, but that didn't seem the time to mention it. I wasn't there to get chummy and make friends, I was there because I wasn't being allowed to leave. As long as I kept that in mind—along with the firm knowledge of what the giant thought he was due from me—I should be perfectly all right. At least until we got back to his tent . . .

When I remained silent the redhead shrugged slightly, and then he headed off past the wagon. I waited until the bracelet yanked me along after him, and then I dragged my feet as much as possible. I'd listened to my brothers' discussions and conquest stories often enough to know that most men found constant disinterest from a woman very much of a turnoff. If the redhead happened to look at it the same, I could be on my way home even sooner than I'd hoped.

We left the campsite to patrolling perimeter guards,

and wended our way down to the river. I expected us to stop as soon as we got close enough to the water, but the giant had other ideas. He moved along the bank until we reached a stand of trees and bushes, and only when we were in the center of it did he stop to put his burdens down.

"First we will share a meal, and then we will share the river," he announced, crouching to open the sack. "You may seat yourself there. I will serve you as though you were guest rather than captive."

The place he'd gestured to was in the grass opposite where he obviously intended to sit, which made the spot one I was best off avoiding.

"Thanks anyway, but I'm not hungry," I said casually, taking in the greenery. "I'll eat once I get home."

"It seems you mean to make this as difficult as possible," he commented, taking the food items out of the bag. "Would it not be best if we declared a truce, at least for the time we spend here? The river is lovely, and it pleases me to have a lovely woman to share it with. It is seldom that I have such an opportunity, and I would make the most of it."

At that point I looked over at him, only to find those very blue eyes now resting on me. His flaming hair spread out behind and below his massive shoulders, one short lock falling onto his forehead. The planes and angles of his very handsome face were set solemnly, and I suddenly had the urge to shiver. That was because I found myself wanting to agree to his request, a dirty trick on his part if there ever was one. If he'd just kept on giving me orders, I would have had no trouble at all ignoring him. Well, there was only one possible response to something like that.

"You know, you do that really well," I observed, trying to sound completely objective. "Sounding sad and wistful and almost lonely, I mean. You must take a lot of female captives, to be that practiced. Do most of them fall for it?"

He didn't answer immediately, not when he seemed to be fighting to control the heavy annoyance that flashed briefly in his eyes. He wasn't happy with me, and that made us even. I deliberately turned away and began to stroll off through the trees, but I'd forgotten about that stupid bracelet. When it yanked me back I almost fell on my head, and I stumbled two or three steps before I was drawn to the ground in the very spot the redhead had previously gestured to, but on my hands and knees.

"You will find sitting a good deal more comfortable than crouching on all fours," he said. "Not that I will allow you to do so should you keep on with your attempt to provoke me. Why do you insist on rejecting all offers of peace and friendship? Are you always so unreasonable?"

"What a nice day this is," I growled, struggling to get myself seated cross-legged while my wrist was all but stapled to the ground. It was ludicrous to have to sit there while some barbarian savage tried to psychoanalyze me, but at least I didn't have to cooperate. I'd said I would not be answering any more questions, and I meant to keep to that.

"Refusing to discuss the matter will not cause it to disappear," he remarked, back to poking around in the sack. "Wisdom lies in acceptance of one's circumstances."

"Accepting the unacceptable is the coward's way of life," I said, letting him know how *I* looked at it. "What wise people do or don't do is *their* business; what I do is mine. If you don't like that, take this bracelet off and let me go home."

He made a faint sound of ridicule. It annoyed the hell out of me that his braceleted left arm was free to move wherever he wanted it to, but my braceleted right was stuck to the ground. How on earth—if we were still on earth—did he manage that?

"Provisions do badly in heat such as this, yet were these things bought from a nearby farm this morning, after we had made camp here," he said, putting down on the grass two squares of what looked like linen, one in front of each of us. "What we fail to eat will likely need to be thrown away, and that cheese is too tasty to merit such a fate. The bread is freshly baked and soft."

By then two portions of the bread and cheese had been placed on the linen squares, and the giant lost no time attacking his share. The white cheese and tan-crusted bread *did* look good, but passive insistence annoys me just as much as the pushy kind. I'd already refused the offer of food, and his pretending I hadn't wasn't going to coax me into changing my mind. Instead of mentioning that, though, I simply looked out over the lake and wondered what sort of wild animals frequented those woods. If our picnic happened to get interrupted by something large enough, I might find it possible to slip away during the confusion . . .

"When one thinks how many go hungry in this world, wastefulness is very nearly a crime," the giant said after a couple of minutes. I looked back to see that he'd already finished his meal, but I couldn't believe the line he was handing me now.

"Not the 'children in Europe are starving' gambit," I couldn't help protesting with a groan. "That one went out with my grandmother, and not even my father had the nerve to use it on us. The usual response my brothers and I gave Grandma was, 'if those starving kids would like it so well, then give it to *them*.' That's a suggestion I also offer *you*, Grandpa."

Since obnoxiousness seemed to annoy the man, I'd decided to be as obnoxious as possible. I really looked forward to being thrown out of camp in disgust, and the way the expression in those blue eyes hardened was very encouraging.

"You have brothers, then," he remarked after a moment. "And you speak of your father and grandmother, but no mother or sisters. This explains your brashness, and having only a father explains your having been so badly spoiled. A man alone too often hesitates to warm the bottom of the child who most reminds him of his lost love. A pity that, as a good bottom-warming would certainly have done wonders with you."

He took the remaining bread and cheese and ate it himself as he continued to stare at me, leading me to wonder briefly if it had been extra food he'd offered me or part of his own meal. But my consideration of that was *very* brief, since I was too busy being annoyed by what he'd said. It was true enough that my father had occasionally spanked the boys but never me. But I hadn't been spoiled all *that* badly, and if the giant decided to remedy what he saw as a lack, he'd need every member of his fighting company to help him do it.

I went back to studying the scenery as he finished eating, not really worried beyond a faint uneasiness. That bracelet gave the giant an edge that went beyond his size, but I'd gotten the sudden conviction that he wouldn't beat up on a woman no matter what the circumstance. That didn't mean he wouldn't resort to other means to get what he wanted, though, but I refused to think about what those other things might entail. I'd be out of there before he could get around to doing more than thinking about them.

It didn't take him long to finish the rest of the food, and then he took something out of the sack and got to his feet.

"Now may we see to bathing ourselves," he said, bending to pick up the blue cloth he'd earlier dropped on the grass. "You may wash the clothing you wear or not, as you please. You will not wear it again. Fael will see to finding proper clothing for you, which will not entice any of my men into foolishness."

"I thought your spreading the word about how dangerous a 'magic' user I am was supposed to take care of that," I remarked, making no effort of my own to stand. "I think you already know I can take care of myself, so what I do or don't wear is beside the point. And if I'm going in that water, how do you expect my clothes to stay dry? If you were waiting for me to strip naked, you can forget about it."

"Woman, you are already all but naked," he ground

out, almost in a growl. "One who dresses as you do cannot claim a sense of modesty. I have brought a jar of soap which you will use on your hair and body, and mean to stand for no more foolishness. Remove your clothing *now,* else I'll do it for you."

His expression said he wasn't joking, and his comment about my clothing made it obvious yet again that we were on different wavelengths. Wearing shorts and a tank top is *not* the same as running around naked, but trying to explain that to a backward barbarian would be a waste of breath. But I'd gotten something of an idea, and since the bracelet was no longer attached to the ground, I got to my feet and tried it.

"What a big brave man you are, threatening to rip my clothes off," I sneered, looking up into those very blue eyes. "I wonder how brave you would be if you couldn't count on this bracelet to restrain me? I knew I shouldn't have been that gentle when I fought you, and no *you* know better than to face me honestly again. There's no doubt about which of us would win."

I'd been trying to shame the giant into removing that miserable bracelet, implying he wasn't man enough to face me without help. If he had released me I would have taken off running, and the way I felt then, his chances of catching me were very low. But instead of succumbing to my ploy and taking that bracelet off me, he closed his eyes and wearily rubbed them with one hand.

"The gods give me strength," he muttered, sounding almost desperate. "The woman takes me for a mindless dolt, who will jump to her bidding as all other men apparently have. What must I do to convince her that I am not as all those others, but *have* come to the end of my patience? Perhaps a short demonstration of my displeasure . . ."

By then his eyes were open again. He had no intention of losing his temper and giving me the chance to get away, which was surprising in addition to being disappointing and frustrating.

"You can't deny it was worth trying," I said with a shrug, working for nonchalance while remembering I was still attached to him. "Why *didn't* you fall for it?"

"Such an attempt is successful only with one who has no sure knowledge of his own worth," he told me, still making use of that hardened stare. "Remove that clothing *now,* for you will not be given the opportunity a third time."

I shrugged again, as though I couldn't care less, but that wasn't anything like the truth. Having all but lived with a man meant I wasn't shy about being naked in front of one, but what I felt at this particular time wasn't precisely shyness. It was more a matter of discomfort—along with the knowledge that Neal, the man I had been sleeping with, had been nothing at all like the giant. Neal had never once demanded anything from me, and hadn't even tried to argue very hard when I'd ended the relationship.

But being uncomfortable didn't mean I had the option of refusing. Something in the way the redhead stared said he was *waiting* for me to refuse, and might even be looking forward to it. That area was private enough for a scuffle to turn into something a good deal more intimate, which meant it was time for me to lay some groundwork I hadn't thought would be needed until later.

"Whether or not you like these clothes, I still have to keep them with me," I said, compromising by bending to open the laces on my running shoes. "I especially have to keep this top, as an indicator of my status. It's not only unethical to keep people from knowing, in my world it's also against the law. Whether or not you pay attention to the warning is entirely up to you."

"For some reason your outlandish speech has turned even more outlandish," the giant said with a frown, taking the bait. "I understood not one word of what you said. To what warning do you refer?"

"What else would I be talking about but this insignia?" I asked with phoney exasperation, brushing at the designer monogram on the left side of my tank top. "Wait a minute. Are you telling me you don't *know* what this insignia means? Or are you simply feigning ignorance so you can blame *me* when you catch it?"

" 'Catch it'?" he echoed, the frown deepening. "Those words have no more meaning than the others. I have never before seen anything like that . . . insignia, nor have I knowledge of what warning it gives. Can you not speak more plainly?"

"Ha! No wonder you kept going on about those 'capture rights' of yours," I said, now pretending to be amused. "At first I thought you were crazy, but now I can see your ignorance is legitimate. Okay, let me say this as clearly as I can: This insignia on my shirt means I've been treated for a medical problem that comes from choosing the wrong sex partner. But the treatment takes a while to work completely, and until then any man who decides he can't do without me will end up catching the same thing. That's the warning I was talking about, but like I said—whether or not you pay attention to it is *your* business."

After taking off my socks and shoes I looked at him, and the thoughtful expression he wore said he finally understood. Granted, the story I'd come up with was more involved than the usual dumb-blonde routine I used, but I'd had to consider the man I was using it on.

"I see," he finally said after a moment or two, looking at me with an unreadable expression. "Should I press for my capture rights, I will find myself in possession of more than a man ordinarily expects. Now that I have been warned, I will certainly keep the point in mind. You may continue with removing your clothing."

I just managed to stop myself from shrugging a third time, which would have changed the gesture from one of unconcern to one of nervousness. I *wasn't* nervous—not exactly, just the least bit concerned. The giant seemed to have accepted my story, but all he'd said was that he'd keep it in mind. It wasn't the concession of defeat I'd been hoping for, but it seemed to be the only thing I'd get out of him. And now it was time to strip the rest of the way . . . without wasting my breath asking him to turn his back. Since there was no chance he'd *stay* turned . . .

Grabbing the bottom of my tank top and simply yanking it off over my head was like jumping into ice-cold water: the faster you did it and had it behind you, the better off you were. Unhooking my bra and shrugging out of it was another effort of the same sort, and then only my shorts and bikini-briefs were left. It was hard not to mutter under my breath as I finished the job, but I had no trouble at all avoiding the giant's stare as I tossed the last of my clothing into the pile.

"If you mean to bring those things with you, best you wash them before washing yourself," the giant remarked. I glanced up to see that he'd turned away from me, and had released the leather holding his scabbarded sword across his back. He'd also removed the dagger strapped to his thigh, and was just then in the process of taking the cloth off his breathtaking body. I had the choice of standing there and watching the way he'd watched while I undressed, or going ahead and starting to wash my clothes. The clothes won hands down, but not because I'm chicken. It's stupid to start something you have no intentions of finishing—and certainly don't want finished *for* you.

I took my clothes and socks and found a good place to sit on the riverbank while doing the washing, trying my best to cover my nakedness with my arms. The air was hot and heavy even under the partial shade of trees, and letting my legs down into the water was heavenly. The river current seemed mild, and a glance upriver revealed a bank that jutted out a number of feet into the river, blocking the current and slowing it close to the bank downriver. It would be really nice for bathing in—once I finished ruining my clothes.

"You seem displeased over the necessity for clothes-washing," the shadow I'd tried to forget about observed over my left shoulder. "Perhaps you feel yourself too good for such menial chores."

"It's the clothes that are too good," I answered without looking up, finally starting with my socks. "They're what the manufacturers call 'delicate fabrics.' They're not used to being treated this way. Where's that soap you mentioned?"

"Here," he said, and his hand came over my shoulder to offer a closed piece of crockery. "Its makers call it the finest soap to be found, therefore should it do little harm to your clothing."

"If it's not liquid detergent made especially for delicate fabrics, it might as well be lye soap," I said, taking the crockery and putting it down by my side. "I'm going to try to fool the clothes by lathering this stuff up first and washing the clothes in the lather, but I don't expect it to work. Clothes like these aren't easy to fool."

"You truly are the strangest woman I have ever come across," he said, and then, with a splash, he was in the river and looking up at me. The water covered him no more than waist high, but under the circumstances that was just high enough.

"Never before have I heard talk of 'fooling' clothing," he continued. "Other women do no more than wash them, and that with little interest and enthusiasm. Also do they usually voice their displeasure with certain actions, even those actions which are necessities. You, on the other hand, accept necessities when they prove unavoidable, and make the best of them. Tell me now what name you are called by."

"Look, do us both a favor and stop that," I said, moving my full attention to the dripping socks I held in one hand. The discomfort I'd felt earlier had increased tenfold, and only a little of that had to do with him staring at me while I sat there naked. "I'm not here because I got tired of the singles scene and wanted to try something different. Unless I'm in the middle of a dream or hallucination, you dragged me here and are now refusing to let me go. With that in mind, I want you to keep your observations and compliments to yourself, along with all friendly conversation. I don't believe in being friendly with men who kidnap me."

"I have heard it said that those who use magic prefer to keep their true names secret," he remarked after a very brief hesitation, disregarding what I'd said. "I would not use your true name to cause you harm even if I were able; I shall, however, give you another name, for I grow weary of calling you 'woman.' From this moment you will be called Wildea, and you, in turn, may call me Tarren."

"I have lots of choices in what to call you, but you can be sure *that* won't be one of them," I ground out, putting one sock down and starting to scrub the other. "I don't know what I'm supposed to have in common with magic users, and at this point I don't even care. Not giving you my name is *my* choice, which you will *not* get around by renaming me. For all I care you can call me 'Hey, you.' I won't be answering to *any* of it."

He didn't respond to that outburst, but if it wasn't amusement I felt coming from him it wasn't anything at all. The nerve of that fool, renaming me to suit himself! I was absolutely furious—and deep down very chilled. The name he'd chosen, Wildea; when my editor, Erin, had begun pestering me about writing in a love interest for the barbarian, I'd spent a couple of idle moments wondering what name she would have. The name had come quickly and had fit well . . . but I could have sworn I hadn't mentioned it to anyone; I hadn't even written it down. And the barbarian's love interest in the new book was called Mavial. The other name I'd decided to save for the woman he really fell in love with in some future book . . .

After I'd finished washing the clothes, I moved to some bushes that stood in a wide patch of direct sunlight, and spread the things over them. With the sun as hot as it was they shouldn't take long to dry, and now it was time to wash *me*. I went back to the place I'd been sitting, sat down again, then slid into the water—completely ignoring the way I was being watched. Prisoners are usually watched, and that was what I had to remember I was.

The water came up to the middle of my chest, and it felt absolutely wonderful. I got my shoulders wet, then remembered the ponytail tie I had on my hair at the base of my neck. I didn't want to lose it when I washed my hair so I turned back to the bank and put it down next to the soap.

"Perhaps it would better matters between us if I were to assist you with your bath, Wildea," a deep voice said behind me, the words a caressing murmur. I'd really been enjoying the silence, and there weren't many things that could have done a worse job of breaking it. I closed my eyes for a brief moment, knowing he was probably just trying to get me to respond to that name, but I'd be damned if I would.

Instead of answering, I ducked all the way down under water, stayed like that for a moment, then came back up with as much of a splash as I could manage. That got me a little more clear standing room, which I was able to see as soon as I wiped my eyes and turned. My personal tidal wave had pushed the redhead back a step or two, and he was busy wiping water out of his eyes.

"Did you want something?" I asked him innocently, a safe enough question considering how close he still was. "If I was hogging the soap, I apologize."

"At this moment my thoughts are not concerned with soap," he muttered, then was able to pin me with a stare. "I am more involved with considering what to do with one such as you, a woman as stubborn as a wall of stone. I have given you my word that you will be returned to your own world in just a short while, and yet you persist in creating war between us. For what reason do you refuse to allow peace instead?"

"That has to be the dumbest question in the history of the world," I said, pushing my wet hair back with both hands. "In the history of both our worlds. You kidnap me and then chain me up, and I'm supposed to forget all that because you've given your word about some nebulous future time? If peace is the kind of reaction you got from previous kidnap victims, I'm afraid they've shielded you from *my* version of real life. But don't worry, by the time *I'm* finished with you, you won't have any delusions left."

I turned with that and began to move away from him and the bank both, needing to put a lot more distance between us. When I looked at him I'd been trying very hard not to *notice* what I was looking at, but I had a lot less in common with that stone wall than he thought. As a healthy female I'd noticed much too much, and it was doing my resolve a lot of damage. The idea of making peace with him was . . . *not* something I could afford to think about, not if I expected to get out of there in less than a year or two. When people make peace they also make up . . . and sometimes kiss and make up . . . or kiss and make love— No, damn it, stop thinking about how good he looks . . .

The rambling of my thoughts was much too distracting, something I discovered when I took another step—and the step wasn't there. Obviously the river bottom dropped off right at that spot, but that wasn't the only problem. The current was also stronger there, which I noticed when I felt it sweeping me away. I floundered around in an attempt to get back to the gentler current and the shallower water, but I wasn't having much success. I was about to be carried downstream . . .

And then suddenly I was being pulled back to safety, led not surprisingly by my right wrist. I had no idea how it was being done, but once again it felt as if a chain linked me to the redhead and he used it to pull me back through the water. I expected the tugging to stop once I was out of the heavy current and again able to stand, but I was drawn all the way back to where the redhead stood, and suddenly his arms had closed around me.

"There has been more than enough of your foolishness!" he scolded, his words harsh with the worry clear in his eyes. "Had I not seen what was happening, you could easily have been swept away! You will not move again from my side, else will you be punished!"

"Let go of me," I snarled, struggling against the arms that held me too tightly to his body. "Let go, you big fool, and I mean *now—!*"

But before I knew it my arms were behind me, one wrist held by his hand, the other by the bracelet, and then he was kissing me. With his free hand buried in my sopping hair I couldn't even pull back, assuming I'd be able to *make* myself pull back. The redhead was like a magnet that had turned me into iron filings, and all I wanted to do was return that demanding kiss in the same way I was getting it. Warm lips covering mine, hot and insistent . . . my breasts crushed against that massive chest . . . my thigh too well aware of how much *he* was enjoying himself . . .

But I just couldn't do it, I *couldn't* give in to him. As long as I knew the man wanted me for something more than just *me,* I wasn't *about* to jump in and make a fool of myself. You can't refuse to answer a man's questions after you let him make love to you, not and expect to be taken seriously. He had his agenda, and a friendly tumble could only strengthen it. My own agenda conflicted with his, and no matter how hard it was I meant to stick to it.

So I stopped the useless struggling I'd been doing and just held as still as the water allowed. If he was the kind to force himself on a woman I'd know about it rather quickly. In a way I hoped he was since I have no trouble hurting someone who has tried to hurt me first. Yet so far he'd done a good job of ruining my willingness to seriously damage him, but maybe that would soon change . . .

Yeah, right. I should have known better than to think he would be that cooperative. The kiss went on for another minute or two, and then he raised his head.

"Stubborn as a stone wall," he said, looking down into my eyes. "Or is it simply a matter of inexperience? Have none of those men you took for your pleasure ever once shared a kiss? Perhaps if I were to give you some instruction before attempting this a second time—"

"Instruction!" I growled, distantly hoping that the flush of red I felt in my cheeks would be taken for anger. That reference to all the men I'd had was embarrassing, referring as it did to that story I'd told him . . . "Of course someone like *you* would think I need lessons. Bigheaded fools have a hard time understanding that all women don't find them as attractive as they think they are. And I'd appreciate being released. I haven't finished taking my bath yet."

He held me for another long moment, his stare inscrutable, and then he let me go. Once I turned away from him I gave silent thanks that he *hadn't* tried to kiss me a second time. Women of stone don't care about being held to warm, hard male bodies, but we flesh and blood types tend to react in a way our minds don't necessarily agree with.

I lathered my body with the soap, and then I wet

my hair again and washed it as well. The soap did a better job on me than it had on my clothes, but I couldn't help noticing that the redhead used soap from a different piece of pottery. Very briefly I considered being suspicious, then shrugged the matter off. There wasn't much soap left in my own pot by the time I was done, and considering the size of the man I could understand his wanting enough of his own to finish the job.

Once I was thoroughly rinsed I moved to the bank of the river. I didn't think I needed any help getting out and I certainly didn't ask for it, but suddenly there were two big hands at my waist, lifting me out of the water. I quickly decided that ignoring the assistance was the best—and only—thing I could do, and simply went to pick up one of the large blue pieces of cotton cloth. The stuff was like a thin, low-grade terry cloth, but it served its purpose, being that I was able to wrap it around me more than once.

The extra section of cloth came in handy to dry my hair with, and by the time I was through the redhead was also out of the water and wrapped in cloth from the waist down. I had the impression he'd used the cloth on his hair before wrapping himself in it, but I didn't know for certain because I'd deliberately averted my eyes from him. If that episode had taught me anything, it was that I had to get out of there as fast as humanly possible. If I didn't . . .

If I didn't, things could become more than complicated. I still refused to believe any of this was real, of course, the only way I could think of to hold onto my sanity. The longer I stayed, the greater the danger of my changing my mind on that score. And I didn't know if I could handle that, I really didn't . . .

Six

Tarren retrieved both jars of soap and returned them to the sack, then brought his weapons from the riverbank to a place on the grass. In truth he should have dressed and rejoined his fighters to make preparations for the attack he knew would take place that night, and yet something held him here by the river.

Something. Tarren laughed silently at himself, knowing well enough what that something was. The woman, the one he had brought with him from the world of strangeness the wizard had sent him to. *She* was what held him here by the river, her presence something he could not yet deny himself. Though she sat studying all things save him, though her anger caused her to speak with a tongue as sharp as a sword edge—he still could not coax himself into returning her to his tent. Had he been prepared to press his capture rights his decision would certainly have been different, yet as matters stood . . .

A sigh escaped from him, one that nearly made him feel the fool the woman had named him. A man's capture rights were *never* challenged once the initial battle was done, not even by the woman involved. In most instances the woman *desired* capture, and encouraged the man to give challenge for her. In those rare instances when she did not, still did she know she must surrender herself to the man who stood victorious. It was the way of things in their world. Only rarely did a man take unwilling capture, and then most often for reasons other than attraction.

He had done so with the woman who held knowledge of what would befall him in this next bout of madness. Anger had caused him to bring her with him, that and the need to be prepared against what would come. And yet once she was here she had seemed so . . . confused and frightened and entirely helpless. To deny the reality of where you find yourself shows a very great fear, and to announce the intention of seeking a wizard alone an even greater one. Tarren had regretted his need to keep the woman and had attempted to reassure her . . .

Only to find himself tossed about like a child. Tarren smiled ruefully at the memory, recalling how shocked he had been to find himself flying through the air and landing painfully hard on the ground and his sword. It had been a forced awakening to the realization that the woman was *not* as helpless as she appeared, and did he not quickly subdue her he would lose all claim to her. For some reason he had not been able to endure that thought, a feeling which went beyond his need for knowledge. Thank all the gods the bespelled manacles had been there for his use . . .

Tarren sat in the grass and made himself comfortable, enjoying the feeling of having refreshed himself. Not quite as enjoyable was the feeling of denial still throbbing in his blood, and yet it was necessary that he restrain himself. He knew well enough that the woman he now thought of as Wildea was not without interest in him as a man, and yet she refused to acknowledge that interest.

That tale she had told him, concerning the pestilence awaiting him should he couple with her . . . At first he had been shocked into believing, and then rational thought had come to his rescue. Had it been true that something ailed her, she would surely have mentioned the fact when the matter of his capture rights had first arisen. That she had threatened dire physical attack rather than speaking of what would have surely kept him at bay meant there *was* no pestilence. For reasons she would not truthfully disclose, his Wildea refused to share herself with him.

His Wildea. Tarren sighed again at such foolishness, for the reason behind her refusal might be found in those two words alone. In no manner did she consider herself his, not even to acknowledge his capture of her. Her most fervent wish was to return to her own world, and he had freely given his word to allow it— after he had privately sworn to himself that he would somehow change her intention. Her accusation of word-breaking had brought him discomfort, and yet circumstance had allowed him no other option. Were he to release her now, she would take herself from his presence and he would likely never see her again.

And that he could not allow. Tarren fought to keep himself from straightening to his feet in answer to the challenge, a challenge he could not admit aloud. Only the gods knew why this woman, among all the rest he had involved himself with, had become the one from whom he could not turn away. It was not her beauty, substantial as that beauty was. Golden hair and green eyes, fair skin tanned by a summer sun, a lovely face, a body men would gladly fight to possess . . .

No, it was not her beauty that drew him so strongly, although the memory of it in its entirety aroused him instantly. He had not been able to keep himself from tasting her lips and pressing her nakedness against his own, and yet she had refused to melt to his passion. He had been with enough women to know when one was taken by arousal, yet she had not allowed herself to be ruled by the feeling. Her spirit had overridden her bodily desires, and *that* was what he found most compelling, the indomitable spirit so rarely found in a woman. Even the few women fighters in his company lacked it to some degree.

And that was why he had chosen to call her Wildea, after the goddess of the same name. Legend held that the goddess Wildea had been born a mortal, and her father had betrothed her to a prince who saw her beauty and coveted it. She had very much disliked her prospective husband, and for that reason had fled the marriage to join a band of outlaws. The prince's father, the king, outraged over the rejection of his son, sent troops to capture the outlaws and the girl.

But the girl and her newfound friends proved impossible to apprehend. The men had been declared outlaw by the very king who sought to recover the girl, and they were wise enough to accept her council on the best way to avoid and defeat the troops. Months went by while the king was made a fool of, and at last he could no longer bear it. In desperation he de-

manded the intervention of the gods, and received it—
only to find it the final blow. The gods had been
watching the matter, and were so delighted with the
girl's courage and skill that they allowed her to bring
down the king before raising her to godhood as one
of their own.

Tarren toyed with a single blade of grass, preferring
not to consider an outcome such as *that*. Happily, in
these latter days, folk were no longer raised to godhood, or so he fervently hoped. Giving challenge to
the gods for the possession of a woman was the action
of a fool, yet Tarren knew he would very likely *be* a
fool of that sort. He would stand in challenge against
anyone for possession of this woman—despite the
large number of difficulties her presence would surely
bring.

Tarren nearly sighed again, but was saved from it
when the girl abruptly rose to her feet and walked
toward the bushes which contained her clothing. The
manacle on his right wrist tingled to inform him of
her movement, alerting him in the event that his attention was diverted elsewhere. Her attempt to have
him remove the manacle had been a good deal more
effective than he had admitted to her, only the realization of who he would be facing succeeding in drawing him back from the brink. No true warrior would
face a nonfighter in anything other than self-defense,
yet a challenge from another warrior was a different
matter entirely.

And warrior the girl was, in spite of having been
indulged to too great a degree in her upbringing. A
strong hand was what she was in need of, to teach her

moderation and self-control. Her attempts to manipulate him had nearly gotten her put over his knee, and might well succeed in the coming days despite his reluctance to bruise her dignity so. Giving challenge was a thing warriors did, and yet one learned a certain wisdom even in that—if one wished to survive.

The girl stood near the bushes turning her clothing, so that the bottom side of it would be exposed to the sunlight. In that heat the clothing would soon be dry, as dry as her lovely golden hair was becoming. Tarren regretted not having brought a comb along for her use, as the heavy golden tresses were already tangled. When they returned to his tent he would offer her his own grooming utensils.

And with that thought he had nearly come full circle. When they returned to his tent his wish would be to offer himself to her, and yet that would be folly indeed. For whatever reason, the girl meant to keep herself from him. If he were to insist that she join him in his furs—which he could easily do even without the aid of the manacle—her stubbornness would insist that she take offense. With constant strife between them he had no hope of luring her interest and willing presence, therefore would indulgence on his part now ruin his intentions for the time when the imminent bout of madness was over.

Assuming he lived through the coming episode, and some accidental misstep did not end him this time. It was for that reason he needed the woman to speak to him, and yet she had now given her word to tell him nothing more. Frustration rose up in Tarren, a frustration all the more vexing in that it seemed impossible to avoid. The woman would not have refused to speak had he released her, and yet to have released her would have meant losing her. How was a maze such as *that* to be successfully traversed—?

"Excuse me," came the woman's voice, and Tarren looked up to see that she now crouched beside him. She also leaned forward and sniffed at him, but happily such strange behavior was quickly explained. "I thought so," she stated after sniffing, sounding much like a child's governess searching out hidden sweets. "I smell like flowers but you don't. Would you like to tell me *why* I smell like flowers but you don't?"

"Surely the answer to your question must be obvious," Tarren responded, somewhat puzzled. "The soap you used is very expensive, formulated as it is for ladies of high position. Its cost would be considerably less did it not leave behind, on dried skin, the scent of flowers, which is due to the magic used in its manufacture. As you used the soap and I did not, for what reason would you expect the aroma to cling to *me?*"

"I think that's the point *I've* been trying to get at," she said, her molten green eyes flashing. "If you'd told me I'd smell like a giant bride's bouquet from using that soap, I wouldn't have used it. Why wasn't I given a choice of which to use? Was it because you decided to make the choice *for* me?"

"It had not occurred to me that a woman would wish to choose other than the best of what was to be had," Tarren answered with bewilderment. "Why does it seem as though you berate me for having given you better than what was kept for myself?"

" 'Better' is a subjective term, even for a shamelessly selfish woman," she replied. "You aren't qualified to decide what's best for me, only I am, so don't try it again. And if the only kind of women you get to know are mercenary ones, that doesn't mean that's the only kind there are. If you ever say something like that to me again, you have my word that you'll regret it."

And with that she straightened and stalked back to the place she had been sitting. Tarren stirred in annoyance, understanding very little of what had been said to him. How he had given her insult this time was beyond him. Yet to question her would be futile, as she continued to prove over and over again. Not a single question of his could Tarren recall having had answered, beyond the very first concerning the attack that would come that night. Under other circumstances he would certainly have admired a woman who stood so unwaveringly behind her word, yet these particular circumstances had long since begun to erode his patience. His dilemma with the madness was the woman's fault to begin with; her refusal to acknowledge the truth of that most certainly did not negate the point, and yet *she* was the one who felt put-upon. How was it that he found such attraction in a woman capable of such narrow-mindedness?

And yet . . . *was* it narrow-mindedness? After a moment or two of less agitated thought, Tarren realized that the woman's fear was most likely at the bottom of her actions. To admit that her writings caused madness in his life would be, to her, an admission that what she found about her was reality. She had insisted quite strongly that it was not, and suddenly Tarren wondered what her reaction would be when she was finally forced to see the truth. It was necessary that she do so, and yet . . . perhaps it would be best to keep her from it after all . . .

The two viewpoints took to battling within his head, so fiercely that all awareness of the world left him. He wished no harm to come to the woman he now thought of as his, and yet the more strongly he attempted to hold to her, the more complex the situation became. She would not speak to him of what lay before him, and because of that his life was in danger. To assure his survival so that he might make her his in some permanent way, he now held her captive in a manner that might well cause her to come to despise him—if she did not already. Or to collapse in fear and madness, an even worse outcome. Should he release her, she would disappear so quickly, he might well come to believe he had imagined her. Had a man ever found himself so completely ensnared?

Then he became aware of a tingling on his wrist. He looked about quickly to see where the woman had gone, and relief flooded him when he realized she had only gone to the bushes holding her clothing. And then much of the relief faded when he saw that she had donned the clothing.

"I had thought you understood that you would not wear those things again," he said to her back, striving for calm. "As you have already gotten into them, you may wear them back to my tent. Once there, you will exchange them for whatever clothing Fael has located for you."

"No, I won't," the woman responded determinedly

as she turned toward him, the blue cloth discarded on the ground near her feet. "These are the clothes I came here in, and they'll be what I wear until I leave again. If you don't like that you can just let me go, otherwise you can lump it. Do *you* understand?"

"In truth, no," he replied, rising to his feet more in answer to the look in her eyes than to her words. "You know well enough that you are not to be released as yet, therefore to walk about one step from nakedness is to ask for complications in a situation already constructed of the same. Fighters are known to take what they desire; a manner of dress which encourages that habit is best avoided."

"If you and your fighters are backward Neanderthals, that's not *my* problem," she countered, folding her arms as she looked up at him. "Even in my own world a man who can't—or won't—control himself deserves to try his games with a woman like me, who doesn't mind showing him what the pain can be like on the other side of assault. If you're worried about whether or not I can take care of myself, don't bother. As long as you don't lend that bracelet to anyone, I'll be perfectly fine."

The look of withering scorn she gave him at mention of the manacle forced Tarren to clench his teeth and fight for control. Each time she sneered at his ability to best her without the manacle's aid, the need to show her the truth grew stronger and more demanding. Had she not been a warrior he would have laughed at her posturing, and yet had she not been a warrior he would have found her considerably less compelling.

"The matter is not open for debate," he informed her tightly. "When we return to my tent there will be proper clothing for you, and you will wear it. Should you fail to don it yourself, I will assist you—and take a small payment for being put to the bother. Think well upon whether or not you care to pay the price."

He turned away from her then to find his body cloth, hoping his words had had the desired effect. The woman had no desire to be made to serve him, therefore should his comment have made her think twice about disobeying.

Her ability as a fighter was not in question, merely her good sense. Not all of his men would present themselves and their desire in a forthright manner, and some might even band together and come at her in a group. Better that the woman add to her dislike of him, than that she be forced to the pleasure of those who desired no more than her body. That his feelings for her would then force him to kill those who had violated her was nearly unimportant beside the indignity she would suffer . . . *that* he would be completely unable to bear. No, better that she despise him than that she be hurt.

Tarren found the decision easily made, much more easily than withstanding the barrage of derision the woman silently spewed. Once he had his weapons replaced he began to gather up the other things he had brought, and saw at once that Wildea had neatly folded the cotton cloth she had used. Yet once again her back was to him, this time as she stood looking across the river, her bearing impenetrable. She had not replaced her odd footgear. He would have questioned her, but knew what her response would be.

"We may now depart," Tarren said after picking up the cloth the woman had used. "Come, Wildea, for there are a number of things I must attend to."

The woman stood as though deaf. She insisted on disobeying him in all ways possible, even refusing to respond to the name he had given her. Another woman would have shared her own name to keep from being addressed by one she disliked. This woman, however . . .

His reluctance to use the manacle had grown, but he had little choice. He therefore clenched his left fist, which once again linked the manacle about his wrist directly to the one about hers. A tug of his arm brought the same to hers, making her know that she would walk or be dragged. The glance she sent him was filled with fury, but she bent to retrieve her footgear and began to follow along behind. Tarren ignored the urge to sigh, and simply led the way back to his tent.

By the time they arrived at his camp, Tarren no longer doubted the wisdom in seeing Wildea properly clad. She had apparently paid no mind to the manner in which his men had inspected her, but Tarren had seen every look and knew that if she stayed as she was there was sure to be trouble. And there was also the matter of the madness beginning, a thing he was able to feel as one feels the touch of a shirt or mantle as it settles in place. The sensation of becoming another man was far too familiar, and although it had not yet settled on him fully, he was beginning to feel its inception.

"Tarren, your arrival is most timely," Fael said as he turned to see him and Wildea enter the tent. "I have now been saved the necessity of carrying these things to you at the river. Ristahr is the largest of our female fighters, and she gladly donated this clothing for the use of your woman. She assured me it need not be returned, for she has not worn the things since the day before she joined us."

"I'm not his woman, and I don't wear other people's castoffs," Wildea said coldly as Tarren rid himself of the blue cloth and sack and moved forward to see Fael's offerings. "You can just take those things back to wherever you got them, and tell the woman thanks but no thanks."

"Give Ristahr my thanks, and tell her these will do nicely," Tarren said to Fael once he had examined the clothing, paying no mind to Wildea's immediate rejection of what she had not even seen. "Await me in your tent, and when I am done here I will join you to speak of what measures I would have us take against this night's attack."

Fael nodded and quickly left the tent, the haste of his departure only a shade less than unseemly. As a fighting man Fael knew the look of a situation about to become a battle, and he clearly had no wish to find himself in the midst of that battle. Tarren would have enjoyed exercising a similar wisdom, but that choice had not been given him.

"Ristahr has sent a perfectly good skirt and tunic,"

he said instead to Wildea, holding the items out to her. "Remove your own things and put these on."

Though the pale yellow short-sleeved, low-cut tunic was almost new, as was the long, full, dark-green skirt, Wildea regarded them as if they were little more than rags.

"If you like them that much, *you* put them on," she said, making no effort to take the things. "For myself, I don't wear skirts, and wouldn't wear one down to my ankles even if I did. And since I won't be here long enough for clothing to matter, let's find something else to argue about. Like just exactly when you expect to act like a real man and turn me loose."

"The topic under discussion at this moment is attire, not departures," Tarren said, struggling to keep his temper in check. "In view of that, there is only a single question to be answered: Are you to change your clothing, or am I to change it for you?"

"I'm not changing anything, and if you try to touch me I'll defend myself," she replied hotly, her green eyes sparking. "This game stopped being amusing about the time you decided to make me a prisoner. Go ahead if you have to, but don't blame me for what happens."

Tarren searched her face to gauge her intent. There was something about the way she stood, one foot somewhat behind the other, arms and hands loose and ready to move. The closer the day moved toward sundown, the tighter the mantle of another man's life drew about him, the more he saw through that other man's eyes . . .

And what Tarren saw—and now recognized—was

that she stood ready to engage him in unarmed combat. The steadiness and confidence of her stance said she was no novice to weaponless combat, something he had not realized the first time he had faced her. But now he was gradually seeing through the eyes of that man whose life he had so often been forced to live, and also was beginning to gain his skill. Not all of it, but hopefully enough of the other's ability with that sort of combat to keep the woman from doing him serious harm.

Tarren tossed the skirt and blouse aside, then began to remove his sword and dagger. His gaze he left resting on Wildea, just as her gaze now rested on him. No longer was there intimacy between them, only battle in the offing. Tarren would sooner have had the intimacy, but first the woman had to be taught to respect him. One learns from those one respects, and lasting love was based on that.

"This has not gone so far that you may not change your mind," he said once his weapons were removed, slowly moving toward the woman. "One who sees reason and relents is wise indeed, for—"

Tarren would have grunted in pain had he had the breath, but the woman's heel in his middle had driven all the breath from him. He had done no more than reach a hand out toward her shoulder when her foot had landed on his torso. He backed up as quickly as possible while straining for air, one hand to his middle, the other somehow fending off her continuing attacks. Somehow . . . he was blocking, a technique of the other's he was able to utilize if he paid it no mind.

Thinking about it sent it back to the shadows, to await the coming of night.

"That's about as gentle as I intend to be," Wildea said as he stood hunched over, pain flashing through his middle. "I'm not enjoying this any more than you are, but I'm *not* going to back down. Take my advice and give it up before we both end up really sorry."

Tarren's first urge was to charge at her as he had done earlier in his successful capture, but the thoughts now entering his mind convinced him of the foolishness of such an approach. Earlier she had not been facing him in ready stance, and if he did the same again she would certainly do him a great deal of damage. So said the thoughts of one who knew, which caused Tarren to growl in frustration. How was a man to teach a woman to respect him, if he lay broken and bloody at her feet? By threatening to stain her clothing with his blood, perhaps?

Lunacy was a fit word for what he now indulged in, but Tarren's self-disgust was too great for that to matter. He knew well enough how effective a manner of battle Wildea used, for during the times of madness he was able to use it himself. But at the moment he could not will himself to use it, and yet he had to defeat the woman without doing her any harm or allowing her to do *him* any great harm. He did not want to give her cause to point a finger of dishonor at him.

By now the pain in Tarren's middle had eased enough to allow him to straighten, which also increased his determination. At base the change of clothing was for Wildea's protection and safety, and that consideration must be uppermost in his mind. It would please him to be respected by the woman he felt such attraction for, but her safety must come before his self-indulgence. She seemed to expect words from him, possibly a concession, but words would best be left for later—after he had accomplished his aim.

He immediately set out to work, though with a good deal more shrewdness than before. He moved directly toward her, but keeping his thoughts from efforts at protection allowed his body to respond unthinkingly with the necessary blocks. Wildea kicked twice low and then a third time high, all of which would have reached him had his arm not performed the proper blocking motions. She then shot a fist toward his chest, a bit below center, and his own ignorance betrayed him. Thinking she could not possibly do him serious harm with her fist, he nearly allowed the blow to land unhindered.

Only at the last instant did the returning knowledge of the madness tell him he was a fool. A heart blow such as that could well paralyze him, possibly even slay him if delivered with enough force. With that finally clear to him, Tarren was able to move back with the blow—which lessened the impact of it only to a small extent. Pain flared in him again—along with anger that a *woman* was in the process of besting him—and then fighting rage forced its way through his blood. He would not be defeated, could not allow himself to be defeated, no matter the pain inflicted on him. Pain was nothing; victory was all.

With a growl, Tarren advanced again. Wildea continued her attempt to beat him to the ground, but blocking protected him from most of the attacks and the rest went unfelt. It was she who gave ground against his advance, she whose resolve began to falter, she who attempted in vain to redouble her efforts. But he refused to be stopped or even slowed, and in another moment he had backed her against the tent wall. Jumping forward then allowed him to close his hands on her arms, but keeping to such a position would have left him much too vulnerable. Instead he spun her about, put an arm around her waist, and tossed her down to the rugs of the tent floor.

"No!" she screamed as he quickly followed, pinning her down with his body. "Damn it, this is no way to fight!"

"From my point of view, this is the best way," he said, immediately beginning to remove her clothing. It was necessary to pull the cloth of her top out of her hands, but once he had done so he was able to toss it aside. The strapped garment she wore beneath the top, a thin and lacy thing of white, was unfamiliar to him, but not so the simple hook holding it closed. That, too, was unclasped and tossed away, and then he reached to her nether clothing.

Pulling both things free of her body at once was wisest, since partially releasing her legs encouraged her to kick. Tarren used the flat of his hand once, hard, on her bare bottom to show his displeasure with her struggling, then finished taking the garments when the shock of his blow immobilized her. They, too, were tossed aside, and then he turned the woman to her back and held her in his arms.

It was far from the wisest thing he might have done, but he could not have denied himself. Desire flared wildly through him as he pressed her naked body to his, an even sharper desire than what he had experienced in the river. To hold her while knowing he might not take her was agony, but to fail to hold her would have been still worse. How soft her skin was, how exciting her unclothed flesh—and how sharp the pain in the thought that he might well still lose her.

"In a moment I will help you dress," he said in the face of her sullen anger. "First, however, I mean to claim my price for having had to assist you to disrobe. And allow me to say how lovely your scent is, as lovely as an armful of wildflowers."

Her immediate sputtering fury was expected, and even more, planned for. When her lips parted in an attempt to berate him, he quickly silenced her with a kiss, a deep and powerful kiss. For the smallest instant surprise caused her to respond, and momentarily their lips met willingly. Then, of course, anger flared in her anew. Nevertheless Tarren continued to kiss her, and only reluctantly pulled away.

"I look forward to the next time you disobey me," he murmured, ignoring her seething outrage. "Each time you do so my price will be higher, and will take longer in the settling. By all means, continue to act as you please."

She glared at him then, but he was satisfied to see a trace of hesitation in her eyes. He had made good on his promise this first time; there was no reason to believe he would not do the same again. If she continued in her desire to keep herself from him, she might well choose to obey him the next time. If he was to be denied, at least he would have her obedience.

Tarren stood and helped Wildea to her feet, ignoring the way she shook his hand from her arm. He fetched the skirt and tunic Fael had brought, allowed the woman to dress in them herself, then gathered up the clothing he had taken from her. He thought there would be no further words from her, but when he reached for his weapons she took a step toward him.

"You can't mean you're taking my clothes *with* you," she protested. "The least you can do is give me my underthings. No one will know I have them on, and then I won't feel naked."

"You and I will know," he corrected, carrying both weapons and clothing to the chest containing his personal possessions. "Had you not forced me to take these things from you, I might well have allowed you to keep the undergarments. Now you must earn their return, or else do without them. The choice is entirely yours."

He might have added that her appearance in the skirt and tunic could not possibly have been bettered by the addition of underthings, but he had no wish to encourage another attack. It would have been indelicate of him to mention how clearly her hardened nipples could be seen through the thin fabric of the tunic, yet not in so enticing a manner as her previous garment had presented. He had noticed the hardening of her nipples as he kissed her, a reaction he chose to see as encouraging to his cause. Perhaps her apparent dislike of him was less thorough than she would have him believe.

"You may use this comb and brush if you wish,"

he said, removing the items from the chest and placing them on a rug. His own comb was of plain wood, sturdy and workmanlike, but not so the items he offered. They were made of carved ivory inset with rubies, the bristles of the brush as soft as a gathering of silk. He had bought the comb and brush many years earlier, with the first of the gold he had earned as a fighter. He had kept them for the woman he would some day marry, and now, perhaps . . .

"My own comb I will take with me," he continued, closing the chest. "I will be absent a while; when I return it will likely be close to dinnertime. There is water in the skin hanging on that peg. Should you require something else, it will need to await my return. You may not, of course, leave the tent during my absence."

It was clear he need not wait for a response from her. Her promise of vengeance was clear in her eyes, which brought him again the urge to sigh. He was now likely even farther away from making the woman his, but there was nothing he might do to change that. It was time to go to Fael's tent, where he might sit upon the rugs and attempt to ease the bruises and aches he would continue to feel for some time.

Tarren paused for a moment just before stepping from his tent, clenched his left fist, and moved his arm in a line across the tent entrance. That line would be a boundary beyond which the manacle on Wildea's wrist would not permit her to go, a precaution he knew was necessary. He did wish to find her there when he returned, even though her temper would surely be further soured. Ah well, there would be another time to find a common ground with her, the gods willing . . .

Seven

The big fool paused in front of the tent flaps, and then he ducked out and left. The tent itself was high enough for him, but the flaps were a little too low. Well, for me they were just fine, and as soon as he'd had a minute or two to get where he was going, I'd prove how fine they were. He'd probably decided to leave a guard outside, but I could deal with that.

As long as the guard wasn't *him*. I turned away from the tent flaps in disgust—self-disgust. I'd almost had him in that fight, had almost won the right to keep my own clothes—and then he'd somehow run right over me. As big as he was, I'd still managed to reach him a couple of times; I knew I had from the way he'd reacted. And then suddenly, out of the blue, he seemed oblivious to my attacks. He just came at me, and then . . .

And then he'd taken away my clothes, and was holding and kissing me the way he had in the river. It was hard to believe that someone like him would consider a measly kiss as a horrible punishment, but he might have been remembering that story I'd told him about my contagion. Or maybe he wasn't quite as interested

in me as he'd acted, which would certainly be fine
with *me*. It wasn't as if I found *him* attractive . . .

Especially after he'd forced me into those clothes;
he'd even taken my underwear! I really did feel naked
under that thin jersey blouse and woven cotton skirt,
mostly because I *was* naked under them—even if they
covered me considerably more than my shorts and
tank top had. They didn't happen to be as comfortable
as my shorts and tank top. And the style of them! The
low-cut pale yellow blouse buttoned up the front and
had cap sleeves. The dark green skirt was very full
and fell to my ankles, and that much material was hot.
Not to mention that the skirt was slightly too big in
the waist; the buttons and hooks didn't close it tightly
enough.

But I'd just have to put up with all that until I got
home. It seemed like the redhead had been gone long
enough, so I went and got my socks and running
shoes. The socks were still damp—which was why I
hadn't put them and the shoes on at the river—but
once I reached the road I was convinced was out there,
I'd have to wear them anyway. Bare feet are fine for
grass—and fighting—but they just don't cut it on
stones and wagon ruts.

But then I was forced to pause and ask myself how
I knew what the road was like. It may be true that
most primitive roads have stones and wagon ruts, but
I could see the road in my mind, just as though it were
familiar from my having used it any number of times.
Just the way that tent felt familiar, now that I stopped
to think about it. But that was ridiculous. This place
wasn't real, so how could . . .

I took a deep breath and decided it was time I stopped kidding myself. This world *was* real, and the reason everything in it felt so familiar was that it was the world I'd been writing about. In theory, that was perfectly possible. Scientists claim there are an infinite number of parallel or alternate worlds existing just beyond our own, where anything you think of can be found. The worlds closest to ours are just like ours with one or two minor differences, but the farther out you go, the more differences you find.

Which had to mean that this world was pretty far out. It was the actual duplicate of the world I'd been writing about, and the "wizard" who had helped the redhead to bring me there was most likely one of its leading scientists. Unsophisticated people tend to confuse technology with magic, a truism I was more than familiar with. I really was in another world, and my surroundings had nothing to do with practical jokes.

But that didn't mean I was ready to believe the rest of the redhead's claims. The idea that he was being forced to do things by my books was absurd, not to mention unheard of. Alternate worlds was a scientific possibility, living out fiction was not. The man was seriously disturbed, but maybe he would pull out of it when midnight came and nothing happened. I hoped so, but wasn't about to sit around waiting to find out. I wanted out of there, and was ready to get it for myself.

Holding my socks and running shoes, I peeked out of the tent from the shadows, thinking it would be better to spot a guard before he spotted me. There were a couple of people near their own tents a good distance away, but no one stationed outside mine. The redhead must have thought he'd intimidated me into staying put. It was time to prove how wrong he was.

I simply strolled out of the tent—or, at least, I started to. Right smack in the middle of the opening it felt as if I'd run into a wall—one that appeared nowhere but in front of my right wrist. I found that out by experimenting, since my left arm had gone past the point where my right one was stopped. I was able to get all of me out of the tent but my right wrist that had that damned bracelet on it. If I'd wanted to cut my hand off I could have left, but other than that I might as well be locked in a cage.

"Damn him!" I growled once I'd given up and gone back inside, then I threw my shoes, one at a time, as hard as I could. The tent was too big and too empty of knickknacks for the shoe-throwing to do any damage, but I'd still been able to imagine I was throwing them at the fool's head. Just because he hadn't made use of the bracelet during our fight, I'd somehow forgotten about it. Not very bright, seeing as he'd used it to confine me there. Right then I really did wish his head was handy for throwing things at.

I paced back and forth for a while to work off some of the anger roiling inside me, but it only worked to a small extent. There was nothing in the big tent to focus on, except the rugs scattered across the floor, four big chests across the back wall, a saddle and bridle set in the lefthand back corner, and a few pegs with various things on them on the wall braces. It was the pavilion-sized field tent I usually wrote about, well used but without the little touches that made it feel like home.

At one point in my pacing I found myself standing above the comb and brush the redhead had offered me the use of. They were a set, a very beautiful and expensive set, and I almost did pick them up and use them. My hair was a tangled mess that *needed* brushing and combing, but not with something given me by *him*. The longer I was forced to stay with him the more I hated him, and I wasn't about to accept *anything* from him. Except my freedom, of course; *that* I would grab with both hands.

After a while I stopped pacing and sat down, but sitting instead of standing makes boredom only a little easier to take. There was nothing to do in that tent but wait, and I've always hated waiting more than anything. Well, more than *almost* anything. There are a couple of things worse, but that tent wasn't a likely place for having to go through a root canal or an IRS audit.

It was dusk by the time the redhead returned, and the interior of the tent had grown dark. He paused briefly just inside the entrance, then walked toward the wall brace on his right.

"Why have you not lit the lamp?" he asked, having spotted me where I lay stretched out on my side on the rugs. I was propped up on an elbow, which must have indicated to him that I wasn't asleep. "I did not mean for you to sit in the dark." he added.

He lit the lamp himself, and then turned back to see that I was now sitting as cross-legged as the skirt he had given me allowed. I would not look at him, and also had no intention of talking to him. My saying anything at all had probably encouraged him to believe I would eventually answer his questions, so the time for fraternizing was over. The sooner he believed he'd get nothing out of me, the sooner I'd be free.

"Our hunters brought in two boar this afternoon," the redhead commented as he moved toward the back of the tent. "They have been roasting for hours, and should soon be fit to eat. There are potatoes and greens as well, and there will also be fresh bread if the farmwife up the road baked this afternoon. I have given instructions that your plate be well filled, as you ate nothing earlier today."

I continued to sit in silence, idly wondering if I was supposed to thank my jailor for offering to feed me. Like I said, I had no intention of accepting anything from him, and that included food. Any appetite I might have had had disappeared, growing fainter the longer I was kept where I didn't want to be. I was beginning to understand why caged animals sometimes starved to death despite an ample supply of food.

"The silence in this tent has grown rather intense," the redhead observed after a short pause. "Also, I see that your hair has not yet been combed. For what reason did you find the comb and brush unacceptable?"

He paused again, undoubtedly to give me every chance to answer. When it became obvious even to him that it wasn't going to happen, he sighed deeply.

"So you have decided to sit about sulking like a child denied her latest whim," he said. "It is clear to me now that my initial assessment of you as having been indulged in your youth was correct."

He almost got me with that. I was half a breath away from telling him off, when all that self-disgust I'd felt earlier came flooding back, this time over my supposed level of intelligence. Succumbing to child psychology used by an ignorant barbarian was truly pathetic.

I concentrated on staring at the rug immediately beyond my folded legs. It was red and blue and orange and brown, a horrible, clashing combination much like the other rugs covering the floor. None of them was especially pretty, just thick and tightly woven enough to make sitting on them moderately comfortable. They also did a great job of making you wish for a decent chair.

"Perhaps you have an end in mind other than sulking," he murmured, suddenly crouched down just behind my right shoulder. "Perhaps you mean to goad me into ordering you to speak, and then to punish you when you refuse. Have you grown curious about what will come after the kiss?"

I couldn't hold back on the ridiculing sound that announced my opinion of *that* theory. It so happened I didn't believe *anything* much would come after another kiss, or if something did it would be just as innocuous. The man was trying to intimidate me, but it wasn't going to work. I shifted away from him, onto the next rug over to my left, leaving him to crouch intimately above empty air.

"Woman, you begin to try my patience again," he growled, obviously not very happy about how I'd reacted to his sexy come-on. And he *was* sexy, I'm willing to admit that much. A man that big, with rock-hard muscle under all that tanned skin, long red hair that made him look dangerously undisciplined, beyond anyone's control . . . If I'd found him in my bed at home I probably wouldn't have kicked him out, but that was the whole point. I wasn't home, because *he* wasn't letting me go.

"I find it a great pity that you were never taught to be reasonable," he went on, that growl still in his voice. "You clearly blame *me* for what has happened to you, and yet, the madness that will come is *your* doing, whether or not you mean to take responsibility for it."

He straightened and went to the back of the tent again, leaving me alone to think about what he'd said. But I'd already done my thinking. I may have been in another world, but certainly not one where my writing affected what went on. The redhead waited for something that wasn't going to happen, and when it didn't I might have my chance to get away. Once I found the scientist he called a wizard, I'd also find the way home. Somehow. I *had* to believe that, otherwise I'd end up as crazy as the man who held me captive.

This was not the cheeriest thought in the world. A crazy man can give you a lot of grief before you get away from him, but my own personal crazy man seemed to have taken to ignoring me the way I was ignoring him. I didn't mind at all, even if it did increase my boredom. I only had to wait until midnight, and then I could well be on my way out of there.

I watched through the tent flaps as early evening waned to full dark, the lamp in the tent getting brighter as the darkness outside increased. The redhead kept quiet and stayed away from me, at least until one of his men came in carrying two metal plates. The plates were piled high with food, and the redhead thanked the man when he took them, and then he brought one over to me.

"Having one's mouth full is an excellent reason for silence," he said as he put the plate down on the rug near me. "You have done well so far in proving your independence and strength of character. To take the matter further would show childishness rather than strength, a point I am sure you are already aware of."

And then he walked away, returning to the back of the tent where he undoubtedly intended seeing to his own meal. I shifted back to the rug I'd originally been sitting on, then moved again to the next one over. That plate of food didn't tempt me in the least, and if the redhead thought I'd be eating it just to keep from being called childish, he'd have to think again. My father had been a strong believer in using child psychology while my brothers and I had been growing up, which meant I'd developed rather strong mental armor against the technique. If seeing food go to waste bothered the redhead that much, he could eat the stuff himself.

One thing I couldn't help noticing as the time passed was how chilly it was starting to get. That was strange, after the heat of the day. I was to the point of wishing for a nice heavy sweatshirt when the redhead finished his meal, took a couple of swallows from the waterskin he'd pointed out earlier, then came to glance down into the plate he'd given me.

"I see you have decided to choose childishness," he

said, looking and sounding strange. He seemed suddenly unfocused and distracted, and his speech was faltering. "The choice is unfortunate . . . but . . . we will discuss it at . . . another time. Now I . . . must sleep . . ."

He stood there for another moment, wavering, not even looking at me, and then he seemed to force himself toward the back of the tent. He went to one of the chests, pulled out two thick piles of what looked like furs, and dropped one not far from the chest. The other he brought with him and dropped next to me on his way to the lamp, and then he turned the lamp down to no more than a soft glow. He stood for a moment as if trying to remember something, then he moved to the tent flaps and tied them closed before returning to the first pile of fur. He took off his sword and dagger and wrapped himself in the fur. Then he lay down and seemed to fall instantly asleep.

I sat there looking at him for a minute, but that was all there was. Not another movement or word, not another comment or criticism. Just as if he knew the barbarian in my book was supposed to be asleep for hours when the attack came . . .

I pulled my eyes away from his unmoving body and silently gave myself a good talking to. Starting to buy into *his* craziness wasn't the way to get myself out of there. All I had to do was wait a little while longer, and then everything would work itself out. Or so I hoped. I reached out for the fur and covered myself with it, but in just a little while I wrapped up in it completely. It really was cold now, and the fur was a necessity rather than an indulgence.

Then I must have dozed off. One minute it was completely quiet except for the sound of the redhead's slow breathing, the next there were shouts and the sound of metal striking metal. I jerked awake, my heart pounding, just in time to see a sword cutting through the leather ties holding the tent flaps closed. Then four men burst in, each of them with a sword in his fist, just the way they do it in the movies. But the grim determination on their faces said they weren't acting, and they'd come to bathe their weapons in real blood, not the Hollywood variety.

I hadn't gotten any farther than sitting up by then, but that didn't seem to matter. It was obvious I wasn't the one they were looking for. Their target was the redhead, and he was not only on his feet, he had his sword in his hands. There wasn't a whole lot of light coming from the lamp, but there was enough to see by.

And what I saw looked like a badly staged dream. Most dreams shift around from scene to scene without making sense, and when you're in the middle of it you never notice. I saw the four men move toward the redhead in deliberate attack, and then they were fighting. There was fighting going on outside the tent as well, which explained why no one came to the redhead's aid. He stood alone against four men . . .

And then the chills really hit me. I was on my feet backing up against the tent's side wall; by that time I began to realize that what I was seeing was exactly what I'd written in the new book. It was midnight and the unexpected attack was under way, and the barbarian was suddenly faced with defending his life against four men who were determined to take it. And the men *were* determined, despite the cautious way they treated their intended victim. They respected him and the weapon he held, but weren't going to let him stop them from doing what they'd come there to do.

I knew that they knew they would not survive the action even if they succeeded. The attackers outside were expected to die in order to give these four their chance, and in the book the four had accepted the fact that the redhead's men would kill them once the attackers outside were seen to. I stood there wrapped in shock as steel struck steel and almost struck flesh, the four men trying desperately to reach their victim, the barbarian defending himself even more desperately with greater skill than the four attackers possessed. It was incredible to watch a swordfight that clearly wasn't being staged. Each of the five men was trying to reach flesh with his weapon, not aiming for mere tactical points. They were serious, and sooner or later one of them would succeed.

If I hadn't been immobilized with shock, I would have seen what was coming. The barbarian in my book took first blood, and suddenly one of the four attackers screamed and went down, opened across the middle at the hands of the redhead. That left the other three shaken, as I'd written, but not so shaken that they retreated, and that was also the way it was meant to go. The way it had been *written,* for god's sake, the way *I* had written it.

Overwhelmed, I put one hand up to my head and the fur that I'd been clutching with both hands swung open and cold air rushed in, effectively bringing me back to my senses. I quickly pulled the fur closed again. No matter the reason for it, no matter my role in it, there was a battle being fought only a few feet away from me. I had to do something.

But I couldn't figure out what that something should be. Jumping in unarmed would have been foolish even if I'd been properly dressed, not when I knew my limitations. There are fighters around who can defend themselves unarmed against a weapon like a sword, but I'm not one of them. Maybe someday I'd be that good, but right now was what I had to deal with and right now I'd end up getting killed. What I needed was a sword of my own, since I did know how to handle the weapon—to a degree. I'd studied half a dozen methods of fencing and had handled as many different swords, though admittedly I'd never been prepared for anything like this.

Aside from that, I had no weapon. The only one in sight that wasn't in someone else's possession was the one next to the dead man, but that was practically under the feet of the remaining fighters. If I tried for it I'd probably get cut down, and even if I didn't I might distract the redhead and get *him* killed. I was on the verge of hopping around in frustration, and not just to warm up my half-frozen bare feet. I *had* to do something besides stand there watching, but what?

A second attacker screamed and went down—right on cue, so to speak—and the fighting heated up. The two remaining attackers had gone beyond desperation, knowing their time was limited. The fighting outside was getting closer by the minute, and if everything really did go the way I'd written it, the attack would soon be over.

The barbarian was supposed to finish off his last two opponents just as another attacker was forced into the tent by outside opposition. The newcomer would be the leader of the attacking force, and rather than kill him the barbarian would knock him unconscious. When the man awoke he would find himself to be the last of his force left alive, and he would eventually answer a few very important questions for the barbarian.

Which meant I didn't have much time if I wanted to help out with what was going on. The faster the two remaining attackers were accounted for, the easier it would be for the redhead to capture the man who would soon be entering. The fighting had begun to drift in my direction, forcing me to retreat toward the direction of the tent flaps. The fighting was moving *away* from the first man to go down, which meant that his sword might now be obtainable.

A glance in that direction proved that it was, so I braced against the cold and dropped the fur, then began to circle around to the abandoned weapon. I made sure to keep as far away from the fighting as possible, of course, which meant I moved along close to the front of the tent. In another couple of minutes I would have that sword, and then—

And then the redhead was on the offensive, advancing faster than he had at any other time in the fight, and his two opponents were too spent to match him. Fencing, like martial arts, is extremely hard work, and they'd been at it for long enough to tire just about anybody. When the redhead attacked as if he'd only just started to fight, the other two tried to disengage and retreat—but he refused to allow it. Two swings of that incredible broadsword backed by almost every muscle in his body, and his opponents abruptly became his late opponents.

I heard hurried bootsteps entering the tent, right behind where I now stood. I began to turn, which can only count as another mistake. If I'd had any brains I would have thrown myself out of the way, but oh, no, not the great galloping heroine. Why get out of the way, when you can simply stand there and give the bad guy a chance to wrap his left arm around your throat? The man behind me did exactly that, and then he laughed as he gestured toward the redhead with his blade.

"Nice swordplay, that," he commented, out of breath himself. "Four were sent to take your life, but instead it was theirs that were taken. Only now does it become your turn, and I must give my thanks for having been provided with this most excellent shield. I truly hope you took a great deal of pleasure from her, for that will prove to be the last pleasure of your life."

The intruder laughed suggestively as he humped into my hip, and that was absolutely it. I'd started out being angry and annoyed at myself, but suddenly all those feelings rerouted to him. The redhead growled where he'd come to an abrupt stop, and his eyes flashed dangerously. I knew the intruder probably had all sorts of plans for me, but when I get mad, things like that don't bother me. I'd wanted something to do in the fight, and now I had it.

Without wasting any more time, I brought my left

elbow back into my captor's ribs, with enough force
to crack one or two of them. He groaned and tried to
reach me with his sword, but my right hand blocked
his arm. He had released my throat to protect his side,
which let me get a two-handed grip on his right arm
and hip-toss him out from behind me. He landed on
his back between me and the redhead, his yell of fear
cut short when he hit the ground. The redhead stepped
forward and kicked him in the face just as he was
trying to get up again, and that put a temporary halt
to his mobility.

Then a bunch of men waving swords stormed into
the tent, led by Fael. The night's fighting was over,
and the only thing left was the questioning of the captive. Adrenaline still pumped through my veins, but
the danger had clearly passed.

"Tarren, seat yourself so that Kergil may see to
you," Fael said to the redhead authoritatively. "He
brought his medications, and all battle is now done
with. The prisoner may be questioned when he has
regained consciousness, but that will not be for a
while. As we are forced to wait, allow Kergil to attend
to you."

Fael seemed to be repeating himself deliberately,
but I can't say it wasn't necessary. The redhead was
giving all his attention to the man who lay sprawled
on the rugs, possibly not even hearing Fael. I didn't
understand the urgency in Fael's voice until one of the
men sheathed his sword and stepped over to the redhead, reaching for the leather pouch he wore slung at
his side. Only then did I see the blood running down

the redhead's left arm, from a deep cut across the biceps. He was wounded, and I hadn't even realized . . .

I suddenly felt lightheaded. More and more men were crowding into the tent, so I got out of the way by going back to the fur I'd dropped. I wrapped it around me as fast as possible and then sat down, before I *fell* down. The thoughts were whirling around in my head without any encouragement from me, and even more, they seemed to be settling into conclusions.

I already knew that the world I sat in was a world other than my own, but I'd just been given absolute proof that it *was* affected by my writing. The redhead wasn't crazy and he'd been telling me the complete truth. What I'd written had happened, almost exactly the way I'd written it. *Almost* exactly . . .

And that was the biggest problem. Accepting the truth about what my writing did was hard enough, but now I also had to accept the fact that when fiction and real life came together, reality had more of a say over how things would go. In my book, the barbarian fought with four men and killed them without getting a scratch. In the fight I'd just witnessed, the redhead had indeed killed the four men, but he himself had been wounded. In real life things like that happened even when the participants *weren't* seriously trying to hurt each other; when they *were* trying, injuries would be inevitable.

And death would be more than a remote possibility. I pulled the fur more closely around me, but that didn't stop the chill seeping into me. The redhead had been wounded only, but what would have happened if he'd tripped on one of those rugs they'd fought on? Reality made that risk legitimate, and the assassins wouldn't have wasted the opportunity. They were *supposed* to try to kill the man; it would have been done before my narrative had the chance to say, "Hey, you can't . . . !"

I felt sick at the thought, and then something came to me that made it even worse. The redhead had apparently been taken over completely by my story, but those around him hadn't been. My narrative said the barbarian wasn't wounded, but one of the assassins had been able to alter that. And the way the leader of the assassins had tried to use me as a shield. That certainly hadn't been any part of the book; the barbarian in my novel is alone in his tent when the scene with the assassins occurs.

So the redhead was being forced into following my story line almost exactly, while those around him had a little more freedom. "A little more" shouldn't have been all that significant, but in this case it was enough to get a man killed. To get the redhead killed. And I'd thought he was a lunatic, with all that talk of the "madness" . . .

The quiet came then, telling me in no uncertain terms that if the redhead died it would be all my fault. He'd tried to explain that, but I'd refused to listen, just the way I usually refused to listen to things I didn't care to hear. That made me even more sick to my stomach, as well as very ashamed. My arrogance had almost caused a man's death, and there was only one thing to do about it, inadequate though it now seemed.

I'd have to wait until the rest of the scene finished playing, but once it did . . .

The man Kergil took care of the redhead's wound, but not with his patient's cooperation. Despite Fael's repeated attempts to get the big man to sit, the redhead stayed on his feet, staring at his captive. He was waiting for the man to regain consciousness, I knew, so that he could begin questioning him. But at least Kergil was able to bandage the arm; I heard him mutter that if stitching proved to be necessary, it would have to wait until the madness passed.

In a couple of minutes the captive began to stir and groan, and Kergil crouched beside him and crushed a bit of hotar leaf under his nose. Hotar leaf was the local equivalent of a truth drug, making anyone who inhales its scent pliable and willing to answer questions truthfully. I'd thought I'd invented the stuff, but it looked like I'd just used something that world already had. Or had my writing about it caused it to come into being?

That was a question I didn't care to dwell on, so I simply listened to the interrogation. The captive told everyone he'd been sent by a man named Agnal Topis of Kesterlin, and his orders had been to kill the barbarian at all cost. He had no idea why he'd been ordered thus, but he wasn't in thc habit of questioning his instructions. He simply followed them, and would continue to follow them for the rest of his life.

That last bit, of course, told the listening men what had to be done with him. Once they were certain they knew all he had to tell, some of the men got him to his feet and took him outside. As soon as they got him to where the bodies of his men had been taken, he would be made into a body himself. When someone tells you they won't rest until you're dead and you have no hope of changing their mind, the only thing you can do is quietly put them down.

Once the man was out of the tent, the redhead announced, "Tomorrow we ride for Kesterlin," and then it was over. I knew it was the end of the chapter, and the next action wasn't scheduled to start until the following day. The redhead took a deep breath as he came out of his "madness" to look around, his right hand gingerly touching his bandaged left arm. Fael and Kergil tried to get his attention then, but he said something to them in a very soft voice, then left them to walk over to me.

"How do you fare?" he asked, crouching in front of me to study my face. "You seem . . . disturbed."

"Probably in every sense of the word," I agreed, unsuccessful in making my speech sound lighthearted. "I . . . have to apologize for what I said to you. You weren't making things up, you were telling the truth, and I really am responsible for all . . . *this*."

I waved a hand vaguely, but there was no doubt he knew what I meant. I wondered in passing how I could be taking it all so relatively calmly, but the answer was obvious. I like to choose my times for having hysterics, and it was still early. Later, once everyone left and I was alone . . .

"And that means I owe you some answers," I continued as he stirred uncomfortably. "The first one is why these men came to kill you. A messenger will reach you tomorrow, while you and your men are get-

ting ready to leave. The messenger will be from Prince
Drant of Kesterlin, offering you and your company
hire. He's heard of your reputation and it's *you* he
wants; if you'd been killed tonight he would not have
hired your company. Agnal Topis knows that, since
he's one of the prince's advisers. That's why he sent
those men, so that—"

"Wait," the redhead interrupted, one hand raised
and a pained expression on his face. "I appreciate your
efforts to assist me, but my head continues to spin
from the effects of the madness. I will ask Fael to
listen to your tale. In the morning, one of my men
will show you the way to the wizard's house. He can
see you back to your own world. Remain here, and I
will send Fael to you."

He straightened out of his crouch and walked away,
leaving me to stare after him rather dumbfoundedly.
Now that I was being reasonable about what he wanted
to know, *he* was being reasonable about letting me go
home. I hadn't really expected that, and I felt off-bal-
ance and uncertain. I didn't belong in that world and
I really did want to go home, but . . .

After a minute Fael approached and smiled encouragingly as he sat down on the rug facing mine.

"Tarren has asked me to listen to what you would
have him know," he said. "Since the information may
well save his life, I shall be very attentive indeed. You
may begin."

"Perhaps you should write this down, as it's a bit
complicated," I suggested, already knowing that Fael
was able to read and write. "That way you won't have

to trust your memory, and can refer back to the notes as often as you have to."

"I would do that very thing, had we the necessary paper," he answered wryly. "There is likely a sheet or two somewhere in Tarren's belongings or mine, but larger amounts can only be found in cities such as Kesterlin. We have little use for writing materials, therefore do we seldom remember to replenish our stock of it. My memory is all we have, but I assure you it is usually quite adequate."

"Then I might as well get started," I said with a sigh, hoping I could keep things simple. "As I began to tell your boss, tomorrow there will be a messenger sent by Prince Drant of Kesterlin. The prince wants—"

"Wait, wait," Fael protested, holding his hand up in the same way the redhead had. "For what reason do you speak unintelligible gibberish?"

"I'm speaking just the way I always do," I protested in turn. "What's so incomprehensible about a messenger from Prince Drant of Kesterlin?"

"About *what?*" he asked, perplexed. "Your words are perfectly clear until you reach what is apparently the necessary information. How can that be?"

"I don't know," I muttered, a familiar chill taking hold. "Maybe for some reason you're being kept from understanding. Is there someone else I can tell?"

He nodded uncertainly, and turned to call the man Kergil. Their medical man was tall and husky, a blond with a bushy red beard and blue eyes, and he came over quickly to join us.

"Kergil, you must seat yourself and listen," Fael said, patting the rug next to him. "The lady wishes to speak of what lies ahead of us, and I seem to be having difficulty . . . taking it in."

"Very well," Kergil agreed with raised brows, obviously having noticed Fael's carefully chosen words. Once he was seated I tried again.

"I'm going to start by telling you about tomorrow morning," I said, and Kergil nodded encouragingly. "A messenger will come from Prince Drant of—"

"Wait," Kergil interrupted, and damned if he wasn't wearing the same confused expression Fael had. "Why are you speaking so strangely? If there is something we need to know, you must say it in *this* tongue so that we may understand. You—"

"By the gods!" Fael interrupted him, frustration clear on his face. "No sense can be made of this!"

I freed my hands from the fur in order to bury my face in them, swallowing down the urge to groan. I had no idea why the two men weren't able to understand me, and also couldn't think of anything to do about it.

"What has occurred to disturb you three?" the redhead's voice came, and I looked up to see that he'd come back. "Wildea, why do you not proceed with your telling?"

"I keep saying that a messenger will arrive tomorrow from Prince Drant of Kesterlin," I told him wearily. "The only problem is, none of you can understand what that means."

"How difficult is it to understand the meaning of the arrival of a messenger?" the redhead asked, perplexed. "Prince Drant will offer me hire, and then . . . what? The details are what I must know."

"Tarren understands!" Fael exclaimed, getting to his

feet. "Once again your words were gibberish, girl, but when Tarren spoke I understood plainly."

"How can he be the only one who understands me?" I demanded. "What's going on? What kind of crazy world do you have here?"

"Clearly the matter is linked to the madness," the redhead said with a thoughtful frown. "Only rarely is Fael influenced by it; my other men are touched to an even smaller extent."

"Well, it makes matters difficult, but that's to be expected, I suppose, in this place. At least there's someone who can understand me, but it looks like you're going to have to *make* time to listen, after all."

"You mistake the situation, Wildea," he said, the words gentle as he gestured for Fael and Kergil to depart. "I would listen if I were able, but as soon as my tent has been cleared of all battle remains, I will be forced to sleep again. I am already feeling the sleep waiting to take me. We will have only a short time in the morning before we go our separate ways. You must tell me what I need to know then."

"But that won't be enough time!" I protested, leaving the fur as I got to my feet to face him. "There are a lot of subplots running through the book, and each one of them hooks into the main problem. Unless you understand how they work you won't understand what's happening around you—and *why* it's happening—until it's too late. That's the way it was written. And my name is Deanne. Deanne Lane."

"Deanne Lane," he repeated, tasting the name in a way that didn't quite seem to be approval. "I appreciate your disclosing that. And I am also aware of the problem of how much there is to know. I would change matters if I could, but it is not possible. What else would you have me do?"

That was the prize-winning question, of course. I did happen to have an idea, but I would have preferred to come up with something else. Only there wasn't anything else, so it was time to prove that I'd gone crazy after all.

"It seems fairly obvious that *you* can't do anything, but the same isn't true about me," I said after letting out a deep breath. "This whole thing is my fault, so I have to do something about it. I—won't go home until you know what exactly you'll be facing."

"No," he responded immediately, startling the hell out of me. For some reason I'd been certain he would jump at the idea . . . "You are not knowingly responsible for the madness, therefore you will not be forced to remain in a place you do not belong. Come the morning, you will go to the wizard Massaelae and ask him to return you to your proper world."

"Why are you being so unreasonable?" I couldn't help demanding, upset at seeing the determination in his cold blue eyes. "You didn't seem to have anything against keeping me here until now, and against my will at that. Now that I'm volunteering, you suddenly object? Why?"

"Because I have no wish to see you dead," he answered simply. "You told me of the man I would take captive after the battle, the one who would tell me who my new enemy was. The matter was obviously written so, and by you. How, then, did you end in a position where that very same man was able to use you as a shield? One stroke of his sword, and *your* blood would have been added to the rest spilled here!"

He was really angry now, and for some reason it was more difficult to meet his gaze. But he was wrong, and I had to tell him so.

"I just happened to miscalculate the time," I explained, working hard to sound self-assured. "I was trying to get to a sword so I could take part in the fight, and I lost track of when the man was due to come in. But what difference does that make? He may have *taken* me as a shield, but he certainly didn't keep me for long. He was supposed to get knocked unconscious, and he was."

"And you freed yourself through the exercise of your great fighting prowess," he said, the words filled with barely controlled fury. "And you would have embroiled yourself in the sword fight, could you have reached a weapon in time. Are you insane, woman? Has it not yet come through to you that this is not a tale told around a fire at night, but *reality?* You could have *died,* and that I will *not* allow to happen. Tomorrow you will return to your own world."

"Will I?" I countered, folding my arms as I looked up at him with sudden anger of my own. "Who do you have around here big enough to force me to do that? You can't do it yourself, not when you have to be here to speak to that messenger, and then get your people on the road to Kesterlin. So how do you expect to make me go back? If I don't tell you what's ahead of you, *you* could die. If you think I can just go home and put my feet up and forget that I'd be responsible, *you're* the one who's crazy. I'm staying here, even if I have to fight everyone in your company to do it."

He regarded me in stony silence for a moment, then he said, "If I allowed you to remain, you would be most unhappy. You would find it beyond you to accept the situation, for I would teach you certain lessons I believe it would be well for you to learn. You, however, would not see it that way, and would quickly regret not having gone home when you were able. Kesterlin is nearly a full day's ride from here, and once we get there there will be no easy return. Go to Massaelae's house in the morning, and go back to where you belong."

I returned his gaze, refusing to be intimidated. He was trying to scare me off by threatening to do all sorts of unnamed things, terrible, horrible things that I would hate but be helpless against. Yeah, right. A man who considers a kiss as terrible punishment is going to do something I can't handle. I became a wall of unshakable resolve.

"So you still refuse," he said after a minute. "Then unfortunately the situation forces me to comply. But you stay under *my* terms, which you will *not* find pleasant. And now I must sleep. See that you do the same, for tomorrow we travel to Kesterlin."

He turned and walked away, and only then did I notice that the bodies of the fallen warriors had been taken out and the bloodstained rugs replaced with clean ones. Tarren's men and the lamps that they had brought into the tent with them were also gone, leaving us alone with the dim light we'd started with. The redhead retrieved his fur, wrapped himself in it, and once again was quickly asleep.

"It's a good thing I *didn't* give him a steady girl-friend," I muttered, going back to my own fur. "Considering that out-like-a-light bit, she'd have to have taken vows of abstinence to stay with him. If this has been going on for a while, he could even be a virgin."

As I lay down, I told myself not to be nasty; what I really felt was terribly ashamed. The redhead had to know the details of my book in order to protect his life, but that had suddenly become of secondary importance to him because he thought *my* life could be in danger. He was trying to get rid of me in order to keep me safe, but I couldn't let him do that. It was *his* life that was most likely to be lost, and I'd be damned if I let that happen.

So he intended to make life difficult for me in an effort to get me to leave; so what? I can take anything I have to in a good enough cause, and this cause went beyond good. I was responsible, so I'd make things right, and *then* I would go home. But not before, no matter what he tried.

I wasn't all that worried. I'd be able to handle him . . .

Eight

Tarren awoke at dawn, relieved as usual to be released from the forced sleep. But not as relieved as he should have been, not after his discussion with Wildea. He sat up slowly to look at her sleeping form, aware of the beginnings of an ache in his left arm. The pain-deadening salve Kergil had used on his wound would soon wear off, and before then the man would want to work some healing on it. It would be best to seek him out now and let him do his work . . .

But Tarren was not yet ready to leave the tent that held the sleeping Wildea. Had the choice been his he would have slept beside her, both of them wrapped in the same fur, unclad bodies touching. Perhaps then his desire for her would have kindled a like desire in her for him. They would then have shared themselves with each other, not simply gone to sleep like uncaring strangers.

Uncaring. Was any word describing his thoughts of Wildea more inaccurate? And was it possible to call *her* anything but headstrong? A tremor of dread raced through Tarren at the memory of how she had nearly been killed, an incident *she* had treated dismissively.

Even in the midst of the madness he had been horri-
fied, and yet she—

He took a deep breath to steady himself. He had
been sincere in wanting her to return to her own world,
and even in this she had insisted on disobeying him.
Her desire to preserve his life moved him, yet did he
know she was motivated only by guilt. But that had
very little bearing on his own feelings. He was willing
to do anything to keep her beside him—short of standing by and watching her be slain. To prevent that he
would see her returned to her own world, which would
certainly mean they would never meet again.

But now the woman insisted on accompanying him,
and in truth there was little he could do to change
that. *He* would have found it possible to carry her over
his shoulder to the wizard's house and then thrust her
through the doorway of mist, but no other member of
his company would have so much as tried. They feared
the High Magic of wizards, and rightly so, but Wildea
would question that. She saw herself as a fearsome
warrior, and in her eyes *that* would be the reason none
would accompany her to the wizard. And it was true,
she did have a certain skill . . .

Yet skill alone kept no man—or woman—alive.
Some few lacked confidence despite the abilities and
were therefore defeated, but by far the greatest number
lacked self-control and that became their downfall.
Fighters who wished to survive took the proper training to remedy these destructive lacks, but apparently
the same was not given in Wildea's world. Or, at the
very least, had not been given to her. Perhaps that had
been because she was a girl child. Many men could

not bear the thought of seeing their daughters or sisters at risk, and therefore *refused* to see the warrior blood in them.

A deliberate blindness which was extremely foolish, for it increased rather than eliminated the risk they feared. Tarren thought of how often Wildea had challenged him, a brashness he would not have tolerated in any other living being. Even with her it had been difficult, and it was necessary to recall that others would not exercise the same restraint where she was concerned. Lessons in equanimity were what the girl needed, and while she remained with him they were what she would get.

Even if the lessons caused her to turn away from him forever. Better that than to leave her as she was, and one day find her lying in a pool of her own blood. Tarren shook his head in an attempt to dislodge the disturbing image, then stood and gathered up his weapons. He had not even properly cleaned and oiled his sword, another outrageous consequence of the madness. He would have to see to it once Kergil treated his wound, that and a number of other things. They would soon be on the road, after all, and moving a company the size of his took effort.

At the tent entrance, Tarren remembered to clench his fist, removing the magical force he had previously drawn in the air with his manacle. It was no longer necessary to confine Wildea to his tent, and although her presence gladdened his heart, he would still have been easier in his mind did she suddenly decide to return home after all. The name she had given for use when addressing her . . . such a name could only be from the strange and alien place she called home. Here she was Wildea, and so she would remain.

And perhaps the lessons he would teach would bring her closer to him rather than drive her away. Should that be so, he would certainly take full advantage of it. The woman was meant to be his, of that he had grown certain; making her know the same would be his major difficulty. But the deed would be far more easily done were he able to hold her in his arms while attempting it. Perhaps there was a way . . . perhaps . . .

Tarren stepped out of his tent into the new day, a smile playing on his lips. During the times of the madness his thoughts and actions were never his own, but there were still the times in between. It was then he would work to make Wildea his own . . .

My own discomfort woke me, and when I opened my eyes it was to see that the sun was up—and already heating the air enough to make the fur oppressive. That was just as well. I had to get up. I had things to do, like describing the details of my book to the redhead.

I'd thought about the situation before falling asleep the night before, and now I was even more convinced that I had to stay. I'd already noticed that the people around the redhead had quite a bit of freedom in what the book made them do—like the assassin who had tried to use me as a shield—but the redhead himself just as obviously didn't.

He should have been willing to have his wound tended to last night once the fighting was over, but

Kergil had had to bandage him without his cooperation. Nothing had needed his attention just then, so
there was no reason for him not to cooperate—except
that the way the book went, the barbarian simply
waited patiently for his captive to wake up. Last night
after the battle, it was like he'd had no choice. I'd
spent enough time in his company to know that he'd
never have done anything as stupid as ignoring a
wound that needed to be dressed if he *had* had the
choice.

So I'd have to stay and tell him the details of the
dangerous parts of my book, so that he could tell Fael
and the others. We'd proven last night that the others
understood what would happen when the redhead
spoke about it, but not when I did. That arrangement
was really frustrating—not to mention unwieldy—but
I'd have to live with it if the redhead was going to
survive. If one small accident would be enough to
cause his death, knowing what was coming should
lessen the likelihood of that accident happening.

I stretched, yawned, and sat up, trying to pull my
mind together enough to justify a claim of being
awake. Being a night person means being totally out
of it until somewhere around noon, and it was a long
way away from that most civilized part of the day. I
looked around, spotted where my socks and running
shoes had ended up, then forced myself to my feet. I
would have preferred crawling over to them to give
my blood a chance to start circulating, but skirts aren't
made to crawl around in. Well, that skirt was the first
thing I'd have to see about changing.

My socks were stiff but dry, and as soon as I had

them and the shoes on I tried the tent flaps to see if I could get out of there. It was a relief when I found that I could, and I was able to walk out and look around for the man whose life had become mysteriously entangled with my life's work. Everyone seemed to be busy packing up the camp, but my unintentional victim sat on a box all by himself, eating breakfast. I headed over to him.

"Good morning," I said on approaching him, trying not to stare guiltily at the bandage—much smaller than the one he had worn last night—on his wound. "How's your arm doing?"

"Tolerably well," he answered, nodding to me in greeting. "Kergil has decreed that this new bandage need only be worn for the rest of today, and then will no longer be required. Are you prepared to tell me what I must hear?"

"As soon as you have the time to listen," I agreed. "But since you're in the middle of your meal, why don't I change clothes first to give you a chance to finish. If you'll tell me where you put my things, I'll even go and get them myself."

"No," he said, still chewing. Just like that. Not, "Tell me first," or, "You can't get to the clothes without being shown," or even, "I like what you're wearing much better." Just a flat, almost disinterested, no. It looked like he was getting an early start on his discouragement tactics.

"What do you mean, no?" I asked. "Those clothes are mine and I'd like to have them. Everyone else around here dresses to suit themselves, so there's no reason why *I* can't."

"Not everyone," he disagreed, still looking completely unconcerned. "Were the choice mine, I would dress in breeches and a shirt and boots rather than a simple body cloth. Should you truly desire your clothing, you may have it—as you leave to find the wizard's house."

"That's unfair," I told him, beginning to be annoyed. "Using my clothes as a way to get me to leave is a dirty trick, but it still isn't going to work. I'll leave after you know what's in the book, not a minute before. The least you can do is give me my underwear. Since I'm cooperating, it's—"

"No," he said again, those blue eyes resting calmly on my face. "If there is something you wish, you must earn it. Now, what will you have to break your fast, which has continued far too long already?"

His question didn't divert me much—until I realized that I still wasn't all that hungry. It was going on twenty-four hours since the last time I'd eaten, but I felt no more than a faint and distant interest in food. And I hadn't even been craving coffee, which was more than ordinarily strange. I usually live with a coffee cup no more than two feet from my hand, but for the last day . . .

"I'm still not hungry at all, although I wouldn't mind some coffee," I said. "Do you have any idea *why* I'm not hungry? It isn't something I've written into this world. I like food too much."

"It is not a state I am familiar with," he answered with a frown. "I had thought your lack of appetite no more than stubbornness, but apparently I was mistaken. Should your appetite not return by this evening at the latest, you will need to force yourself to eat. One cannot live without sustenance in this world, and perhaps your appetite merely needs to be reawakened. As for coffee, we have used up our supply and need to purchase more when we reach the city. In the interim, a pot of chai stands there."

He pointed to a nearby fire, where a rather primitive container stood on the stones surrounding the flames. I walked to the spot and reached for the pot handle, which was just short of being too hot to touch, but I still managed to fill one of a nearby cluster of metal cups. I tasted the stuff tentatively. Chai appeared to be tea, which was a definite disappointment.

"If you don't get new supplies soon, I may never wake up," I commented as I turned back to the redhead. "But that's not the reason I came over here. Are you ready to listen to those details yet, Your Majesty, or do you have something else you'd like to disagree about first?"

"Sarcasm will not be tolerated," he responded, once again looking up at me with those ice-blue eyes. "You were told you would find your time here unpleasant, but would nevertheless be required to obey if you remained. You have until my company is prepared to leave to change your mind. While you remain, I am to be addressed as Tarren, and now you may begin your tale."

"That's really big of you," I murmured with a friendly smile after taking another sip of that too strong, unsweetened tea. I could see he was trying hard to drive me into blowing up and walking away, but that wasn't going to happen. If I left without telling him everything he needed to know, he could die, a hard and brutal truth all the pushing in the universe wasn't going to make me forget. Besides, just because someone decides to give you orders doesn't mean you have to obey them.

"The messenger from Prince Drant of Kesterlin will get here just as you and your company are ready to leave," I continued before he could reprimand me again. "The prince had been informed of your presence here, a routine report he gets on all travelers across his realm. Yesterday the prince discovered the theft of a possession he considers extremely important. His father had given him a ring of quartz, to be worn only when vital decisions are to be made, and that's what was taken."

"The ring is magic, then," the redhead commented after swallowing a bite of bread and cheese. "Magical objects are very much in demand in Kesterlin, for the city encourages the presence of mages. Most of them are below wizard level, but some . . . Which of them is responsible for the theft?"

"None of them," I answered with a headshake. "The culprit is not a magic user, though the prince will be led to believe differently for a while. He sends for you and your company, intending to send you after the ring. He knows your—the barbarian's—reputation for honesty. The ring could have been stolen in the first place only if some of his guards accepted a bribe, so he can't depend on any of *them* to find and return it."

"A sensible precaution," he commented with a nod. "And yet I still fail to understand. If the ring is *not* magical, for what reason would its return be so vitally important?"

"It's important because *he* believes it is," I said. "It does nothing but sit on his finger, but because he believes it has some kind of magical power, he always makes the right decision. He has the ability to do that all on his own, but what he lacks is confidence. His father knew that, so he gave him a phony magical ring to embolden him. But this is all beside the point, not to mention unnecessary for your survival. Can I get back to the main storyline now?"

He gestured his permission in a mock-regal sort of way, with faint amusement in his eyes.

"As I said, the prince hires you and installs you and your company in one wing of his palace," I continued. "He has his agents out looking for clues to the ring's whereabouts. It takes them about a week to conduct their investigation, and their information leads you to the thieves' and assassins' guilds, and both of their headquarters are protected by magic."

"For what reason would assassins be involved in the matter of a stolen ring?" the redhead demanded. "And for what reason would there be a need to look about for clues? The first one to be questioned should be this Agnal Topis, the man who sent the assassins against me last night. Was there not some link between him and the theft, he would not have sought my life."

"He's nothing but a red herring," I ground out, confused by his questioning as well as frustrated. "He sent those assassins after you because he doesn't want you and your men involved, not when he's already made a deal with another company. He's one of the prince's closest advisers, but he wants more power than he has. If he can get to the ring first he'll have that power, so it's essential to him that his own hirelings are the only ones out looking for it. He'll make another couple of attempts on your life at the palace, but neither of them will be successful."

"One hopes," he said dryly. "But that fails to explain the reason why I keep from speaking out against him, or where the assassins' guild enters the matter."

"You don't speak out against him because of the obvious regard the prince holds him in," I answered. "You realize you would not be believed, especially as it is your word against his, and you have no proof to back up an accusation. Agnal Topis can always claim the assassination attempt was made in his name, without his knowledge, to ruin his reputation. And if you don't say anything, he might not know *you* know the truth. Which could be to your advantage."

"But he must know I am aware of the truth," the redhead replied. "None of his men returned from their mission. He will assume the assassination attempt was thwarted, that the men he sent are dead. That one or all was forced to acknowledge who sent them. Another reason for those additional attempts against my life, which you failed to provide any details about."

"Which I *wouldn't* have failed to do if you didn't keep interrupting," I said exasperatedly. "And before you do so again, the clue leading to the assassins' guild is planted by Agnal Topis's allies, still hoping to get rid of you. You suspect it's a trap, but you still have to check it out. It might be a legitimate lead, and if so, you can't afford to ignore it. The prince has a very important decision coming up, and he needs the ring to make it. If he makes the wrong decision, his entire princedom will suffer."

"And without the ring, he will certainly make the wrong decision," the redhead pronounced sourly. "The intelligent course would be to seek for the thief among those who would not suffer from the prince making the wrong decision. Or is such a concept too simple for a work such as yours?"

"If you mean simpleminded, you're right," I answered. "The real villain behind the theft isn't someone who benefits directly from the prince not having the ring, but someone who thinks he'll benefit indirectly. He's wrong, of course, but he's not bright enough to see that. Are there any more tangents you'd like to go off on? It's not like *I'm* losing the thread of the damn book myself, so feel free to keep confusing the hell out of me."

"The use of strong language by a woman is extremely unattractive," he said, finally rising to his feet. "And before we both lose all understanding of what will occur, we had best leave the topic for a while. Is there anything you wish in my tent before it is taken down and put in a wagon? Perhaps the use of that comb you refused yesterday?"

I shrugged as if to say I didn't care one way or the other, but that wasn't entirely true. If my unkempt hair bothered him—which apparently it did, since he kept mentioning it—I was annoyed enough with him to want to keep it like that. I hadn't realized how hard it is to *describe* a book to people. There are so many little threads that have to be woven in. And having to fend off a barrage of questions and comments didn't help much, either. If the big idiot had just sat there and listened, I *wouldn't* have forgotten to explain the two attempts on his life that would happen at the palace. Pretty soon I wouldn't even need a comb for my hair— It would all be gone after I'd torn it out in frustration.

"I will get you the comb once my trunks have been loaded into their wagon," he said. "When you are done with it, do not attempt to replace it in the trunk yourself. The spells guarding each lock are minor, but are still able to do considerable harm."

"Since that *is* something from the books, I'm already aware of it," I said with another shrug, then looked at the men emptying his tent in preparation for striking it. "Those men who are seeing to your possessions—didn't a couple of them replace the stained rugs last night? I hadn't realized you kept so many servants in your camp."

"We have no servants at all here," he corrected, his eyes never leaving me. "Those men have apprenticed themselves to various members of my company, their aim being to learn the skills of a fighter. For part of the day they take instruction in weapons, and the rest of their time is spent in doing what needs to be done around the camp. They pay for their lessons with the sweat of their brow, which makes those lessons more valuable to them. One learns more from a lesson paid for in sweat than from one paid for in gold."

"If you say so," I commented sweetly, refusing to

argue the point as he seemed to be expecting me to do. Under other circumstances I probably *would* have argued, but right now he wanted nothing more than a good reason to leave me behind. Arguing everything he said would have supplied that reason, and I really didn't want to have to follow him on foot.

It didn't take the apprentices long to clear the tent of trunks and rugs, and then they took down the tent itself. They were mostly very young men, but one or two looked to be well into adulthood. They worked as fast as possible, since the rest of the camp was already struck and the sun was already well up. And then the sun bounced off my wrist with a gleam, reminding me of something that did need mentioning.

"By the way, you can have your bracelet back now," I said, holding up my right wrist and turning it a little. "Since I'm free to go or stay as I please, there's no longer a reason for me to wear it."

"But a reason does remain," he said simply. "The reason is that *I* wish you to wear it, and so you shall. If you dislike the idea—"

"I know, I know," I interrupted in a growl I couldn't hold back. "If I don't like it I can always leave. But the point is I do intend to leave, only not at this moment. And if you don't stop trying so hard to get rid of me, I'll save my book the trouble of killing you by doing it myself."

"You may make the attempt if you wish," he said, amusement in his eyes. "A fighter is often faced with attempts to slay him. Should you decide to make the attempt, Wildea, you had best hope that you accomplish your aim. If you fail, you will have me to answer to."

"So you've said," I answered dryly. "As *I've* said that my name is Deanne Lane. I won't respond to the other, no matter how long you persist in using it. I don't intend to hear it again even if you happen to say it."

"Refusing to hear it will not make it any less yours, Wildea," he countered, enjoying himself entirely too much for my liking. "It has now become time for you to either make for the wizard's house or to climb into the wagon where I wish you to be. After this, you will no longer have your own choice in things."

"As opposed to the way it's been up until now?" I asked, then snorted. "You're mistaken about the matter of choice. People *always* have a choice about what they do, as long as they're willing to pay the price of that choice. I've always been willing to pay; so don't say I didn't warn you. If you try to push me too far, *you'll* be the one regretting it."

"There is a great difference between being willing to defend oneself and daring another to test one's skill. The next challenge you give me I will accept, Wildea, so it would be prudent of you to think before you speak."

He headed off toward the line of wagons then, and after a very brief hesitation I followed. I didn't quite understand what he meant by challenging him, not when I had simply been telling him where I stood. I considered asking for an explanation, then shrugged off the idea. His tone was vaguely threatening, but I was getting used to threats that didn't come to anything.

The wagon he led me to was tarped over about two-thirds of its length; the canvas cover stretched over arched braces protected his four trunks and the numerous rugs he'd had on his floor. The redhead climbed into the wagon, went to one of the trunks, then came back out holding the carved ivory comb.

"This is for you, and you will ride in the back of this wagon," he said, handing me the comb. "The rugs will provide you with comfort, and the canvas will shade you when the sun climbs high and hot. I believe the moment approaches for the arrival of the messenger of which you spoke, therefore I must leave you. We will speak again later, once we are on the road to Kesterlin."

And then he picked me up and set me in the wagon before turning and striding away. He was obviously being pressured by the advance of the book, which turned out to be a fairly lucky thing. He'd startled me by picking me up that abruptly, but even more he'd surprised me with how much strength he used so effortlessly. He was a formidable man, and maybe I *would* be smart to watch what I said to him.

I paused to take a substantial sip from the cup of chai I had managed to keep from spilling when he'd lifted me. The redhead may have been under pressure from the book, but he'd still taken advantage of the situation in an effort to make his threats sound more real. He'd been trying to show that he was strong enough to do just about anything he pleased to me, so I'd better behave the way he wanted me to.

I shook my head as I went back to find a place to sit on one of the piles of rugs, wondering how long he would keep that up. He seemed more than ordinarily anxious to be rid of me, as though he didn't believe I really would leave as soon as I told him about the book. Well, if that was his problem, he was worrying for nothing. As soon as he had what he needed, he'd get his wish and I'd be gone.

I put my cup of chai down on the wagon floorboards beyond the rugs, then studied the comb he'd given me. It was a very beautiful comb, but I still didn't know whether I'd be able to use it. It reminded me of the day before, when the man who owned it had seemed so very interested in me. Personally interested, and not just because I was responsible for his trouble. But that had probably been no more than his way of trying to get me into bed. I'd put up a fight, and now all he'd wanted was to see me leave.

And for some stupid reason, that was distressing. It wasn't as if I found *him* more than physically attractive, after all, so I didn't understand *why* his attitude bothered me. But it did, which is why I hesitated to use that comb. I was being childish and stubborn but my reasons were clear. It belonged to a man who really wanted me out of his life. Every time I looked at the carved ivory I thought of that. And for some reason, being out of his life hurt. In any case, if that life he wanted me out of hadn't been at stake, I would already be gone. But I owed him the answers he needed, so I'd stay there long enough to supply them.

And after that I *would* leave, just as fast as I possibly could. Which, in a way, I wished I could do right now. I hate being where I'm not wanted, but it certainly wouldn't be for much longer. And then I'd be out of his life, which seemed exactly the way he wanted it.

Nine

Tarren put Wildea in the low wagon, then let the rapidly descending madness direct his steps to his horse. The stallion had already been saddled and awaited him, a welcome but surprising sight. He had last seen the animal tied to a post outside of the wizard's house, and since Tarren had not returned for the mount, Massaelae must have returned him.

His stallion reached a sleek black nose forward to greet him, and Tarren stroked the animal's neck a moment before preparing to mount. The entire company was either mounted or in wagons, proving *he* was the laggard. They should already have been on their way, the insistence inside him proclaimed, and he'd best be about it.

The stallion, Flatterer, was well rested and eager to be on the road, and Tarren allowed him to move ahead as a signal to the others. Their order of march would be the usual one, with riders both ahead of and behind each of the wagons. Had they been expecting opposition in large numbers it would not have been the same, but there would not be such opposition ahead. If there were, the woman would surely have mentioned it.

"Tarren, I believe I see a rider ahead, just off the

road," Fael said after riding up on his side. "It must surely be the messenger the woman spoke to you of, and yet I see nothing of the red cloak of officialdom."

"Likely the man attempts to disguise his presence," Tarren forced himself to say. "In another moment I will be taken by the madness, and then you must see if you are able to warn me—that is, the one the madness makes me become. If not . . ."

And then the words and thoughts of the moment disappeared, leaving him to wonder what he and Fael had been speaking of. Ah, well, it could not have been very important, Tarren concluded, not when they rode for Kesterlin to learn why assassins had been sent against him. The road was only a short distance ahead. But what manner of man approached, riding toward them alone? He was well-dressed, but also well covered with the dust of his travels.

"Fael, halt the column," Tarren said, his eyes narrowing as he studied the approaching rider. "And look about carefully for any signs of an ambush."

"Tarren, this must surely be the messenger from Prince Drant whose coming was foretold to me," Fael said slowly and carefully. "I cannot now explain in what manner I was advised of this, but know you that it is true. Will you trust my word?"

"Always have I trusted your word," Tarren replied, glancing at Fael quizzically. "This time will be no different, though I expect an explanation from you once the stranger has gone. And now let us see if your information proves correct."

Tarren pulled his stallion to a halt and awaited the newcomer, giving the man all his attention. How curious it was that Fael would know a thing he did not, an event that had never before occurred. He would listen closely when the time came to learn the reason behind the oddity, yet now it was time to listen to the man who approached.

"I believe I address the warrior Tarren, leader of the well-known fighting company," the stranger called from where he halted, a good ten feet away. "If this is so, I would approach and speak with you privately, sir."

"I am Tarren," Tarren allowed, seeing how carefully the man kept his hands from his weapons. "You may approach and tell me who *you* are."

"I am called Gol," the man responded once he had closed the distance between them. "I am a special messenger of Prince Drant of Kesterlin, may he rule forever. His Highness has ordered me to bring you this."

He handed Tarren a folded thickness of paper. Tarren, being unable to read, took the missive and passed it to Fael giving his second a meaningful glance. Apparently Fael *had* been told the truth. The messenger Gol seemed prepared to protest Tarren's handing away of the document, and then thought better of it. What sense was there in insisting no other was to see the writing, when Tarren, unassisted, could *not* read it?

"It seems we are being offered hire by Prince Drant," Fael said after a quick perusal of the message. "The sum mentioned is indeed princely, and the request is most courteously put. Shall I read it aloud?"

"Later," Tarren replied, his gaze remaining on the messenger. "For what reason would Prince Drant hire a company such as mine? His generals command a dozen companies and more, and he commands his generals. What use has he for me and mine that cannot be accomplished by others?"

"That, sir, is for the prince himself to discuss," Gol responded evenly. "If you will give me your reply, I will carry it immediately to the prince."

"Tell him we will be in Kesterlin before dark," Tarren said, his expression concealing the curiosity he felt. "I will thereafter be honored to listen to what requirements he has. Hopefully they will be such that will allow me to accept his hire."

"Sir, I will carry your word," Gol said, then turned his horse and rode off. Flatterer nearly followed, eager to race the messenger's mount, but Tarren held him back. They would need to keep to a good pace to reach Kesterlin before dark, and Flatterer would need all his strength.

"That horse has clearly not run all the way from the city," Fael remarked as his own mount danced. "The man surely used the prince's posting houses along the way, which supplied him with fresh mounts."

"And which will certainly do the same for his return," Tarren added. "With that in mind, send out scouts to be certain we find nothing of a surprising nature awaiting us along the way. After that we will discuss who gave you such excellent information."

Fael grunted and rode off to give the necessary orders, and then Tarren felt himself being slowly released from what had held him so tightly. Gradually the madness receded, and he was himself again.

Their plan had worked; Tarren, even in the midst of the madness, had heeded what Fael had told him. That meant he would indeed be forewarned during the occurrences, and would not need to trust his life to pure chance. It was apparently impossible to change the progression of the book as it had been written, but foreknowledge would allow him to be prepared for what occurred, rather than being taken by surprise— which was where the greatest danger lay.

Tarren stretched a bit, pleased with the way things had gone. When next the madness took him, Fael would need to speak of some secret magic which gave him knowledge of what was to occur. Though he were taken by the madness, he would believe Fael, he would listen to his second. This last encounter had been proof of that. Another event was now behind them, and he would be free until they reached the city. Or at least he hoped he would be free. Once they were on the road, he would question Wildea again.

He hoped she'd refrained from giving him further challenge. Tarren sighed as he allowed Flatterer to move forward again, wondering which would this time bring him more difficulty, the new madness or the creator of the madness. He had done everything possible to discourage the woman from accompanying him, but her stubbornness had exceeded his determination. It would be untrue to say he was not delighted with his failure, but his worries over her safety remained.

The meadow under Flatterer's feet led quickly to the road, and even before Tarren reached it his scouts rode past him. They would take to the woods on either side of the road and spread out. It was unlikely the company would succumb to ambush, not after their recent attack by assassins, but laxity in guarding oneself was foolish. Far better to make the effort unnecessarily than to end up regretting the oversight.

Tarren waited until the entire company was on the road before he left Fael at the head of the column and rode back to the wagon that carried his belongings. *And* that carried Wildea—her presence there was meant to be significant, a message to his fighters that Wildea was under his protection, that any claims on her would be personally contested by him.

Tarren peered into the wagon and saw Wildea sitting on a pile of rugs, the cup of chai in her hands, her expression revealing her to be lost in thought. She still had not used the comb—why did she persist in such behavior? Perhaps she sought a way to defy him without running the risk of a direct challenge. He cleared his throat.

"Ah, you're back," she said suddenly in her odd way of speaking, roused from her thoughts. "Are you ready to listen again, only this time *without* extraneous questions? The more you divert me, the more likely it is that I'll forget something important."

She had left her chai cup and had come to the wagon side, perching on it with a hip as she leaned her back against the canvas brace. The way the wagon jounced along the road made her position somewhat precarious, a fact Tarren believed she knew. But she had clearly chosen to be unconcerned with risk. Again, perhaps, to defy him.

He moved Flatterer closer to the side of the wagon,

leaned over, and snatched her from her perch. Her squawk of surprise and indignation made him grin as he settled her sideways across his saddle. His left arm supported her back, his right hand held to her thigh just above the knee, and her own hands gripped his shoulders in fright for a moment before she forced herself to release him.

"That wasn't funny!" she snapped, dots of red coloring her fair cheeks. "Either give me a horse of my own to ride, or put me back in the wagon!"

"No," he replied evenly, finding it delightful to have her so close to him. "Our conversation will be held much more easily this way, and there are two things I must ask before you begin again. The first is, are we to be attacked on our way to the city? After having sent the assassins last night, it would make sense for Agnal Topis to follow up with an ambush today."

"Topis can't afford to do that, and *he* knows it even if you don't," Wildea replied indignantly. "The assassination attempt occurred before the messenger reached you, which means anyone could be responsible for the attack. An attempt today would be brought to the prince's attention; he'd conclude that someone was trying to keep him from hiring you and your company, and he wouldn't hire another without knowing who was responsible for eliminating yours."

"I see," he murmured. "Your writing tends to be intricate indeed, more's the pity. Now I would know of the two attempts against my life which will come in the next week. When are they to happen, and what will they consist of?"

"Look, I don't know about you, but I'm very uncomfortable like this," she said, squirming some small amount in his lap. "I also happen to be here for just one reason, and that *isn't* to get you turned on. If you want—"

"Turned on?" Tarren interrupted, wondering at the phrase's meaning. "How are you using those words? They seem to make very little sense."

"That depends on your position at the time you use them," she muttered, then raised those very green eyes to his face. "In *my* position, it isn't hard to tell that you're enjoying having me in your lap. But you can forget about scratching that particular itch, at least with me. I don't take well to the role of handy female."

"Handy female," Tarren mused with a grin, finally understanding to what she referred. "But you most certainly *are* female, else I would not be experiencing the—itch. And were you not the one who insisted on accompanying me, no matter the discomfort I warned would be yours? You were told your presence here would be under *my* terms, and you agreed to that. Are you now attempting to define what my terms must be? Surely you understand that that happens to be *my* prerogative?"

"Yes, but that's not—" she began, frustration in those lovely eyes, but Tarren had no intentions of allowing her to continue.

"Then you see that the matter involves more than the concept of 'handy female'," he went on, riding over her attempted protest. "You have already agreed to my terms, no matter what they may be. Should I wish to extend those terms, as I mean to do once we have reached the city, you have no grounds for protest. Is that not true?"

"It's true only as long as I want to stay and tell you about the book," she answered after something of a hesitation, a flush now spreading across her cheeks. "If I decide to say to hell with it and leave, it's no longer true."

"You were also told that once we left camp you would no longer have the choice," Tarren quickly pointed out. "And yet I feel in the mood to be generous. Although what occurs in my life *will* be your doing, you may overlook that and go your own way right now. Should that be your wish, I will set you down so that you may follow this road in the opposite direction. Is that your wish?"

"Damn you!" she growled, controlled fury now heating her gaze. "You know I can't just turn around and walk away, not when your dying would be *my* fault! You're using my sense of responsibility against me, and that *stinks!*"

"Was it not you who said we all have choices in this life?" he countered, filled with relief that she would not be leaving him. "Also you said that certain choices demand a price, and you have always been willing to pay that price. Is the price now beyond your means?"

She stared at him in seething silence, hating that her words had been thrown back at her but unable to argue the point. Or apparently unable to argue it. Tarren was certain she would find another stance to take, but for the moment she had conceded that she was his. But not yet his in the way he wished her to be.

She would come grudgingly to his bed, but once there she would find herself held in the arms of a man who offered his love as well as his body, desiring *her* love rather than just her body. If she was truly meant to be his, he would find it possible to convince her of it.

"So the price is not too great for you to pay," he concluded after a moment, knowing better than to leave the matter unresolved. "Once we are settled in the city you will need to do so, but at this moment I require no more from you than conversation. Tell me of the two attempts there will be against my life."

"The first one will occur tomorrow night, after a lavish dinner party the prince throws in your honor," she replied after the briefest pause, as though another matter had momentarily taken her thoughts. "Topis will have a servant make sure your wine cup is never empty, but he's not just going to be counting on getting you drunk. The servant will also be drugging your wine, but subtly, to make it *look* like you're drunk. By the time you get back to your apartment you'll be ready to pass out, and that's when the assassins will try to jump you."

"But I defend myself successfully?" Tarren asked, the doubt he felt too strong to be kept from his voice. "How am I to do that, when it will be professional assassins I face?"

"They won't be professional, and you won't have to do it alone," she responded, showing a faint frown. "Topis will think you'll be easy to take, so he'll hire a few of the palace bullies to finish you. Because of that you'll manage to hold them off until some of your men come to help you and—God, it never occurred to me how much of a disadvantage I was putting you at. When you write something like this it doesn't matter, because you know it will turn out the way you want it to. But when someone is forced to *live* through it, there can't possibly be any guarantees. What if there's an accident, and one of them gets you . . . ?"

"Calm yourself, Wildea," he said quickly, putting his arms tightly about her to warm away the shudder that shook her body. "You could not possibly have known this would happen, and now that I have been warned there will be little chance of an accident occurring. Tell me why Agnal Topis will not hesitate to attack me in the palace, when he dares not attack me on the road today."

"Today he's one of the only three people beside the prince who know the prince means to hire you," she answered, for a moment making no effort to push away from his chest. Her cheek rested against him, and the palms of her hands, and—"By tomorrow night everyone involved in and around the palace will know, so the risk of being found out is minimal. Besides, he won't be doing all that hiring and bribing himself, so no one will be able to point a finger at him even if they're caught."

"Unfortunate," Tarren commented in a mutter, struggling to pay attention to something other than the woman he held. He had wanted her almost from the first moment he laid eyes on her, quickly coming to know her as the woman destined to be his. Now, holding her so close, it was difficult to think of anything but that. He had never been a man to deny himself, but he had also never forced himself on a woman. It was a measure of his desperation that he had gone so far as to maneuver Wildea into his bed, and he had best be satisfied with that. For the moment.

"What of the second attack?" he asked, now desperate to divert his mind. "When does it come, and under what circumstances?"

"It happens in the afternoon, before the evening you're supposed to start checking into the leads the prince's agents have found," she replied, taking a deep breath after leaning away from him. "This second time the assassin will be female, and killing you will be her second priority. The first will be to compromise you, an effort to show the prince how easily you're distracted from what's really important. Once she's done that, *then* she's supposed to kill you. But you, of course, aren't taken in by her wiles, so you're neither compromised *nor* killed."

"Nor, apparently, allowed the prerogatives of what should be a man's by right," Tarren added dryly, finding it impossible to keep silent. "By that alone, I should have known the author of the madness to be a woman. Men and women will likely always see these matters differently."

"And what difference is that?" she asked, a dangerous glint to her green eyes. "Why is it a matter of man versus woman, when the point should be the same no matter *who's* writing it? If you don't rape a male assassin trying for your life, you have no right to rape a female trying the same thing."

"I find it unnecessary to rape any female, assassin or not," Tarren replied. "What you seem to have difficulty in comprehending is that I would do nothing more than slay *anyone* attempting my life. But if that anyone came with smiles and swaying hips, offering me pleasure should I choose to take it, then what came afterward before the slaying would be no more than just. Those who offer themselves, male or female, have no grounds for complaint when the offer is accepted."

"Maybe so, maybe not," the woman said begrudgingly. "I still don't agree with you, but that's beside the point. What you have to remember about the second attack is that the woman won't be armed with a conventional weapon. She'll have a poisoned pin hidden in her clothing; that's what you'll have to watch out for."

"I will need to speak to Fael of both incidents, for I, myself, will have no memory of what you tell me," Tarren said with a nod of agreement. "Is there any other thing I must know concerning this period of time, the week before I begin efforts to retrieve the ring? We may speak of what comes afterward later, once Fael and I have made plans to take us through these first hazards."

"There's no other danger I can think of," she said, her brow wrinkled in thought. "We reach the city about an hour before sundown, Gol meets you at the main gate, then he and his escort lead you to the palace. While your people are moving personal possessions into the rooms you've all been given, the prince greets you and introduces you to his advisers. After that, you're on your own until the morning, when the prince sends for you and explains his problem. His letter contained nothing in the way of specifics."

"Once the messenger had left, I was able to read it

for myself," Tarren said with another nod. "Only when the madness is working strongly am I unable to read, a lack I am undisturbed by while it is present. I will return you to the wagon now, and then speak with Fael."

"Wait a minute," she said as he began to urge Flatterer closer to the wagon. "I'm a good rider, and I'd like a mount of my own. And I'd also appreciate something else to wear. I do *not* do well in skirts."

"Riding in the wagon will do you little harm," Tarren replied. "Also will you continue to wear what you have been given, for at the moment there is nothing else to offer. When a choice becomes available, however, you will then need to earn the new things. We will speak this evening of what the earning will entail."

Annoyance tinged with outrage flashed in her eyes before Tarren swung her back into the wagon, holding to her until her footing was firm. Tarren quickly urged Flatterer back toward the head of the column, before she found yet another thing to demand of him. The demands were, of course, only a response to having been refused in whatever requests she had put, the expected reaction of one chafing under unfamiliar restrictions. The apprentice fighters his company took on usually behaved the same.

But their situation was not identical to Wildea's. The girl had been raised to be willful. It was a practiced trait. Restraint and control under all circumstances was what the apprentice fighters were taught, and that would also be taught his Wildea.

But first he would need to take his thoughts from the memory of how her body felt beneath his hands, the thin cloth of her clothing doing little to impede his appreciation of her. His arousal was full because of those things, but also because of the memory of her distress at his situation. Many folk in her place would have shrugged with lack of concern over his plight; they would not, after all, have been *trying* to do him harm, and therefore would feel no guilt over the results of their doings.

Wildea, however, felt full responsibility, despite his assurances that the fault was not hers. Her concern was not for a situation that might come to prove embarrassing or awkward for *her,* but one that might turn deadly for *him.* She was a woman, then, who considered others besides herself, one with compassion and conscience to match his own.

And then another thought came to him, of how she had known the name of the prince's messenger without having been there during his brief visit. Had he doubted her ability to speak of what would happen, his doubts were now no more. She *knew* . . . as he needed to know. And when the madness had run its course he would find some suitable reward for her selflessness, which at this time he could not afford to acknowledge . . .

By the gods, but his life was becoming even more entangled than her writing!

Ten

The procession didn't actually stop at lunchtime, it just slowed down to give people the opportunity to eat. Some sort of dried meat was handed out by a few of the apprentices, but I still had no interest in food. Brooding was what I was into at the moment, something I'd been doing since the redhead had returned me to the wagon. The man was taking advantage every which way he could, and that fact was getting me mad as hell.

But some of his actions were disturbing on a level that really alarmed me. Since the man now knew he wasn't going to be rid of me any time soon, he'd decided to make the best of my being there by ordering me into his bed. He'd just about made it a condition of my staying. I'd be damned if I was going to sit back and be dragged into his bed . . . even if I wanted it . . . and I certainly didn't want it . . .

If I'd been somewhere private I would have screamed out loud, the frustration was that intense. All right, so I found the man physically attractive; did that mean I had to continually wobble back and forth about whether or not I wanted sex with him? Because his attitude and actions proved that that was all it would be for him. A roll in the hay, a quick tumble, a fun time. And that wouldn't have been so bad, except—except I seemed to *want* something more.

Want, that was the key word. If I could just figure out what I really did want, it might not be so bad. What I thought I wanted was to tell the man what dangers he had ahead of him, and then take myself home. It was what I should have wanted and had wanted—until he'd pulled me into his lap. All I'd been aware of then was the big body I was so close to, those hands burning me right through my clothes. And when I'd suddenly realized what a terribly dangerous position I'd put him in with that first attack, he'd put those arms around me and had held me until I'd stopped shivering.

All of which made me want to shiver even more. He'd taken the trouble to tell me again that none of it was really my fault because I hadn't done it on purpose. And he wasn't just saying that, he really meant it. None of the men I knew would have reassured me like that, not even if they thought it was true. They would have used the guilt to manipulate me, not simply taken advantage of my sense of responsibility. *He'd* used my own words to back me into a corner, but that meant he was actually *listening* to what I said.

I took a deep breath and shifted around on the pile of rugs, trying to add up all those buts and ands. They seemed to mean there was more to the man than a great body and handsome face, and that was why I was interested in more than just sex with him. But what more could there be, when I would be going home soon and would never see him again? Even if he'd wanted to see *me,* which I knew he didn't. It wasn't possible for anything real to grow between us, not when we *literally* came from two different worlds.

So it was fruitless to think about anything developing between us; it just wasn't possible. That meant I should be avoiding him to keep the complications to a minimum, but he wasn't *letting* me avoid him. He'd made it clear that tonight he would drag me to bed, unless I could think of a way to stop him. But in order to think of things, you have to *want* to think of them . . .

"Lady, are you well?" Kergil asked after jumping back. He'd jumped back because I'd come to my feet so fast, startled into being ready to defend myself. I had no idea what he was doing there, or how he'd appeared out of thin air.

"You almost gave me a heart attack." I answered, trying to get my pulse back down to where it belonged. "Don't you know better than to sneak up on people who are thinking? Where did you come from?"

"I came from my horse, who is currently tied *there,"* he said, pointing to the back of the wagon. "I did not realize how deeply your thoughts were occupied. I come at Tarren's direction, for he was told that once again you have refused food. Do you feel ill?"

"No, it just so happens I don't," I said, sitting again on the pile of rugs after tugging up that skirt. "I told the man there was nothing wrong with me, so all he's done by sending you here is waste your time."

"At the moment my time is my own," he said with a smile, picking out his own pile of rugs to sit on. "There are worse things I might do with it than spend it in the company of a lovely woman. You say nothing ails you, and yet I sense a . . . great unhappiness about you. There *is* something, but apparently you have chosen not to speak of it."

"I'm unhappy about a lot of things, this wagon and these clothes being only two of them," I said, wishing I hadn't finished the chai in my cup. The stuff tended to grow on you. "But since your friend the redhead is responsible for those two as well as most of the others, you'd probably rather talk about something else. Even just listening to criticisms of the boss has been known to get people in trouble."

"Tarren knows my opinion of him," Kergil said with a shrug, studying me with serious blue eyes as he leaned his forearms on his thighs. "And as a free man, I may listen to anything I wish. Why do you never call Tarren by name? I thought the lack strange last night—or this morning, if you prefer—and now you do the same again. It seems there is more than simple anger toward him that accounts for it."

"Why do you keep saying things like that?" I countered, looking at the man directly. "Has your boss been talking to you?"

"Tarren has said nothing of what lies between you," Kergil denied with a headshake. "As the matter is personal to the two of you, he *would* not. What I know I know from my talent, that of healing. One day I will develop it properly, by apprenticing myself to a sorcerer-healer. Until then, I use fewer spells and more herbs."

"Fewer *spells?*" I echoed, thinking I ought to laugh at the joke. He was kidding, wasn't he? "You're not saying you perform magic? Magic isn't real, it's just something you find in books and movies."

"How can you doubt the reality of magic?" he asked with a small laugh. "It touches everything in this world, and although I remain mostly untrained, the ability I was born with has still found a number of ways to exercise its existence. But—what are 'movies'?"

"They're— Never mind." It didn't seem like a good idea to go into *that* topic right now, not when we had only just started on one I needed to get straight on. "Let's stay with this magic thing. I know I treat it as real in my books, but I've always thought of it as a . . . psychological trick of sorts. You have people watching your house through small, hidden windows, say, and if anyone breaks in, your watchers spring traps on them from their hidden room. Then you say it was magic that protected your house, and people are too afraid to come back and learn the truth. That has to be the way it works."

"Then would you care to explain the 'trick' that allows Tarren control over you through the manacle you wear?" he said, the question gentle and patient as he pointed to the bracelet on my wrist. "He used it to make you follow him to the river yesterday, did he not? Explain that, Lady."

I couldn't explain that, and not because I hadn't tried. Alternate worlds aren't hard to accept after the first shock passes, not when even science admits the possibility of their existence; magic, though, is another matter. I'd finally decided the bracelet was too complicated for me to figure out how it worked, simply disregarding the fact that a society with such sophisticated technical know-how would show signs in other ways. I still wasn't quite ready to call it *magic,* though.

"You seem to require proof more easily seen," he observed, his amused smile evident even through that bushy red beard. "Perhaps this small spell will convince you."

He reached toward me with one finger, speaking some words in a language I couldn't recognize, let alone understand. As his finger touched the top of my head I drew back, but not before experiencing the oddest sensation—sort of a soundless crackle and tingle, one that seemed to course through me from head to feet. I had no idea what had happened, except that the experience had been like getting a *slow* charge of static electricity from somebody, one that didn't unsettle you the way a static shock usually does.

"There," Kergil said, looking satisfied as he took his hand back. "Folk tend to recover more quickly when they feel properly groomed. It proves a useful tool to those of us who labor in fighting companies such as this one, where there are none to carefully tend the bedridden. The spell is one most ladies' maids would prize, but it nevertheless falls most fittingly under healing. Are you not pleased with the result?"

I looked down at myself, trying to figure out what he was talking about. It took a minute before I noticed that the skirt and blouse I wore were no longer stained with my sweat from the heat of the day, or even from the chai I'd spilled when the wagon had hit a rut in the road. And then I noticed a thick strand of my hair, which was hanging over my left shoulder.

The last time I'd noticed that strand it was all snarled and flyaway from not having been combed. Now it was smooth and shining, as though it had been brushed three or four hundred strokes. I touched it gingerly with my left hand, expecting it to *feel* snarly even if I saw something else. But when it felt as smooth as it looked and touching the back of my hair showed *it* felt the same, I couldn't help snatching my hand back as if I'd been burned.

"Have no fear, the spell cannot be undone from the touch of your hand," Kergil said with a chuckle. "Allow me to say how lovely you look. Tarren should be very pleased."

"But I don't *want* him to be pleased," I objected. "I'm here for just one reason, which has nothing to do with his likes and dislikes. With that in mind, I want you to take it back."

"Take it back?" he echoed in bewilderment while I braced myself for another dose of sorcery. "Why would you ask for something like that? In any case, it is impossible."

"But if you did it, you should be able to *un*do it," I protested. It was already mid-afternoon, and the sun had disappeared behind the clouds of the coming rain. I'd forgotten to tell the redhead about the rain, mostly because it hadn't been in the first version of the book. Rewrites have always been difficult for me, but now the point that had to be remembered was that we were almost to the city. Once we got there and into the palace, I'd be face to face and alone with a man who'd wanted to take me to bed even with uncombed hair . . .

"Wildea, in my present state of learning I know of

no spells to reverse grooming," Kergil said gently, obviously trying to calm me down. "I apologize most profoundly if my use of the art has upset you, for a healer's magic is meant to soothe rather than disturb. You say you have no wish to look more beautiful for Tarren; although your reasoning escapes me, I may point out that all is not lost. Once the rain arrives, you may undo my efforts simply by standing out in it."

"My name is Deanne," I told him distractedly, and got up to pace in the bouncing wagon. It wasn't bad enough that I had *real* magic to worry about and try to make myself believe in. Now I also had my looks to consider, something I'd never bothered about before. Kergil's suggestion about standing out in the rain was very reasonable—except that I knew how cold that rain was going to be. And what if the redhead realized I couldn't have possibly gotten wet by accident? He was sharp enough to take that conclusion and jump to the next, which was that I'd done it on purpose just to make myself less attractive to him. That in turn would mean I'd given up all say over whether or not we went to bed together, which was something I *couldn't* do. Damn it, how was I going to get out of that mess?

"I believe I begin to understand," Kergil said suddenly, and I turned against the lurching of the wagon to see him studying me again. "You are afraid. But not of Tarren. You are afraid of yourself. The more attractive Tarren finds you, the more your own feelings toward him will strengthen, and *that* is what disturbs you so deeply."

"Is there anyone in this world who *isn't* a part-time

psychiatrist?" I couldn't help asking, mostly to keep from saying something more . . . revealing. "How I feel and why I feel that way is *my* business, and now I think I'd like to be alone. If you're not in the mood to get back on your horse, then I'll take him."

"I believe Tarren has refused you a mount of your own, has he not?" Kergil's words were very smooth as he rose to his feet, but he lost no time doing it. "You would not truly disobey him to *that* extent, would you?"

"If you didn't already know the answer to that, you wouldn't have gotten up in such a hurry," I pointed out, folding my arms. "And at least you're right about me not being afraid of your boss, but I think I've just gotten an idea about the rest. I'm going to set a deadline, and after that I'm gone. If he listens to me before then, he'll know how to protect his life. If he doesn't, whatever happens will be his fault rather than mine. Letting him use my own conscience against me is stupid, and I thank you for helping me to see that."

"*I* helped you to see such a thing?" Kergil demanded, his expression suddenly anxious. "I said nothing to bring about such a conclusion; so why has the fault been laid at *my* feet?"

"Fault?" I repeated with a happy smile, delighted to have found something to divert him from too-accurate guesswork. "That word presupposes blame, and therefore someone who would blame you. Who could that be, I wonder? Certainly not your boss, since you're a free man who does as he pleases. I wonder how often the redhead does as *he* pleases—with free men who mess up his plans."

"Were you to accuse me of influencing your decision, Tarren would not believe you," Kergil said, his firm tone making him sound like a man trying to convince *himself.* "And why would you do such a thing? Merely out of annoyance over my speaking the truth to you?"

"Your version of the truth," I corrected, refusing to back down. "It doesn't happen to be what *I* consider true, but that won't stop you from telling it to your boss. Then he'll decide he can do anything he pleases to me, which is another version of someone else's truth and one I don't intend to have spread around."

"My leaving now is indeed an excellent idea," Kergil said after closing his mouth with a snap. "Before my presence causes any further decisions to be made. It has been—an experience."

And with that he headed for the back of the wagon, climbed over to pull his horse closer by the rein, and then he jumped for his saddle. He made it, too, something he hadn't taken the time to worry about before his hasty departure. A moment later he was gone from sight.

I went back to my pile of rugs, pulled up that stupid skirt again, then sat back down. I mulled over the encounter with Kergil. The healer had asked me why I didn't use the name Tarren, but I wouldn't have answered under any circumstances. The reason was admittedly strange, but I couldn't seem to get around it.

Tarren was someone *I* had created, someone I'd made up for a very special reason. I'd never thought of him as real, but sometimes a writer has closer ties to a character than a parent has to a child—or a wife to a husband. He linked up to me on a level that no one living could ever have reached, the ultimate dream man, fantasy lover, and perfect match. No one in the world could equal him—at least no one in *my* world.

But now I found myself in another world where a living man went by his name, and in one or two ways the living man was better than my creation. My own dream man would never have acknowledged or wanted me, not when I'd never written myself into his world. But this man *did* want me. Even if it was just for sex . . . I knew that if I got involved with him I'd probably forget the temporary nature of his attraction. He'd slip through and touch all those unreachable parts deep inside myself, and I'd end up hopelessly in love with a man who had only a passing interest in me.

Which, all things considered, was very wise of him. I had no interest in taking up permanent residence in some backward, fictional world, and my own world had very few uses for the head of a fighting company who used a sword. Neither of us fit into the other's place, so the only practical solution was to not get involved. Toward that end I would continue to call him everything but Tarren. I needed to retain my literary detachment . . .

I got up again and walked to the brace holding up the canvas, then looked out at the countryside we passed. It was pretty even under clouds, stretches of wood scattered across quiet meadows filled with birds and field mice and rabbits. The road we bounced along was half stone and half rutted from wagon traffic, and about a dozen company fighters on horseback rode between my wagon and the next. It was horribly primitive compared to what I was used to, but somehow it was also incredibly attractive. In some strange way it felt like home, a home I knew only slightly but which waited to welcome me should I decide to give in to its lure and stay.

But it *couldn't* be for me, not when there would never be anyone to share it with. I stood and stared at it for a while, then went back to the pile of mats to do some very necessary thinking.

Eleven

It was about an hour before sundown when we reached the city; as it was in my book. It was also pouring rain, the kind of heavy, steady downpour that makes you doubt it will ever end. The rain had already been going on for more than an hour, and the fighters riding behind my wagon had put on poncho-like hooded garments to protect them from the deluge. The things might have also been of use against the growing cold, something that was starting to get to me. I'd draped a rug around my shoulders, but it was too short and thick to really be effective.

The procession stopped briefly at the main gates into the city, where I knew the redhead was being met by Gol, the prince's messenger. Gol and his small escort then assumed leadership of the caravan, and their honored guest rode with them. We had to pass through four of the five city districts before we reached the inner one where the palace was, and Gol and his men were eager to get back to where it was dry and warm. That was why they were hurrying, a circumstance which brought on the incident the redhead would be blamed for—

"Oh, damn," I muttered, suddenly remembering *why*

I'd added rain to the plot in the rewrites. It was to provide a logical reason for the hurry, not to mention muddy puddles everywhere. When we got to the third district, the one that contained the large market area, there would be a mage on the streets who was unhappy over the need to walk home through the rain.

And as he walked, a number of horsemen passed him in the street. The horseman closest to him—who would be the redhead—would send a large splash of water sheeting at him, drenching him more thoroughly than even the rain had managed to do. He would be outraged, thinking it an insult, and would cast a spell after the unsuspecting horseman. The spell would cause the redhead to have a series of very embarrassing yet comical accidents, a fitting repayment to the mind of an ill-used magic user.

And I'd forgotten to tell the redhead about that. I muttered a few nasty descriptives of my intelligence under my breath, but when you came right down to it the fault hadn't been mine alone. If the redhead hadn't kept distracting me with questions, I might have remembered the rewrite I'd done at my editor's request. Of course, since it wasn't a threat against his life—and I hadn't really believed that magic was a factor—I might not have, but that still made it a fifty-fifty matter of responsibility. *I* wrote the damned thing, but *he* hadn't let me talk about it.

I went so far as to get to my feet, thinking I'd call one of the fighters following the wagon and then send the man to warn the redhead. Then I remembered that the redhead was the only one able to understand me when I spoke about the book, and even if I sent someone to bring him back it would probably never work. Right now he was being moved by the plot of the book, and that plot demanded that he ride with Gol and his men, matching their pace. Someone trying to call him away from that would probably be ignored the way Fael had been ignored when he'd spoken about the wound the redhead wasn't supposed to have gotten.

I sat back down on my pile of rugs, still cold but no longer thinking about that fact. My mind was too busy trying to figure out how I would tell the redhead what I'd forgotten to tell him about, or even if I *should* tell him. When those accidents—designed to make him unbend and be more human—started to affect him he'd hate it, possibly even more than the threats to his life. Many people would rather die than be publicly humiliated, and for all I knew he was one of them. It would also be a great chance to see just how thoroughly he believed that what happened to him wasn't really my fault . . .

I took a deep breath as I leaned back, preferring not to wonder if he would decide to kill me. *I'd* want to kill anyone who did to me what was going to happen to the redhead, but maybe he was a better person than I am. Considering the size of him and the sword he carried, I sure as hell hoped so. But would my chances of surviving be better if I told him, or better if I didn't? Keeping quiet would mean I could claim it was all *his* fault that I'd forgotten, and what was more important, anyway? A little embarrassment never really killed anyone . . .

I finally put off a decision by deciding to wait and

see what happened, and spent the rest of the trip sightseeing. I knew how the city was arranged and had even described it in the book to a certain extent, but there was a lot of it I hadn't thought about at all. The place had been designed and carefully planned by the current prince's great-great-great-grandfather, a "fact" I thought had been of my design. Now it seemed it really was a fact, one I'd somehow *picked* up rather than dreamed up.

The street we followed was neatly cobblestoned and more than wide enough to let two wagons pass each other going in opposite directions. There weren't any sidewalks in that district; the cobblestone streets ended four or five feet from the buildings. Some of those buildings were two-story and some were three, but all of them were built with the upper story or stories wider than the lowest, to create an overhang and a protection from the elements, of sorts, for the pedestrian.

That first or outer district was the largest, and also the poorest. We were being taken by the scenic route, but I knew that the district was crammed with sheds and booths and shops in various stages of disrepair. The residents of the district with actual houses to live in comprised the upper-class poor; those who occupied a room behind their shops the middle class, and those who slept in the street the lowest class. There were a lot of members of those three classes, but then there usually are. The current prince's ancestor had expected that, and had planned accordingly by giving them the largest district.

The second district was mostly warehouses and

guildhalls, a place of industry. Smithies and stables alternated with taverns in one section, and another held city government offices near private manufacturers. There were also residential houses, but no private homes. It was a more prosperous district than the first, primarily because of the businesses.

The third district contained the marketplace, filled to bursting with every kind of shop or stall you could think of. There were also dozens of food and drink booths, not to mention places of entertainment. Plays, circuses, music shows, costumed and naked, with dancing and without, even some with audience participation. There was also a section reserved for the nobility, where it was possible to sit down after an hour or two of shopping or attending a performance, and be served the sort of drinks and snacks that befitted your station by servants who knew their place.

The fourth ring in was primarily the residences of the well-to-do, merchants and mages and high officials. There were also a number of exclusive—and expensive—shops, high-class eating places, and a large theater for serious dramatic productions. This district had streets that were cobblestoned all the way up to the various buildings and residence gates, to avoid the mud problem other districts had in wet weather.

By the time we reached that district we'd already passed a man walking alone, one who was soaking wet but who wore an expression of grim satisfaction. I watched him over the side of the wagon until we'd left him behind, then sat back with a sigh. It was definitely done, and now I had to decide when and how to tell the redhead about it. Or maybe I could just wait and let it happen, and then claim ignorance and innocence. But no, not when he "felt" when my plot took over his life. Damn. If only I'd written a scene where he was chained hand and foot . . .

I sighed again over lost opportunities, then peered through the rain at the large houses surrounded by well-tended grounds in the innermost district. This was where the prince had his palace, in the exact center of the city and surrounded by the estates of his nobility. No one without a title was allowed to own a house in this district, and titles weren't easy to come by. The prince's ancestor had allowed room for a few new nobles to be made, but not many. That was to keep his descendants from handing out titles like treats on Halloween, and thereby watering down *all* titles. It seemed to have worked, since there was still supposed to be some land unclaimed in that district.

Riding through the circles of the city took a lot longer than talking about it, but the procession finally reached the palace and slowed. The place was absolutely enormous, and we circled around the main front entrance until we were all the way around and almost near a back corner. We slowed then, and finally my wagon pulled in under a wide marble overhang next to an entrance into the palace. Gol and the redhead stood next to that entrance, and even as I made my way carefully over the sopping wet wood of the end of the wagon, I could hear their conversation.

"This stable was built to house the horses of the retinue of a visiting ruler," Gol was saying. "It should therefore be adequate for your company's mounts, and the wagons, once emptied of personal property, may be left beside the stables."

"And this entire wing is to be ours?" the redhead said. "The prince is most generous. How many rooms does the wing consist of?"

"It consists of three corridors, but I do not know how many rooms there are," Gol answered. "Your own apartment is to the left of these doors and straight ahead, the one directly across the corridor to the right. All these rooms on this entrance corridor are part of the wing, all the ones beyond your apartment and opposite to it on the righthand corridor down to the next corridor, and the rooms on both sides of that corridor to the next cross-corridor. Are you understanding my descriptions?"

"With some small effort," the redhead answered dryly. "And our meal this night will be provided by the palace kitchens?"

"Yes, and the morning's meal as well," Gol agreed. "His Highness wishes you and yours to have a comfortable stay, even should you choose not to take his hire. His Highness believes in showing people the benefit of cooperation rather than the drawbacks of refusal. The efforts of one who works unwillingly are most often better done without."

"A wise man, the prince," the redhead commented, not even looking in my direction as I climbed over the wagon's tailgate. "We will appreciate the night's comfort before he and I speak tomorrow. I will be sure to give him my thanks."

"Which he is certain to enjoy having," Gol replied solemnly. "His Highness is pleased when people voice honest appreciation. There are servants in your apartment who will fetch anything you require, and now I would like to take you there. My men will return to show yours where they and all personal possessions are to be taken."

The redhead nodded and turned to follow Gol inside, which gave me the chance to look for the safest way off that wagon. Climbing around in a long skirt can get you killed, but jumping isn't always the best idea, either. A long step down to a metal bracket seemed the only option, and I had already started to take it when an arm circled my waist and got me down without any more fuss. I already knew the arm didn't belong to the redhead, but when I turned to see who it did belong to, I was surprised.

"Tarren wishes to speak to you when the current time of madness releases him," Kergil said without expression as he took his helping hand back. "He and I spoke for a time before we reached the city."

"What a friendly group," I observed, noticing how closely the man watched me. "Thanks for the help with the wagon. Maybe I can return the favor sometime."

"Have you no interest in what I told Tarren?" Kergil asked as I began to turn away. "You still seem distraught, but in a somewhat different manner. Perhaps you anticipate a less than friendly discussion, since my version of what occurred reached him first."

"First isn't always best," I countered with a grin, then took pity on his growing agitation. "Relax, Kergil, I was only kidding about trying to get you in trouble. I won't even mention your name to your boss, so you can stop worrying about it. If the big man finds himself unhappy about anything, the only one he'll be looking for is me."

"And that disturbs you, but not in the expected way," he said with a frown. "Almost does it seem that you discount Tarren, a foolish course of action, no doubt. Wildea—should you wish someone to speak to, I will override my better judgment and accommodate you."

"You really should learn not to volunteer for things before you find out just how much trouble they can be," I said, ignoring the sympathy in his eyes. "And this is the last time I'm going to say this: My name is Deanne, and the next person who calls me anything else will hate what happens to him. Do all of us a favor and spread the word."

That time I finished turning and walking away, even though he tried to stop me again. Talking to people in this world got me agitated, and sitting around alone just thinking got me agitated. That didn't leave many options for nonagitation. If I'd needed a reason to leave, that would have been one of the best.

Going through the entrance into the palace put me in the first corridor Gol had mentioned, the first one of the three making up that wing. The redhead's apartment was to the left, I knew, and when I turned in that direction I wasn't surprised at the crowd gathered in front of the apartment. The prince had shown up right on time to greet his guest, accompanied by his three most valued advisers. I stopped on the fringes of the group, leaning against a wall and looking around until the brief discussion would be over.

It's strange how different visualizing something and actually seeing it can be. I'd described the palace in fittingly grand terms, marble-walled and floored and impressive in all dimensions, but that didn't tell the story by half. Twelve-foot ceilings meant the marble went *all* the way up, and eight feet of corridor width put a lot of that same marble under your feet. And it stretched at least the length of a football field all the way down to the first cross corridor. There were glass-mantled lamps on the walls, large oil paintings, and at least two small but beautifully carved tables, one holding a jeweled vase, the other a miniature bust in what looked like gold.

And the carvings in the heavy wooden doors along the corridor! Each one seemed to tell a story, and I couldn't help wondering if all those scenes, taken together and in order, made up a cohesive narrative. While I was there I knew I'd have to find out, but right now the discussion was breaking up and I had a book of my own to get into. I tugged up my dratted skirt, something that had gotten to be well beyond annoying, and turned back to the dispersing crowd—to find that I was being stared at quite openly.

The prince and two of his dignitaries and four guardsmen were just starting to turn away from the redhead and Fael and some of *their* people, but the third of the prince's companions was looking straight at *me*. He was a tall man of about forty, in fairly decent physical shape and easily considered handsome with his dark hair and light eyes. His trousers were dark blue silk, his tunic cream silk, and his short coat light red silk. It was that short, light red coat that proclaimed him and the other two royal advisers, but this particular adviser was named Agnal Topis.

And for some reason he was staring at *me*. There was no expression on his aristocratic, well-schooled features, but the look in his light eyes was speculative. What he could be speculating about I couldn't imagine. Our eyes met for a single instant and then he was gone, walking away with the prince and the others. I'd had the impression he'd expected me to avoid his gaze rather than meet it, and if so I disappointed him. I hadn't liked him on paper, and seeing him in the flesh hadn't done anything to change my mind.

"The place you want lies in the other direction," a voice said from behind me as I watched the prince and his group walk away up the corridor. "Tarren should soon be himself again, and when he is he wishes to speak to you."

"What did he do, leave messages with everyone in the company?" I asked as I turned to look at Fael. "I hope all this eagerness for conversation means he's ready to listen to the rest of the book. I've decided he doesn't have all that much time left before his chances run out."

"That, I think, is what he wishes to discuss," Fael said, looking annoyed. "What he faces is your doing, but now you say you mean to leave him to face it alone and without warning or assistance. Is that your concept of making amends?"

"*He* said none of this was my fault because I didn't do it on purpose," I pointed out, making no attempt to avoid his gaze as I stared up at him. "Why would

I have to make amends for something that wasn't my fault in the first place?"

"It would be . . . out of a sense of responsibility, yes, a proper sense of responsibility," Fael came back, now looking relieved that he'd found an answer to my question. "What occurs may not be your fault, but it certainly is your responsibility. For what other reason did you remain here rather than return to your home?"

"Well, it wasn't to have the chance to entertain your boss," I said, watching for and seeing the flicker in his eyes that said he knew what the redhead intended. "And since there seems to be enough room for everyone in this place, I'd appreciate your finding a small corner of it for *me*. I'd like to have someplace quiet to sleep tonight, but if it's too much trouble, don't bother. I can always go looking on my own."

"That would be another matter for you to discuss with Tarren," Fael said, eyeing me cautiously. "But I would strongly recommend against wandering about opening doors. One can never be sure what lies behind a closed door."

"That's a consideration only if one tends to worry," I said, suddenly deciding to play the pushy, unconcerned kind of broad most people can't stand. "Are you the sort to worry, Fael, or are you smart enough to just live life as it comes?"

This time he simply looked frustrated without answering, probably wishing he could take a swing at me. It had come to me that annoying the hell out of the redhead's closest associates might get me out of there faster. If the redhead's people were up in arms about having me around, he just might sit down and listen to the rest of the book and then step out of my way. Before I had to explain about a series of very embarrassing accidents. I should have a day or two before the first incident, so the idea was more than worth trying.

"Come," Fael said, gesturing to me. "If Tarren has not yet returned to himself, the wait will not be long."

I made sure he saw my shrug and grin before he turned away, two indications of obnoxious amusement that stiffened his whole body and probably had him grinding his teeth. I ambled along behind him, setting my own pace rather than matching his, and that meant he had to stand and wait like a servant after opening the door to the redhead's apartment for me. That, of course, really gave him something to grind his teeth over.

Again, walking into the redhead's apartment was both a familiar experience and a surprise. The entertaining and reception room was enormous, with lots of couches and chairs and small tables scattered across the marble floor. Straight ahead were silk-hung terrace doors which led to a private garden, dingy and dark now with pouring rain and enveloping night beyond them. Crystal-mantled lamps bathed the room in a soft golden light, and the fire in the gilded hearth flickered invitingly.

The redhead was engaged in conversation with someone who wore the pink tunic of an upper-class palace servant, so I headed to the roaring fire in the giant fireplace. Just because I hadn't been directly out in the rain didn't mean my clothes weren't damp, and that fire was just what I needed. Besides, I wanted some time to adjust to the sights of the palace. What a place! There were probably more paintings in that one room than I had in my whole house . . .

There was a wide carpet very much like dark brown fur arranged in front of the fireplace, and I discovered that the front edge of it was as close to the fire as it was wise to get. Half a tree seemed to be burning, and the golden screen stretching from one end of the hearth to the other emanated heat. And a good chunk of the wall over to the left of the fireplace had been made into bookshelves, all of which were filled with impressive-looking tomes.

I turned around in front of the fire to give the back of me a chance to warm up, and saw the servant that had been talking to the redhead heading for the door. But that didn't mean the redhead wasn't still engaged in conversation. Fael had taken the servant's place, and seemed to be in the middle of describing what a bad girl I'd been. I could see the agitation in his gestures, but the two of them were too far away for me to hear what was being said. Well, that didn't matter much. As soon as Fael was through, I'd undoubtedly be given a recap.

By that time I was stretched out in a chair not far from the fire. The redhead clapped Fael on the shoulder as he saw him to the door, said something that Fael accepted with a sigh and a nod before leaving, and then the big man was on his way over to me. I couldn't help watching him as he crossed the floor, his every movement filled with confidence, so big and beautifully muscled and handsome that almost any red-blooded female would have licked her lips in reflex reaction.

And his expression made me swear that the next time I created a main male character, he would be short, thin, nervous, and a pacifist hermit.

Twelve

"It seems, woman, that you have had a busy day," the redhead said as he stopped in front of my chair to look down at me. "First Kergil comes to me in a state rivaling the aftermath of battle, and now Fael does the same. How many others may I look forward to seeing in a like condition?"

"If I'd known you'd be looking forward to them, I would have arranged a lot more," I answered comfortably. "Maybe by this time tomorrow I can even manage to add the prince to the list."

"Perhaps the boredom of the trip has driven you to such," he replied dryly, and then, surprisingly, he grinned. "I apologize for that, and will certainly do all I may to change the situation—as soon as dinner is over and the time has come for . . . relaxation. Until the food arrives, would you care to join me in a tour of this modest apartment?"

"No, I would *not* care to join you," I answered hastily, refusing to notice the hand he'd offered to help me out of the chair. "The only thing I'm interested in doing is talking about the rest of the book, which also ought to be *your* first priority. I'm sure Kergil told you you have only two days to hear it, and after that

I'm out of here. Fael, likewise, should have told you I've asked for my own quarters, so now you know how I feel about after-dinner 'relaxation.' If we're not going to be getting you caught up, I intend to be elsewhere."

"And is that all?" he asked mildly and politely as he folded his arms. "Have you no further opinions to express?"

"Now that you mention it, there *are* a couple of other things," I obliged, deciding it was time to get a little pushier. "Those clothes you're holding for ransom are mine, and I want them back *now.* I could also use a pair of long pants and a warm shirt for the nights, but I won't be able to pay you for them until I get home. As soon as I do, I'll write into the narrative the delivery of a pouch or two of gold. And tomorrow I'm taking some time off to run, just to fool myself into believing my life is still normal. I had to pass on it today, but tomorrow there won't be any traveling in the way."

"What is it that you mean to run from tomorrow?" he said, his tone still mild. "Can it possibly be the word you gave, to do as I say if you were allowed to accompany me? Or perhaps you mean run *to* something, such as an excuse or two concerning your withdrawal from our bargain? Is dishonoring one's vow done often in your world?"

"As a matter of fact, it is," I hedged, trying not to sound defensive or apologetic. "But that has nothing to do with the fact that you're just taking advantage of my sense of responsibility. I didn't—"

"This same road has already been ridden too many

times," he interrupted, holding up one hand. "Rather than help to wear a rut through down to bedrock, I will ask only a single question: Did you, or did you not, agree to obey me if I allowed you to accompany me to this city?"

"I didn't need to be *allowed*," I countered, forcing myself not to fidget or squirm under that stare. "I told you you didn't have anyone big enough to make me go back to the wizard's house, and you conceded the point. If you'd tried to leave me behind I could have followed you, so there was no—"

"Followed me on foot?" he interrupted with a snort of ridicule. "For the entire day? And how would you have entered *here,* through the line of palace guards? These things you say are foolishness, woman, so permit me to repeat: Did you or did you not agree to obey me if I allowed you to accompany me?"

I felt so cornered that I almost glanced around furtively for a place to run and hide, and the idiocy of that thought was all that saved me. It reminded me that the best defense is a good offense, and right after that was when the idea came.

"As a matter of fact, your question, as put, isn't true at all," I said, wondering how I could have missed the point before. "Our deal wasn't simply for me to tag along, but for you to *listen* while I came with you. So far you've interrupted me at every turn, and you've gotten me so confused with your questions even *I'm* losing track of what happens when. You're asking for obedience? I'd say my letting you keep my clothes and my riding in that stupid wagon qualifies for that. So until you keep up your end of the bargain, we'll do things *my* way."

I could see he didn't like that last addition at all, and that was just the way I wanted it. If obnoxiousness was the key with his men, it ought to be the same with him. He stood staring down at me for a moment, the look in his eyes saying his mind was busy with thought, and then he nodded.

"Very well, I am willing to grant your point," he said, making it sound like a major advancement. "I will listen, and *then* you will obey me. And this will now be a *firm* agreement between us, one with conditions and penalties. Should you once again seek to avoid *your* part of the bargain, you will incur a penalty."

"Well, my agent usually does my dickering for me, but I still know the rules of the game," I returned. "If we're going to make a formal agreement out of this, we first have to *discuss* the terms. Like who gets what if they uphold their side of the contract, and what *each* loses if she—or he—doesn't. That could take quite some time, and you don't have that much of it left. Especially if I change the deadline to tomorrow at noon."

"What can possibly have brought you to this deadline matter?" he demanded, exasperation over my newest idea quickly evidencing itself. "Only this morning you would have fought my entire company to keep from being sent home, and now you shorten the imminence of your departure with every sentence. And defy me with every word."

"Life's a bitch, isn't it?" I commented pleasantly

but *without* the grin that probably would have started a real fight.

Once again he fell silent, and this was annoying. He was playing the part of the honorable gentleman unjustly accused of villainy by the town lunatic. That was nonsense, of course, since by his own admission his intentions were anything *but* honorable. And I was no lunatic! And then he was saved by the proverbial bell in the form of a knock on the door. A moment after the knock the door opened, and a bunch of pink-tunicked servants entered with trays.

"Chai and coffee, to occupy us until dinner is brought," the redhead explained solemnly, then went over to watch as the servants arranged the contents of their trays on a waist-high sideboard carved with dragons. I realized I could use some liquid refreshment myself, so I went over and joined him. As soon as the servants bowed and left, I grabbed the opportunity to rid myself of a nearly forgotten burden.

"Here," I said to the redhead before he could take more than a step toward the drinkables. "I've been carrying around this comb you gave me since I left the wagon, and I'm giving it back before I forget and leave it somewhere. I don't like the idea of losing other people's property."

"You need not have carried it with you," he said, looking as if he were sorry he'd taken it without thinking. "Had you left it in the wagon, it would have been brought in here with the rest of my possessions. Or you might have kept it. It would have pleased me to see it taken as your own, and still would. Keep it as a remembrance of me and my world for when you leave us both."

He held the comb out to me, the beautifully jeweled comb of carved ivory that I hadn't been able to make myself use. I stared at it for a long moment, wishing I *could* take it, but it was exactly what he'd called it: A memory of a man and a world that I would soon be turning my back on. Keeping it would be a thousand times worse than simply using it, so I quickly shook my head.

"Thanks anyway, but I have lots of combs at home," I said, trying to make the whole thing sound trivial. "I'd rather leave with nothing more than what I brought with me, and not just because taking things back with you from alternate worlds is supposed to cause trouble. I just like to travel light."

"What trouble might there be from a simple comb?" he asked mildly. "And how are those of your world to know where it comes from? I promise you, it carries no caution that it was produced with the aid of foreign wizards."

I laughed at that, realizing that even technologically backward societies might have problems with cheap foreign competition, but still shook my head.

"What books there are on the subject all claim that the . . . *natural vibrations,* I guess you can call it, of something like that comb would be different from the vibrations of things in *my* world," I quickly improvised, drawing on only a small part of what I'd been reading since childhood. "That can cause all sorts of trouble, ranging anywhere from disturbing the very foundations of my world's universe, all the way down to attracting the attention of unscrupulous people who want to take advantage of *your* world. It just isn't worth the risk."

Of course, I didn't mention that all those possibilities were discussed in books of science *fiction* rather than scientific journals and such. It was something the redhead didn't need to know, not if I wanted to keep some semblance of peace of mind. And every time he got as close to me as he now was, I needed every bit of peace of mind I could get.

"Perhaps you have the right of it," he allowed, still sounding mild as he moved forward to put the comb down on the sideboard near the drinks. "I would not wish to see your world disturbed by so foolish a thing as a comb. Nor mine ravaged by unscrupulousness. Which will you have, chai or coffee?"

"I think I'll try the coffee," I decided, moving closer to the sideboard myself. "I'm beginning to feel the onset of caffeine withdrawal, and it's about time. I usually have trouble going two hours without a cup in my hand, and here it is going on two days. And those little cakes also look interesting."

"You may not have those," he said, stopping my reach for one by smacking my hand. "Your appetite till now has been nonexistent, and I will not have what little of it has returned ruined by sweets. When you have finished your dinner, we will speak again of dessert."

"Look, Daddy, I'm a big girl now," I said as I rubbed my hand. "If I want to eat something, I'll damned well eat it."

"No, you will not," he said firmly, setting a beautiful and delicate ceramic mug filled with black coffee down near me.

"Let's make a side deal," I sighed while he poured piping hot chai into a cup for himself. "Since this has nothing to do with our main subject of negotiation, we ought to be able to come to agreement. I'll stay away from those chocolate-cream-stuffed cakes over there just to make you happy, but *you* have to give me something in return. Something like . . . oh, say, taking this bracelet off. Since there's no longer a reason for me to wear it, you'll be getting what *you* want for no cost at all."

"I see no reason for making a deal of any sort," he answered, turning to face me again with his cup near his hand. "A mature adult knows when a thing being done is in his or her best interests, and accedes to the necessity without needing to be coaxed. A child, however, considers its own wishes above all necessity, and must be made to obey despite its unwillingness. As you act the child, so will you be treated, until the time your actions prove you otherwise."

I was about to hotly deny the accusation, when the calculating part of my mind told me to shut up and think for a minute. It was obvious the big redhead disliked the idea of someone acting "childish," and that was too golden an opportunity to pass up. It would be a lot easier keeping him at arm's length if he didn't *want* to be closer, and this new idea worked in well with the obnoxiousness I'd already been cultivating. It also had its risks, of course, but remembering who I was dealing with made a big difference. That smack he'd given me must have been a fluke, something he

would *not* do again, since his idea of punishment was
to kiss me. A kiss would be bad enough, but nothing
compared to finding myself sharing a bed with someone I both did and didn't want. That vacillation was
really killing me . . .

I reached to the crystal bowl of sugar standing near
the pitchers, shoveled some into my coffee with a
spoon, and stirred it, then took a cautious sip. There
was a giant mound of annoyance standing silently to
my right, one I looked at only out of the corner of
my eye. Before the redhead could continue his chas-
tisement, there was another knock at the door.

A single servant entered, leading some of the men
from the company, the men carrying the redhead's
trunks from the wagon. The boy Lamor was with
them, struggling to hold up his end of one, but he
wasn't too occupied to give me another distrustful
look.

"Where would you have us put these, sir?" the servant asked the redhead, leading the procession into the
room. "Your bedchamber has ample space, as does
the bathing room. Your dressing area, however, might
well become too crowded."

"Find wall space in the bedchamber to put them
against," the redhead decided, then stood watching the
trunks being carried past. With his back turned I had
the perfect opportunity, but not to attack him as Lamor
seemed to be waiting for me to do. It was a lot more
satisfying to grab one of those cream-filled cakes and
stuff it in my mouth, the chocolate cream flowing out
in all directions when I began to chew. It tasted even
better than it looked, and even if he noticed that a

cake was gone, the redhead would have no complaint coming. After all, he was the one who had turned down my deal.

By the time his men and the servant trooped out again, I'd swallowed the evidence and had gone to another overstuffed leather armchair to sit down. When the door closed behind our latest visitors, the redhead removed the sword from across his back and took a chair opposite mine. I expected our previous argument to continue, but he surprised me.

"So in a week's time I will begin to work on the problem of finding the prince's ring," he said after sipping his chai. "Tell me of the dangers waiting in the guildhalls of the thieves and the assassins."

"The thieves' guildhall is the easier of the two, but that's not saying much," I answered. "Considering what its membership is like, it's heavily protected *against* thieving. Fael points that out to you, so you decide you have to change your mind about stealing anything, even stealing the ring *back*. Since the magical protections are triggered by intent, you can avoid them by really and honestly intending to do nothing that can be considered thievery."

"But complications enter to make the matter more difficult and dangerous," he said matter-of-factly. "This I know from personal experience with your books, therefore I await the details of what goes wrong."

"It's impossible for anyone to keep their thoughts under rigid control for very long," I responded, trying to ignore the heat of the guilt I could feel burning in my face. I *did* make a habit of having things go wrong for him as often as I could, something a reader would easily understand, but someone who had to live through the trouble couldn't be expected to be as broadminded.

"You keep to your decision not to steal anything until you've searched most of the guildhall," I continued after clearing my throat. "But then you come to the offices of the head of the guild, and happen to think about how much valuable information it probably contains. If the ring was taken by one of their people and the deal had been made through the guildhall itself, the name of the one doing the hiring would be in the records. That name may lead to the villain behind it all, and then your work would be over. But you can't read, so you'd have to take any records you found to someone who can—and that thought does it. Your intentions have become suspect, and the protective spells are immediately activated."

"And why, save that it would make life far too easy, do I fail to *bring* someone able to read?" he asked next. "Surely you have an excellent reason for sending someone so ill-prepared into so dangerous a situation."

"The presence of two people would increase the likelihood of having compromising thoughts," I said, feeling worse and worse by the minute. My explanation was not entirely defensible. Damn! This was a lot easier on paper! "Look, how was *I* supposed to know that—"

"So I find myself there alone, and a spell is activated," the redhead said, interrupting my attempted apology. "What does that spell entail?"

"A guardian in the form of a . . . a sword fighting

by itself," I said, trying to keep my tone even. The redhead's stare was so cold and accusing. . . . "It—it tries to cut your—hands off, the standard punishment for a—thief. And it comes close to doing it before . . . before you realize there might be something invisible holding the sword. It's the uh, only chance you have, so you go ahead and, uh, try for the invisible something, and end up . . . getting it. When it dies it turns visible, and you see it was only a man."

"Only a man I cannot see wielding a deadly weapon," he stressed sourly. "And the situation is such that I cannot even warn myself with a note, for with my memory of what you say will go my ability to read. And should I slip, or have some other mishap before realization of the truth comes to me, I could well die no matter *what* was written. Is there more to be faced, or did you find that one small contest sufficient?"

"That's the only thing there," I managed to say, really beginning to despise myself. "After the, uh, man is dead, you look through a ledger on the guild head's desk. You can't read it, but one item on the last page is a symbol rather than a word. You won't know it at the time, but that symbol eventually leads you to the thief of the ring."

"Assuming I survive to see it," he qualified. "And what, dare I ask, occurs in the guildhall belonging to the assassins? Surely not so simple a thing as another invisible opponent. Perhaps this time the sword itself will live."

I tried to go on with the briefing, but my eyes closed with shame and my throat tightened. What he would face in the second guildhall—and unnecessarily—wasn't something I could talk about right now, and maybe not ever. It would be horrible for him, and he could end up really, truly dead, and all because I'd let my imagination run wild for a few hours one afternoon. He hated having to sit there and talk to me as if I were someone he *wanted* to talk to, and I couldn't blame him. I hated me at least as much as he did, and suddenly I just had to find some place to hide for a while.

I put the mug on a nearby table as soon as I got to my feet, and then I was hurrying toward the hall door. I couldn't see very well through the blur of tears, but I wasn't really crying. Hating yourself is frustrating enough to make you *want* to cry, but you know you don't deserve to have that release so you don't allow it. My throat burned and there was a dull pain inside of me, and when I felt two arms catch me before I could get past I even managed to struggle a little. But I didn't have the right to fight free either, not to mention the fact that those arms were like two bands of steel.

"No, small love, do not weep," he whispered as he hugged me tightly to his chest. "The fault is mine and I apologize for having given you pain. Anger makes fools of men, and the man who forgets that is the king of fools. I truly do not blame you for what was done, I merely attempted to use the discussion as a punishment for disobedience. Your great-hearted sense of right and wrong, however, has turned this more into torment than punishment, and I cannot continue with it."

I shook my head, knowing he was lying but unable

to get the words out. He was supposed to be so big and strong, but the real truth was he just couldn't stand to see a woman cry. He'd been absolutely right to act the way he'd been doing, and I didn't deserve any comforting lies. Besides, he had no reason to want to punish me . . .

"You doubt me?" he asked, the words still a murmur. "How can you doubt one who is known to never break his word nor speak a lie? But that refers to the other; the real truth is that *I* am far from the perfection of the one you write of, for I am only a man. But as a man I give you my word, the fault here is not yours. Come, let me convince you that I mean what I say."

He moved me back with him a couple of feet, and then he sat down and pulled me into his lap. I felt absolutely wretched and didn't *want* to be in his lap, but he refused to let me go.

"Here, see?" he asked, holding me tightly to his chest and pressing my head down to his shoulder. "If I truly believed my difficulty was your deliberate fault, I would not find it possible to hold you so close and tenderly. There are those in the world who treat enemies as though they were friends, but I have never found myself able to do that. If I thought you deserved to be blamed, I would have let you leave."

His left hand held my head down on his shoulder; his right arm circled my body and kept me in his lap. But it also kept me pressed up against his chest, and the heat of him reached me even through my clothes. As upset as I was I couldn't stop my own body from flaring wildly in response to his nearness, a raging desire for him that terrified me. My left hand was flat against his chest and my right pressed into his side, but instead of helping me to push away from him, they seemed glued in place. His body was so hard and warm and strong, but I wasn't supposed to want him. Not only would I be a fool to get involved, but I also didn't deserve any rewards for what I'd done.

"To tell the truth, I find it rather fortunate that you and I are not enemies," he murmured, then touched his lips to my forehead. "It would crush me to have a woman such as you as my enemy, and not solely because I love the scent of wildflowers. The scent is more enticing on you than it would be on any woman I have ever met."

He meant the perfumy odor left by that magical soap, something I'd forgotten about despite Kergil's grooming spell. The odor must be fairly obvious to anyone who hadn't gotten used to it the way I had, and his noticing it just made things worse. I didn't *want* to "entice" him, not for a million reasons, not even if my body *was* trying to change my mind. I raised my face to tell him that, but unfortunately took too long choosing the right words. Those ice-blue eyes stared down at me for a heartbeat, and then all words were blocked off by two demanding lips.

And demanding was the word. The other times he'd kissed me were like weekend holidays compared with this. Now he was more than serious, and before I could stop myself I'd already begun to respond. It was as if I really needed to believe he didn't blame me for what he was being put through, and kissing me was proof of it.

I not only met his demand, but added a good bit of

my own. I knew I shouldn't be doing it, knew I was being a fool, but the whispers trying to tell me that were very faint and far away. Much closer at hand and taking all my attention was the feel of his mouth on mine, the way his arms held me, the way my own arms had found themselves around his neck. I was being an absolute and utter fool, but I couldn't bear the thought of having that kiss end.

And it didn't end, not for a very long while, not until I became aware of the movement of his hands, one of which was stroking my hair and back. The other, his right, had opened the buttons on my blouse and was toying with my left nipple. I heard myself moan as his fingers sent thrill-tinged shivers through me, and felt like I was drowning in them. All thoughts of stopping him were buried under an ocean of need . . .

Another stretch of mindless time passed, and then a new sensation grabbed my attention. I hadn't realized that the giant's hand had left my breast until it reached its new objective, under the skirt and a long slide up my leg and thigh. I gasped as his fingers probed at me gently, trying to find out if I was as ready as he'd been for quite some time. Since the answer was an emphatic *yes!* I thought I would lose it then and there, but all he did was tickle me a little and lightly kiss my lips.

"Best we now take ourselves to the bedchamber," he said, his voice a thick rumble of arousal. "The servants enter this room much too freely for my liking."

He lowered his head for a moment to kiss the nipple he'd turned so hard, and then he was on his feet and carrying me in his arms. I couldn't quite understand how he'd managed to get up so easily while still holding me, but that was a faint and distant question. My main concerns were hanging on to make sure I wasn't dropped as he strode along, and forcing myself *not* to demand that he move faster. Pride was a secondary worry, right now a long way behind the need for self control. *That* was what I tried to regain, but my body kept refusing to allow it.

The redhead reached the bedroom and turned to close the door, and despite the way I hadn't been able to keep from kissing his neck I got a sweeping glimpse of the room. Almost as huge as the outer one, it was dimly lit but obviously richly furnished. There was carpeting on the floor, another giant fireplace, chairs and tables—and a huge bed in the middle of the floor. But the bed seemed plain and drab in comparison to the rest of the room, canopied and curtained in a drab, dark tan, what I could see of the bedding the same plain, awful color.

It was definitely strange, but I discovered rather quickly that I didn't care. As the redhead strode toward it I kicked off my shoes, but had to use one hand to get rid of the socks.

When we reached the bed he put his knee on it, then swung me through the curtains before putting me down. It was darker inside those curtains than I would have liked, but that wasn't important at all. What *was* important was the way he stretched out near me, closing the curtain behind him with one hand. That made it completely dark, of course, but not for long.

"Oh!" I yelped. The bed we lay on had suddenly burst into yellow and red flames, high and flickering flames that lit the interior of the huge canopy. I tried to get out of there to keep from being burned alive, but the redhead laughed and held onto me. It took a moment to realize that we weren't being burned, not even singed a little despite the flames all around us. I didn't understand what was happening—and then I noticed what had become of the curtains.

Instead of material curtaining the bed, we were now surrounded by pouring rain. Sheets and waterfalls of rain, the heavy but muted sound of it merging with the gentle cracking of a warm and friendly fire. That we lay on the fire and that the downpour wasn't outside didn't seem to matter, not even when I looked up to see that the canopy had turned to a brightly burnished gold. I couldn't help feeling the least bit overwhelmed, and the redhead chuckled softly.

"Clearly you have never seen a spell such as this," he said as he smoothed back my hair. "Those of the upper classes offer their guests the choice of what they will sleep and make love on, and the spell is set to match mood and desire. Our mood can be seen in the curtains, and our desire in the bed itself."

With that his lips went to my breasts, well exposed by the opened blouse. He kissed first one nipple and then the other, then began to use his tongue as well as his lips. I moaned and buried my fists in his hair, and he chuckled without stopping what he was doing and then added the touch of his hands under the skirt, and along my flesh. As I closed my eyes, the flames roared even higher.

He removed my skirt and threw it somewhere, and I couldn't help thinking it was damned well about time.

But at least his body cloth was already gone, so he was able to gather me in his arms as he moved between my knees. Then his mouth was on mine again, trying to swallow me as I did the same with him.

And that turned out to be a lucky thing for me. Distantly I felt his desire search around a little before it found the place it wanted, and then he began to enter me—slowly. If I could have I would have urged him to hurry—and then quickly would have changed my mind. He was so *big* . . . so very hard . . . it hadn't felt like that my very first time. It was faintly frightening, faintly intimidating . . . and then it was totally beyond description.

He began to stroke me, slowly and gently but very definitely, and I knew there was nothing to fear. When I raised myself up to meet his thrusts and move with them, he increased the speed of his movements. But slowly and carefully, making sure I was with him before he continued on. I had never experienced anything like it, and for an instant could have cried because he wasn't the first to come to me. I *wanted* him to have been the first, but then I realized it didn't matter. In a very real way he *was* the first, and no other man would ever be able to affect me the same after him.

This time I was lost to mindlessness a very long while, a world of exquisite sensation that built and climaxed, built and climaxed, over and over. The red-head joined me in that once, early on, but it hadn't been the end of our time, only a very brief intermission. He seemed to have a *lot* of desire to work off, and the flames crackled high around us all the way through to the end. When he joined me for the second time, the flames finally died down to hot glowing embers.

"Ah, Wildea, my own," he said softly after he'd caught his breath a little, leaning over me as he rested on his forearms to either side of my body. "You are the most magnificent of women, just as I knew you would be. Your response to the love I gave was more than I had ever imagined possible. When we have recovered ourselves, we will bathe before sitting down to dinner, and then we will take pleasure in each other again."

He kissed me then, more of a leisurely caress than a peck, and then withdrew to lie beside me. My hands had been on his arms till then, feeling the smooth flow of rock-hard muscle under his skin, but that wasn't all I'd felt. Even after all that time, effort, and release, it was obvious he could have been ready again very quickly. Myself, I felt annihilated, flattened and drained and without the energy to move even an inch. It had been a time of incredible pleasure, but I'd never had such a workout.

The two of us lay side by side on the soft quilt, doing nothing more than breathing, but after a moment the redhead reached down and took my left hand to fold into his larger right one. The gesture was something else no one had ever done before, and his hand-holding disturbed my far-from-restful state of mind. All those thoughts I'd had, about wishing he could have been the first man to have me and then deciding he *was*—I was more than just beginning to fall in love with him, and that couldn't be allowed to continue.

I raised my right hand to push back sweat-soaked hair, trying not to flinch from the silent tongue-lashing my conscience was giving me. *Now see what you've done,* was the way the furious lecture went, *you've really screwed things up! You let your feelings of guilt destroy your defenses, and then you let him take you to bed. Now he's talking about doing it again later, not to mention holding your hand like an infatuated teenager. But it's you who feels like the teenager, and you're thinking like a two-year-old. Aren't you supposed to be leaving him behind in two days? And weren't you getting tired of the way he keeps ignoring what you want and just satisfies himself? He may share that satisfaction in bed, but what about when you're out of bed?*

Those were three excellent questions I'd asked myself, and it didn't matter that it was stark fear that made them so good. The redhead had enjoyed our little tumble even to the point of offering the usual compliments about how good I'd been, and was now holding my hand to make those compliments seem more real. For me, though, it had been more than a passing good time. The thought of doing it again was terrifying, not because of the act itself, but because of what the act would do. I didn't need a useless love reinforced to the point where it—and I—would shatter like brittle glass when we were finally brushed aside. Or when circumstance brushed us aside. I *had* to go back to my own world, if for no other reason than to let my father and brothers know I wasn't dead.

So there was no chance at all of anything permanent happening between me and the man lying beside me.

What I had to remember was that he'd started out trying to comfort me, and had ended up getting me hotter than those flames the bed spell had produced. It could have been an accident, just something that happened, but the chance of that was as good as the chance of someone flying simply by flapping their arms. He knew what he was doing when he began that first kiss, so I had to know the same: once he got his hands and lips on me, I was dead meat.

This meant I had to do my damnedest to stay well away from him. And to get back to the obnoxiousness that he disliked so much. I had to make him decide that he didn't *want* me in his bed, and then I'd have at least a fighting chance to go home sane. Or relatively sane. No one in any world in either of our universes would ever consider anything about my situation sane. Including the fact that I was actually starting to feel hungry at last . . .

Thirteen

Tarren lay beside Wildea among the glowing coals of his desire, more satisfied than he had ever been in his life. The woman touched more than his physical being, excited and fed more than the ordinary urgings in a man. She was beautiful, strong, intelligent, feisty, stubborn, independent—all which he admired and desired in a woman. Now that he had had her for the first time, he felt more determined than ever to have her for eternity. And her response to his lovemaking brought him the conviction that she felt the same.

He reached over and took her hand, needing that physical link to make up for the one he had so recently and reluctantly abandoned. He had used the woman hard, harder than he had ever allowed himself to do before, and Wildea was clearly near the end of her strength. Not that she had not urged him on and on almost to the end of his own strength. The woman demanded all he had to give, and would likely demand even more once she had had time to rest.

But for the moment her silence disturbed him. He ran his thumb over the back of her hand as he watched her reflection in the polished gold of the canopy above them, and the sight of her disturbed him even more.

Wildea seemed lost in thought, but not, it seemed, over the pleasure they had shared. So serious she looked, and so sad . . .

Tarren nearly took her in his arms and demanded to know what disturbed her, but an instant's thought kept him silent and unmoving. His Wildea responded badly to demands, and he would not tolerate angry words tarnishing the splendor of what they had shared. Best would be for him to stoke his patience full, and then attempt to coax the knowledge from her. In the fullness of time she would have enough trust in him to speak freely of what disturbed her.

"I have heard talk of the magnificence of the palace's bathing rooms," he murmured in her ear after another moment. "Are you ready to join me in seeing if the tales are true?"

"I suppose so," she replied noncommittally, yawning as she pulled her hand from his, then sat up to rub her face with both hands. "I suppose it will serve to pass the time. A brief respite from the boredom of this world."

Tarren frowned and sought to restrain himself from speaking precipitately. He sat up. He had been about to demand how she could speak of boredom at such a time, but such a protest seemed very . . . defensive. He knew very well that she had shared his pleasure; there had been enough women in his life for him to know the true from the feigned.

He watched her as she groped for the bedcurtain joining. "I myself found the time in this bed most diverting, and had hoped that you considered it the same."

"Oh, hey, sure, it was great," she quickly assured him, a glance over her shoulder showing him an extremely sincere expression. "There's nothing like a man with a good case of the hots to set the old blood flowing faster, but like they say, you can only spend so much time in bed."

By then she had found the joining and had parted the curtains, so Tarren followed her out of the bed. Some of what she had said escaped him, but not the heart of the matter. She had indeed found her own satisfaction, but seemed less than impressed. Had the experience truly been so much less for her than for him?

"Which way is this bathing room?" she asked as he got to his feet. "There are so many doors in this room, it looks like Grand Central Station."

"Most likely the bathing room is through there," Tarren replied, nodding toward the wide double doors beyond the bed. "The others lead to dressing rooms, one for each of us, and we have been asked to make full use of the clothing to be found in them. The clothing will fit perfectly, since they, too, have had a spell cast on them."

"I never realized how handy magic really is," she said, rubbing her bare arms as she began to hurry toward the double doors. "Too bad they don't use it to make this mausoleum a little warmer, but I suppose you can't expect primitives to catch the finer points."

Tarren followed after her woodenly, wondering that she would say such things in his hearing. He was a member of the society she spoke of with such scorn, and surely she knew her insults disturbed him. Where was the woman he had brought into that room, the woman who had ached and nearly wept with a guilt that only her own sense of honor made hers? He had begun to comfort her, had found he could not resist tasting her lips, then had been taken by the surprise of her response. Where had she—?

The bewildered question ended in mid-sentence as the answer quickly filled Tarren's mind. The woman he had brought to the room was there in front of him, her delightful bottom the most pleasant beacon he had ever followed. It was what she said that failed to ring true, and therefore most likely *was* untrue. His Wildea lied with every word she spoke, but undoubtedly for a purpose. He had only to discover that purpose, and then her true intentions would become clear. Obviously the matter related to what had saddened her previously, the matter he had meant to coax from her . . . that was even now locked within her.

Wildea threw open both doors and hurried through, and Tarren was able to see that the bathing room was indeed where he had thought, with a large pool to swim in to the left, a smaller bathing pool with hot water to the right, and private sanitary facilities behind the gilded wall straight ahead. In point of fact all of the room's walls were gilded, with blue-veined marble under foot. Plush lounges stood about with small tables beside them, a sideboard held glasses and liquid refreshment, and the lamps on the walls lit the windowless area well.

"At least it's warmer in *here*," Wildea said as she disappeared behind the privacy wall. *"Yes!* Indoor plumbing! The acme of luxurious living, along with

Now, for the first time...

You can find Janelle Taylor, Shannon Drake, Rosanne Bittner, Sylvie Sommerfield, Penelope Neri, Phoebe Conn, Bobbi Smith, and the rest of today's most popular, bestselling authors

...All in one brand-new club!

Introducing KENSINGTON CHOICE,
the new Zebra/Pinnacle service that delivers the best
new historical romances direct to your home,
at a significant discount off the publisher's prices.

As your introduction, we invite you to accept 4 FREE BOOKS worth up to $23.96

details inside...

We've got your authors!

If you seek out the latest historical romances by today's bestselling authors, our new reader's service, KENSINGTON CHOICE, is the club for you.

KENSINGTON CHOICE is the only club where you can find authors like Janelle Taylor, Shannon Drake, Rosanne Bittner, Sylvie Sommerfield, Penelope Neri and Phoebe Conn all in one place...

...and the only service that will deliver their romances direct to your home as soon as they are published—even before they reach the bookstores.

KENSINGTON CHOICE is also the only service that will give you a substantial guaranteed discount off the publisher's prices on every one of those romances.

That's right: Every month, the Editors at Zebra and Pinnacle select four of the newest novels by our bestselling authors and rush them straight to you, usually *before they reach the bookstores*. The publisher's prices for these romances range from $4.99 to $5.99—but they are always yours for the guaranteed low price of just *$3.95!*

That means you'll always save over $1.00...often as much as *$2.00*...off the publisher's prices on every new novel you get from KENSINGTON CHOICE!

All books are sent on a 10-day free examination basis, and there is no minimum number of books to buy. (A postage and handling charge of $1.50 is added to each shipment.)

As your introduction to the convenience and value of this new service, we invite you to accept

4 BOOKS FREE

The 4 books, worth up to $23.96, are our welcoming gift. You pay only $1 to help cover postage and handling.

To start your subscription to KENSINGTON CHOICE and receive your introductory package of 4 FREE romances, detach and mail the postpaid card at right *today*.

We have 4 FREE BOOKS for you
as your introduction to
KENSINGTON CHOICE
To get your FREE BOOKS, worth
up to $23.96, mail the card below.

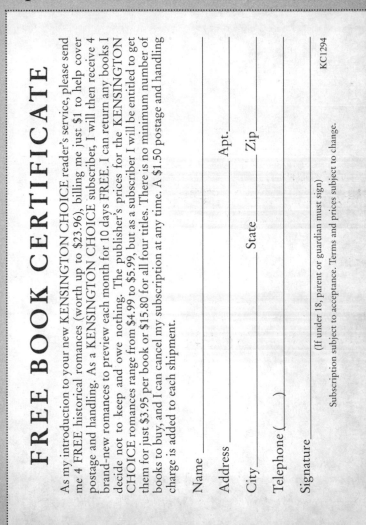

FREE BOOK CERTIFICATE

As my introduction to your new KENSINGTON CHOICE reader's service, please send me 4 FREE historical romances (worth up to $23.96), billing me just $1 to help cover postage and handling. As a KENSINGTON CHOICE subscriber, I will then receive 4 brand-new romances to preview each month for 10 days FREE. I can return any books I decide not to keep and owe nothing. The publisher's prices for the KENSINGTON CHOICE romances range from $4.99 to $5.99, but as a subscriber I will be entitled to get them for just $3.95 per book or $15.80 for all four titles. There is no minimum number of books to buy, and I can cancel my subscription at any time. A $1.50 postage and handling charge is added to each shipment.

Name _____

Address _____ Apt. _____

City _____ State _____ Zip _____

Telephone ( ) _____

Signature _____

(If under 18, parent or guardian must sign)

Subscription subject to acceptance. Terms and prices subject to change.

KC1294

We have
4
FREE
Historical
Romances
for you!

(worth up
to $23.96!)

Details inside!

a basin and pitcher for small wash-ups. But I'm not getting into that water unless I find some towels."

"Why would there be . . . towels?" Tarren asked as he closed the doors, certain she referred to drying cloths. "There is a grooming curtain. What more can be considered necessary?"

"What's a grooming curtain?" she demanded, appearing from behind the privacy wall.

Tarren regarded her with curiosity, again aware of the differences that separated them. *"This* is a grooming curtain, hanging here beside the wall. When one is done bathing one steps through it, emerging dry and combed. The spell is quite simple."

"I'll bet," she said, eyeing the curtain. "It reminds me of that simple doorway you hauled me through not long ago. Misty, silverish; it clashes with these god-awful gaudy walls. God-awful gaudy golden walls. How's that for a tongue twister? All right, where's the soap that *doesn't* leave you smelling like flowers?"

"Most likely over there," Tarren replied, pointing to a shelf holding seven or eight ceramic jars. "Those on the end are undecorated, therefore it can be assumed that the soap in them is unscented. But using it will be the only true test."

"What have I got to lose?" she asked with a shrug, heading for the soap shelf. "At worst it will make me smell like something other than flowers. At best it'll take the original scent away, and then I can smell like a person again instead of a blossom. And I do believe that that water is hot."

She directed her gaze toward the smaller pool, and then she walked to it holding the soap jar, using her toes to test the water's warmth. Tarren had long since noticed how unconcerned she appeared to be with her nakedness, something that failed to hold true for *him*. Her body was marvelous, so lean and toned and rounded . . . full breasts and flat belly, gently swelling hips and slender thighs . . . thighs that had held to him with such strength . . .

Tarren took a deep breath to regain control of himself, then also walked toward the heated pool. It would be foolish to expect the woman to greet him as warmly as she had earlier, now that she seemed bent on plans of her own.

The heated pool was certainly large enough to accommodate them both, with plenty of space between them, and Wildea made it clear that that was what she desired. She soaped and scrubbed herself vigorously, discouraging closeness, so Tarren decided to see to his own washing. The faint ripples in the pool suggested that the water was continually renewed and refreshed, again a matter of magic. The prince's encouragement of the magic users in the city had reaped for him substantial benefits.

Once their bathing was done, they left the pool for the grooming curtain. Tarren would have preferred to swim first, but his own hunger as well as Wildea's obvious disinterest kept him from making the suggestion. When she hesitated at the curtain's opening, Tarren moved past her and stepped through first to demonstrate how easily it was used. He stepped through with water dripping from him, his wet hair tousled, but once on the other side he stood dry and neatly combed. He turned to see Wildea following his example. When she had emerged from the curtain, she shivered.

"I don't think I'll ever get used to that weird tingle," she muttered. "A slow charge of static electricity without the pain, and who needs a hairdresser?" Then she looked up directly at him, her dry hair falling smoothly about her shoulders. "Where did you say those guest clothes were?"

Tarren led her from the bathing room and pointed out the dressing area on the far side of the chamber, then went into his own dressing room just beyond the bathing room. Under other circumstances he would have worn his own clothing, but Wildea's presence and his desire to defy the madness made him change his mind. He meant to dress to the teeth, and be a most resplendent sight at dinner.

In the end Tarren settled for opulent simplicity, choosing dark tooled-leather boots, cream-colored cord breeches covered with faint golden embroidery, and a wide-sleeved tunic of teal blue embroidered in the same color. The tunic's collar stood out against the red of his hair, and with the help of the candlelight reflected from the blue of his eyes. Tarren grinned at his reflection, certain that Wildea would find him most impressive—and a fit companion, no matter the finery she chose for herself.

The bedchamber was empty when he left the bathing room, so he paused at one of his trunks to find a modest gold medallion and chain to hang about his neck. The medallion would bring out the gold embroidery in his breeches, and add to his overall splendor. Tarren chuckled as he headed for the entertaining room, finding his sudden preoccupation with his appearance amusing. Some men never thought of such things—until a woman wrought the change in them. But not just any woman . . . a very special woman . . .

Tarren expected to find Wildea in the entertaining room, but a quick look about showed the place empty. A moment of immediate concern caused him to look at the manacle on his wrist and think the word, "Where?" and then his concern was laid to rest. The manacle drew his arm up to allow his finger to point back toward the bedchamber, showing that Wildea had not yet come out of her dressing room.

"Have you forgotten how women enjoy an entrance?" he murmured to himself with a relieved chuckle. "Allow her the time to gild her beauty, for the wait will surely be worth it."

Tarren felt expansive with contentment, for he was able to imagine himself waiting for Wildea in a home of their own. He had enough gold to build a house nearly the size of that palace, and had even found a lovely valley to build it in. The land around there was rich, and many men would work it eagerly for a share in the profits from the crops, and the promise of protection from him and his fighters—not to mention for houses of their own where they might raise families. All Tarren had needed to begin the venture was a woman to share it with him, and now he had found her. If only he could be certain he would *keep* her . . .

A knock at the door interrupted his thoughts, and then servants were entering with their dinner. The timing was too perfect to be happenstance, and had most likely been spurred by his appearance in the entertaining room. If that was another indication of the use of magic, Tarren was content to allow it to continue. Magic was indeed useful when used properly, a point the prince clearly attempted to make.

The servants began by bringing in a table and two chairs, and then a white linen-and-lace cloth for the table. Then came the place settings, including silver and crystal. Last came the food itself, covered platters by the seeming dozen, which were set down along the center of the long table. The plates had been set at either end, and when all the food was brought, two servants remained while the others left. The covers on the platters would keep the food hot and fresh until he and Wildea were ready to eat it, no matter how long that took.

No matter how long that took. Tarren felt his mind repeat that phrase over and over as the minutes passed, his belly near to growling with hunger. It was certainly true that women took longer preparing themselves than men did, but there were limits to what was reasonable. Tarren had paced all around the huge entertaining room in an effort to divert his appetite, but now he had returned to his starting point near the table and diversion no longer worked. He was *hungry,* by the gods. Perhaps Wildea had fallen asleep in the midst of dressing . . .

Abruptly he made up his mind to see, but took no more than two steps toward the bedchamber before Wildea appeared. Tarren was tempted to consider the "coincidence" yet another indication of magic, but Wildea seemed unable to perform magic in his world. And the timing smacked more of contrivance, a conclusion supported by what the woman wore. A plain gray cotton lounging robe it was, sloppily belted and seemingly slept in for a week or more, to judge by the creases and wrinkles. She had also braided her lovely golden hair in a single plait down her back, and those odd shoes of hers once again covered her feet. All in all she looked rumpled and unappealing, not to mention annoyed.

"Nothing in that closet is any good," she announced as soon as she saw him, all but dragging her feet as she walked. "I went through every bit of it three times, but that didn't help. I don't like any of it and I refuse to wear it."

"There must surely be enough clothing in there for a company or two of women," Tarren said, remembering the racks of tunics and breeches and trousers and coats available in his own dressing room. "Do you mean to say there was not one dress able to catch your fancy?"

"*That* was the trouble," she replied belligerently, stopping to look up at him with annoyed green eyes. "They were all *dresses,* and I've already told you how I feel about skirts. I shouldn't have set a precedent by putting on that first one, but that can be remedied. I won't wear another one no matter what."

She moved past him toward the table then, leaving him to seethe with his own annoyance. He had looked forward to seeing her in a richly made gown, the sort of gown he also looked forward to having made for her by the dozens. It was what a man did with his gold for the woman he loved, but this woman wanted nothing to do with that, and dismissed with contempt anyone who attempted to persuade her otherwise. It was enough to give a man second thoughts concerning what *he* wanted . . .

A deep, calming breath allowed Tarren to follow her to table, and despite her costume he stood and waited until Wildea had been seated by her serving man before he took his own seat. The long table made conversation unwieldy, and the immediate beginnings of the meal added to that. Chilled fruit began it, followed by chilled fish with a spicy sauce, and then chilled soup. Next came thin and succulent cabbage filled with a meat mixture and baked in a sauce, breads and cheeses, cuts of beef, venison, and boar, roast quail, and stuffed eggs. There were also three kinds of cheese sauces for the vegetables as well as drinking cups of soup and hot fish preparations, and by then even Tarren's appetite found it necessary to surrender. Had there been ten at the table rather than two, no one would have walked away hungry.

Tarren took his glass of wine and leaned back in the comfortable chair, for the moment ignoring the sherbet which had been put in front of him. The sherbet was meant to clear his palate for whatever desserts had been prepared, but dessert was another thing he meant to put off for a while.

At the thought of dessert he looked over at Wildea, wondering if she had eaten anything at all. He had been displeased earlier to discover that she had disobeyed him and eaten one of the cakes brought with the coffee and chai, and that anger had led to his foolish behavior with her. The disaster coming from his attempt to punish her had led to unexpected pleasure, but beyond all that lay the question of whether or not she had this time eaten.

And to Tarren's surprise, it seemed that she had. The plate before her was on the verge of being emptied, and even as he watched she finished the last of its contents. Her servant stepped forward then, but not to refill her wine glass. Fresh coffee had been brought with the meal, and it seemed that Wildea had drunk that rather than wine. Even as her cup was refilled she was in the process of refusing sherbet—but not the chocolate-and-cream confection that followed. *That* she accepted, and after a swallow of the coffee she set to consuming the dessert, savoring each bite with her eyes nearly closed.

Tarren found it impossible not to be taken by the sight, delighted to see a grown woman who took as much pleasure from sweets as a small child. He would have been just as delighted earlier, had he not been so concerned that she would starve and fade away before his very eyes. Now that she was safe from such a fate . . .

Now that she was safe his amusement left him, for he was once again faced with the problem of her behavior. There was little delight for him in that, nor in the way she had taken no notice of the clothing he had been so pleased with. Nothing beyond her own wants and needs seemed to occupy her—and her insistence on leaving in two days' time. At first he thought he would refuse to allow that, but now . . . perhaps she was not the woman he had thought her . . .

He grew despondent at the thought, so much so that his thoughts drew him away to a place that was a good deal easier to bear. That place contained the woman he felt such love for, the woman he would gladly die for, and in that place she also loved him. They stood hand in hand on a private balcony of their house, watching the sunset on a warm summer's evening, sharing each other's presence and a love that could be felt even in the silence . . .

"Hey, did you fall asleep?" Wildea's voice broke him out of the pleasure of his dream. "I asked if you were ready to continue with our discussion."

It was her writings she meant, and she had left her chair and come to stand by his without his having seen it. The two servants looked to him for instructions, so he dismissed them and then took a chair near the one Wildea had taken earlier.

"By all means, let us continue with our discussion," he said once the door had closed behind the last of the serving men. "The only difficulty is, I cannot remember where we left off."

"I can," she said after taking a sip from the cup she had carried with her from the table, having reclaimed her earlier place of sitting. "We were up to what you'll face in the way of opposition in the assassins' guildhall, and it won't be pleasant. There are a lot of traps and tricks waiting, but you manage to bypass those with very little trouble. You get within one corridor of the guild head's office, and that's when you're suddenly face to face with a masked man holding a sword."

"That cannot be all there is to it," Tarren said, well beyond being weary of such doings. "Were he the hall's only protection, the hall would soon be without it and him both."

"That's exactly how you feel when you face him," she replied with a nod, the look in her hooded eyes bleak. "The two of you cross swords and he's skillful, but you're better and you kill him. He goes down with your sword through his heart, and you circle the body to continue on your way. You take only a couple of steps when you hear something behind you, and turning, you find *two* masked men with swords. In addition, the body on the floor has vanished."

Realization dawned slowly on Tarren's face. "You cannot mean that killing a masked man allows him to double himself," Tarren protested, appalled. "Woman, that would be obscene! Defeating your enemy would mean strengthening him, and not defeating him would mean your death. How could you have conceived of such a thing?"

"Those not so personally involved call it creativity," she muttered, then seemed to force herself to continue. "You find out about the doubling when you kill the two new fighters, then stand and watch them become four. The four jump to their feet and attack you, and you have no idea what to do. Even if you manage to kill the four, you'll then have eight to face. You seem to be stuck but good, and that's when Mavial appears."

"Mavial is a woman's name," Tarren observed suspiciously, watching Wildea closely. "What? Am I so taken with this woman's beauty that I find myself transformed into a hero *able* to defeat eight men? Perhaps I rescue her with my left hand the while I defend us both from sixteen men with my right?"

Wildea rolled her eyes. "When you first see her you can't tell anything about her beauty, because she's also dressed as a masked assassin. As a matter of fact, she *is* an assassin, but she isn't there to help her guild brothers. She scatters a magical powder in the air, then helps you to defeat your four opponents. This time when they go down, they don't get up again."

"Her powder counters the multiplying spell," Tarren said with a nod. "But for what reason does she do this? She cannot truly be there to assist *me,* therefore she must be in the employ of my enemy."

"That's what you at first believe, but it doesn't happen to be true," Wildea said. "Mavial tells you she's trying to find out who hired the assassins who were sent to your camp, that group you and your people killed. Her younger brother was among them, and he told her before he left that he and the others expected little or no trouble. They'd been told that their target was a fat and wealthy merchant, a man too cheap to hire an adequate guard force. Her brother wasn't yet good enough to go up against members of a mercenary company and expect to survive, so whoever sent him just about murdered him in cold blood. She wants to know who that was, so she proposes the two of you work together to find your common enemy."

"And this is the truth?" Tarren asked doubtfully. "She aids me as she says she will, and keeps from turning on me until we find our enemy?"

"She doesn't even turn on you then," Wildea answered. "She became an assassin because her only other option was prostitution, but she hasn't lost her sense of ethics. You tell her what she wants to know in thanks for her having saved your life, and she repays your honesty by working with you. And when it's all over, you offer her a place with your company."

"Does she accept?" Tarren asked, his curiosity aroused. "She must surely be hideous to look upon or uninterested in men, but does she take the offer?"

"The book ends before she gives you her decision, but as for her looks and . . . interests"—and here Wildea's voice grew notably softer—"Mavial is a real beauty, which is why she goes masked most of the time, and she likes men just fine. In fact, she likes . . . *you,* and you . . . feel the same."

For a moment Tarren was too wrapped up in the surprise of these novel happenings to notice the silence that suddenly descended on them. Wildea sat and sipped at her drink, averting her eyes from him. A part of him still desired her attention, but only as she *had* been, not as she currently was. He wished she would see *him,* not her displeasure with the world around her. He longed for her to speak to him with affection, not exasperation and annoyance. Even now she paid him no mind—now that she had told him of the woman he would meet—

Tarren would have groaned aloud, but announcing one's stupidity to the world is no easy matter. Wildea had just told him of the woman he would meet, a woman he would find interest in. No wonder his attentions to *her* had been unwelcome; he was destined to meet another woman, one who would catch his eye. And Wildea meant to return to her world, but would leave him with a woman of his own world. How dishonorable it would be for her to encourage his attraction, and then leave him bitter and hurt and unable to return the affections of the woman fated for him.

So she had chosen to make herself *un*attractive in his eyes, and then would be able to leave without hindrance. Tarren rubbed at those eyes with one hand, distantly wondering how mortal man—or woman— found the strength to accomplish such a thing. Most especially when the woman was far from disinterested herself. So quickly she had responded to him, far too quickly for a woman who had no feelings for a man . . . But *her* feelings would do *him* ill, and that she refused to allow. Far better that she leave him to the happiness that would come, and return home without once speaking for herself.

"Is something wrong?" Wildea ventured in a small voice, having chanced a glance at him. "Are you . . . angry with me again? Not that I would blame you—"

"No," Tarren said decisively, and then he softened his tone as he looked at her. "No, sweet, I find no anger for you within me. Was the dinner to your liking? Were you able to eat a good portion of it?"

"It—was fine," she responded, momentarily startled by his change of subject. "And yes, I managed to eat more than I thought I would. Not only was the cooking excellent, it must be the first time I've ever eaten anything without preservatives. If it doesn't kill me, I'll probably end up healthier. Don't you want to know how Mavial happens to be at the assassin's guildhall just at the time *you* get there?"

"The matter is no lucky happenstance, *that* I'll wager," Tarren replied, now looking Wildea over in a new light. He should have noticed how carefully disarranged she was, how deliberately unbecoming she had made herself. Or tried to make herself. To him, she was always beautiful. "Your writings may give me a great deal of trouble, but never are they contrived to the cry of 'coincidence!' "

"You almost sound like a fan," she said, a faint, sad smile softening the line of her mouth. "But you're right about it not being a coincidence. When Mavial hears who her brother has died attacking, she thinks you'll be by sooner or later looking for the identity of your enemy. So she spends her nights in the guildhall, waiting until you show up. When you do she saves your life, and afterwards is surprised to learn you already know who hired the assassins. She expects to have to buy the information she wants; when you simply give it to her because she saved your life, she's so impressed she decides to join *your* efforts."

"Does she attempt the life of Agnal Topis as soon as she learns his name?" Tarren asked, more than simply curious. The point was an important one, for it would tell him how far the woman Mavial might truly be trusted.

"Her first urge is to go after him, but then she realizes that that will disrupt *your* plans," Wildea responded. "You also make no effort to keep her from taking her revenge whenever she feels she has to, and that helps her to make up her mind. She gives you her word that she'll wait to make Agnal Topis pay for her brother's life, and she keeps that word."

"Then you have given me a true and valuable ally, and I thank you for it," Tarren told her as warmly as possible. "Now I know the matter will end with less difficulty than previous ones. Should you need proof of your lack of guilt, this would surely be it."

"Right," she muttered, for some reason looking extremely uncomfortable, and then she shook her head. "But I think knowing what's going to happen will help even more. Once you and Mavial join forces, things begin to move a little faster. She knows a lot of people in this city, most of them denizens of the night. With the help of one of her friends you locate the thief who stole the ring—only he's been killed. That gets *his* associates angry, because his employer was supposed to have paid him to leave the city, not killed him. Before you know it you have an army working for you, made up of thieves and assassins."

"Better and better," Tarren said with an approving nod, trying again to lighten Wildea's mood. It was well nigh painful to watch her struggling to atone for what had never been deliberately done, and he meant to end the session soon. But first she must be allowed the easing of her mind.

"Your army finds the leads, and you and Mavial follow them," she continued, her expression now intent. "The prince's men have been coming up with information that makes it seem that a very powerful magic user is behind everything, but what your secret army picks up doesn't agree with that. The prince insists that you follow a particular lead that Agnal Topis supposedly considers important—he's talked the prince into agreeing with him—but it turns out to be a trap. With Mavial's help you spring the trap, then drag the leader of it in front of the prince. The prince's sorcerer puts a spell on the man, and *he* tells how

Agnal Topis set everything up and the situation has nothing to do with the missing ring."

"But Topis manages to talk himself out of the accusation?" Tarren asked, hoping he was wrong. "I will need the details of the trap, but first I would know what becomes of Topis."

"He *tries* to talk himself out of trouble, but this time the prince isn't having any of it," Wildea answered with a small grin. "Mavial has also found out about that mercenary company waiting to step in when *you* fail, and you and she volunteer to bring back that company's leader to be questioned with magic. Topis panics at the suggestion, and in the prince's eyes that makes it unnecessary to get the confirmation. He tells Topis to get out and stay out, and walks away from the man rather than listen to any more lies."

"An excellent turn of events," Tarren said with satisfaction, crossing his legs. "Facing disgrace and a diminishment of power is always worse than death for one of his sort. Does he flee the city, or remain to plot against the prince?"

"Oh, he stays to plot, which is the last mistake he ever makes," Wildea said meaningfully. "Now that he no longer has the prince's protection and support, Mavial is free to pay him a visit. Before she leaves, she makes sure he'll never cause grief to anyone ever again. After that the two of you give all your attention to the stolen ring, but run into a dead end. No one who would profit by the prince's making a wrong decision can be linked to the theft even distantly, so you are at a loss as to what course to pursue. Then Mavial happens to ask if it's possible that someone simply wants *any* wrong decision, not just that particular one."

"Which gives me cause to think upon the matter," Tarren said with a nod. "This, most likely, is where that symbol from the thieves' guild head's ledger comes into play. Do I interpret the symbol, or remember it?"

"Remember it," she replied, glancing at him as though he were in truth a brilliant leader of men before banishing the expression. "You saw it during your time here in the palace, but don't make the connection until you stop thinking about ordinary profit from a mistaken decision. Then you realize that the symbol is really the sigil of one of the noble houses, and you saw that sigil the second night you were in the palace, at the dinner given by the prince in your honor."

"Which will be tomorrow night, before the first attempt on my life here in the palace," Tarren said with a slow nod, seeing the pieces come together. *"That* is the reason for the dinner, not merely to allow the servant to drug my wine. Now I begin to understand. And to whom does the sigil belong?"

"It belongs to the house of Gisten, and its new head, Lord Rimin," she replied. "Rimin is a man in his mid-twenties who inherited the place as Head of the House when his father died unexpectedly. He isn't a true plotter, just someone who isn't very bright. Flatter him a little, and he lets you lead him around by the nose. As soon as you see that, you start to look around for the one doing the leading. There's a little more trouble, but then Rimin leads you to her: the princess Elial, Prince Drant's wife."

"Do I survive the accusing of her?" Tarren couldn't help flinching as he asked the question. Prince Drant was known to be in love with his wife, and to accuse a man's beloved is no easy thing—

"You don't accuse her," Wildea said with that faint, sad smile upon her again. "Mavial makes the suggestion and you agree, so you go to the prince and tell him you've discovered that his ring is hidden right in the palace itself. The prince has his sorcerer cast a finding spell, and they follow it to Elial's apartment.

"Drant is brokenhearted, but when they find the ring hidden among his wife's personal possessions, he can't lie to himself. He knows how ambitious his wife is, so he has her put under a truth spell and she confesses everything. She intended to wait until Drant made the wrong decision, which he would have done without the ring, and everyone was up in arms. She would then have Drant assassinated and take his place, and would immediately reverse his decision. Everyone would see how well she did, and the city would suddenly have a popular princess on the throne instead of a prince."

"And this Rimin of House Gisten?" Tarren asked. "What was to be *his* role?"

"He thought it was to become the new prince," Wildea said with a small snort of derision. "That's what Elial told him, so that's what he believes. He doesn't realize that for *him* to take the throne would be to disentitle Elial and Drant's young sons, and she has no intention of doing that. She *wants* her eldest son to inherit, but only after she finishes her reign—as princess, not as a short-term regent. Once she's found

out, Rimin tries to save things by having some men he's hired attack you and your company. He's under the muddleheaded impression that defeating you will free his ladylove, but neither happens. Your people win the fight, and Elial stays in trouble."

"Ambitious women upset my innards," Tarren said with a sigh and a grimace. "A man has difficulty enough with the ordinary sort, but ones with ambition—" He shook his head. "Most often they allow nothing to stand in their way, and full fighting companies are more easily faced or opposed. What becomes of the princess when Prince Drant has the entire truth?"

"That's something no one ever finds out," Wildea said with a small shrug. "She's never seen again, and no one knows what the prince has done with her. The only thing I can tell you is that it's many years before he marries again."

"And then the madness is finally over," Tarren said, reaching up to stretch behind his head and yawn. "There are still a large number of details we must review, but that will have to wait for another time. It has been a long day after a short night, and tomorrow morning I will need to speak with the prince. Best we retire now, so that I do not yawn in the man's face."

"Yes, that *would* tarnish your image just a little," she agreed, her smile still small but considerably more amused. "Have a good night's sleep, and we'll talk again tomorrow after you see the prince."

Tarren hesitated, not quite certain what to say. He longed to hold Wildea in his arms again, and yet . . . "Why does it seem that you mean to do other than join me in bed?" Tarren asked at last, watching as Wildea rose and walked to the coffee pitcher to refill her cup. "When we spoke earlier, we agreed that bed-time was to be looked forward to."

"You decided that," she corrected mildly. "What *I* said—and before that—was that I wanted my own room to sleep in. Surely you remember our discussion about that after you spoke to Fael."

"It would be difficult to forget," he granted her, immediately vexed. "But surely *you* recall what we shared in my bed. Why may we not share the same again?"

"Because I don't want to," she replied, turning to gaze at him mildly after replacing the pitcher. "I don't need any other reason than that, so don't expect to be given one. Tonight I want a room of my own, and tomorrow I want clothes *I* find acceptable. I'm tired of being put off, talked around, and ignored, and I won't accept it any longer."

"This is the most difficult you have been yet," Tarren told her as he stood, frustration turning his voice to a growl. "No least willingness to discuss the matter, nor even to argue. I dislike being presented with this side of you, and am tempted to simply carry you to my bed and kiss away your protests."

"I think you know that if you try it you'll get something other than kisses from me," she told him, those green eyes resting directly on him, her tone still mild. "You won the last time we fought, but that doesn't mean you'll win the next time. I've found that most people who think they want a fight change their minds when they pick on someone who's *willing* to fight."

"Is this the way your people see the thing?" Tarren asked, surprised enough to be temporarily diverted. "That only those who are unwilling to fight are the ones to be challenged? Now do I begin to see," Tarren muttered, rubbing at his face. "Rather than trying to challenge those about you, your behavior attempts to avoid unnecessary strife. I had thought you knew full well what you did, but apparently you do not."

"What's *that* supposed to mean?" she asked after sipping at her drink, faint curiosity in the question. "What did you think I was doing when I really wasn't?"

"I thought you realized you were among fighters, who see your 'willingness' as an offered challenge," he explained gently. "Here, fighters challenge only other fighters, who *will* respond when provoked. You must learn, Wildea, not to offer what you do not wish accepted."

"That sounds like advice on another topic entirely," she responded with a drawl, "and advice I don't happen to need. But as applied to fighters, I'll certainly keep it in mind. Why don't you go to bed now, and we'll continue this discussion tomorrow."

Tarren stared at her for a moment, the abrupt return to their original disagreement giving him pause. If he pressed the matter, there would surely be a fight. Battle was not what he wished to share with this woman; therefore there was but one thing to do.

"There is no need for you to seek elsewhere for a place of your own," he said, bowing to the inevitable as gracefully as possible. "Follow me, and I will show you."

She raised her brows and kept her distance, but made no effort to refuse to follow. He led her into the bedchamber, and then to one of the many doors she had earlier remarked upon. This one stood to the left of the bathing room doors, and behind it was the small, lamplit servant's room he had expected to find.

"That looks like it'll do the job," she remarked when he stepped aside to allow her access to it, simply peering in and glancing around. "Do I have to ask if there's a lock on the door?"

"I believe you know a lock is unnecessary," he replied, fighting down feelings of exasperation. "As your desire—or lack of it—has been made perfectly clear, your rest will be undisturbed."

"Good," she replied brightly. "If you think I'm bad now, you don't want to know what I'm like when I'm dragged out of a sound sleep. I'm going to finish the rest of that coffee before turning in, and I'll be sure not to wake you when I come through. Pleasant dreams."

The smile and nod she sent were suitable for giving to a stranger, and then she was returning to the entertaining room without a backward glance. Tarren watched her move, tempted to follow her, but then dismissed the idea. Her current mood of distancing herself from him would almost certainly cause her to begin a discussion of the writing's details he had not yet been given. Since that would run contrary to his own plans, best would be if he simply took himself to bed.

But first he would need to swim in the cooled water of the larger pool, to calm his body's demands for the woman of his heart—who refused to listen to her own.

Fourteen

A persistent beam of sunlight dragged me awake, and when I found I couldn't avoid it I gave up the idea of sleeping any later. That tiny room must have been meant for a servant, but it still had a window in addition to a very comfortable bed. There was also a wooden chair and a small clothes chest beside the ordinary double-sized bed, as well as a single lamp on the wall.

I took a couple of minutes to pull myself together. Sitting up and putting my head in my hands got the sun out of my eyes, but did nothing for the desire that invaded even my dreams. How I had wanted to join the redhead in his flames and rainstorm again, and I woke up with an ache of longing. I'd thought he was attractive in just that body cloth; when I walked out of the bedroom and saw him dressed like a prince, I'd almost lost it. Some clothes *do* make you want to tear them off . . .

But clothes had nothing to do with the way I felt about the man. I sighed as I rubbed at my eyes, remembering how he'd acted more than the way he'd looked. It went beyond simply showing the manners of a gentleman; it had to do with his gentleness and understanding, and the tender, almost sweet way he sometimes touched me, as though I really meant something important to him, as though I were special . . .

Although I couldn't mean those things to him, not really. Okay, I had no doubt that he'd enjoyed himself in bed with me and would again if he were given the opportunity, but something inside me insisted it wasn't love that he felt. It had some connection with the way he kept calling me Wildea, the name I'd given the barbarian's one true love. Being called that upset me, but it was clear by now that he wasn't going to stop doing it—or anything else, for that matter. Any and all stopping would have to be accomplished by me.

And that conclusion ended all desire to continue thinking about the man who had touched me far too deeply.

I threw the covers aside and reached for my socks and running shoes, putting them on before sliding into that robe I'd found. Foot coverings were a necessity when walking across uncarpeted marble, at least in the chill of night. Daytime might be different, but I wasn't prepared to find out. What I *needed* to do was get out of that world, before its discomforts—and natives—drove me to the point of talking to myself.

The bathroom facilities were nothing more than two carved and polished lengths of curved wood suspended over a channel of constantly running water, but indoor plumbing is welcome no matter how primitive it is. After using it I took a quick dip in the heated pool, then passed through the grooming curtain. I was still unaccustomed to that tingle, but the outcome was worth it. I tried throwing my socks through to see if they would be freshened like they were by Kergil's spell, but it didn't work. I'd have to wash them by hand—as soon as I found something to take their place.

After getting back into my things, I went to the closet of women's clothes again. Last night there hadn't been anything I could wear that wouldn't have had the redhead all over me in seconds, and I didn't expect that to have changed. But I did need something to wear in order to go *looking* for neutrally unarousing clothes, and I'd had an idea. Even women who never wore anything but skirts sometimes had to ride a horse, and that meant *divided* skirts. That item would have to do.

The lamps came on in the closet when I stepped inside; I looked for their power source to no avail— magic again. People who lived in that world probably took it for granted the way we did electricity. The closet was bigger than the room I'd slept in, and contained row after row of gowns, dresses, skirts, and blouses. I bypassed the really richly decorated gowns, and began to check the dresses and skirts.

It took a while, but I finally found what I was looking for. What had at first looked like a high-waisted skirt in pearl-gray jersey was actually a riding skirt, and the red silk blouse hanging right in front of it seemed to be the top half of the outfit. The blouse had a high collar in back and elbow-length sleeves, but the sleeves fell long in layers away from the arms, and the front showed a lot less cleavage than the gowns and dresses. Compared to the other blouses it was downright modest.

Taking the skirt and blouse off their holders brought a surprise. Below the items, on the floor, was a pair of red boots that matched the blouse perfectly. The heels on the boots weren't very high or particularly narrow, meaning they were meant for riding. I picked them up, intending to at least try them, and got another surprise. They were thickly lined with something like the same jersey of the skirt, which meant I didn't need to wear socks with them. I could wash my own socks, and let them drip dry.

Generating intense concern for the state of cleanliness of my socks let me forget about my real problems for a while, but by the time I was dressed and ready to go out into the entertaining room the dodge no longer worked. I had to stop and put a hand to the wide skirt sash around my middle to stop the fluttering, but that wasn't anything like a permanent solution. As soon as I saw the redhead the fluttering would start again, but I'd just have to learn to live with it.

I was all but holding my breath when I walked out of the bedroom, but discovered immediately that I needn't have bothered. The redhead was nowhere in sight, and only a single servant waited near the new, much smaller table. A number of covered dishes said that breakfast was waiting, but once again I wasn't in the least hungry. All I wanted was coffee, so I dismissed the servant and sat down to brood.

I'd forced myself into admitting that I *had* to leave at the end of the next day whether I wanted to or not, when there was a knock at the door. Leaving my cup on the table next to the chair I went to the door and opened it, but didn't recognize the man who stood there. He was short and slender and fussy-looking, the kind of man who never seemed satisfied with the world around him. He frowned as he looked me over with very little approval, then pulled a hankie from his sleeve and gently touched it to his nose.

"I happen to be terribly allergic to flowers," he stated in an accusing voice, apparently blaming me for the condition. "You would do well to take heed of that. First thing tomorrow, and definitely *not* after breakfast, you will present yourself at the apartment of the High Adviser Agnal Topis. I will be there, and will give you further instructions at that time. Are my orders clear in your mind?"

"Oh, absolutely," I assured him solemnly, then watched him nod before turning and walking away. His comments about flowers had confused me for a minute, but only for a minute. I closed the door and went back to my chair, shaking my head over the colossal gall of that Agnal Topis character.

Obviously Topis had taken a *good* look at me the day before, and now wanted his turn at playing house for a while. He'd assumed I was the redhead's current bed bunny, and since the redhead was due to be killed tonight, he'd arranged to take over my custody tomorrow. That he actually believed I'd take his secondhand orders and show up at his apartment tomorrow said something about that culture—or maybe it was just the man. Some people believe they can do anything they like, even if there are laws against it.

But Agnal Topis wasn't anyone I cared to worry

about, and wouldn't have been even if he wasn't soon
due to get his comeuppance. More to the point was
the redhead, and how I would manage to stay away
from him for almost two full days longer. I could see
him deciding last night not to push the point of my
sharing his bed again, but somehow I doubted that his
show of patience would last.

I grabbed the coffeecup and gulped down some of
the still-hot brew, trying to get a grip on myself again.
Little tingles were running up and down my entire
body, brought on by nothing more than the thought of
him. If he ever touched me again . . . It wasn't just
physical desire that I felt, no, I couldn't have *been*
that lucky. I also wanted comfort from his arms, approval from his eyes, and words of love from his lips.
Not just desire but love, the kind of love most people
only get to dream about.

But those were the very things I couldn't *afford* to
have from him. I still couldn't stay in his world or
expect him to come to mine, so what was the point
of falling in love with him? Or encouraging him to
fall in love with me? Besides, I'd watched him last
night while I was telling him about Mavial. It was
obvious how intrigued he was—before he'd remembered he was with a woman he expected to take to
bed again. After that he didn't show nearly as much
interest, and perversely that had hurt. He couldn't wait
to meet Mavial, but didn't want *me* to know it.

And that was all that had let me insist on a bed of
my own, the pain of jealousy brought about by a character *I'd* written. The redhead didn't yet know anything
about her, really, but I did and also knew he'd be very

much drawn to her. He'd even make love to her, and I *had* to be out of here by then. It was hard enough just thinking about it, and I wasn't even in love with him yet . . . well, not *completely* in love with him . . .

Another knock at the door saved me from going on with that thought, so I left my cup and chair again and answered the door for the second time. This time it was a pretty woman about my age, maybe just a little bit older. She had dark hair and sparkling brown eyes, wore a dress of brown and gold silk, and smiled shyly when she saw me.

"Excuse me, but I would know if the fighter Tarren is in," she said in a friendly, eager way. "I have heard so much about him, it would be unthinkable not to make his acquaintance now that he is here in the palace. *Is* he in?"

"Not at the moment," I answered, suddenly even more depressed than I had been. Mavial would also have heard of him . . . "I believe he's with the prince right now, so he could be back at any time. Would you like to come in and wait?"

"Oh, that is most kind of you," she accepted with a radiant smile that made her really lovely, coming in when I stepped aside. She was of average height and size, which meant she had to look up at me. "I am Drant's sister Drinna, and that of course means I know the wait may be a bit longer than you expect. Drant does love to go on and on at times."

Her smile had turned merry, but I was still surprised. She was a princess, but hadn't even bothered to mention that in passing. And she certainly wasn't one of *my* characters, or I would have recognized her.

I'd been hoping a visitor would distract me from my problems, and I seemed to have lucked out.

"I'm sure the meeting will be over before lunch," I said. "I'm Deanne, and as your temporary hostess I get to ask if you'd like coffee or chai."

"Chai would be nice," she answered, following me to the sideboard. "Are you the fighter's . . . companion?"

"No, it so happens I'm not," I said, appreciating the delicate way she'd put that. "You could say I'm his . . . literary adviser. I'll be leaving soon. It looks like the chai is still hot, so you're in luck."

"Why would you consider it luck?" she asked, watching while I filled a cup for her. "The sideboard will keep hot things hot and cold things cold. Are you not familiar with the spell?"

"Truthfully, no," I said, turning to hand over the cup of chai with a smile. "I come from a long way away from here and my people accomplish the same thing without using magic, so I'm still not used to it."

"Your—unusual—accent told me you were from another land," she said with a small laugh as she this time followed me to the chairs and my own drink. "I very much enjoy meeting people from other lands, yet have little or no desire to travel. A homebody, Drant calls me, and he is right. For that reason he will not marry me to just anyone, but only if an alliance is absolutely necessary. Until that time I will happily remain here and paint."

It was surprising to find a fellow artist there, and even more surprising when Drinna said she had a painting hanging in that very room. We went over together to look at it, and surprise gave way to astonishment. The painting was *good;* I could almost hear the roar of the falls it showed, and smell the flowers on the bank in the foreground. We returned to our chairs to discuss painting, Drinna talking and me listening. If not for magic her palette would have half the number of colors it did, she said, which briefly made me feel glad there *was* magic.

The time disappeared behind our conversation, and after telling me about painting Drinna pumped me about writing. I made sure not to mention the reason I was there or how it related to the redhead, but aside from that had a very good time talking about my craft. We had just gone to the sideboard for the third refill of our cups, still exchanging information enthusiastically, when the hall door opened without a knock and the redhead came in. He closed the door behind him while looking at our visitor—who had abruptly fallen silent—which meant it was time for introductions.

"Drinna, this is the man you came to meet," I said as the redhead walked toward us. "This is Drinna."

"Your Highness," the redhead said, proving he knew who she was and stopping a few feet away to bow. "You honor me with your interest. And may I say how lovely you both look."

Drinna smiled happily at that, but the redhead's eyes were on *me* when he said it. "As soon as I have dressed," he continued, "I mean to take you to visit some of the city's clothing shops. There you will purchase what you wish rather than needing to go searching for it. Your Highness, if you will excuse me for a few moments?"

He bowed again as Drinna nodded her agreement, then she watched him stride toward the bedroom. The pink in her cheeks said she'd had no trouble noticing how much of him was visible around that body cloth, and possibly she felt the least bit disappointed that he meant to dress. I also would have preferred not to have him dress, but for an entirely different reason.

"Oh, how lovely!" Drinna exclaimed once he had disappeared into the bedroom. "He means to take you shopping. I do hope you will allow me to recommend a shop or two, so that you may get exactly what you wish."

"Why don't you come along with us and show me," I said, acting on the idea as soon as it came to me. The redhead had been so pleasant he *must* be up to something, which meant I had to protect myself any way I could.

"I *love* shopping," she answered with a delighted laugh. "I also tend to indulge myself a bit too often, therefore will I have the satisfaction without incurring the cost. Are you quite sure no one will mind my accompanying you?"

"Oh, I'm positive," I assured her, as sincere as a used car salesman. *"I'll* certainly enjoy the company."

"Then I *will* accompany you," she agreed excitedly. "And some of my brushes could do with replacement, so I, too, will shop. I must have my carriage brought around, and must pick up a coin or two. May we meet outside the entrance nearest these rooms?"

"Certainly," I said, then saw her to the door. I really did like her, and hadn't invited her just to have someone to put between me and the redhead. She seemed to be as alone as I felt, so the outing ought to be pleasant for the both of us.

I went back to the coffee cup I'd refilled, but the redhead didn't keep me waiting long. He came back out of the bedroom dressed in tight black pants and boots and a wide-sleeved gold silk shirt embroidered with black. He'd also found a black medallion and chain like the one he'd worn in gold last night, and if I hadn't been braced for the sight of him I probably would have dropped the coffee cup. All dressed up he really did look like a woman's dream prince, that long red hair framing those broad, silk-covered shoulders. And that was another difference between him and my character. Tarren the Barbarian never dressed like that.

"We can be on our way now," he said, then looked around. "What has become of the princess Drinna?"

"She went to get some money and arrange for her carriage," I said after taking a last sip and putting the cup down. "I invited her to accompany us. You don't mind, do you?"

"Likely, good manners demanded it," he allowed with a sigh. "Now it seems fortunate that I permitted Fael and Kergil and Lamor to accompany us. They will assist me in seeing to the safety of you both. Do you mean to ride with Drinna in her carriage?"

"No," I answered, then had to ignore his immediate brightening. "Shall we go?"

He agreed immediately with a courtly grace that also seemed to belong to someone I didn't know, but there wasn't much time to consider the matter. It took only a minute to get to the side entrance we'd come in by, and we were the last arrivals. The redhead's men stood around holding horses, a liveried man stood beside the two horses of Drinna's dark brown carriage, the princess herself stood beside the carriage, and four uniformed guardsmen stood behind the carriage, waiting with their own mounts. It looked like our shopping trip had become an expedition, but the redhead didn't seem surprised.

"It delights me that the princess has her own guard," he murmured as we walked toward the horses. "That means her brother values her enough not to leave her safety in the hands of strangers. I will mount first, and then assist you to your place."

"Wait a minute," I said, stopping him from turning toward his stallion. "What 'place' would you be referring to?"

"Why, your place before me on my horse," he answered, his brows raised slightly in puzzlement. "Did you think I meant to ride you behind me like a sack of oats? You did say you would not be joining the princess in her carriage . . . Have you changed your mind?"

"No, I haven't changed my mind, but I'm also not riding with *you*," I said. "I've already told you I can ride. I want a horse of my own."

"You cannot mean to cause everyone to wait while a horse is found for you," he said at once, making it sound as if I were being totally unreasonable. "I realize the carriage would make you feel pampered and foolish, too much like a delicate, helpless female, therefore do I offer a place on my own mount. It will not be for long, and Flatterer is more than capable of carrying us both for such a short distance. Come, let us not waste any further time."

He smiled as he put his hand out to me, and damned if I didn't almost return that smile and give him my own hand. I actually had to clench my teeth to keep it from happening, even though something told me he knew exactly what he was doing. It was all part of his plan, which meant I had to stick to my own plan.

"Not wasting time sounds like a good idea," I said, ignoring his outstretched hand. "With that in mind, you have a simple choice, which goes as follows: either I get my own mount, or the bunch of you can leave without me. I'm tired of being manipulated into doing things *your* way."

He parted his lips to say something, but must have realized I wasn't kidding. "Very well," he conceded with a short breath after another moment. "You shall have your own mount. Wait here."

His movements looked annoyed as hell as he headed for his men, undoubtedly because his plans were in ruins. He'd *wanted* to get his hands on me under circumstances where I couldn't complain, but it hadn't worked out. That nonsense about how helpless and foolish I'd feel riding in the carriage had been an absolute giveaway, and if I'd fallen for it I would have deserved whatever I got.

"His horse is called Flatterer?" Drinna said from beside me, having come up without my noticing. "How did he come to be given so strange a name?"

A glance at her told me she wanted to ask a different question, but was much too well-mannered to do it. I smiled at her tactfulness.

"His stallion is named Flatterer because of a habit he has," I told her, another point I knew all too well because I'd written it. "The horse tends to be really friendly with anyone who comes near him, acting as if that person is someone he likes and wants to be pals with. But just let that person try to climb on his back. His current owner is the only one who was ever able to ride him without getting thrown, and the horse has *not* given up the habit, so ignore any advances he makes. He does *not* think you're the best human ever born, and will *not* give you a ride just to show how much he likes you. And yes, your redheaded friend over there is trying to back me into a corner I don't care to be put in."

"Obviously, my curiosity was a shade too—obvious," she said with a blush, her expression rueful. "I had thought . . . since you shared the apartment with him . . ."

"That I was sharing other things as well?" I finished when she didn't, and her blush deepened. "Well, it so happens it doesn't *matter* whether or not I'm sleeping with him. It still would not give him the right to ignore my wishes and opinions. And if I *was* sleeping with him, do you think he'd be trying so hard to find a reason to put his hands on me?"

"That point had not occurred to me," she answered, blinking in surprise. "Of course! The man attempts to coax you into his bed by first coaxing you into his lap. You find him less attractive, then, than he finds you?"

"Attraction or the lack thereof has very little to do with it," I told her, refusing to let myself sigh. "He may or may not believe it, but I really won't be around much longer. I have to go home, and there's not much chance of my ever coming back. Under circumstances like those, would *you* let yourself get involved with a man?"

"That would depend quite a lot on the man," she responded, and her expression grew rather sad. "The thought of leaving a man like Tarren behind would be painful, and yet one must also ask if he would *allow* himself to be left behind. You may well leave him, Deanne, but what is there to say that he will not finish my brother's commission and then ride after you to claim you for his own? Would your father refuse to give you to him?"

The thought of my father face to face with a man who wanted to "claim" me was almost too comical for words, especially a man as . . . unusual as the redhead. My father would probably try to throw him out—except that the redhead never would follow out of his own world. Which was all to the good, since he needed a woman of his own world to get together with. And he'd have that woman with Mavial.

It took me a while to notice that I hadn't answered Drinna's questions, and by then she'd obviously given up expecting an answer. We stood without speaking until another horse was brought from the nearest stable. The redhead himself led the bay over to me.

"You may have the loan of this gelding for the day," he said, barely concealing his glare. "Should you prove unable to handle him, however, you will ride with me with no further argument."

"There's no reason I won't be able to handle him,"

I responded, stepping forward to take the rein he held. "Unless there's a burr under his saddle, in which case I'll come looking for you."

Our eyes held as I passed him, and then I gave my attention to mounting the bay. The animal began to dance as I settled into the saddle, but that was just eagerness to get some exercise. I used my knees and the reins to settle him down, and then looked at the redhead—who was in turn looking at my riding skirt and shaking his head.

"I would ask where that article of clothing came from, did I not already know," he said, raising his eyes to my face to give me a sour look. "A spell that responds to the desires of ordinary mortals must surely respond even more strongly to the talented. And yes, I see now that you *can* ride, so let us be on our way."

Everyone was busy either climbing into a carriage or mounting a horse, so while making sure my stirrups were set to the proper length I had a minute to wonder what he'd been talking about. What did a spell have to do with what I was wearing, other than making it the right size to fit me? He seemed to have been suggesting that I somehow manipulated the spell to produce what I wanted, but that was ridiculous, *I* couldn't do magic, and didn't know enough about how real magic worked to even try.

We started out from the palace, heading toward the gate that led to the fourth district. The gate was at least a mile away from the palace, a distance that translates into about twenty city blocks for urban dwellers like me. Of course, the area wasn't divided into blocks or streets the way other districts were, not when it made up the estates of the nobility. There were well-tended roads dividing those estates, and each of the roads led to a gate to the next district.

The wall dividing this innermost district from the next was about twenty feet high, made of intricately designed metal lace. It was really pretty to look at, but that wasn't the reason for its design. In the event of invasion of the city by hostile forces, the gateways would be blocked by sliding across a section of metal wall that locked *into* the opposite side of the gate. Once all the gates were closed, the spell inherent in the wall's design would flare to life, turning the wall into a highly charged electrical fence. That the electricity came from magic rather than machinery meant it was wild and uncontrolled, but that was a benefit rather than a drawback in a defensive wall.

We passed through the gate without any of the guards trying to stop us, of course, and not only because we had palace guardsmen with us. Getting *into* the area was so hard, that getting out of it again never took a major effort. The guardsmen were there just to keep idlers from blocking the gate and bothering those who lived in the area. The gateways themselves were bespelled, and anyone who didn't belong in the area was unable to go through alone. You needed to be in the company of someone who did belong, or had to have legitimate business there.

And that was supposed to be a clue for the redhead when it became time for him to figure out who stole the ring. A random thief couldn't possibly have gotten into the area, not to mention the palace itself, without the help of a member of the nobility. I almost called the redhead over to tell him that, but it was actually unnecessary now that he knew exactly who was responsible. And in addition to the fact that I'd decided to stay as far away from him as possible, he was also riding next to Drinna's carriage and talking to her. The princess seemed to be enjoying herself, and I had no reason to interrupt her good time.

The fourth district *was* divided into streets, but since the wealthy and influential lived there the streets were wider than average. They were also relatively empty at that time of day, since those who weren't still sleeping had already gone to take care of whatever business they had. The few people we passed only glanced at us, then continued silently on their way.

Soon, we were all pulling up and dismounting near the very large stables built right against the next wall. Every gate had a stables like that, with a shop renting pull-carts directly across the way. If you weren't able to walk—or were simply too good to do so—you rented a pull-cart with a comfortable seat and let one or two of your servants or relatives pull you around. The carts were relatively small and narrow, and with human beings rather than animals pulling them, no one was in danger of getting run over.

Once we'd left our mounts and walked through the unguarded gate, I found the noise and bustle almost a physical presence. People from all over the city—not to mention from the countryside—came to shop for necessities as well as luxuries, and the place almost looked like Times Square on New Year's Eve.

"The shops I would recommend are to the right," Drinna said, her guardsmen spreading around the both of us as she stopped beside me. "After you have chosen what you wish, we shall have lunch at a neighboring establishment. There should also be far fewer people."

The redhead had heard what she'd said, so he nodded and gestured his men into leading out. The boy Lamor wasn't as big as the other three, but he did his best to hold the line as they moved forward. Drinna and I followed them as closely as possible, to keep from having to batter our own way through the crowds. In this district people did tend to stare at us, but only until we reached the Silver and Gold Line. Beyond the line there weren't that many to do the staring, although the area was far from empty.

"I tend to be very grateful for the Silver and Gold Line, although when I think of the throngs the thought shames me," Drinna said softly after taking a deep breath. "The Silver and Gold Line will permit no one without silver or gold to pass, unless they accompany someone else who has one or the other. It means a respite from the shouting, jostling numbers who even overwhelm themselves, but it also keeps out those who would simply enjoy seeing what there is to strive for. When people are denied the sight of what success can bring them, too often they give up hope."

"I never thought of that," I said, trying to reconcile that perceptive observation with my own world's latest trend against "conspicuous consumption." If you don't see what breaking your back can earn you, why would you bother doing it? Just for the fun of it? Where's the incentive? When I'd created the idea of the Silver and Gold Line, I hadn't been thinking along such lines. It looked like I'd have more than a little rethinking to do when I got home.

"In any event, there is the first of the shops I mentioned," Drinna said, pointing past the shoulders of the men ahead of us. "Their ballgowns are absolutely the best to be had anywhere, most especially if you let them do their unique embroidery work. There is never even a single stitch out of place, and they will fit the gown to you as you have never been fitted before."

"That sounds like an excellent suggestion to me," the redhead commented, having stopped once we were all beyond the press of the crowd. "A beautiful woman should have one beautiful ball gown at the very least, and it would undoubtedly please you to have clothing of your own here."

"I *do* have clothing of my own here," I reminded him, the feeling of being ganged up on bringing on immediate near-panic—and an automatic effort at self defense. "That was my clothing you walked away with and keep refusing to return. Besides, I don't expect to be here long enough to *go* to a ball. Drinna, do these wonders of yours also have pants and shirts in my size?"

"Do they *have* them?" she echoed blankly, as though I were speaking another language. "There are no seers among their lot, therefore they could not possibly have garments already made up for you. First you must choose your material, then you must be measured, and finally you must come for one or more fittings. Only magic could provide you with clothing more quickly, and magic is a service no clothing shop provides."

I squeezed my eyes closed and shook my head hard, hoping to loosen some of the hardening of the brain I must have been suffering from. Of *course* those clothing shops would have nothing already made up. Their civilization wasn't even up to K-Mart level, not to mention Bergdorf. I wondered what I could have been thinking of, and then suddenly I knew.

"Why did you agree to take me shopping *here?*" I asked the redhead after opening my eyes again, not caring that I sounded accusing. "You knew I wanted something now rather than a month from now, so why didn't you say something? Like telling me where your female fighters get *their* clothes?"

"I have no idea where my female fighters obtain their clothing," he answered innocently. "For all I know, they take them at swordpoint from suitable victims. How would it harm you to choose the material and be measured for a gown? You need not worry over wasting gold, as I have little else to spend it on. Will you deny me the pleasure of at least pretending that you will remain longer? A small pleasure such as that would outweigh a good many larger distresses."

Because of the almost-pleading way those ice-blue eyes looked down at me, he nearly had me. On the surface he was asking for a favor that would outweigh some of the awful situations my writing had forced him into, and I couldn't consider that at all unreasonable—until I stopped to think about what that favor was. He wanted me to let him *pretend* that I would stay longer than another day and a half, but the next step would surely be for me to pretend along with him. Since I couldn't let that happen, there was only one answer I could possibly give.

"It's nice to see that some people are still rather easily pleased," I said, forcing myself to look straight at him. "But I like to buy off the rack. Custom made items are too much of a hassle."

Behind the redhead, the boy Lamor looked confused, Fael stood with one hand shading his eyes, and Kergil shook his head as he sighed. They were all upset by the way I treated their leader, and their leader was even less happy about it.

"Without doubt, you are the stubbornest female ever to have lived," the redhead growled, making Drinna jump in alarm. "You resist my every effort, especially the ones which are to *your* benefit. Can you say with full truth that you have no interest at all in being held in my arms?"

"I can do better than that," I countered, stepping back fast before he could put those arms around me. "I have no *intentions* of being held in your arms, so you'd better give it up. I want to return to the palace."

"Stubborn," he growled, and then he straightened and shook his head. "No, we will not return to the palace. Princess Drinna has not yet made the purchases she intended, and my men and I would like to look about a bit. At the very least we will remain to lunch here."

Depression settled down on me then, but I had to wait until I could sit somewhere and brood about it. Drinna led the way to the booth where she bought her art supplies, and the proprietor told her about some new paints he'd just gotten in. While she looked them over I took the opportunity to look around, but didn't see anything unexpected.

The booths and shops in this area were mostly silk-walled or covered, as opposed to the canvas or thick cotton used beyond the Silver and Gold Line. The wood of the booths was also better quality, and the large silk tents that comprised the better shops were also more brightly colored. Most of the people passing us had bowed or curtsied to Drinna, even when she wasn't looking in their direction. Afterward the passers-by tended to put their heads together, probably trying to figure out who the rest of us were.

Or at least who everybody but the redhead was. *He* was recognized, the way people pointed and whispered making it an absolute certainty. They were probably wondering what he was doing with the prince's sister, and why there was another female tagging along. The female in question was wondering the same, but she'd already gone contrary enough times today.

"Did you eat what breakfast was left for you?" my nemesis murmured from only a couple of feet away. "The madness took me too quickly this morning, else I would have waited and seen for myself."

"Why, of course I did," I answered, watching the play of bright sunshine on a dark blue tent across the street. "I ate everything there was, but I must have looked at the empty platters too intently. The servant grabbed them away, then left with them and the table. I guess he was afraid I'd eat them too if he gave me the chance. But I was really much too full, so don't expect me to repeat the performance at lunch. After all, I do have to think about my weight."

"So you ate nothing," he concluded with a sigh, getting just the message I'd wanted him to. "And you mean to continue like that. I had hoped the small amount of exercise you had— Well, the mystery is not to be solved easily, it seems. But after lunch we will leave the princess to return with her guard, and will go ourselves to a remnants and secondhand booth in the larger section of the market. There, perhaps, you will find trousers if you'd like to fit you."

"You've changed your mind?" I asked, surprised. "Why? And how is it you suddenly know what you said you didn't know only a few minutes ago?"

"My knowledge comes from Fael and Kergil," he answered, reaching out to brush back a strand of my hair and almost making me flinch. "It was they who spoke of the shop, telling me our female fighters often need to resort to such a place when first accepted into the company. I *had* not known, else I would not have brought you to *this* section. It was not my intention to lie to you."

This time there was nothing in the ice-blue eyes looking down at me to suggest anything but the simple truth. That made it a good deal worse, of course, at least from my point of view. I would have preferred being able to think of the man as devious and unreliable, someone interested in nothing but getting what *he* wanted. Now . . . I couldn't quite manage to think of what to say, and then Drinna saved me by coming over with her purchases.

We had to retrace our steps a short distance to reach the food establishment Drinna recommended, a place not far from the Silver and Gold Line. It was a bright yellow silk tent with tables both inside and out, though the hot sun overhead had made most of the shop's patrons take shelter inside. The shop's servants pushed two tables together for the six of us to use, Drinna's guardsmen standing around doing their job rather than joining us.

Once we were settled Drinna started to tell us about the wonderful new paints she'd bought along with the brushes, but I couldn't keep my attention on her words. I watched the crowds hurrying about only a few dozen feet away beyond the Line, noticed that the food shop we were at was really becoming crowded, and wondered why I felt so strange. It was partly because of the redhead and what he'd said, but something made me believe that that wasn't the only reason. It was almost as if I'd forgotten something, something important and maybe even critical . . .

But then a servant came with cups of a complimentary drink called shab, a delightfully cool concoction made up of chopped ice and a mixture of fruit juices. What mixture of juices you got depended on where you had the shab, and some places even served different mixtures at different times. The shop's current mixture was a bright red in color, but a sip didn't reveal to me just exactly what was in it. Cherries, certainly, maybe even raspberries with a touch of peaches, and—

"How odd," the redhead said with a frown just as the servant with the tray headed for him. Drinna and I had been served first, and as the most important male there, he would be next. Drinna sat at the end of one of the small, square tables, and I sat to her right with Kergil to my right. The redhead sat at the other end of the tables, with Lamor to his right and Fael to the boy's right and Drinna's left.

"How very odd," the redhead said, beginning to look uneasy. "Almost it seems that the madness is about to descend again, but that cannot be. Surely it was not meant to do so until tonight, when . . . when . . ."

I choked on the shab, suddenly remembering what I'd forgotten, but it was much too late to do anything about it. The redhead wore a distant look that said he'd been taken over by the book, and the servant with the tray of cups filled with bright red shab was heading right for him. Those embarrassing accidents the redhead was slated to have, courtesy of the magic user he'd splashed on our way into the city . . . I hadn't gone into too much detail about the incidents and I'd expected the first one to take longer in coming about. But that first one happened in the city, in front of a large crowd of people . . .

And now was when it was going to happen. I knew that as I watched the servant stumble, his attempt to catch his balance causing his arm to fly up. At the end of the that arm was the hand holding the tray of cups, and as the arm and hand went, so did the tray. Or at least the cups did, and two of them went straight for the redhead. It was going to be horrible, I knew it was, and I couldn't watch.

Clapping my hands over my eyes blocked out sight of what happened next, but it didn't keep me from hearing the sudden burst of laughter from all around. I knew I'd be better off if I *continued* to keep from looking, but something about the laughter forced me to drop my hands.

Two of the cups had been deposited atop the redhead, one of them standing inverted in his lap, the other balanced upside down on top of his head. The one on his head was leaking red juice all down his face and hair, and looked like a silly little hat *meant* to be laughed at. Which everyone was doing, except for the servant who had tripped, me, and the redhead's three men. Drinna was fighting hard *not* to laugh, and not having much success.

And then the redhead came up out of his chair with a roar, sending both cups flying. He was furious, so much so that he even seemed beyond speech. But when he stood he knocked back his chair with his legs, probably the worst thing he could possibly have done. His roar had startled a servant passing behind him, causing the servant to turn in his direction. The next moment his chair *hit* the servant, not hard but hard enough to cause the man to stumble like the first servant—with almost the same results. This time it was a pitcher of something blue that splashed him, from mid-back all the way down to his boots.

After that, the people around us were in definite danger of hurting themselves, so hard were they laughing. The redhead now had a soggy seat to match a runny front, and people had even gathered at the Silver and Gold Line to watch the spectacle. For myself, I would have been happy to drop through a hole in the ground, but the Fates had decided I couldn't be that lucky. The ground under me refused to open up, the distant look faded from the redhead's eyes, and then he was glaring directly at me.

"You!" he growled, the word almost drowned out by the glee of the crowd. "This is *your* doing, and this I will *not* forgive you for!"

He turned and stomped off then, pausing only to grab the clean cloths brought on the run by a third servant, Lamor and Fael in his wake. Rather than watch him disappear I covered my eyes again, wishing I had at least a dark closet to hide in, and Drinna touched my arm.

"How can he possibly put the blame on you, Deanne?" she asked, sounding more upset than amused. "With my own eyes I saw the servant stumble, something that could not possibly have been your fault. When we return to the palace I will speak to him, and insist that he apologize."

"Why should he apologize when he's absolutely right?" I asked, feeling totally defeated. "It *was* my fault, but I didn't deliberately keep from mentioning it. With everything else going on I forgot, but he'll never believe that."

Drinna stared at me, baffled, but I managed to divert her attention to the lunch we had gone there for. I just sat silently and drank shab, looking around at the bright, sunlit booths and shops, trying to figure out where I would sleep tonight. I couldn't go back to *his* apartment, not after that scene. It was amazing he hadn't tried to kill me.

My editor had wanted something to make him less perfect and untouchable, but what that something was had been *my* choice. And I'd chosen this . . . If I'd been alone, I would have buried my head in my arms and spent some time wishing that he'd not only tried to kill me but had done it.

Fifteen

Tarren stalked into his apartment slamming doors behind him, but even the slamming did little to cool his fury. He had never been so enraged in his entire life, and if anyone had spoken even a single word to him he would have struck them at the very least. Had anyone else laughed, he would have killed without hesitation or regret. Humiliation does exceedingly well in removing all traces of humanity from a man.

The feel of his clothing against his body added to his rage, a wet and sticky clinging that strove to drive him out of his mind. And the stickiness clung to his face and hair even though he had used those cloths provided by the eating establishment in an effort to wipe himself clean. Clean. Considering the way he felt at the moment, he might never feel clean again.

He threw open the bathing room doors and went inside, then immediately began to strip off his fouled attire. The awful stickiness had even reached his swordbelt, and the gods alone knew what state the sword itself was in. But that could not be his primary concern, not with his body so completely covered with the same substance. Once his clothes lay in a heap, he hurried to take down a jar of soap and then plunged into the small, heated pool.

It took more than one scrubbing, but after a time he finally managed to remove all traces of stickiness from both body and hair. The constantly renewing hot water was able to soothe him to some extent, so he moved to a ledge, lay down upon it, and put his head back. Only then, with his eyes closed and his mind free of rage, was he able to consider. How could she have done that to him, without warning or regret? Did she truly have so little feeling for him that she could pass such an incident by with nothing in the way of comment?

That Tarren had not expected such treatment made it all the worse, as if she had reached out to caress him and then had slapped him in the face instead. Could he have been wrong in believing she had more than casual feelings for him? Did she really and truly wish to leave him in one more day, and had chosen this method as very clear proof of her position?

Tarren spent quite a long time soaking and brooding, finally bestirring himself when he recalled the dinner that he must attend that night. Sooner would he have remained in the apartment to think dark thoughts of disappointment and betrayal, but once again the choice was not his. At least this time he knew what to expect, he allowed, partially diverted as he stepped through the grooming curtain. And were his plans to work out properly, a good deal of difficulty would be avoided.

"Like the difficulty of preserving my life," he muttered as he padded barefoot across the bedchamber to his dressing room. But what benefit would there be in having that life, when the woman he desired above all others would be elsewhere than beside him? The thought of going on alone was extremely depressing, but less so than the thought of taking a different woman to wife. Nor would it be fair, to wed a woman he would never love as he loved Wildea . . .

The brooding took him again briefly, and when he returned to the world about him it was to discover that the time for the dinner must be nearing. He had donned the body cloth and the broadsword of his alter personality, and currently left the dressing room as barefooted as he had entered it. Ah well, the sooner the dinner and its aftermath came, the sooner they would be behind him. Then his life would be his own again for a time, and he would be able to . . . to . . .

Watch Wildea ride out of his life forever? Ache for her presence everywhere, not simply in his empty bed? Think about the woman he would soon meet, a woman who would never be *his* woman? Tarren found that he had left the bedchamber without noticing, and now stood in the entertaining room near the sideboard with coffee and chai. The pitcher of coffee had been replaced with fresh, but there was no Wildea in the chamber to drink it. After all this time, why had she not returned? Had she already gone, or had there been trouble in the market district after he had left?

Suddenly alarmed, Tarren strode toward the door out of the apartment. The madness would surely attempt to take him over soon, but he would not allow it to do so until he knew Wildea was safe. Sooner would he see his soul ravaged than have harm come to her, and he would *not*—

Sudden knocking brought Tarren up short, perhaps two strides from the door. Relief flooded him at the thought that it would be Wildea, and he pulled the door open, only to find Kergil waiting there. He recalled that Kergil had remained behind at the market with Wildea; alarmed, he quickly pulled the healer inside.

"Where is she?" Tarren demanded as he closed the door. "She could not have departed the city already; she gave her word to remain."

"She *has* remained," Kergil said, inspecting Tarren closely. "She now wanders about the corridors of the palace, refusing to return here although she has no other place to go. I followed her for a time, then left her to come here. Tarren—do you still feel that you will never forgive her for that—horrible incident?"

Tarren parted his lips to demand an explanation of Kergil's words, but then memory returned of what he had said to Wildea after the incident in the city. His pride and dignity had been severely brutalized, but to say such a thing to the woman he loved—!

"I have no need to ask if *she* believes I continue to feel so," Tarren said instead with a sigh, turning from Kergil to walk slowly back toward the sideboard. "I spoke in anger, man—no, more in rage, and words spoken so can never be called back. Though I would gladly do so if I could, even though she let me face such humiliation without warning."

"Tarren, it was not deliberate," Kergil said earnestly, following along behind. "I myself heard her say so, and saw the horror she felt at what befell you."

"The incident disturbed her?" Tarren asked, brightening as he turned to Kergil again. "She felt no amusement, no satisfaction? Are you certain of this?"

"As certain as a man can be," Kergil replied, studying him again. "You thought otherwise?"

"I *feared* otherwise," Tarren admitted, relief flooding his features. "I had thought she disliked me enough to allow something of this sort to occur, but now that may not be so. She may indeed feel for me what I feel for her, therefore you are to find her and return her to this apartment. I will arrange for dinner to be brought her, and will speak to her after the madness has left me. And after the incident scheduled for when I return here. Be certain she knows to remain in the bedchamber—better yet, in her own bedchamber—until she is told she may come out."

"Her *own* bedchamber?" Kergil blurted, then belatedly held his tongue. He, undoubtedly like many others, obviously believed that the woman shared Tarren's bed as well as his apartment. That it was not so would come as a blow to them and their exalted opinion of him, but Tarren found the situation amusing.

"Yes, her own bedchamber," Tarren confirmed, turning again toward the sideboard. "There is a servant's chamber in the apartment, and she has taken it for her own. She insists she has no feelings for me, and refuses to allow me to do so much as touch her. Before the incident I doubted this stance, and now do so again."

"I doubt it as well," Kergil agreed, following again. "I would wager she has yet to call you by name, a point I brought up with her during our journey here. I suggested that that was done by her in an effort to keep from admitting her feelings, and although she denied it I continue to believe the same. Will you allow her to leave after tomorrow, as she continues to insist she will?"

"I cannot allow her to leave, and yet I cannot force her to remain," Tarren said with a sigh, pouring himself a cup of chai. "An ordinary woman would be easily held, yet my Wildea is no ordinary woman. I would not be forced into conflict with her, but have as yet to think of another method of keeping her."

"Something will surely come to you," Kergil said, refusing his own cup of chai with a headshake. "The gods would not have allowed you to bring her here and give her your heart, only to steal her from you again. Such a thing would not be right, and men of honor—as well as the gods—live by what is right."

"May it be as you say," Tarren fervently agreed after sipping at the chai, and then he felt a ripple touch the world and run through him. "By fire and thunder, I fear the madness is about to descend again. Go and find her, Kergil, and be sure she knows I harbor no ill feelings toward her. I must speak to a servant about her meal, and would ask that you see to her partaking of it—if she allows you to. It would not be wise to press her too strongly. Once you are done with her, speak to Fael concerning the details of our plan."

Kergil nodded in agreement and turned toward the door, leaving Tarren free to call for a servant. Even as he pulled the cord another ripple shook his body, threatening to wipe his mind of all true memory. This

Tarren fought against until the servant arrived, and was able to give his orders and retain control of himself until the man left. Then, at last, he permitted the madness its way with him, so that the time of it might be more quickly over. Afterward . . .

. . . Afterward? Tarren the Barbarian wondered at the word floating alone in his mind, along with the hint of memory of a very special woman. The barbarian fighter would have joyed to know such a woman, but unfortunately had never encountered her. Perhaps some day . . . He smiled at the pleasant thought and promise, then walked toward the door to the hall. The prince awaited him now, but after the dinner in his honor . . . how was one to know what afterward might bring?

I finally let Kergil talk me into going back to the redhead's apartment, but only because I was cold, hungry, and tired—and I knew *he* wouldn't be there. I'd walked the halls and corridors of the palace for hours after discovering that every room in our assigned wing was occupied. I could have gone to Drinna's apartment since she'd invited me, but I hadn't been in the mood to make anything up about what had happened and couldn't tell her the truth. So I'd walked around all alone, trying to decide whether or not to leave that very night. I really wanted to, but first I had to detail the various attacks that awaited the redhead. After that there would be nothing to keep me there . . .

"Ah, I see that your meal has been brought," Kergil said after opening the apartment door and glancing inside. "It will be my pleasure to keep you company while you eat."

"Thanks anyway, but I'd prefer to be alone," I said. "It hasn't been the sort of day that makes you *want* company."

"Girl, you must believe that I speak the truth," Kergil said. "Tarren regrets the words he threw at you in the market district, and tonight will tell you so himself. You must give him the opportunity to do so, else he will likely never forgive himself."

"Oh, he'll get the chance, and then I'll tell him the rest of what he needs to know," I agreed, already planning just how and when I would leave. "I suppose we'll be able to do it when he gets back."

"When he returns there will be the attack," Kergil said very low, glancing around to make sure no one was listening. "Tarren wishes you to remain in your own bedchamber until it has been seen to. He will send someone when it is safe for you to come out. If you are certain my company would be a burden, I will take my leave of you now."

I nodded my thanks for his understanding and went into the apartment, but I could feel the frown his reminder had given me. The redhead would be attacked tonight, and I'd almost forgotten all about it! Instead of thinking about what was important, I'd been walking around concerned over a few words and some hurt feelings.

Kergil had disappeared up the corridor, so I closed the door and headed for the servant standing near the table holding a chair. I wanted to stop in the bathing room and wash my hands before sitting down, but there was no reason for him not to begin serving. I felt hungry enough to start chewing on the table, but the reason why I was hungry again after only a single day wasn't as important as deciding what I would do tonight. I couldn't let that attack just happen, not when the redhead would be practically reduced to helplessness. I'd come up with a plan, and try to make up for that afternoon.

The meal was delicious and I ate most of it, but my attention was on strategy rather than food. I knew when the attack would come, of course, but the scene had been written from the redhead's point of view—which meant he knew nothing about where the three men came from. Dizzy and disoriented from the drugged wine, he would only be aware of the men once they attacked him. Whether they entered the apartment before or after him remained to be seen.

But I meant to be there to see it *whichever* way it went. I pulled myself out of my thoughts long enough to thank the servant and dismiss him, then I went into the bedroom. The first thing I needed was a weapon, to keep from being a liability rather than an asset, so once in the bedroom I went to the redhead's dressing room. I *knew* he had more weapons than the broadsword he wore across his back, since he'd had one on just that afternoon. I hadn't seen the thing on my earlier trip to the bathing room or in the bedroom itself, so that left the dressing room.

And that's just where it was. I saw the swordbelt lying on a low, padded bench, and once I went over and picked it up I could guess who had put it there. The leather of the belt smelled lemon-oily and gleamed, which must have meant it had needed to be cleaned after the fiasco in the marketplace. The hilt of the sword was spotlessly clean except for a thin film of what looked like powdered chalk, undoubtedly added to facilitate the wielder's grip. The blade itself was polished between its two cutting edges, and those edges as well as its point were acceptably keen. It would do just fine—if I found it possible to put the rest of my plan into action.

Putting the sword and belt back on the bench, I left them temporarily to go prowling through the lines of clothing. It was all men's clothing, of course, and in the redhead's outrageous size, but the comment he'd made earlier today about the spell on the dressing rooms had given me an idea. If it worked there'd be no need to go looking for pants again, not even if I stayed a year.

I finally found what I wanted behind all the fancy outfits, a pair of breeches in some stretchable jersey-like material, and a comfortable long-sleeved tunic to go with it. The pants were light blue and the tunic dark blue, and they were exactly what I needed—if I could do something about their size. As it stood, I could have fit two of me in each one of the things. And thinking about the swordbelt, *it* could use a little trimming down as well.

On the way out I passed a pair of very soft kid leather boots in black with no heels to speak of, so I took them along. Carrying everything across the room to my dressing room took only a minute, and then I hung up the clothing, arranged the boots below it, and added the swordbelt. Everything in that room was supposed to fit *me*. If the spell worked the way I hoped it did, the garments would be transformed into a perfect fit in no time.

After arranging everything I went back to the entertaining room for another cup of coffee, not only to give the spell a chance to work but also to think about a hiding place. It was a toss-up between skulking behind a piece of the furniture in there, and lurking behind the bedroom door. After thinking about it for a few minutes, I decided on lurking behind the door. That way the three attackers were less likely to trip over me if they got there first, leaving me free to jump out at the *right* moment, not stumble out at the wrong one.

With that decided I forced myself to sit still and finish the coffee, and only then went back to the dressing room. I didn't quite hold my breath until I got there, but only because it didn't occur to me. I was too busy worrying, but as soon as I walked in I knew my worries were over. Even the boots and the sword-belt had been scaled down to my size, so I was all set and in more than enough time. It would be another couple of hours before the redhead got back, so I even had time for a bath.

While I soaked I could finalize my plans for leaving the following night. By then I'd have done everything possible to save the life of a man I'd endangered, and my conscience would be clear. I stood there in the dressing room, watching my fingers pull at the soft sash around my waist, fighting to believe that there *was* no reason not to go.

* * *

Tarren the Barbarian walked carefully along the corridor toward his apartment, staggering some but in no real danger of falling. To watch him one would think he had had far too much drink, and that was just what any watchers were meant to believe. In full truth Tarren had had a good deal less wine than he had the capacity for, and all had so far gone exactly as planned.

It still was not clear to Tarren what magic had given Fael his information, but Tarren's second had intercepted him before he had reached the prince's dinner party. At that time Tarren was told that Fael had learned of a plan to assassinate his leader, and the first of the plan was to drug Tarren's drink. Fael, with Kergil's help, had substituted something harmless for the drug in the bribed servant's possession, therefore was it necessary that Tarren pretend to be drugged. In such a way the assassins awaiting his return to his apartment would not be warned and frightened off.

Nor would they be allowed to survive and be given another opportunity to try for his life. Tarren chuckled as he lurched along, appreciating the humor in the thing. Agnal Topis, who had arranged this assassination as well as the attack against his camp, would have no idea where his plotting had gone wrong. Tarren the Barbarian would be deemed invincible even when in his cups or drugged, and thereafter few would be willing to face him. That end alone was worth the effort to attain, for Tarren deplored the need to slay lesser warriors.

In due course the door to Tarren's apartment came into view, and along with it came a very odd thought.

The face of a woman appeared faintly in the thought, a woman Tarren had never met. And yet it seemed that he *had* met her, and had once even made love to her. The thought which had just come insisted that the woman would now be in his apartment, but would be safely out of harm's way. His concern must be to make certain her safety continued by seeing that none of the assassins escaped, and that he meant to do.

Tarren fumbled at the apartment door before succeeding in opening it, then he lurched inside while swinging the door shut behind him. Fael and some others of the company had secretly entered the apartment hours earlier, and now hid at various points in the very room he had just entered. Whether or not the assassins would also enter before his arrival was unknown, therefore Tarren made no effort to look about the room. He made his unsteady way to a chair which stood too openly for anyone to hide behind it and attempted to seat himself, then permitted himself to remember the sword scabbarded across his back. The sword would need to be removed before he might sit, an excellent reason for having both scabbard and weapon in his hands.

Once he had settled himself in the chair, Tarren put his head back and pretended to shut his eyes. In reality he closed them to slits, and silently watched for what would happen. Although the wait might well have been long, the assassins of Agnal Topis apparently had little in the way of patience. A mere handful of minutes passed, and then the door to his apartment was being silently and slowly opened. The assassins were being cautious then, much good it would do them.

When the assassins had made certain that no resistance awaited them, they staggered inside with the look of fools showing off a nonexistent prowess. There were three of them, Tarren saw, and the third to enter obligingly closed the door behind him. What occurred in the apartment would now be kept among those already in it, at least among those who survived.

"See how besotted the fellow has become," one of the three said with a laugh, gesturing toward Tarren. "This will be as simple as child's play."

"It would not have mattered even if he had remained alert," another said, he who had entered first. "We would still have been able to slay him, or at least *I* would. There are few about who dare to face me with weapons."

"Had *I* the cousin you have, there would be just as few willing to face *me,*" the third said in a petulant and petty tone. "It is *he* whom all fear, not your vaunted skill with a sword."

"Do you two mean to stand here all night and bicker?" the second demanded as the first began to hotly argue what the third had said. All three were dressed well and expensively, more like fops than assassins, which Tarren had come to believe was the truth. These three had come to prove warriorhood by slaying a man who had become incapacitated, undoubtedly the *only* way any of them would test their skills.

"No, we shall *not* stand here all night," the first announced frostily, glaring at the third. "We will see to the business we have, and then we will go to a place where we may each show what skill we do and do not possess. Is that clear?"

The last of the boy's words—for boy he seemed—were addressed in particular to the third who had spoken. That one looked sullen but defiant as he nodded with feigned unconcern, and then, suddenly, the question was answered aloud by another.

"It isn't clear to *me* why you'd need to go anywhere else to prove how good you are," a woman's voice said clearly in a drawl. "You *do* have someone here willing to face you."

By then the woman had come forward, and Tarren was able to see her by moving his eyes to the left. Tall and blond and slender and beautiful, she was undoubtedly the woman whose visage he had imagined earlier. But now she wore light blue breeches and a dark blue tunic which clung to her form, soft black boots which fit her also like a second skin, and a swordbelt wrapped tightly about her hips. But it was not the swordbelt alone which named her warrior, a truth the three would-be assassins attempted to deny.

"You expect me to accept the challenge of a bed-warmer?" the first asked with a ridiculing sneer, the other two supporting him with their laughter. "A pity you must now share the fate of *that* lout, but be assured you will not be sent on to the next plane of existence without a last warming—or three. We will consider it an additional reward for our efforts."

"Boy, you sound really dangerous," the woman drawled after the other two had added their laughter. "Why don't you show me something, big man? Like just how serious you are about acting rather than talking."

And with those words she drew her sword, an action that showed she was no stranger to the weapon. The three intruders noted that fact as well, paled with the realization of having an actual, competent opponent, and then everything seemed to happen at once. The three drew their swords almost as one and went for the woman, clearly meaning to overwhelm her with numbers. At their first step Fael and Kergil and two other fighters from the company jumped from their places of hiding and attempted to interfere, but they were nearly on the far side of the huge room. Only one fighter was close enough to assist the woman, and he lost no time in doing so.

Tarren drew his broadsword as he leaped out of the chair, tossing away his scabbard as he hurried to join the fight. The woman had beaten off the first concerted attack, but would certainly have difficulty with the following ones. Tarren began to step in front of the woman, to draw the attackers to himself, but the woman refused to allow it! She shouldered him aside—shouldered *him* aside!—and continued to face the three alone. Apparently, his assistance was unwanted!

It was difficult to know how one was to react to such a thing. Tarren was indignant over having been rebuffed, and yet concerned over the safety of the woman—who might well think him taken by the drug! Tarren had not considered that, and now he recalled another time this woman had attempted to assist him. The attack against his camp, the one which had begun this adventure . . . How could he have forgotten such a magnificent woman . . . ?

Fael and the others were nearly up to them, and the three attackers had yet to notice them—or himself, who was supposed to be their prey. Their entire attention was on the woman, who fought quite well despite a seeming lack of experience in facing such opponents. Her confidence was full, and yet she seemed to pull the blows which would have ended her inept opponents one after the other. So the confident woman warrior had never killed . . .

Which meant that Tarren *must* take over if the fighting was to end from anything other than exhaustion. Fael and the others would not take the three in the back, and at the moment it seemed unlikely that they would turn to face the newcomers. The woman before them took all their attention as they took hers, and that told Tarren what must be done. Rather than attempt to insert himself, he put an arm about the woman's waist, swung her behind him, and swiftly took her place.

The three would-be attackers were startled by his abrupt presence in place of the woman, and the instant relief upon their faces suggested they believed him incapacitated by drink. That belief lasted no more than a moment past their first attack, and then each, one after the other, were no longer able to experience feelings. The last crumpled to the floor as the second twitched in the last throes of death, and all was done as it needed to be.

"Tarren, good work!" Fael called as he and the others approached, more slowly than before.

Tarren nodded, feeling the persona of that other man falling away from himself. With the end of the attack came the end of the madness, but not the end of anger. That came full upon him with each returning memory, and once he had taken a deep breath he turned with that anger toward Wildea. "And you, woman! What did you think you were about, risking yourself in such a way? What if they had harmed you?"

"They were going to do more than just harm *you*," she countered, but with something very like bewildered confusion. "I couldn't stand by and just let it happen . . . You aren't drugged? When you first came in I thought you were."

"The pretense was for *their* benefit," Tarren told her, not much mollified. "With Fael and the others already here according to plan, all was as we wished it to be. You, however, were to remain in your bedchamber, and not to emerge until called. Had you done as you were told, there would have been no confusion and no risking of yourself. Do you truly believe I would have wished my life saved at the expense of yours? You should not have done as you did."

"Well, excuse me," she responded, the words and her manner suddenly quite stiff as she resheathed her sword. "I shouldn't have intruded. I certainly won't make the same mistake again. Have a good evening."

She turned then and marched into the bedchamber, but not to remain there, Tarren knew. She would put herself behind the closed door of her own quarters, and he would see no more of her tonight. Tarren sighed, realizing that he had handled the exchange badly, but there was little else he might have done.

Worry turns a man mindless, and worry the woman provided in plenty.

"I fear you will now find it much more difficult to apologize," Kergil said from beside him, and Tarren turned to see that the bodies of the three assailants were already being seen to. Fael had gone to the door to call others of their company, and the two men who had already been there carried the first of the bodies behind Fael. "And where, may I ask, did the woman find the breeches she has been seeking?" Kergil added.

"How is a mere man to know?" Tarren asked in turn, the words sour with the knowledge that Kergil was correct. He, Tarren, was to have apologized to Wildea, not all but shouted at her, and now he had that to apologize for as well. "Wildea being Wildea, it does not surprise me that she has gotten exactly what she wished to have. But at the moment I would prefer not to know her manner of procuring it. It would doubtless make even more trouble between us, if that were possible."

"Perhaps tomorrow will provide an opportunity for calmer talk between you," Kergil suggested sympathetically. "And yet not the first thing in the day. It might be best to allow the woman some time to herself before broaching the subject of apology."

"As I must spend some time with the apprentices of the company, I shall take your advice," Tarren decided after indulging in a deep breath. "But I will not leave the woman entirely to her own devices. Have Fael assign those who will watch this door, and follow if the woman leaves. They are not to interfere with her movements, but they *are* to follow."

"They should be extremely relieved that they are not to interfere," Kergil said wryly. "Had the woman had true battle experience, even you would not have had the opportunity to keep the lives of those would-be assassins from her."

"Yes, I saw the same myself," Tarren agreed, then went to find a cloth with which to clean his sword. Indeed he had seen the thing, and he felt pride despite the worry he had been caused. Now, he had only to find a way to explain the matter to Wildea, who likely would not care to hear *anything* he had to say. Ah well, tomorrow was another day . . . and it would *not* be her last there, the gods willing . . . it would *not* be!

Sixteen

I slept somewhat late the next morning, if for no other reason than to let the redhead leave the bedroom before I had to walk through it. I'd also had some uneasy dreams about that sword fight, but more out of frustration than guilt. I hadn't done anything to feel guilty about, even though I should have. Those three had meant to kill the redhead, and if he hadn't only been pretending to be drugged . . .

But he *had* been pretending, so I'd been wasting my time trying to protect him. I stopped to push one hand through my hair in an effort to forget the humiliation of that, of finding out that he and Fael had figured out a way to keep him from being drugged. I'd thought they simply arranged to have fighters in the room . . . Being warned about what would happen had obviously helped quite a lot, which meant there really *was* no reason for me to stay longer than tonight. After I dressed I would go out to the entertaining room and give the redhead the rest of the details he needed, and that would be it.

I used the bathing room as quickly as possible, then went to my dressing room. I'd left the tunic and pants in there the night before, hoping they would be fresh-

ened for wear today. I'd sweated more than a little
during the sword fight, and would have preferred not
to have to put on too-well-used clothes. Finding that
they *had* been refreshed was pleasant, but not quite
the high spot of my day. As I carried the things back
to my room, I couldn't quite figure out what *would*
qualify as a high spot.

Once I was in the clothes I resisted the impulse to
stay in my room a little longer and went out to the
entertaining room. I felt as reluctant as ever to face
the redhead again, but for some reason I was also
hungry. Whatever it was that had affected me since
I'd gotten to this world had apparently worn off, and
now my body was expecting food on a regular basis.
Playing the coward might have made me miss breakfast, so I went on out—to find breakfast waiting, but
not the redhead. The servant waiting with the food
told me the redhead had left to work with his fighters,
which gave me nothing to do but eat.

After I breakfasted the servant left, and then I really
had nothing to do. I walked to the terrace windows
and looked out at a beautiful day, but that didn't
change the nothing. I thought about the redhead going
out just *now* to work with his fighters, only hours before I was due to leave. Did he think I was bluffing,
or that I'd stay longer if he sat down to listen five
minutes before I was due to walk out the door? I didn't
know, but there was one way to avoid that if it turned
out to be true. I would get some paper and ink and a
pen, and write out what I'd intended to tell him.

Ringing for a servant brought a girl knocking on
the door almost immediately, and when I told her what

I wanted she nodded and left again. Ten minutes later there was another knock, and thinking it was the girl with my supplies I opened it. Instead of the girl it was the small, thin man from the day before, the one who had been sent by Agnal Topis and whom I'd managed to completely forget about. Once again his expression said he was totally displeased with me, but he wanted to make sure I knew it so he added some words.

"You were ordered to be elsewhere than here this morning," he told me immediately with heavy disapproval. "For what reason have you disobeyed those orders?"

"I don't believe you're back here again," I said, in no mood to play games with him today. "Do you always go where your boss sends you, no matter how stupid it makes you look?"

"You are the stupid one, to speak of matters you know nothing about!" he snapped, the color rising in his sallow cheeks. "Nothing concerns you beyond obeying orders, and that you have not done. What consequences arise from your obedience is for others to see to, therefore are you to obey at once!"

"I have a better idea," I said, looking him up and down in the most insulting way I knew. "I'm going to send your boss a message, in words of one syllable so you won't have any trouble remembering it. And if you like, you can even take it personally."

I pronounced my message slowly and clearly then, and this time his face ended up mottled. He was also speechless when I closed the door in his face, probably never having been spoken to like that by a woman before. Actually, I rarely used language like that, but this time it was well deserved.

Five minutes later it *was* the serving girl at the door, and she had a hefty supply of paper, with a pen, ink, and sand. I'd been afraid that world was still at the quill stage and had been picturing myself sitting with a knife in order to constantly sharpen the quill's point, but it wasn't that bad. The pen had a steel tip, and although it had to be constantly dipped in the ink, it didn't have to be sharpened. I set everything down on a table, pulled over a chair, and got to work.

Even with learning how to use the pen, putting down the details of the attacks and dangers still ahead of the redhead took only a little more than an hour. I'd also had to sand the pages in order to dry the ink, but that took only another minute or two. Then I sat there staring at the rest of the blank paper, lured by it the way blank paper always lures me. I felt the urge to write on that paper, but starting another book right now wasn't very practical. Besides, I remembered about that beautiful day outside and thought about how long it had been since the last time I'd gone running. Just about the last time my life had been normal, was the answer, and I was beginning to *need* some normalcy.

" 'And as she sat at the table thinking, two odd things happened,' " I wrote idly, just to fill up some of that blank paper. " 'The first was a servant knocking at the door, bringing a tray of chilled fruit juices. Once the servant was gone she went into the bedchamber, and discovered that all of the giant's trunks stood open. In the third trunk lay the clothing he'd taken from her, and she was able to take it back.' "

I smiled at what I'd written, wishing it could be just that easy. If it ever was I'd certainly go running, in the perfect place I'd found. It would—

I jumped at the sound of a knock on the door, and before I was able to get up to answer it, the door opened. I stared as a servant in a pink tunic walked in, carrying a tray.

"Chilled fruit juices for your pleasure, lady," the man said with a bow, then headed for the sideboard without seeing my openmouthed disbelief. It couldn't be true, it just couldn't be, it was nothing more than coincidence. I held to the table with one hand until the man was gone, also just about holding my breath, trying to believe that bit about coincidence. It was possible that that's all it was, but there's a big difference between possible and likely. There was a way to find out, of course, but it took a while before I could force myself out of the chair to try it.

I got as far as the closed doors to the bedroom, then dithered there another couple of minutes. I'd never considered myself chicken before, but I'd also never been faced with the possibility of having done something very like magic before. I mean, the servant had come with the juice; if the redhead's trunks, which had been firmly closed, now stood open . . . I ran both hands through my hair, took a deep breath, and straightened up, then opened the doors fast.

I almost went back out again. All four of the trunks stood along the righthand wall, and every one of them stood open. If I were the type to feel faint I probably would have felt faint. Instead I walked into the room slowly, trying to see if I were somehow imagining things. Maybe the trunks *weren't* open, and I was just hallucinating . . .

But I wasn't. The third trunk did contain my running clothes, and when I reached in slowly and gingerly I was able to pull them out. My underwear was folded neatly underneath, and I was able to take that as well. Then I just stood there staring at the things, wondering how that could possibly have happened. All I'd done was write one silly paragraph, and not even on purpose. I'd thought it was more like idle wishful thinking, a fun daydream that was never supposed to really come true.

But it *had* come true, just the way my books came true for the redhead. I suppose I'd been thinking that I had to be home in order to affect this world, but obviously it wasn't so. I tried to see how I felt about that, but my feelings still seemed to be in shock. Now I needed to run even more than I had, to settle everything to the point where I could understand and handle it.

Digging out my socks and running shoes from the dressing room wasn't hard, so it wasn't long before I was dressed and ready to go. It felt odd to be wearing underwear, shorts, and a tank top after the last few days of skirts and things, but it was certainly too hot out for running to be comfortable in anything else. When I was ready I went back to the table in the entertaining room, and wrote, " 'And after she removed her possessions the trunks closed again, making it seem as though they had never been touched.' "

Then I put the sheet of paper under a chair, and left the apartment.

I turned after closing the door behind me, and only then saw the three male fighters who happened to be lounging around a little way down the hall. The way they looked at me I expected them to say something, like a "suggestion" to go back into the apartment, but they didn't. I matched their silence as I walked past them to the end of the corridor, then glanced back as I turned right. The three hadn't said anything but they *were* following, which meant the next half hour or so should be interesting.

Two more corridors down I turned left, and at the end of *that* corridor was the area I'd found the night before during my wandering. At that point the palace had a long stretch of what looked like a pillared porch, with archways at intervals leading back into the palace proper. The overhead kept the direct sunlight off anyone walking along the porch, and the thing was wide enough for two sports cars to have passed each other. For a single runner it was delightful, especially since it was paved rather than marbled, with a dark substance that felt rubbery to walk on. If it was tar softened by the heat, it wasn't so softened that it trapped me or came off on my shoes.

I hadn't passed anyone but a couple or three servants on my way there, but I also hadn't lost my three shadows. They stood watching while I loosened up a little, probably also looking at the porch that stretched a good long way into the distance. Depending on how long it really was, I intended to run it back and forth until I'd done three miles. I'd know its length once I got to the end of it the first time, but right now it was time to start.

I'd wondered if my three shadows were going to try following or simply wait until I got back, and I quickly discovered that they'd chosen the option of following. But my three shadows probably didn't know a six minute mile on a regular basis so that was the wrong decision.

The third of the three managed to trail along for quite a distance before he gave up, finally stopping to bend and gulp air the way the other two had already done. I didn't quite laugh out loud as I kept going, but only because they were going to have to tell someone that they hadn't been able to stay with me. But I did have things to think about, so I dismissed the problems of my shadows and concentrated on my own.

To my right as I ran was the palace, but to my left, across a good span of grass interrupted by occasional linking paths, was a long series of stables. Behind the stables I caught glimpses of what looked like fenced-in corrals, with horses moving around in them. It all looked so normal and ordinary, grass and buildings and horses, but hidden behind the banal and everyday was that one ingredient my own world didn't have: magic.

The heat was starting to bead on my forehead, so I wiped the sheen of sweat away impatiently and then realized that that was part of what bothered me. Being able to do something is no big deal, but if you have any intelligence—and imagination—you worry about consequences. If I suddenly discovered that I could build some technological marvel I'd get a kick out of it—until I stopped to wonder what turning on the marvel would do. When the possibilities range between improving the world and destroying it, any normal person would hesitate before throwing the switch.

But I'd thrown the switch on magic without even knowing I was doing it, and that was the frightening part. I'd ended up getting juice and my clothes out of it, but what if I'd written something a lot less innocuous? What if I'd written about disaster or murder—or even a lack of sweat when I ran? A human body that doesn't sweat ends up dying. So what would have happened if I didn't know that, but wrote it anyway?

Consequences were the things to worry about with magic, especially when, for the most part, you'd never really thought about it before. I'd always believed people had to be trained before they could use the stuff, but the training probably had more to do with using it safely and effectively. Coming from a world without magic I hadn't realized that, but now I did. If I sat down and wrote something with unseen consequences, I'd find out all about it rather quickly.

At that point I discovered that I'd reached the end of the porch and had turned to run back without really being aware of it. I'd judge the distance and stop after I'd done what felt like three miles, and afterward I'd go somewhere to sit down and cool off, and try to decide if I ought to risk writing anything again except under conditions of absolute emergency.

I was about half way back to my starting point when I ran into something unexpected. Two men stepped out of an archway from the palace and two more joined them from behind a pillar, but they weren't my former shadows with reinforcement as I immediately assumed. As I neared them I saw that the four men were strangers, and the grins they wore weren't the sort that suggested light hearts and innocent good humor. They were spread out in a way that said they weren't going to let me go past, or even around them, without trouble.

"I see the gods truly favor us," one of them said when I was close enough to hear. "Our delivery will be made, but not before we take a short . . . entertainment stop. He will never know the difference, for if this one is a virgin then I am the same."

The other three laughed at that comment, but I found very little amusement in it as I was forced to stop. I didn't know what sort of delivery the four had in mind, but it was fairly obvious that I would enjoy it as much as I'd enjoy the rest of their intentions.

"You may not know it, folks, but you're in my way," I said as neutrally as I could, remembering what the redhead had told me about a fighter's view on challenges. And these four *were* fighters, not like the three last night. They all wore the same sort of breeches and shirts and swordbelts, but the important difference was attitude. A blowhard with a weapon is still a blowhard who may or may not use it, but a fighter is a fighter even without that weapon.

"That is our intention," the same one of the four said, a slightly bigger man than the others. "There is one of position and power who desires your possession, girl, and our task is to make his wishes come true. Come with us now and make no fuss, else it will be necessary to chastise you."

"Oh, I see," I said with a pleasant smile as my heart thudded and I set myself. "You want me to make your job easy as well as fun. Sorry, guys, but I don't think so. You'll have to do it the hard way."

The four men were amused again, which hopefully meant my defensive stance meant nothing to them. Being female has one great edge, in that most men will discount the possibility of your being able to do anything to them. Capable men are even more likely to think that way, so there was a decent chance that I'd be able to break through their line. And I *had* to break through, otherwise I'd have had it.

"So you mean to make us earn our entertainment, do you?" the spokesman asked indulgently, still enjoying himself. "Very well, then let us begin immediately."

And with that he jumped at me, obviously intending to end the fight even before it got started. But I'd been more than half expecting something like that, so I was ready with a side kick right into his middle. By following immediately with a second kick I was able to knock him back into two of his friends, and then I headed for the hole in their line that the skirmish had made. The last one, to my right, tried to stop me, but putting a shoulder into him got him out of my way. He'd obviously never had to defend himself on the subway at rush hour, but his loss was my gain.

Once I was in the clear I took off, running smoothly and only a little faster than usual. The adrenaline pouring through me tried to insist that I run flat out, but that would have been stupid. Staying at my regular pace would let me keep going as long as necessary, rather than end up drained and exhausted in no time at all. I heard cursing behind me and the pounding of boots to say that at least some of the four were in pursuit, but hopefully that would do them no more good than it had my original shadows.

After a minute I risked a glance back, and wasn't at all happy with what I saw. The four running men were strung out in a line, but only the last two looked like they were suffering. The first two, one of which was the man I'd kicked, were coming on strong, and with their longer legs they just might be able to catch up. And on top of that, I had no idea where I was running *to*. Back to the apartment? But there were no locks on any of the doors. To ask for help from some of the redhead's fighters? After all the trouble I'd given them and their leaders, there was no guarantee they *would* help. I seemed to be on my own, which wasn't turning out to be the benefit I'd always considered it.

It took a moment's thought, but it finally came to me that I had to go back to the apartment and get the sword I'd used the night before. By then I should have no more than two of the men to face, possibly even just one. That way their undoubtedly greater ability than what the men last night had had might let me hold my own, at least until I was able to force myself into trying to kill them. The thought of doing that made my hands shake and my mouth turn dry, but it would be a matter of them or me. *If* I could make myself do it.

And then I was so startled I nearly stumbled and fell. A body jumped out of an arch just ahead of me, followed by two more bodies. For an instant I thought the men behind me had somehow gotten ahead, and then it registered who the men were. Two were former shadows—and the third was the man who had made them be shadows in the first place. After stepping past me the redhead gestured his men into going for the two stragglers, and then faced the nearer two ambushers himself.

"You seem to be in the midst of seeking something," he growled as the redhead drew his sword, the two men coming to a screeching halt not far from him. "Allow me to congratulate you on having found something extremely specific."

"You would be far wiser to turn and walk away," the spokesman for the opposition panted as he reached for his own sword. "No woman is worth incurring the displeasure of the high and powerful, and one of those is whom we labor for. Step back and close your eyes, man, and then go seeking another female for your bed."

"Your advice is undoubtedly filled with wisdom, but I prefer to ignore it," the redhead countered, the words hard and completely inflexible. "My own advice would be that you withdraw, *now,* before you learn that the high and powerful can do nothing to protect you from a sword's edge. How will you have it?"

"Not as *you* wish," the man answered, and now the second had joined him, also with sword in hand. "Our reputations rest on performing this small task. Should we fail at it, no one will ever again entrust us with anything of greater importance. We do as we must, but *you* have only to withdraw to avoid the conflict. We will have the woman who now stands behind you."

"You may have her only when I no longer stand in your path to her," the redhead replied, his inflexible tone unchanged. "Come and do as you must then, and the gods take pity on he who relies on a lesser ability."

The two men took a better grip on their weapons, and then they came at the redhead together. His sword blurred and glinted as it swept their attack aside, and then they were all in the midst of trying to kill each other. I stepped back just a little even as I fretted, unable to help and not wanting to make things worse by tripping the redhead. His two fighters were already engaged with the other two men about twenty yards back, so he was on his own.

And that fact was killing me. Last night he'd swept through the three idiots in about a minute and a half, but now he was engaged with two *real* fighters who weren't in the "script," so to speak, and he would not find winning quite as easy. While I stood there and just watched, like every other typically helpless female. It was *me* he defended and risked his life for, and I couldn't do a single thing to help.

The fighter on the redhead's right attacked high while the one on the left swung low, obviously expecting that one or the other of them would connect. The redhead used his sword to block high as he jumped, then he came down with both booted feet on the low sword trying to backsweep. The man on the left was pulled forward by that, and an instant later was knocked back again by a wide fist filled with a heavy hilt.

Which left only the man on the right, still on his feet and armed, to face the redhead. The man looked bothered and almost disbelieving, and it came to me that he probably hadn't believed what was said about the redhead. But then the man dismissed his disturbance and the fight was on again, which gave me an idea about where he and his three friends had come from. That other fighting company, the one Agnal Topis wanted used instead of the barbarian's . . . He'd decided to give them a side job while they sat around waiting.

The man facing the redhead was determined to do that job, using a skill that couldn't be called negligible. The two of them fought hard, steel ringing against steel as they blocked each other's attacks. Neither of them would back down, I could see, and the fight would go on until one of them died. I was still trying to think of something to do, when it suddenly became unnecessary. The redhead moved incredibly fast, too fast for his opponent to counter, and then he no longer *had* an opponent. His sword went straight through the man, who died trying to scream.

But the next instant the redhead was down! The second man, the one he'd hit with his fist and hilt, had jumped up with a rock in his hands and had hit the giant in the back of the head. The redhead crumpled to the ground a moment after the man he had killed, and the one who had hit him started for the sword he'd lost earlier. That sword had been kicked aside to get it out of the way of the fighters, but it wasn't that far away.

I'd almost done my own screaming when the redhead was hit, but fury rose in me so fast that I couldn't utter a sound. Instead I ran after the miserable coward who had struck from behind, and just as he was bending for his sword I jump-kicked him as hard as I could right in the face. He went down without a sound, possibly dead of a broken neck, but right now I couldn't care about that. The redhead . . . what if his skull had been crushed . . . I'd die if it was . . .

I skidded to a halt next to the redhead and went to my knees beside him, more terrified by the way he lay unmoving than I'd been when facing those four men alone. I took his face in both of my hands and leaned down to him, trembling with fear.

"Please don't be dead," I whispered, too afraid to check his pulse. "Please be all right. Tarren, tell me you're all right. Tarren, please . . ."

Those ice-blue eyes blinked open to stare at me, and there was the strangest look in them.

"Wildea," he murmured. "You called me by my name . . ."

And then his hands were behind my head, pulling me down to join his kiss. A tender kiss, so tender. I'd been so worried, and now my relief was sublime. We kissed for a seeming eternity, and then I finally realized what he'd said. I'd called him by name—and I had. My insides dropped when I understood that and I tried to pull completely away, but he seemed to be expecting something like that.

"No, you may no longer deny the truth," he said, refusing to let me go. His voice was gentle and his smile as tender as the kiss had been, but his eyes said he would *not* accept any contradictions. "Your feelings for me are the same as mine for you, and we shall discuss the matter fully in a short while. First we must see to this incident we are in the midst of."

I got up when he let me go, wondering what I would say when we "discussed the matter fully." He winced as he sat up, one hand going to the back of his head, and then he also stood and looked around. His two men had won against the third and fourth attackers, and were now on their way over to us. Also, from the other direction, the third man who had been my shadow now led other members of the company toward us. They looked like they'd been running at some point, but now they walked along wearing grins.

"We shall not dispose of these bodies ourselves," the redhead—Tarren—said to his men as they reached us. "In a moment you will summon members of the palace guard, and inform them of this attack against my woman. Should they wish one to ask questions from, send them to my apartment. She and I will be there, calming her fears and soothing her upset."

"Calming her fears," one of the men chortled, the one who had gone to check the attacker I'd kicked. "Fear seemed to be the farthest thing from her mind when she put this one down."

All the other men chuckled in agreement, but I still felt queasy. I'd actually killed someone, and knowing the man would have killed Tarren if I hadn't done it didn't help as much as I'd hoped it would. Oh, I knew I'd do it again if Tarren's life were at stake, but I couldn't imagine ever getting used to it.

"Do not mention that the woman took that one," Tarren said, nodding toward the body I'd made. "We would not wish to confuse the guardsmen, nor warn any future attackers. She and I will leave now."

He put his arm around me, and urged me back in the direction from which I'd come. But not to go back to what I'd thought I would. I now had an entirely new problem, and there was no doubt it would turn out to be two or three times the size of the rest.

Seventeen

Once Tarren and I were out of hearing range of the others, he said, "To take a life is never easy, small love, but the first is ever the hardest for those who have a great deal of humanity within them. The illness you feel will be remembered to the end of your days, but in time it will fade enough to be bearable."

And his arm around me tightened in comfort, although how he'd known what I was feeling . . . But he did know, and what he'd said to make me feel better had helped—but only as far as that one subject went. In every other way his understanding made me feel miserable, not to mention scared down to the bone. I half expected him to say something else, but he kept silent until we reached the apartment and went inside.

"You may be curious about how I appeared so fortuitously," he commented after closing the door, heading for the sideboard with the drinkables. "To answer your probable question, I returned here earlier to discover you and those I had assigned to your protection gone. I used the manacle we both wear to find the direction in which you had gone.

"When I reached the porch area, I discovered your guards. We all of us began to walk in the direction in which you had gone, when we saw armed men in the distance ahead, obviously awaiting one who would return. Not knowing precisely how many of them there were, I sent one of my men for additional fighters and took the remaining two with me. We were able to arrive soon enough to keep them from recapturing you, and the rest you know. Including, I presume, the reason this difficulty occurred in the first place."

"What do you mean by 'the reason'?" I asked, distinctly uncomfortable. Maybe if I hadn't left my shadows behind, those four wouldn't have started anything . . . "I didn't set out specifically to leave your men behind. I went there to run, and that's what I did. Is it supposed to be my fault they weren't able to keep up?"

"You know well enough where you were at fault," he answered, turning back to look at me with a mug of chai in his hands and anger in his eyes. "How you were able to reclaim those garments I know not, but to run alone in those clothes . . . Someone with authority—the 'high and powerful' person mentioned by the fighter—saw you and decided he wished you for himself, and sent his men after you. Because you disobeyed me four men are now dead, one of them through your own efforts. Is this not a matter which merits punishment?"

"It most certainly is not," I countered, hating the way he now looked at me and distantly wondering how he could think about kissing me when he wore such an expression. "Your description isn't the way it happened at all, so it doesn't matter *what* I'm wearing.

In another few hours my actions won't be of concern to you any longer."

"Your actions will be of concern to me for the rest of eternity, as will you yourself," he said, putting his mug back on the sideboard and then suddenly pulling me to him. "And as for the matter of your leaving . . . I feel certain that you cannot leave, no more than I can allow it. You spoke my name at last, the miracle I have been praying for, and now cannot deny my love. You feel the same, Wildea, and I live for the day that you say those words as well."

He lowered his head and did kiss me, and just as I knew would happen, once again it wasn't possible for me to refuse to join in. I did love him, terribly and painfully, but how was I supposed to say that? And when? Just before I returned forever to my own world? The pain I felt increased, but so did my no-so-sudden desire for him. His kiss was fire now, passionate rather than tender, igniting my flesh and blood from the very first spark. I held to him fiercely as we tried to merge our souls with lips and tongues, and all thought of leaving in a few hours became completely impossible.

I was just about ready to lead him into the bedroom when we were interrupted by a knock at the door. We parted reluctantly and not very quickly, but eventually Tarren was able to go over and see who it was. He opened the door, and when he stepped aside I could see an officer of the palace guard who looked rather uncomfortable about being there.

"Your pardon, sir," the officer said to Tarren, also sounding uncomfortable. "I was told to interview you concerning—that is—the difficulty of a short while ago—"

"Come in," Tarren said, but somehow it sounded more like an order than an invitation. The man obeyed, and when the door was closed behind him, the redhead continued. "My woman was set upon by ruffians, and had I and my men not been there she might well have been carried off. I find the incident inexcusable."

"Indeed, sir, it most certainly is," the officer hastened to assure him. "Neither I nor my men are acquainted with the dead men, and inquiries have been instituted. And yet, one must pause to ask. Can the thing have been done by cause of the woman's—ah—attire? Surely any man of full red blood would find her—extremely attractive."

The man had glanced at me once and then had looked hastily away, not repeating the action when he made the suggestion. I was about to jump into the conversation with both feet, when Tarren beat me to it.

"Most certainly she is attractive," he granted, but his voice had hardened. "That, however, is no excuse for what occurred. One might expect—not condone, mind you, but expect—such a happening in one of the outer districts of this city, but here in the palace? And it is necessary to add a fact: the one who faced me with a weapon spoke of the high and powerful, and intimated that he acted for one such. Had he spoken a name I would not now be here conversing with *you*. I suggest you do your utmost to locate the man, if for no other reason than to save his life."

The officer was even more flustered now, and his

repeated agreement had an element of worry to it. He knew Tarren wasn't talking just to hear himself talk. The big redhead meant every word, something I knew as well.

Which meant I had another large problem. *I* knew who was behind the kidnapping attempt, but if I mentioned the name of Agnal Topis, Tarren would go after him. That in itself would add to the danger he had to face, but what would happen to the plot of the book he was being made to live through? Would he end up looking insane when he accused a dead man of things? Or *would* Agnal Topis end up dead? What if Tarren tried to kill him and couldn't—but *he* had nothing keeping him from killing Tarren? Whichever way it went it would probably be horrible, and that meant I had to keep my mouth firmly closed.

The guard officer stayed only a little while longer, and his relief when he left was strong enough to see. Tarren closed the door behind him and came back toward me, glancing at the cup of coffee I'd poured and was sipping from.

"That was a less than satisfactory interview, yet it came at a most opportune time," he said, going toward the bell pull rather than coming back to me. "I have not lunched yet, nor can you have. First we will eat, and then we will see to other things."

I had no need to ask what those other things were, not when I couldn't deny that I wanted it at least as much as he did. But I also couldn't argue about lunch, much as I would have liked to. I was definitely starting to get hungry again, just as if I were back living my usual, ordinary life. I sighed as I sipped my coffee, wondering if anything would ever be usual or ordinary again.

A servant came quickly and took the request for lunch away with him, which let Tarren come back toward me again. He eyed me as he came, but not with much in the way of satisfaction.

"Now back to the matter at hand—your feelings for me," he said, stepping closer to put a big hand to my face. "You feel love for me and I feel love for you. When two people feel so toward each other, they commonly make a life for themselves together. As the madness will soon be permanently over, you and I will do the same."

"And just pretend we don't come from totally different worlds?" I asked, stepping back from his hand to make thinking a little easier. "Would you be just as ready to do it in my world rather than here? My world has thousands of things yours doesn't, but the one thing it doesn't have is fighting companies who use swords. How great would you find our life together if you had to come to *me* for anything you wanted?"

"For what reason would we need to live in *your* world?" he asked, his eyes showing him to be seriously bothered. "Here I am a wealthy man, with a fighting company that can easily be turned into a guard force when I begin to establish myself. There is much land under no one's protection, and the people fear to establish farms and villages for they know the unprotected suffer depredations from the lawless. I have waited only to find the proper woman before I do that very thing, and now I have found her. Anything your world might offer, it will give me a great deal of pleasure to match."

"Really?" I said, stepping back from his step forward. "Then you won't have any trouble providing television and movies on video, a telephone and microwave, a computer and central heating and air conditioning? Those are just a handful of the things my world has, and I know you don't even know what they are. This world doesn't have the technology to support them, and won't have it for centuries. You don't miss them because you've never had them, but I would because I did."

"Is this truly what disturbs you?" he asked, making no effort to pretend he really did know about the items I'd mentioned. "A handful of *things,* possessions which might be pleasant to have but need not *be* had? Is not building a life with the man you love more important than any possession? Can anything *be* more important than shared love?"

I didn't answer those questions, and not simply because I agreed with him. Possessions *weren't* that important, but what he'd said about loving me . . . No matter how I felt about *him,* I couldn't quite bring myself to believe that he really did love me. The point that had been bothering me . . . it suddenly came to me that his love had something to do with my having written the books, so once the current "madness" was over his love would certainly be the same. If that wasn't so, he wouldn't have kept calling me Wildea. If I expected anything else I'd be crushed when it didn't happen, and I couldn't let myself be crushed.

Sometimes it *isn't* better to have loved and lost, not when the pain would be unbearable.

The silence grew to be rather awkward, but before I felt compelled to make *some* kind of answer, there was a knock on the door. It seemed the servants had arrived with our lunch, so the time for private and personal discussions was over. I hadn't been able to look at Tarren during the silence, but I could imagine what his expression was like. Disappointed and hurt, the same things I would be feeling, but *he'd* get over them. As soon as this last book ran its course, he'd certainly be over them.

Three male servants had been sent with the trays of food, and only later did I realize that two of them were probably supposed to have left after delivering the trays. Depression kept me from paying much attention to anything but sitting in a chair at the table, so I missed any sort of byplay that might have gone on. I'd forgotten about my running outfit, which the men of that world seemed to like so much. The outfit is the most likely reason the two additional servants stayed, which made the resulting incident doubly my fault.

Unsurprisingly, the hunger I'd been feeling had completely disappeared, but this time I knew why. I toyed with the coffee cup I held, miserable over what I'd said to Tarren, but I couldn't admit I'd lied. If he knew possessions were as meaningless to me as they were to him, he'd renew his efforts toward an end that would never come to be. Once the book ran its course his love would do the same, and then I'd be left all alone to remember the dream. *He'd* be free of it and me together, and then—

The crashes and shouts almost made me jump out of my skin, and I actually did manage to spill some coffee on my thigh. But a couple of drops of coffee were nothing compared to what happened to Tarren, and as soon as I saw the mess I understood *why* it had happened. That spell the angry magic user had cast against him—it was manifesting again the way it had yesterday, and the results were even more spectacular this second time.

It seems to be against some sort of law for lunch in a palace to be sandwiches or plain salads. We'd been brought soup and meat and vegetables and sauces and all sorts of involved dishes, a whole lot of it liquid or semi-liquid. Even without a spell hanging around to make trouble, you usually have to be at least a little careful with things like that. And three men were really too many for careful serving, especially if they were sightseeing rather than paying attention to what they were doing.

The crashes were the result of everything spillable that had been brought—soup, sauces, gravies, syrups—ending up spilled all over Tarren. Tarren yelled and jumped up, the servants yelled and jumped back, but none of the yelling or jumping did any good. Tarren was covered in goo and glop, and I felt absolutely appalled. When I'd written the scenes I'd considered them mildly amusing, but now . . . all I wanted to do was hide, which was the best idea I'd had in a long while.

With the three terrified servants crowding around

the man they'd almost drowned, I slipped away from the table and out of the room, heading for my own small room. If there had been anywhere else to go I probably would have gone there instead, even if Tarren did deserve the satisfaction of finding me and yelling. Or finding and killing me, something I couldn't have blamed him for. Of all the stupid, mindless things to do to somebody, even in a book . . .

After closing the door, I lay down on my bed to brood about the serious lack of a decent sense of humor which I'd discovered in myself. I stared at the ceiling, wondering if I could get away with blaming my editor Erin for the mess, but that didn't seem too practical a solution. Erin wasn't here at the moment, and if she had been she would have pointed out that she'd just asked for something to lighten the grimness of the books a little. *I* was the one who had come up with the idea of the mage and his spell—

"So you *are* in here," Tarren said after opening my door without knocking, startling me into sitting up. He was an absolute mess, all over sticky-looking rather than just plain wet. "I have but a single question, which you *will* answer in full. Why have you done this to me, *why?*"

"It—was felt that my barbarian was too—lucky, and dignified, and—too much a winner," I groped, trying to give him the answer he really did deserve. "Some people thought he was—too stuffy, and a little farce would make him seem more human. Besides, I needed something for the female assassin Mavial to rescue him from besides the trap. When they leave the assassins' guildhall they go to a tavern, and this sort of thing happens again. Mavial realizes it *has* to be magic when she sees how outrageously improbable an accident it is, and she speaks to some of her friends. They help her to locate the magic user, she sweet-talks him, and the spell is canceled. When that happens, the barbarian is very grateful."

"I can well imagine," he commented, the words extremely dry to match what I could see of the look in his eyes. "What I still fail to understand is why this occurs in the way it does—and what I might have done to deserve having such a spell cast at me."

"That's right, you don't know all the details yet," I reminded myself, then told him the reason for the thing. Once I'd gone over the basics, I added, "And there's a definite pattern to watch out for. As long as there are three or more strangers around to witness the occurrence, the spell is almost guaranteed to come into play. If just one of those servants had left, this might not have happened."

"Might not have?" he echoed, trying to raise a sauce-covered eyebrow. "As you are the one who conceived of this—this—*amusement,* you should know for certain."

"I can't be certain without knowing whether or not *I* count as a stranger," I pointed out, flinching a little over his choice of words. "The fact that we were served once by two servants suggests I'm not, but that would have to happen more than once before I became sure."

"And the reason nothing of the sort occurred when I dined with the prince and his people?" he asked, still far from happy. "There were considerably more than three strangers present *there,* and yet there were no mishaps. Could we have found an oversight in your perfectly constructed creation?"

"It isn't an oversight, it's a deliberate omission, and it isn't mine," I said, feeling a flush beginning to rise in my cheeks. "The prince actively supports magic users in this city, so they've returned the favor by routinely making certain no spell of theirs manifests in his presence unless it's meant as something *pleasant* for him. They don't want to upset him, you understand, not even with the *sight* of someone else being gotten even with."

"A pity their compassion is so limited," he said, just stopping himself from leaning a syrup-covered shoulder on the wall. "I wonder if matters would be different if *you* had wished them to be. At the very least you might have warned me."

"But I didn't because I forgot," I burst out, getting to my feet to glare at him. "If you want to think I forgot on purpose then go ahead and think it, I just don't care anymore. I told you there were too many things working against any kind of a relationship between us, and now maybe you'll believe me. If this doesn't prove it, nothing will."

"This proves only that you have much too low a sense of humor, woman," he countered as I turned away. "Not to speak of an abominable sense of timing. In any event, it aids nothing for you to sit sulking here in your chamber. Justice demands that you make amends."

"I am *not* sulking," I stated as I quickly turned back, beginning to be annoyed as well as horribly embarrassed. "Besides, what makes you think I *want* to make amends?"

"Your wants, by rights, should have as little weight as mine in this situation," he said, those blue eyes showing determination again. "Fair is fair, Wildea, and as you caused this nauseating and humiliating condition, you may now bathe me to rid us of it."

"Bathe— Oh, no," I denied with an immediate shake of my head, not so far out of it that I didn't know what he was doing. He'd obviously realized that the mess was making me think about leaving again, and tonight as originally planned rather than at some nebulous future time.

"You refuse to bathe me?" he asked, trying to raise that eyebrow again. The goo in his hair was beginning to drip down the side of his face, and he wiped it on an already-stained sleeve. "Your sense of honor accepts the doing of such a thing as this without also requiring an effort to balance it? I find that difficult to believe."

"I don't care *what* you believe," I said, refusing to be a fool. "I may be responsible for what happened to you, but this is one time I have no interest in making up for it. You can take that bath yourself, and my advice would be to hurry. Some of that stuff looks like it's about to harden into a permanent shell."

"Fair is fair, Wildea," he repeated, apparently ignoring everything I'd said. "I feel certain the lack of a balancing action will eventually shame you, and I would save you from that. For that reason you *will* bathe me, whether you wish it or no."

He turned and walked out the door with that, and

for about one instant I thought he was expecting me to follow him voluntarily. Then the bracelet on my wrist began to drag me after him, and I cursed my stupidity for having forgotten about it *again.* Then I switched to cursing *him,* but that did as much good as commenting on my stupidity. No matter what *I* wanted, I was dragged after him into the bathing room.

"You may remove that clothing out here, or I will remove it in the pool," he said after closing the door behind the both of us. "And fetch a jar of soap from the shelf, one of the jars on the left. I have already begun to leave a trail of drippings behind me, and have no wish to extend it farther about this room."

Even as he spoke he was already starting to get out of his own clothes, a horrible thing to watch, not to mention do. All that stickiness and glop smearing and spreading every which way—! I turned away to spare my stomach, but refused to feel sorry for Tarren. He'd dragged me in there against my will and I was too mad to feel pity for anyone except, maybe, for me. He'd decided to ignore everything I'd said against a relationship between us, deciding I was wrong even though he lacked all the facts. He would force me to touch him, and then everything would be fine from *his* point of view.

So cooperative was another thing I refused to feel, but there was no sense in kidding myself. If I didn't get into that giant bathtub by myself, he would use the bracelet to drag me in. With that in mind I toed off my running shoes, then dumped the socks on top of them. Shoes don't do well with a bath, and just sitting in that hot, steamy room was bad enough. But they'd come back from the wilting, a lot faster than they would from a dunking.

By then Tarren was groping his way into the heated pool, groping because he'd smeared his face even more and it was obviously difficult for him to see. The water in the pool swirled, clearly ready to carry away the gunk and return him to the way he'd been, which meant I had only another minute or so to help out the vengeful part of my feelings. I'd gotten an idea, so I hurried over to the shelf holding the jars of soap. Taking a jar from the right and replacing it with one from the left balanced the shelf properly, and from a distance no one should be able to see that the replacement jar lacked the small flower of the one I took to the side of the pool. If this didn't teach the man not to ignore what I said and then assign me chores, nothing would.

As soon as Tarren was in the water he submerged himself completely, running his hands over his face and then into his hair. The water was no longer clear and inviting, but the messy murkiness didn't last too long. Slowly but definitely the swirling cleared it away, and then Tarren was out from under it and wiping his eyes.

"Ah, the blessed relief," he said with a sigh, then looked around himself. "The water will soon be clear again, and then you may join me for the scrubbing. Have you decided that *I* will be the one to remove your clothing?"

"I don't want it removed," I stated, deliberately looking only at his face. "And I don't want to get in there with you. With most of that glop gone, there isn't any *need* for me to be in there with you."

"But there certainly is a need," he countered, looking up at me with those ice-blue eyes. "Most of the—glop—is indeed gone, but the complete feeling of being clean again will not return until I have been scrubbed all over with soap. That is the task *you* will perform, to balance your having created the need for it. As you may now enter the pool, you must remove your clothing yourself or see it soaked before *I* remove it."

"I'm not taking anything off," I gritted out as I felt a preliminary tug at my wrist. "And neither are you."

I returned his stare in a way that hopefully said I wasn't joking, and that was the absolute truth. I was desperate to keep to my resolve about leaving, but Tarren was determined to make me change my mind again. If he touched me that resolve would certainly start to crumble. Once we touched, though, I would be back to having no rational say over my actions.

"So you mean to fight me again," he said, using both hands to push back his long, sopping hair as he glanced at the soap jar I put down near the edge of the pool. "Very well, then, let us fight."

And as soon as the jar was firmly down on the marble, I was pulled so hard by the wrist that I went stumbling into the pool. The water closed over my head even as I fought to get my feet under me, and I almost managed to get straight. My feet were just about to touch when the bracelet pulled me hard again, and a moment later there were two massive arms folding closed around me.

"This sort of fighting I find extremely pleasant," Tarren murmured as soon as I was no longer under water, giving me almost no chance to clear my streaming eyes. "With clothing or without, Wildea, your nearness is a precious gift I shall always be delighted to have. It occurs to me that my dismay over this incident most likely caused me to be too short with you when we discussed it, and apologies are therefore in order. I would not wish you to become cross with me."

I knew what his apology would consist of so I struggled to free myself, but water and a giant opponent don't do much to help, not to mention that I still couldn't see. His hand came out of nowhere to raise my face, and then his lips were on mine, coaxing and insisting that I follow his lead. I tried to hold out, I really did, but all my feelings for him exploded out through my skin, refusing to be held down. There was a broad, bare chest under my hands, giant arms holding me close and tight, soft lips that were also hard and demanding against mine. It was impossible to refuse to join him, no matter how desperate the rational part of me was to do it.

This time he kept the kiss going for quite a few minutes, taking his time and simply enjoying the merging of our mouths. For me it was a matter of desperation again, but this time it was to get what I could while it was still available. When he finally ended the kiss I was both glad and sorry, and utterly in love.

"All right, enough," I finally surrendered after discovering that it was impossible to break loose or make him stop touching me. "You're an absolute bastard, but you win."

"That happens to be untrue," he commented with a grin as he released me. "My birth was completely legitimate, with not even a hint of scandal. You may begin by washing my hair."

I went for the soap jar while muttering nasty things about back-seat bathers, and remembered only at the last instant that my revenge on the man was already partially taken care of. The small flower on the side of the jar that I wasn't letting him see meant the soap was spelled to leave the scent of flowers after the user was dry. Tarren would hate it when he found out about it, but would also find it impossible to do anything to get rid of the scent. It was only just beginning to leave *me,* and I'd used the stuff days ago.

I had Tarren lie sideways on the resting ledge while he held to the edge of the pool, and I was able to wash his hair that way. After a minute I was forced to admit it did need seeing to, since some of the sauce and whatnot had gotten glued to the long strands in any number of places. I would have done better with a decent shampoo than with that soap, but I finally managed to get his hair clean. Then I directed him to the broad steps leading down into the pool.

Once he was settled along the wide step, I began to wash his body. This was the part I really hadn't wanted to do, not when every time I touched him I wanted more and more to continue touching him. The thought of leaving was already hard enough; how was I supposed to do as I should when dreams of staying kept blinding me to what was right and sensible? I couldn't, and that made me wild, even more so when I saw the way Tarren looked at me. He knew exactly what I was going through, which had to be why he'd insisted on putting me through it. He meant to do anything he had to to keep me from leaving, even cheat and blackmail.

This got me even wilder. Once the book ran its course he would find himself very *un*interested, leaving me all alone to cope with loving someone desperately who didn't love *me*. I *knew* that would happen, I was sure of it, but he would never accept it. It didn't agree with his current beliefs, so he would reject it out of hand without even considering the possibility. Or thinking about how much pain I had to look forward to . . .

By then I was really crazy, in all meanings of the word. The broad, rock-hard arms and chest under my hands had turned my mouth dry with physical desire, the warm bath water had made me realize even shorts and a tank top were too much in the way of clothing, and the insanity my thoughts had been building grew higher and higher. I *knew* I would end up getting hurt, but without proof Tarren would never believe it. I loved him but I also began to hate him, and that suddenly made me determined to find something to show how I felt.

I could see that Tarren had noticed how desperate I was getting; his body had lost some of its languid relaxation, and the look in his eyes had turned somewhat wary. He seemed to be expecting to be attacked. I suddenly shoved him away and hopped out of the pool. He lunged and grabbed my arm where I promptly swung around and slapped him across the face.

Tarren stood speechless but I could see the fury rising in his eyes. It was nothing compared to my own, which was coupled with fear and desire. I had the urge to run and had pivoted to retreat to my room, when he grabbed my arms with his hands. His grip was powerful and frightening and I was afraid I had gone one step too far, that I would really see the barbarian I had created. Instead, Tarren's furious face softened and he gently released me and stepped away.

Helpless, I realized I hated myself. I loved him and I had slapped him, and while I doubted that my hand did any physical damage, I knew the action had wounded him more than any sword. I hated myself so much the hatred was pain and the tears in my eyes made seeing impossible.

The sobbing took me by surprise, but I had never felt so desolate in all my life. I hated myself and what I'd done, hated everything that was happening, and was terrified of the loneliness that lay ahead. That more than anything else made me sob, to know how terrible life would be without the man I'd just begun to love. I knew he would be gentle and polite before he left me, but he *would* leave to continue his own, real life. I had no place in that, and the truth of that knowledge tore me apart.

"No, beloved, do not weep," his deep, gentle voice came, and then those arms folded around me to hold me close to him. "You are confused and unhappy, I know, but you must have faith in me. I will guard our love and see that nothing harms it, and we will live out our lives together, blissful in each other's arms. Do not fear to love me, for I will never betray you."

I had no idea how he knew so much about what I felt, but none of that kept me from feeling even worse. What he'd said, about trusting him and having faith . . . he had no idea he *would* betray me, through no fault of his own. The sobs came even harder as his hand gently pressed my cheek to his shoulder, and I clung to him against the desolation I would have to face. It would not be his choice but it would happen, and I couldn't bear knowing it.

He spent a short while trying to comfort me back to some kind of calm, and when it didn't work he became concerned. He coaxed me out of the tank top and bra and left them in the pool with the rest of my clothes, then lifted me in his arms and carried me out. He held me as if I were a small child, which was perfectly fitting since that was the way I felt. He carried me through the grooming curtain to get us dry, and then he left the bathing room.

I really had no idea where he was taking me, and felt some faint surprise when it turned out to be my own room. He put me down on the bed and sat beside me, then bent to kiss my forehead.

"This may not be the best of times for me to remain with you," he said with a troubled expression as he smoothed back my hair. "My efforts at reassurance have obviously failed, and it may well be my presence which continues your tears. If this is so and you wish me gone, you will not need to insist. I would prefer to remain and hold you close, but will leave if that is what you require to return to yourself. It was not my intention to give you such hurt—"

"No, you didn't," I whispered as I took his hand in both of mine, refusing to let him blame himself. "Everything is *my* fault—or will be my fault—and none of yours. Please don't go."

I don't know how he heard the faint, uneven words through the crying, but he did hear them and what's more he listened. Instead of leaving me alone before it was absolutely necessary, he moved me farther onto the bed then lay down beside me. It was the size of an ordinary double bed which means it was too small for him, but he didn't seem to mind. He gathered me to him and held me in the way most women dream about, with serious concern and love and the clear intention to do nothing I wasn't prepared to cope with.

I thought at first that lying with him like that would make things harder for me, but surprisingly it made them easier. The sobs eased off and went away, and then so did the tears. I lay in his arms with my eyes closed and my cheek against his chest, the warmth of his body reaching through to the chill emptiness inside me. I had never felt like that with a man, so safe and important and really wanted, three of the many components that made up love. It wasn't meant to be mine for long, but as long as it *was* mine I couldn't help but respond.

And after a while I began to respond in another way as well. I would give him back his freedom as soon as the time came, but until then I wanted to make love to him very badly. And it wasn't as if he were unwilling, or that I'd decided to lie to him. I would simply refrain from telling him a truth he would refuse to hear anyway, and whatever time we had together would be pleasant.

And more than pleasant. When I stirred in his arms he loosened his hold, enough so that I was able to reach up and put my arms around his neck. The kiss I began was quiet and gentle and he accepted it in the same way, but then I began to kiss his face and neck. When I bit his ear a little he made a sound deep in his throat, then shifted to lie flat on his back when I showed that I wanted him to. He'd been wonderfully patient and understanding, and now it was time for his reward.

I let my hands stroke his body gently as I kissed him all over, slow, lingering kisses that I alternated with tasting him. His body was so deliciously hard all over, his tanned skin tight and healthy and wonderfully alive. His hands massaged and caressed me as I kissed lower and lower, his breathing heavier and definitely uneven, a murmuring sound of pleasure encouraging me to continue on.

I moved my kissing from his belly to his thighs, and now the sounds I heard were more like groans than murmurs. His body rose up beneath me, trying to direct me to where he wanted me to go next, but I had my own ideas about that. At another time I'd certainly give him exactly what he now asked for, but now I lacked the self control to do anything of the sort.

So instead of simply kissing his readiness, I straightened, straddled him, and captured him whole. The sensation was exquisite, exactly what I'd been dying for, and his hands came to my thighs even as he groaned in deep pleasure. He knew he was about to be ridden, and clearly wanted the ride to be a hard one. I did my best to oblige, feeling the pleasure shoot through me but after a short while he must have felt there was something missing. He reared up, threw his arms around me and rolled us over.

At first I thought I might scream with pleasure from the strength of his thrusts, but his kiss ended that idea. I nearly clawed his back while he stroked so deep he touched the very center of my being, our mouths sharing our souls back and forth. I had never given a man so much nor had so much *from* him, and the time continued on into that forever made only for two. It was a magical time in a magical world, and I was no longer capable of thinking about when it would end.

Forever lasts a long time, and when it finally ended I knew what truly being satisfied means. But between lovemaking and crying I was exhausted. I was able to stay awake long enough to share a last, sweet kiss with Tarren, and then I was gone to the world.

Eighteen

Tarren waited until his woman was asleep, then he quietly left the bed. Once again he was in need of a washing, but this time to rid him of love sweat. Not that he would have minded staying as he was and even, perhaps, adding to what was already on him. But Wildea had fallen asleep, and that bed was so very *small* . . . The next time he would do well to be certain they were in *his* bed, so that he might sleep too if he wished.

He covered Wildea with a sheet and then left the room, soundlessly pulling the door closed behind him. His body felt more satisfied than it ever had before after leaving a woman, but the worry in his mind refused to allow him to enjoy the afterglow. He had discovered that his woman did indeed love him as much as he loved her, but there was something disturbing her so deeply that it refused to allow her to acknowledge that love. It had felt to Tarren as though she feared to give herself over to loving him, but why?

The mystery occupied his mind while he quickly rinsed himself in the pool, dried by going through the grooming curtain, and then went to find clothing. A simple tunic, breeches, and boots sufficed, then he returned to the entertaining room to see what he might salvage from the disaster of lunch. His insides were prepared to rumble their protest over having been denied, but the meat and cheese and bread which had been left behind quickly quieted them. The spillage had been cleaned and the rest of the food removed, but what had been left would more than suffice.

Tarren brooded and thought as he ate, missing Wildea's company but having decided against waking her. After the crying she had done she needed the sleep more than food, crying which had shocked and disturbed Tarren deeply. Some women cried as naturally and easily as they breathed, using tears to get what they wished in the way of assistance or pity. But Wildea was not such a woman, and her tears must surely have surprised her as much as they did him. At first he had thought she wept from the short, well-earned punishment he had given, but that theory quickly disproved itself. What the woman had done was one with whatever disturbed her, and his response to her actions had seemed to be other than what was expected.

"How could she believe I would truly give her hurt?" Tarren muttered after sipping at his chai, the conclusion he had suddenly come to when first seeing her tears. She had clearly believed his punishment would be severe, and then had wept bitterly when her expectations had proven false. That, too, was beyond his understanding, that she would find disappointment when he proved to be other than a beast. And yet, the way she had made love to him showed something other than disappointment . . .

Tarren growled with frustration, but was able to make no sense out of what had occurred. Wildea had attempted to completely deny her desire for him, but then had begun their lovemaking herself. That should have pleased Tarren, but instead it worried him. Wildea had still not *spoken* of her love, and until she did so he would be a fool to believe that matters were settled between them. Or to assume that she would stay merely because she had ceased to mention leaving.

One swallow emptied his cup of chai, and then Tarren rose to leave the apartment. His fighters assigned to guard her would need to be alert against more than the minions of the unknown man who desired her, and that he would tell them himself. Almost did it seem that he was in the midst of a campaign, but the object of his maneuvers was not a stronghold or even a city. It was the heart of a woman he wished to take and keep, a far harder task than the taking of a city. But he would succeed, by all the gods did he swear it. One day the woman would be his completely, as he was ever hers.

I awoke to a tickling at the side of my neck, and then the tickling moved to my cheek. By then I knew I was being kissed rather than tickled, and sleepily I reached out to capture the one doing the kissing. He did other things even better than he kissed, and I was beginning to want those other things again.

"No, little one, that must be left for later," he said with a chuckle, two big hands taking my face between them. "We have been invited to take dinner with the princess Drinna, who will have no more than one servant present. When the matter of my difficulty with that magic user was explained to her in detail, she agreed at once."

"She's nice," I said, reluctantly giving up the idea of more sex. "What time is it, and why did you let me sleep so late?"

"It is late afternoon, and you needed the sleep," he said, moving back when I let him go. "I would not have awakened you even now, save that the maids are here to assist you in dressing. They were sent by the princess, and seem to believe it will take quite some time to prepare you."

"How long could it possibly take to shower—*bathe*—and then jump into some clothes?" I asked with a yawn as I sat up. "For me, fifteen or twenty minutes usually does it."

"That question must be answered by the maids," he said with a smile, his eyes unmoving from my face. "Since I have never been prepared by a crew of them, you may wish to share the answer with me once you know it."

"I'll do that," I promised with my own smile, joining him in ignoring the scene we'd gone through earlier. There would be no more scenes like that, even if I had to kill myself to make it happen. Whatever time we had together would be *pleasant* and fun.

He gave me a brief kiss before he left, and my lips remembered the touch of his all the way into the bathing room and the sanitary facilities beyond. When I came out again all thoughts of kissing were banished, as the four maids had come into the bathing room and were waiting for me. They were really nice girls, friendly and eager to be of help, and persistent in administering that help. I was coaxed and urged and *pushed* into doing things their way, and by the time I realized I should have defended myself against their sweet and helpful attack, it was already too late.

I was bathed and combed and dried and massaged, pampered in a way even the most expensive salon in my world couldn't have matched. Everything about my toilet was done slowly and carefully and meticulously, just as if we had all the time in the world. I might have started out not wanting the treatment, but long before it was done I had changed my mind completely. Being pampered like that is almost as good as sex, and depending on your partner, maybe even better.

When we finished in the bathing room we shifted to my dressing room, where I was encouraged to choose a gown and shoes. I hesitated for a second or two, thinking how much more comfortable a blouse and pants would be, but I discovered I was in the *mood* to dress up. So I chose a gown of coral silk and silver lace with silver shoes to match, and let the girls help me get into it. The silk was as tight as a second skin and cut low enough to guarantee that everyone knew I was female, and the lace pretended to make the rest look perfectly respectable, only it didn't. It enhanced rather than muted the coral silk, and I looked great even to me.

Although I refused to wear a corset. I couldn't believe women still let themselves be tied up in those things, and the girls were upset until they saw how well the gown fit without one.

When I was dressed they put my hair up into a complex crown of braids and curls, but that wasn't the end of it. One of the girls had left the dressing area, only to return with three velvet boxes in dark blue. The gentleman waiting for me had asked that I favor him by wearing the trinkets in the boxes, she said, so we opened them up to see if those "trinkets" would go with my outfit.

While the girls gasped and oohed and aahed, I granted the fact that silver-set diamonds would have gone with just about anything I might have chosen to wear. The necklace and earrings matched, of course, and had to be worth a couple of large fortunes. The third box contained matching hair ornaments, which the girls immediately began to add to the crown they'd built. By then I'd already decided against refusing the loan. If Tarren wanted me to wear his jewelry, I would do it. It wasn't likely to kill me, and would add to the pleasure he got out of our time together.

Tarren was waiting in the reception room, and he actually did a double-take when he saw me. His own finery was just as impressive as on the other occasions he'd dressed up, this time consisting of reddish-brown boots and breeches, a cream-colored shirt, and a tight, short vest that matched the pants. Both were embroidered with a coppery-red thread, and so was the wide-sleeved shirt, which opened down to the middle of his chest. Around his neck he wore a bronze medallion of some sort, which complemented the color of the embroidery; perhaps it was red gold.

"You look . . . dazzling," he said after a long moment in which he simply stared at me, dumbstruck. "I had thought your beauty to be considerable to begin with, but now . . ."

I was flattered, but also somewhat taken aback by his response, and I could actually feel myself blushing under his overwhelming admiration.

"You look rather dashing yourself," I managed with a small laugh as he moved closer. "I think I might have done you a favor by putting the barbarian in nothing but body cloths. You look great in body cloths, but in clothes like these you would have had hordes of women chasing after you. A man like you would find it a bit of a nuisance being chased by hordes of women, wouldn't you?"

"They would certainly get in the way," he said seductively. "Particularly when one's desire turns to only one woman, one remarkably beautiful woman . . ." He raised a finger and ran it caressingly down my cheek. "How long do you believe it would take the maids to restore you to this condition after a short . . . interlude?"

"Long enough to make us late," I responded without hesitation, but responded nonetheless. I suddenly didn't much care if we *ever* made it to the dinner, and Tarren, no doubt realizing this, let his hand drop with a sigh.

"You have chosen an inopportune time to cease refusing me," he grumbled, only partly in jest. "As we are to be the princess's only guests, it would be unforgiveable if we were late . . . but perhaps I could find it possible to shift the entire blame for the matter onto *you.* I am only a man, and when your lust over-powered your sense of propriety, I was helpless to deny you. You forced me to bend to your desires, despite my unwillingness, and ruthlessly had your way with me. Hmmm . . ."

"And people call what *I* come up with fantasy," I said laughingly, tickled by his scenario. "But as helpless and scrawny as you are, it might just be believed. Let's try it and see."

"Ah," he said, his expression darkening comically. "I understand your intention now. You mean to lure me to excess as a means of taking revenge on me for capturing you. You will not cease until my reputation is ruined and I am a mere shadow of the man I was. I will not let that happen. Take your desires firmly in hand, woman, for they will not be satisfied. At least not until we return."

He smiled then and I laughed, and took his arm as we left the apartment. Drinna was alone when we joined her, and she poured drinks for us as Tarren told her how virtuous he'd been in the face of my treacherous efforts to entice him. We all laughed at that, setting the mood for the rest of the evening. The dinner was pleasant, we were all very happy, though several times I caught Tarren staring at me as though we were quite alone, a definite gleam in those very blue eyes. Dinner was handled by a single serving man, and his presence in the room occasioned the only sober moments of the entire evening.

Drinna was very animated, and seemed amused by the intimate looks Tarren was throwing me.

"You may not have shared his bed before this, but

tonight will surely see it done," she murmured too low for Tarren to hear just before we left. "If you attempt to refuse him *now*, after he has seen you like this, he will certainly carry you to his bed over his shoulder."

"I wonder if he'd *rather* do it like that," I murmured back with a smile, curious about the point. "As long as he really does wait for agreement first—which he does—what's wrong with making it better for him?"

She raised her brows and shrugged, which I took to mean that she didn't know and wasn't sure she wanted to find out. I considered her reservations silly and decided to find out anyway, but that decision turned out definitely rash. Once we got back to the apartment and Tarren understood I wasn't refusing—only teasing—he did carry me to bed over his shoulder. And then proceeded to "have *his* way with me."

The very next morning, I came out of the bathing room to find Tarren acting rather strangely, but as soon as I understood what that strangeness was about I knew I was in trouble. He stood in the middle of the bedroom sniffing at his arms and shoulders and hair—which meant he'd finally noticed the scent of flowers. Apparently he'd been too distracted to notice until now, but that doesn't mean he was confused about what had happened. He seemed to know exactly what—or who—the cause of his smelling like that was, and didn't hesitate an instant in coming after me.

I may have been stupid enough to do something to bring him after me to begin with, but I wasn't about to just stand there and let myself be caught. Naked or not I ran dead out, and made it into the entertaining room ahead of him. Considering the size of the place that should have done some good, but Tarren wasted no time in cornering me and then carrying me back into the bedroom. I spent some effort hoping he was carrying me to bed, but that wasn't what he was in the mood for.

He spent more than a few minutes lecturing me about deliberately doing things I knew people would dislike then punished me with kisses. I promised to be good only if he would continue kissing me, to which he obliged.

And the last of that seemed to set the pattern for the next few days. Tarren and I rode together all around the inner district, took long walks around the palace, had our meals together—and made love every time we felt like it. He told me all about his family and what his childhood had been like, and I contributed occasional stories about me and my father and brothers. But nothing about the way I really felt toward my family. He had no need to hear that, and my time in his world had produced at least one benefit: I no longer had to decide about that barbecue. By the time I got home, the weekend event would be long over.

I did my best to ignore the passage of time, but when the day the second attack was due began, I knew it. I came out of the bedroom to find Tarren seated at the breakfast table, no servants at all in sight. When I took my own seat, he reached out to take my hand.

"There is something we must discuss," he said, touching my cheek gently with his other hand. "It pains me to upset you, but this day must be spent in something other than pleasure."

"Because this afternoon is when you'll be attacked

for the second time," I said with a nod, squeezing his hand briefly before letting it go. I needed a cup of coffee, and not only because it was relatively early. "If you're worried about me being in the way, you don't have to be. Drinna wants me to come over to see her latest painting, so that's where I'll be."

"You relieve my mind considerably," he said, reaching for his cup of chai. "Already I can feel the tendrils of the madness swirling toward me, a definite beginning of what will soon occur. You will, of course, remain with the princess until I send for you."

"Of course," I agreed, lying in my teeth. When that female assassin came after him with her poisoned pin, I would be right there to make sure she failed the way she was supposed to. This second attack would be a lot more serious than the first, and I wasn't about to take any chances with Tarren's life.

"Why am I suddenly less reassured?" Tarren asked slowly, studying me as I sipped the coffee. "From another woman that calm agreement would mean nothing but acquiescence, yet from you . . . I have grown suspicious, Wildea, and the task of dismissing that suspicion is yours."

Those ice-blue eyes tried to force mine into a guilt reaction of some sort, but a girl growing up with a father and four older brothers learns at an early age how to project innocence any time she needs to. Especially when confronted by a strong, suspicious male.

"You were probably just expecting me to argue," I told him reasonably, then gestured with my coffee cup. "If that's what it is, I don't mind obliging you. Rather than being with Drinna, I ought to be *here*, making sure nothing goes wrong. In fact I'd prefer to be here, so—"

"No, enough," he interrupted, raising one hand. "Your time will be spent with the princess, and then there will be no difficulty between us. You *do* know how unpleasant any such difficulty would certainly be?"

I nodded with a sigh, and that satisfied him completely. He'd threatened to punish me if I disobeyed him, and I'd backed down like a good little girl. It seemed unnecessary to mention that I'd rather face him angry than dead, and I'd worry about his punishments when and if the time came to face one. With the subject closed we began to have breakfast, and a very tasty meal it proved to be.

After breakfast, I dressed—in black leather breeches, dark blue shirt, and short, soft-soled black boots—and kissed Tarren before leaving the apartment. I also wore the swordbelt I'd "borrowed" that first time, now a permanent part of my wardrobe any time I went out alone. Tarren had insisted on it, and I'd seen no reason to argue. Wearing a visible weapon did quite a lot to eliminate casual trouble, as everyone knew you don't wear a weapon unless you can use it. Men who might otherwise have tried to come on to me didn't, which made life a lot less complicated.

"Dee!" Drinna exclaimed when I was shown into her workroom. "I expected you somewhat later."

"But this is the time you asked me to be here," I pointed out as I looked around. "Why would you expect me to be late?"

"For the reason that the last time you came, you mentioned that Tarren enjoyed returning to bed after breakfasting," she answered with a grin. "As he seems the sort of man to insist in a way difficult to argue with, I assumed you would certainly be delayed."

"A safe assumption," I agreed with a laugh, enjoying the memory of the ritual Tarren and I had begun. We'd discovered that it was a great way to start each new day, especially when we were both comfortably filled with breakfast. "But today he has serious and important things to do, so I got out of the way as quickly as possible. Where's the new painting you wanted to show me?"

"There," she replied, pointing to a large, covered canvas. "I had not expected it to be done so quickly, but the thing refused to release me until I had completed it. I also consider it my best work yet."

She led the way to the rag-covered canvas, and when she uncovered it I just stood there and stared. It was absolutely marvelous, but it was also confusing.

"I don't understand," I protested once I could speak again. "It's Tarren and me the way we looked that night at dinner, but we never posed for this. How did you do this?"

"It is no mystery," she said with a very pleased laugh. "I have the ability to reproduce what I see, and the two of you were seen all that evening. I mean to present this to the two of you when you marry, but felt I had to show it to you first. Will Tarren like it as well as you do?"

"He'll probably love it even more," I answered automatically, suddenly feeling cold and ill. The painting was meant as a wedding gift for a wedding that would never take place, but I couldn't very well tell Drinna that. And although I would have given anything to take the painting home with me when I left, I knew I'd never be able to manage it. It was much too large, and in a strange way also seemed unfinished.

"There should be background in the painting," Drinna mused as she studied it with me. "I intended from the first for there to be background, but whatever force refused to let me leave the figures unfinished, also refused to allow the addition of a background. Perhaps that will change once the date of the wedding has been set. I understand from Tarren that the two of you will decide on a date once he completes the commission he has from my brother."

"When did he tell you that?" I asked, turning to her with a frown. I had a feeling I knew why there was no background to the painting, why Drinna hadn't been able to add one. Tarren and I weren't *meant* to be together, not anywhere. The lack of a background showed there wasn't any place at all where the two of us belonged together, and never would be.

"Why, he spoke of the proposed wedding only yesterday," she said, surprised by my reaction. "His words were so filled with assurance and certainty that I assumed the two of you had discussed the matter and agreed. Was I mistaken?"

"No, the mistake was his," I muttered, wondering how many other people he'd mentioned the same thing to. "He did tell me he wanted to marry me, but there's a problem he refuses to acknowledge the existence of. I will have to leave soon, and once he finishes your brother's commission he won't be interested in marrying me any longer."

"I . . . can think of nothing to say," Drinna sympathized, her expression and one hand to my arm offering whatever support she was able to give. "Are you absolutely certain of this? As Tarren's feelings for you are incredibly clear to anyone with eyes, I find your statement difficult to believe."

"Could I bother you for a cup of coffee?" I asked, changing topics quickly. I couldn't continue.

She apologized for not having offered refreshments sooner, and then led the way to her sitting room. We stayed there and drank coffee and talked about nothing until lunchtime, and then we sat down to the meal. My appetite had long since gotten back on schedule, but I would have skipped lunch if I hadn't known I would need its fortifying later. I had something to do, and meant to be fully prepared.

I stayed for only a short while once lunch was over, telling Drinna that I needed to take a long walk to think about some things. Since she couldn't have helped but notice my distraction during the visit, she simply told me to come back if I felt I needed someone to talk to. I hugged her in thanks for the offer, and then I left. I'd need to sneak back into my apartment, and to do that I'd also have to lose the shadows I wasn't supposed to know were there.

Tarren had acted as if he wasn't having his people follow me any longer, but I'd known they were there from the very first time I'd gone out alone. As I walked down the corridor now, away from Drinna's apartment, I could have put an X on the spot where each of the four was trying to keep out of sight. But I pretended I was all alone, and headed for a corridor that led in a certain direction.

My running outfit was now somewhere I didn't know about, but I hadn't had the time or the interest for running during the past few days. I still had other things to occupy my attention, but sometimes a little running is the best thing you can do to solve one of your problems. At least it was worth a try, and if it didn't work I'd think of something else.

Occasional people passed me along the corridors, and most of them nodded politely or smiled. I did the same, pretending I was simply walking rather than going anywhere in particular, and certainly wasn't heading toward Tarren's apartment. In point of fact I was headed in the opposite direction, but not walking aimlessly. I needed a particular section of corridor, and hoped like hell that no one would be in it. If there was my plan was ruined, and I *would* have to think of something else.

I strolled along, completely unconcerned for the benefit of those who were watching, and turned into the cross-corridor I'd been heading toward as if it was just someplace else to walk. Actually it was one of the very few *short* corridors in the palace, and as soon as I turned into it and saw no one who would be able to see *me,* I immediately began to run. I had to hold my scabbard to keep it from beating me to death, but the soft-soled boots I wore made no more than a whisper of sound as I ran, and I tore around the next corner at top speed.

And no one was there either! Luck was really on my side, but now wasn't the time to crow over it. I ran as I had never run before, and took the first left as soon as I reached it. Once into *that* corridor I slowed, and then worked at getting my breath back. Since I should have been out of the short corridor before my shadows got to it, they would have no idea which way I'd gone if they hadn't seen me in this *last* corridor. I was sure they hadn't, and the lack of pounding bootsteps coming close confirmed the guess. I'd made it away in the clear, and my shadows were shaken.

I spent the walk back to Tarren's apartment wondering if my abandoned bodyguards would search the palace for me, or try knocking on every door in that short corridor first. The way I'd disappeared *could* have given them the idea that I'd gone into one of the rooms there, and I hoped it had. It would keep them occupied while I was busy elsewhere, an elsewhere I didn't want anyone to know about. Things might go so well I'd be completely unneeded, and if that happened I'd stay hidden and sneak back out later. What Tarren didn't know wouldn't hurt either one of us.

The corridor outside the apartment was deserted when I got there, proving the assassin hadn't arrived yet. She would have a lookout posted in the hall to warn her when her victim was approaching, a single knock on the door that would let her get ready to start the act. I slipped through the door myself *without* knocking, knowing that Tarren was right now with the prince and hearing about the leads the prince's agents had found. If he'd planted some of his men in the apartment I'd have to forget about the possibility of staying unnoticed, but a quick glance around showed no one at all.

Which meant I was free to hurry to my dressing

room, the place I'd decided to lurk this time. The assassin would wait for Tarren in his bedroom, handily close to his bed, and I couldn't remember if I'd told Tarren that. I was sure I must have but I wasn't *certain,* and that was another reason for me to be there. If I *had* missed mentioning the point and Tarren had his men hide in the entertaining room, they might end up too far away to help if they were needed.

Once in my dressing room I turned down the lamps that had magically come on, then was able to relax a little. I sat down not far from the latest half dozen outfits I'd liberated from Tarren's dressing room and hung in mine, reflecting that he still didn't know where I was getting all those pants outfits. I'd refused to tell him when he'd asked, knowing better than to tempt him with the idea of leaving me with nothing but dresses to wear. He liked seeing me in dresses and I'd even worn a few for him, but switching to them exclusively was absolutely out.

If I'd had too long of a wait I might have started to climb the walls, but my timing had been really good. The assassin must have gotten to the apartment just after me, since it wasn't very long before she slipped into the bedroom. I peeked around the dressing room door to see her hurry to Tarren's bed and wind a silken cord around one of the posts, then also wind it around her raised wrists. That way it looked as if she were tied to the bedpost facing outward, a tempting gift left for the use of the owner of the bed.

A couple of minutes later Tarren entered the room, but he stopped short when he saw the busty blond tied to his bed. She wore a see-through silk blouse in yellow with a matching skirt and was barefoot, but he wasn't noticing the barefoot part. There was too much else about her to notice, including the fact that she was a real blond. Tarren took his time noticing everything of interest, and the faint grin he wore annoyed me. Intellectually I knew his grin was *my* doing, but emotionally the blame was all his.

"How odd," he commented as he resumed walking, now directly toward the blond. "I feel certain I would have noticed had you been here when I left earlier, so I find it necessary to ask from whence you have come. Perhaps you were meant to be elsewhere, and have simply lost your way."

"I have been left here to serve your pleasure, sir," the girl answered in a smooth voice, moving her body in a way that showed she liked the idea. "Prince Drant is the most generous and understanding of employers, and wishes to show his appreciation of your efforts in advance. I was ordered to tell you that, and now I ask to be released so that I might demonstrate that appreciation along with my own."

Her grin was very nearly a challenge, and the way she looked Tarren over set my teeth on edge. He wore his barbarian body cloth, of course, so there was a whole lot of him to see.

"Your offer is tempting, wench, but I have matters of importance awaiting my attention," Tarren said, walking in my direction to reach a table to put his broadsword on. "Your appreciation will therefore need to be demonstrated another day. It surprises me that the prince, generous though he undoubtedly is, would fail to realize this."

"The prince knows well enough that you would never do such a thing by your own choice," the blond purred, moving her body again as soon as Tarren was back to looking at her. "It is for that reason I was sent, to assure you that a brief time of pleasure is more than acceptable. Come, sir, release me now and I will show you just how great a pleasure is possible."

"You may show me you know the way out of this apartment," Tarren said, already walking toward her. "I have no need of distractions now, pleasant or otherwise. After a week of boredom, the prospect of action at last is more attractive than any woman."

A week of boredom! I echoed silently but indignantly, knowing he wasn't talking about his time with me but still finding it personally insulting. And the damned fool was walking right up to her, ready to untie a woman who wasn't really tied. When he reached up to the ropes, apparently seeing nothing of the way her right hand freed itself, I lost it entirely.

"Move away from her, you idiot!" I snapped as I stepped out of the dressing room, reacting like those people in movie theaters who yell at the actress to stay out of the basement where the slimy monster is. "Can't you see she isn't really tied, and that she's after something other than your pure, sweet body?"

Of course, I regretted the words immediately, especially when Tarren just turned to stare at me with a frown. The blond was momentarily startled, but then her right hand continued its movement down toward her skirt, reappearing an instant later holding a three-inch pin.

"Look out!" I yelped to Tarren as I began to run toward them. "That pin she's holding is poisoned!"

That part of it got through to him, and the pin missed him by a hair when he managed to dodge back. By then the blond had also freed her left hand, and she used it to balance herself as she kicked at the back of Tarren's knee. He grunted and staggered, and her right hand swung around in an effort to bury the pin in him. She might have managed it, too, if I hadn't already reached them. I grabbed her wrist with my right hand and pressed the nerve above her elbow with my left, and she screamed and dropped the pin.

But that didn't end it. Her right leg came up in a side kick that reached my middle hard, and I went back and down with no breath and a good deal of pain. As soon as I was out of the way she recovered the pin, then went after Tarren as if she were stalking him. Which she was, and seriously.

But Tarren wasn't just another helpless victim. He stood ready with feet apart and hands up, and when she kicked and then tried to stick him he was able to block both attempts. His return kick almost got the pin in his leg, and I almost choked trying not to yell. I couldn't afford to distract him again, not when I couldn't even sit straight, never mind help.

The two enemies continued to perform their deadly dance of attack and defense, and no one came rushing into the room to help. Tarren was on his own, and I just about held my breath until he blocked her latest jab at him, then managed to punch her in the face. She went down like a pole-axed cow, and I knew that

that would be the end of it. Her fall would stick the pin in *her*, and she would never wake up again.

"You, woman, I know you," I heard, and looked up to see that Tarren was speaking to *me*. "I have seen you before, and would know . . . know . . ."

His words trailed off as confusion covered him, which had to mean he was coming out of it. It had felt strange—and strangely eerie—to have *the barbarian* recognize me, but a moment later I had no time to worry about it. The real Tarren was back, and to say he was furious was putting it mildly.

"Wildea, what do you do here?" he demanded as he rushed over to kneel beside me. "No, do not attempt to regain your feet until I have sent for Kergil. You may well have been injured on the inside."

"Don't worry about it," I told him, trying not to wince as I moved. "I've been kicked before, and once even got a broken rib. It may hurt a little now, but I'll be back to normal in no time."

"It pleases me to hear that," he growled, looking at me with ice flames in those eyes. "As soon as you *have* returned to normal, you must tell me at once. I will then be able to put you over my knee again and teach you the folly of lying and mindlessly rushing into danger. And the lesson will *not* be as short and gentle as your first taste of it."

"It wasn't my fault," I said at once, privately deciding that I would have to be hurt a lot worse than I'd thought at first. He wasn't joking about that "lesson," and I *really* didn't want to have to rely on my ability to defend myself. With other people it was no problem, but with *him* . . .

"It wasn't *my* fault, it was yours," I said, trying to maintain a sense of injured dignity. "How would *you* feel if I made *you* promise to stay away while someone tried to kill *me?* You'd hate the idea and you'd lie about staying away, you know you would. So why would it be all right for *you* to do it, but not me?"

"It would be fitting for *me* to do such a thing for the reason that I am not in love with *me,*" he stated, making no effort to excuse such ridiculous logic. "To see *you* risk yourself is completely unacceptable, and it will not happen again. You have my word on that."

With that he stood and headed for the door, leaving me with nothing to say. You can argue against logic, but he'd made the effort to show that his feelings were anything *but* logical. He opened the door and called, and a moment later some of his people appeared in the doorway. They *had* been hiding in the entertaining room and they *had* been too far away to know their help was needed, but that didn't seem to be the time to point it out to Tarren.

He had two of his men see to the body of the assassin, and the third was sent after Kergil. I'd made it to my feet by then, but I wasn't allowed to stay on them. I was gently lifted into two strong arms and carried to the bed, but not for the usual reason. Once in the bed with my swordbelt taken, I was ordered to stay there until Kergil arrived and examined me, and again there was no way to argue.

Kergil arrived rather quickly, but the intensity left his expression as soon as he'd poked and prodded a little. Actually he was very gentle, and seemed to be checking me out with more than just his hands and eyes. When he was through, he turned to a nervously hovering Tarren.

"She should rest for the balance of this day, but I believe she will be fine," Kergil said to him. "The injury was no more than one might expect in fighting practice, and the woman is fit enough to have withstood more than she did."

"*I* am not fit enough for her to withstand even as much as she did," Tarren returned dryly, giving me a look that had very little amusement in it. "Clearly, her lesson in proper behavior must be postponed, but she will have it without fail. To disobey me about what clothing she wears is not the same as disobeying about endangering herself."

"That matter, happily, is between the two of *you*," Kergil said firmly as he headed for the door. "As I am not really needed here, I may now go to meet the lovely lady whose acquaintance I have recently made. We mean to spend the remainder of the afternoon together, and as she has no interest whatsoever in becoming a fighter, I fully expect to enjoy the time considerably. If you will excuse me?"

The last was accompanied by a bow for Tarren, but Kergil didn't even wait to be answered. He simply headed for the way out, and Tarren turned to give me a speculative look.

"A woman who has no interest in becoming a fighter," he mused, just as though the idea really appealed to him. "I had considered Kergil wise before this, but now he has risen considerably in my estimation."

Fael arrived then to call him away, which means he

missed the face I made in his direction. He was definitely unhappy with me, which meant I'd have to stay out of his way for a while. But not *too* long a while. He was scheduled for a really rough time before the coming night was over, and I fully intended to be there to help.

Lying in bed fully clothed and alone is boring, but it did take a while for the pain in my middle to ease up. The blonde had caught me with a good one, but I hadn't been lying when I'd said I'd had worse. And for a lot less reason than saving the life of the man I loved. I also meant to be fully recovered by the time I was needed again, so I rested without complaint and even ate dinner from a tray when it was brought. After that I took the opportunity to nap a little, since Tarren was ignoring me completely.

I awoke from the nap feeling good as new, and also having the feeling that it was already dark out. Nothing in the way of sound came from the entertaining room, but there was no sense in taking any chances. I slipped out of bed, moving slowly out of deference to the slightly sore muscles in my middle, and tiptoed to the door. Opening it a crack showed that the room was empty, so I was able to stop tiptoeing. I had plenty of time, since Tarren wasn't due to get to the thieves' guildhall until the wee hours of the morning.

With that in view I took some time to freshen up, then went out to the reception room. The clock there said it was only just past nine, so I poured a cup of coffee and sat down to do some planning. I'd searched everywhere for my swordbelt and hadn't been able to find it, but that wasn't going to keep me in the apartment. If I couldn't find a sword or borrow one I'd do without, and I had no worries about being sent back to the apartment in chains when I showed up at the first guildhall. That would be Tarren the Barbarian who saw me there, not Tarren the man who knew me; the first Tarren might get curious, but he would *not* go freaky and protective.

When I finished my coffee I took one more look around for a sword, but finally gave it up and headed for the door. Tarren would be out in the city by now, waiting for everyone to leave the first guildhall so that he could sneak in. I intended to be there before him, and I didn't even have to ask directions to find the place. I knew where both guildhalls were, and had even included directions in the book. I pulled the hall doors open and stepped out—

—and discovered that I *couldn't* step out. All of me passed through the doorway but my right wrist, the one still wearing that damned bracelet. Tarren had done it to me again, just the way he had in his tent. Somehow I was locked in without a single lock being used, for the second time being held captive where I didn't want to be.

And being turned furious, which goes without saying. I went back into the apartment and slammed the door, then spent some time stomping around and using some very unkind descriptions of Tarren's ancestry and personal habits. But getting mad didn't accomplish anything, so I forced myself to pour a cup of coffee and sit down to think.

I spent more time fuming than thinking, but eventually my attention was taken by a corner of white peeking out from under one of the nearby chairs. It was enough to make me wonder what it was, but as soon as my mind asked the question I *knew* what it was. The piece of paper I'd used to write on that time, writing which had gotten me fruit juice delivered and all of Tarren's trunks opened. Trunks *opened* . . .

As soon as I got the idea I was out of the chair and rushing around, looking for the pen and ink I hadn't used since the day they were brought. I found them along with the stack of paper and sand for drying the ink on the desk not far from the refreshment sideboard, ready and waiting to be used again. I'd long since given Tarren the pages of details I'd written first, but what he'd done with them I had no idea.

Rather than taking a new sheet of paper I retrieved the one under the chair, then sat down with it at the desk. Messing with magic again made me nervous, but I had no choice at all. Either I got that blasted bracelet off, or I was stuck in that apartment until Tarren let me out. Assuming he *lived* to let me out.

That thought made up my mind for me, so I dipped the pen in the ink and wrote, "As soon as the ink dried, the bracelet clicked open and fell from her wrist. She was finally and permanently free of it, and what's more there was no longer any soreness in her middle from the earlier fight."

I'd added that last bit as an afterthought, and as I sanded the words I hoped they would come true. I also wondered how long it would take for the ink to dry, and found out the abrupt way when the bracelet on my wrist suddenly clicked and fell away. The small residual ache I'd been feeling also abruptly disappeared, which made the experiment a complete success.

"Yes!" I breathed, only just remembering to take the piece of paper with me when I left the desk. Putting it back under the same chair ought to keep it just as safe as it had been until then, safe and out of Tarren's sight. What he didn't know would keep me free, and I didn't have much time. The thought came that I should have also written something about finding a sword the next time I looked, but I didn't go back and add it. As long as I got to the guildhall on time, I'd make do with or without a sword.

I was no more than three steps away from the door when someone knocked, but that didn't mean anything. I wasn't about to be stopped or slowed down no matter who it was, since it couldn't possibly be the one man who *could* slow me down. I reached the door and pulled it open, then had to hold tight to my temper. It was that ridiculous little man Agnal Topis kept sending around, and even though he hadn't appeared in a while I was still extremely annoyed.

"I don't have the time for you right now," I told him, staring in a way that said I wasn't joking. "Get out of my way, or I'll go straight over you."

"I rather doubt that," he said with a sniff, and then there was a small cloud of dust in front of my face. I had just enough time to wonder what it could possibly be, and then the world turned black and went away.

Nineteen

When the last assassin was truly and finally dead, Tarren found it necessary to stand still and simply breathe for a time. First an invisible attacker, and now attackers who multiplied rather than died when they were slain. At the last there had been four of them, and if not for the woman who had come to his aid, he would certainly not have survived the coming of eight.

The woman. Tarren moved his eyes to her, and was surprised to find that she was auburn-haired rather than blond. And although she was large for a woman, she still appeared smaller than the blond female he had expected. Though why he should be expecting a blond female, he had no idea.

"You have my thanks for having saved my life," he said to the woman as soon as his breath had returned. "I am Tarren, and I would know to whom I give my thanks."

"I am Mavial, and you would be wise to withhold all thanks until you learn my reason for having assisted you," she replied in a low and throaty voice that touched his interest deeply. "Also you must know that I am a member of this guild, although not part of its defense. I have come for reasons of my own, which deliberately included your rescue."

"You are an assassin, then," Tarren said, fighting to keep the distaste from his words and expression. Mere hours earlier he had nearly fallen to a female assassin, and for that reason—as well as a general disapproval of assassination—he was less than pleased to owe his life to this one. "What did you mean, that my rescue was deliberate?"

She told him her story and answered all of his questions, and by the time they left the guildhall he was beginning to believe it just might be possible to trust her. They went to a tavern to continue their discussion, a definite mistake on his part caused by the growing desire to know her a good deal better. Mavial was like no woman he had ever met—save one—and yet that one was less than real. But she *had* been real, he would have sworn to it, even though confusion usually accompanied her appearance . . .

But there was no confusion to the mistake he made in entering the tavern, for the unknown magic user's spell soon had half the drinkables in the place spilled all over him. The uproar of laughter quieted quickly enough once he stood and glared around, but Mavial showed no laughter that needed to be stilled. Instead she looked thoughtful, and agreed to see him again at another time and place, one where he would *not* find himself in danger of drowning.

Disgust rode with Tarren until he was halfway back to the palace, and then the confusion came rolling over him again. When it was gone he was returned to his real self, and satisfaction took the place of disgust.

The blond female his other self had expected to see was still safely in his apartment, and *he* had survived to return to her. She would undoubtedly be extremely unhappy with him, but first and foremost she would be unharmed.

"Tarren, you are yourself again," Fael said, from his place riding beside him. "Do you wish us to stop so that Kergil may see to you?"

"For a wonder, I have no wounds," Tarren replied, turning his head to nod briefly at Kergil, who rode on his other side. "How did you know I had returned to myself?"

"I have often witnessed the transformation," Fael retorted, clearly amused. "As you are unwounded, I take it that the other recalled my warnings and admonitions."

"He did indeed," Tarren agreed with a nod. "He knew at once that it was an invisible opponent he faced, and therefore had little trouble besting him. The warning about the multiplying opponents would have done little good if not for the woman. He—I—would not have survived."

"And a rather interesting-looking woman she was," Fael said after clearing his throat. "It was little wonder that the other found her so . . . intriguing."

"He did indeed find her intriguing, and now I understand the reason behind my Wildea's upset," Tarren said with a sigh. "Had I not met Wildea first, I, too, would have been attracted to this Mavial. Her pull is *very* strong, but even the other's thoughts went first to Wildea when Mavial appeared. There is no true competition between them, but how am I to convince

Wildea of this? I now believe she expects me to turn from her and take up with Mavial, but that will never happen. No matter *how* attractive the female assassin may be."

Tarren muttered this last, but those riding to either side of him had surely heard. They made no comment, however, and he did not elaborate on the observation. It almost seemed that it had not come from him but from the other, even though the madness had passed. He pushed the thought aside and focused on what awaited him at the palace—namely a bath and Wildea.

When they made their return, his men saw to the mounts and Tarren went directly to his apartment. The spilled drinkables coated him, therefore he hurried to the bathing room. Only when he was clean again did he realize that he had not passed Wildea on his way through the apartment, which meant she had likely taken to that small bedchamber again to show her anger.

Tarren sighed as he passed through the grooming curtain and then headed toward his dressing room. Dealing with Wildea would not prove easy, but it certainly had to be done. And clothed, definitely clothed. A naked man attempting to speak reason to a woman was at a great disadvantage, most especially if she were a clothed woman. Perhaps it would be best if he recalled the punishment he owed her, and reminded her of it as well. She seemed less prone to stubbornness when a lesson for disobedience loomed.

After Tarren had dressed, he went immediately to the small bedchamber. The door to the chamber stood slightly ajar, and that disturbed him. Did Wildea lay within in tears, hurt rather than angered by what he had done? But what choice had he had, when she could well have been slain? He pulled the door open prepared to tell her just that, but there was no sign of her in the chamber. Tarren glanced into each of the chamber's storage chests and even looked under the bed, but Wildea was not there. He was certain he had not seen her in the entertaining room, so where could she be? He strode back to the bathing room to look in the sanitary facilities, then went to each of the dressing rooms in turn, but the woman was not about.

He was about to look under his own bed, when he suddenly recalled the reason she *had* to be in the apartment. The manacle they both wore, and the restriction he had put on hers. To find her, he simply had to direct the manacle to take him to her. Relief flooded him when he did this and was led toward the entertaining room, a room he had thought to be empty. The infuriating creature must have hidden herself there to punish him, but they would soon see which of them gave or received punishment.

Tarren was faintly annoyed as he followed the manacle's pull across the entertaining room, but all emotion disappeared behind shock when he saw Wildea's manacle lying on the floor. How she had managed to remove it was beyond him, but when he bent and picked it up, there was no doubt. The manacle was a mate to his, and Wildea no longer wore it.

Which meant she might be anywhere, even in the city and attempting to reach the guildhalls! This second shock was a good deal stronger than the first, and Tarren felt the blood drain from his face at the thought. The next instant anger reanimated him, and he strode toward the door to rouse his fighters. *Why* had he relied so completely on the manacle, why had he not stationed watchers in the corridor despite having used it? He was a fool, and if some ill befell his Wildea, the fault would be entirely his.

And then he nearly stumbled, and stopped within two steps of the door. The thought had come that she might have left the city entirely, to return to her own world. What would he do if that were the case? That she was a sorceress could not be denied, not after she had freed herself from the manacle. How did a man carry a sorceress back to a place she had no wish to be? The ache in his heart nearly felled Tarren, and he left the door and slumped disheartened into the nearest chair.

"What am I to do?" he whispered to the empty apartment. "If she has left me for good and always, what in the name of every god will I do?"

There was no answer to Tarren's tortured question, but he managed to force himself back to his feet. First he must be certain that Wildea had not attempted to follow him into the city, and if she had not then he would . . . would . . .

I woke up with a faint headache behind my eyes, but it seemed to be fading rather than developing. By the time I managed to force my lids apart it was just about gone, but then confusion took its place.

I found myself lying on my back in a large bed, but it wasn't Tarren's bed and I wasn't simply lying there.

It was almost as if I'd been arranged in place, and struggling to sitting showed me even more. The bed-clothes around me were gold and white, I'd been dressed in what seemed to be a nightgown of pink lace, and the room was unfamiliar. There were thin, delicately engraved chain bracelets around each of my wrists, and around my ankles. I couldn't imagine how I'd gotten there—and then I remembered the fussy little man and Agnal Topis's interest, neither of which had been in my book.

"If you begin to cry or make a fuss of any sort, you will be punished," I heard, but in a woman's voice. I located the woman in a chair not far from the bed, a woman most easily described as a middle-aged battleaxe. The expression on her face said she was used to pushing people around. Dark hair and eyes matched her long black dress; I felt like a costumed doll next to her.

"Women don't have to do that any more," I commented, looking casually around at the rest of the room. Richly furnished but on the sparse side, as if the place wasn't used all the time. "Cry or make a fuss, I mean. In this modern day of ours, we're free to tell people what to do with themselves instead . . . Damn it, it's full daylight out!"

I'd just seen that through some windows on the far side of the room, windows that were covered with metal filigree or something, but which still let the light in. *Day*light, which meant Tarren had gone through the dangers of the night before by himself!

"Mid-morning, in fact, which means you have only a few short hours to wait," the woman replied, looking faintly disturbed. "The man you will serve will be here this afternoon. You would be wise to spend the time considering how you will please him, to avoid the worst of the discipline he will subject you to. Your behavior thus far has greatly *dis*pleased him, and he will see you crawl on your belly in apology."

"I hope he holds his breath waiting for that to happen," I commented, disgusted by the delighted anticipation I'd heard in the woman's voice. "And you might do the same. Where have you put my clothes? I'll feel like an idiot if I have to walk out of here dressed in this stupid pink lace."

By then I was already shifting to the side of the bed, intent on getting out of there no matter who I had to go over to do it. I started to stand—and then fell back when my ankles suddenly locked together! My wrists did the same.

"What walking you do will be at the decision of your betters," the woman said with smooth viciousness, getting out of her chair to come closer—and show me a bracelet identical to my four around her wrist. "Your refusal to obey the High Lord has earned you full restraint, the implications of which you have just experienced. At the moment *I* wear the controlling band, but when the High Lord arrives it will be he who wears it. And who gives punishment in my place."

I'd managed to sit up again by then, so when she swung a hard, open hand at my face I was able to lean back a little and avoid the slap. At the same time I raised both legs and kicked her two-footed, which sent her flying back to fall over a different chair. She shrieked, but unfortunately was not knocked unconscious. Her movements were slow and painful as she picked herself up, and the hatred in her eyes was backed by fear.

"When the High Lord arrives, he will see that you pay for that," she croaked hoarsely, strands of hair sticking out around her face. "I will demand that he deal as harshly with you as possible, and I have been in his family's service long enough to be heeded! Even though he has little need to be urged to such action. Whores of your sort are worthless, and deserve whatever is done to them!"

She turned and headed for the door. When it slammed shut I leaned back and put my hands over my eyes, trying to blot out the sight of my surroundings.

The feel of those bracelets around my wrists and ankles was so slight that I barely knew they were there—except for the fact that I still couldn't separate them. I'd tried with all my strength—backed by desperation—but all I'd accomplished was to dig the engraving into my flesh. If I'd been tied with rope I might have managed to chew my way loose in true, adventure-fiction fashion, but how did you chew through seamless metal . . . ?

I let the nonsense simply fade out of my mind, the chill of fear pushing in so hard there was just no way to stop it. There's a limit to what anyone can do tied hand and foot, and that little becomes a lot less when magic is involved. When Agnal Topis got there I'd be at his mercy; right now I could see no way to avoid it. I couldn't get myself loose, and even if Tarren had survived the night, there was no way for him to know where I was. We certainly weren't in the palace any longer, and I'd been so clever about freeing myself from his bracelet . . .

I sat up again, but only because panic was making me feel sicker and sicker. I'd never told Tarren that it was Agnal Topis who was behind my attempted kidnapping, and if there had been any guards in the hall outside his apartment, Topis's fussy little man would never have come to the door so openly. On top of that was the problem I'd worried about before, the one concerning what would happen to the progression of the book if Topis was hurt or killed. In order to do anything to me he had to come close, which meant I could always get lucky.

But good luck for me might be devastating for Tarren, and I had to guard against that. But I couldn't see myself letting Agnal Topis do whatever he pleased to me. Strong fear will force me into defending myself no matter what the consequences, and killing someone is so frighteningly easy . . .

I used my palms to rub hard at my eyes, trying to chase away the beginning of terror. You can't think when you're terrified, and thinking clearly was what I *had* to do. If I could get out of that room and whatever house it was in, my problems would be solved. And I *could* get out, if there happened to be paper, pen, and ink in that room. I'd almost forgotten about that again, but now the memory was firmly back.

Renewed hope let me struggle to my feet, but hopping around was a nightmare. It's damned hard keeping your balance without counterbalancing with your arms, which means I had to hop close to the wall and use *that* to keep me from falling. Going around pieces of furniture was the most fun, but I'd spotted a desk to encourage my hopes. It took forever to reach it and I was puffing like a Sunday runner, but I finally eased myself into the chair in front of it.

I then proceeded to discover that I'd wasted my time *and* effort. The desk had a couple of knickknacks as well as a candle and holder, but its drawers were so empty it had obviously never been used. It was there just for show, part of the furnishings in a room never used for anything remotely related to business.

Disappointment made me want to cry, but frustration was stronger and that made me want to break something. There *had* to be a way out of that mess, there just had to be. I refused to accept the possibility that there wasn't. I looked down at my hands resting in my lap, seeing my body through that open-patterned pink lace, and closed my eyes in pain. I'd go mad if Agnal Topis forced himself on me, and that was *not* melodrama talking.

I sat there with my eyes closed for quite a while, having nowhere else to go and nothing else to do. Once the door to the room opened and a man looked in, and I caught his surprised expression when he saw me in the chair. For a moment he seemed ready to admonish me, but then he shrugged and closed the door again. Behind him I'd been able to see other men, obviously on guard duty in what had looked like an anteroom. Great. Even if I managed to hop out there, the two armed men would have been two too many.

The hours went by as I sat in that chair. Noon came

and the only thing I had been able to accomplish was a few stomach growls—I was hungry. I was in the midst of rejecting the tenth desperate plan my imagination had come up with, when I heard something beyond the closed door that sounded like talking. Two people were having some kind of conversation in the anteroom, which probably meant at least one of them had just arrived. The men on guard hadn't worn any sort of uniform, but hours worth of silence said they were too professional to gab while on duty. That could mean their High Lord had just arrived.

My heart began to thud and I almost stood up, remembering only at the last instant that I would be better off seated. A simple push would knock me over if I stood, and I didn't want to be knocked over . . . The babbling in my mind stopped as the door opened, and it sure as hell *was* Agnal Topis who walked into the room. He carried a jeweled goblet and looked extremely pleased with himself.

"Well, at last," he said, looking me over as if I were a steak dinner with all the trimmings. "You were some small amount of trouble, woman—which you shall certainly pay for—but now you are mine. A pity you went to all the trouble of taking yourself over there. Now you will need to return yourself to the bed."

I really wanted to say something about how good his chances of seeing that were, but I happened to notice that he wasn't wearing the control bracelet the woman in black had had. He'd been in too much of a hurry to go looking for her, then, which meant he also didn't know what I'd done to her. Suddenly it seemed time to start being creative, to see how possible it was to rattle his cage but good.

"So, the trap worked after all," I said with a faint, cold smile as I negligently looked him up and down. "I told them it never would, but apparently they know you better than I do. You really did go for it, and now it's about to close tight on your leg."

"Trap?" he echoed, "What can you possibly be speaking of? And to whom do you refer?"

"I doubt if you need *me* to tell you who your enemies are," I answered with a low, mocking laugh. "Or maybe you do, otherwise why would you have made the colossal blunder of coming here?"

"You anger me, woman!" he snapped, his face coloring with embarrassment. "Of course I have no need to be told who my enemies are! But I *will* be told of this trap you prattle about. As it was I who had you brought here, how is it possible for the situation to be a trap?"

"Your having me brought here was the very beginning of the trap," I said, trying to think fast. "They knew you would see me and want me, and the more difficult it was, the more determined you would become. Why, I'll bet you even believe you got me out of the barbarian's apartment without anyone knowing about it."

"No one *does* know," he insisted, but his voice and eyes showed doubt. "But what difference can it make even if someone *has* found out? I am untouchable by all save the prince, and *he* believes me to be a man of virtue. Any accusation would be seen as an attempt to ruin my reputation, and would fall on deaf ears."

"Barbarians are notorious for attacking rather than accusing," I said, now showing even more amusement. "The man actually believes I belong to him, and isn't at all interested in sharing me. When he breaks in here and finds *you* with me, his sword will touch you despite your being untouchable. That, of course, will be the end they've been aiming for."

"Those ill-born maggots!" Topis growled, his handsome face twisted in fury. "They think to be rid of me, but their little plan will fail. Before that barbarian arrives I will be gone, but first I *will* have a generous taste of the bait in this trap."

He threw away his jeweled wine cup and started for me, and rather than waste time cursing his stubborn, one-track mind I got myself to standing. The first step had been to get him to believe my story, and that was done. Now I had to prove that trying anything with me would be too time-consuming—and painful—and I'd have it made.

But that was a worry for later. Right now Topis was in the midst of striding up to me with all the confidence of a man about to have some fun with a woman who was tied hand and foot. He really thought he was safe, but the attitude was premature. As long as you're willing to take what comes from your actions, you can usually manage at least a gesture even in a situation like that. As soon as he was close enough and reaching for me, I slammed the back of my right hand down on his nose. He yelled and brought both hands up to protect his aching nose and streaming eyes, and I sat down again and then used both feet to kick him hard in his libidinous intentions.

This time Topis screamed as he flew back and down, ending up on the floor with one hand to his nose and the other to his crotch. He was in a fair amount of pain, I knew, but the question was if it was *enough* pain. Would he decide to get out while he could still hobble, or would he pause first to get some of his own back? I waited as he moaned pitifully, and then he began to struggle to his feet. My mouth had gone dry, especially when he looked at me with what could only be described as murderous rage, and then—

And then there was suddenly the sound of a sword fight outside the bedroom door. Topis turned pale and stopped in his slow walk in my direction, then he turned and hurried a little in the opposite direction. He shuffled to the bed, and a touch to the headboard opened a small door in the wall beside it. Topis disappeared through the hidden door without a backward glance, and I was finally able to breathe freely again.

There was shouting and the sound of more than two or three swords being used, but I couldn't imagine who it might be. I had just decided to hop over to the door no matter how hard a fall I was risking, when the swordfighting stopped almost as abruptly as it had started. Someone called out orders and there was the sound of running feet, and then the door was opened fast. I was on my own feet by then, but when I saw who it was I collapsed back into the chair with my mouth open.

"Wildea, are you all right?" Tarren demanded, striding over to me as he resheathed his sword. "Have you been harmed in this place?"

"This outfit is pretty miserable," I babbled in answer, too shocked and relieved to know what I was saying. "The lace is irritating me in the worst way— Tarren, how did you get here? You couldn't have known *anything* about what happened to me."

"You seem to have been born with the luck of ten ordinary women," he muttered, bending to examine the bracelets on my wrists and ankles. "I nearly gave you up entirely, thinking you had returned to your own world. Remain here, and I will have my people search for the controlling band."

"A tall woman in a black dress is wearing it," I supplied to his back, and he nodded to acknowledge the information before passing it along to someone outside. Through the doorway I could see what looked like bodies on the floor, the results of that fight I'd heard. It was too bad none of the now-late guards hadn't said or done something to show they deserved to die. It would have made *me* feel better, even though their deaths were the fault of no one but Agnal Topis.

"I was able to find no trace of your whereabouts, nor clues to suggest where you had gone," Tarren said as he came back toward me. "We searched for the remainder of the night to no avail, but just past breakfast time the answer came knocking on my door. It was Princess Drinna, coming to pay you a visit."

"How could *she* have known?" I asked, happily letting him take my hands between his own. I hadn't realized how much I would miss him, how much being with him had come to mean to me.

"She knew because she was a witness of sorts," he answered. "She informed me she had come for a late visit the evening before, having felt disturbed over a thing you and she had discussed that morning. She would not mention what the discussion entailed, yet felt she would be unable to sleep unless she spoke with you again. When she entered our corridor she saw one who ran errands for this Agnal Topis standing at our door, and then she saw him enter. Believing she would be intruding she returned to her own apartment, but still felt she must speak with you. She visited again perhaps an hour later, but received no answer to her knock. That was the reason she returned so early this morning."

"Because she was concerned," I said with a nod. We had become friends so quickly . . . "I'll have to think of some really special way to thank her. If she hadn't been there, you never would have known to look for me in Topis's house."

"But you are *not* in the house of Agnal Topis," Tarren said, surprising me all over again. "The wife and family of Topis live in his house, and Princess Drinna assured me he would never have you taken there. What she failed to know, however, was where he *would* have you taken."

"Is that what you've been doing since breakfast time?" I asked. "Searching for this place? No wonder you called me lucky. You could have still been searching a week from now."

"*No* one has luck enough to be found during a random search of that sort," he said, letting one of my hands go in order to reach a finger to one piece of the pink lace. My left nipple was under that particular piece, and once he confirmed that, he nodded. "A more effective method to locate you was found, and *that* brought us here."

"Well, don't stop now," I protested, mostly to take my mind off the way his finger tickled back and forth across the lace. "What method?"

"That will be discussed when we return to the palace," he said, his finger still moving even as his eyes rose to mine. "Along with the matter of the manacle you wore. Had you not found some way to remove it, you would not have been able to be removed from the apartment to begin with. Should some way *have* been found, it would then have proven impossible to hide you. All returns to your determination to disobey me, and nearly were you lost forever because of it. In truth, I had *thought* you lost forever."

He stopped touching me completely after saying that, and I felt a sudden rush of shame and looked away from him. It hadn't even occurred to me how worried he must have been. It was a good thing he wasn't meant to keep loving me, because I didn't deserve that love. Everything has to be *my* way, and that was unfair. Tarren deserved someone a lot better than that, and I was really glad he'd be getting her.

"Tarren, here is the controlling band," Kergil said as he came into the room, distracting me from thoughts of self-hatred. "The woman who wore it was found in a room at the back of the house, and apparently she took her own life. A dagger was plunged into her breast, her own hand still wrapped around its hilt. She must have known the end was near."

My clothes were found not long after that, and since the wrist and ankle bracelets had been removed I was able to get dressed. I felt so depressed at the coming loss of Tarren I spoke to no one at all, and barely noticed it when we left the house. It was located in the third district between two large storage warehouses, and had probably been perfect for its owner's purposes. Any noise in that house would have gone completely unnoticed, just the way no one had seemed to notice the sword fight which had killed six men.

I wasn't the only one wrapped up in private thoughts, so our ride back to the palace was a silent one. Once we got there the men saw to our horses, and Tarren and I went directly inside. For some reason I expected the apartment to look different, and when it didn't I found that vaguely disappointing—just like everything else, especially me. Tarren waited until I poured myself a cup of coffee, then gestured to a chair.

"Come and sit here, Wildea," he said quietly, his expression grave. "There is something of very great importance which we must discuss."

What I really wanted to do was apologize to him in a way that would mean something, but now that I very much needed the words they just weren't there. So I went to the chair and sat in it, and after removing his swordbelt he took the chair opposite mine.

"A thought has come to me of late, a very disturbing thought," he began, looking down at his hands clasped between his knees. "I have . . . told you many times of my love for you, and . . . although you seemed to be enjoying my company, you have never said the same to me. Wildea: have you remained with me simply to see to the resolution of the difficulty you consider yourself responsible for? Do you mean to leave me as soon as this latest madness is done?"

He'd raised those very blue eyes to my face, and the pain in them was almost unbearable. I wanted to run to him and hold him and make him believe everything would be all right, but he had more than earned the right to the truth.

"Tarren, you just aren't looking at it properly," I said with a sigh. "How I feel and what I want simply don't matter. Once the book runs its course, you won't be feeling for me what you do right now. Even during periods of lull, the book still affects your life. It isn't love you're in the grip of, it's my writing, and every time you call me Wildea you make that more and more clear. Once the—'madness'—is over, you won't *want* me to love you. You'll be too busy getting on with a normal life that will never be interrupted again."

I knew it was the truth and inevitable, but it still hurt to say it. He would stop loving me, but I would never stop loving him no matter how long I lived. I couldn't tell him that, of course . . .

"Let me see if I have understood you correctly," he said slowly, and I glanced up to notice his faint frown of concentration. "You believe that my feelings for you are caused by the fact that you are the author of the madness, and once the madness no longer affects me I shall no longer feel the same. Is this your meaning?"

"You've got it," I said, fighting to keep my voice even and the tears out of my eyes. "Wildea is the name I invented for Tarren the Barbarian's one true love, a character I hadn't yet had the chance to write into any of the books. Somehow my being here has you confusing me with that character, but once the whole thing is over, the confusion will go with it."

"And I will find myself no longer in love with you," he said, nodding thoughtfully. "Are you absolutely certain this will occur? That once the madness has ended for good, my feelings for you will end as well?"

"Yes, I'm certain," I said with my own frown, finally noticing how strangely he was acting. "We've both said it and even rephrased it a couple of times, and it still comes out the same. Repeating it over and over won't change it."

"I had wondered why you resisted giving yourself to me completely," he said, for some odd reason now looking happily relieved. "Nevertheless, you were, and are, completely mistaken. When the madness ends, my feelings for you will remain as strong as ever. I am able to prove what I say."

"How?" I demanded, silently calling myself a fool for having wasted my breath telling him a truth he refused to accept. "How could you possibly prove something like that?"

"With no great difficulty," he answered, his grin wide and sure. "I am able to prove it by the fact that the madness has already ended."

Twenty

"That's not possible," I told him flatly. "The book is only about half over, so how can it have ended?"

"I know nothing concerning the how of it," he returned, leaving his chair to come and crouch in front of mine. "All I know is that the end of madness is an experience I am more than familiar with, and this is what I felt late this morning. It was for that reason I asked of your intentions for when the madness ended. Now that it has, I cannot bear the thought of losing you."

I stared at him, dumbfounded. Had the link between our worlds been broken because I'd spent so much time in his? I didn't know, and I didn't even care. All I cared about was whether or not he was right.

"Tarren, there's a way you *can* prove that the madness is over, and I mean to me," I said, dying to reach out and touch him. "Are you willing to do it, even if it might prove the opposite?"

"What would you have me do?"

"Call a servant and order a meal," I said, almost losing myself in his eyes. "A meal to be served by *four* servants."

Surprise flickered in the depths of those blue eyes,

but he didn't have to ask for explanations. If, for whatever reason, the book really had ended, the spell he'd been under should have ended as well. That wouldn't be true during periods of lull, like the time we'd spent together, but once the book was over so would the spell be. As, I prayed, it was.

Tarren straightened without hesitation, and went to ring for a servant. I couldn't remember ever being so anxious about a meal in my life—except for that family barbecue—and it was ridiculous that I also felt hungry. Granted, I wasn't used to missing two meals in a row, but didn't my appetite have *any* sense of the dramatic?

If my appetite didn't, the rest of me did. I refilled my coffee cup twice while we waited, then had to pay a hasty visit to the sanitary facilities. By the time I came out, the meal had arrived; everyone was waiting for me to be seated before it was served.

Tarren seated me without a word, then indicated that the meal could begin. I'm sure the four male servants wondered why so many of them had been asked for this time, but none of them put the question aloud. They simply did their job, and they were marvelously efficient. Not one drop of the various soups and sauces and dressings that Tarren had ordered was spilled, not even on the tablecloth.

The longer that held true the more Tarren and I grinned at each other, and by the time the meal was over we were actually laughing aloud. The servants must have wondered about *that* even more, but once again they didn't ask. They gathered together the remnants of the meal and left, and Tarren closed the door behind them and turned to look at me.

"That has to be one of the best meals I've ever eaten," I said to his questioning look. "So well-balanced, so well-cooked, so—*neat.*"

"Then you believe!" he said with a great laugh, striding over to take me in his arms. "You are my beloved, my *Wildea,* and you will never leave me?"

"Not as long as you still want me," I said into his grin, then decided to get the rest of it said as well. "Even though after the way I've been behaving you *shouldn't* want me. Tarren, I'm really sorry about the way I worried you, and for not even realizing that you *would* be worried. You should punish me for that, and if you do I promise I'll forgive you."

"It relieves my mind to hear you say that," he replied, not the answer I'd been expecting—or hoping for. "You have indeed earned a great deal of punishment, but we will discuss the matter at another time. At the moment there are other things awaiting our attention."

The first of those things turned out to be a visit to Drinna. He'd had one of his people let her know that I'd been found and was all right, but he was right in believing that I'd want to see her myself and thank her. As we walked along the corridor toward her apartment, I spent some time wondering if Tarren had been serious about punishing me. I couldn't deny the fact that I'd given him a lot of grief, but if he decided to spank me again . . . The thought was intimidating, so I quickly pushed it away. I had enough of the intimidating to think about under the heading of making a life with him.

Drinna was delighted to see me back and unhurt, and I hugged her in thanks for the help she'd given. I also promised myself again that I would find some way to repay her for her kindness. We stayed for a while and talked, but during the time a thought occurred to me. I couldn't ask it with other people around, but as soon as we got back to our apartment I put a hand on Tarren's arm.

"I should have asked this before, but I didn't," I said to the questioning in those beautiful blue eyes. "Now that you know it was Agnal Topis behind my kidnapping, what do you intend to do about it? The prince still considers him a trusted adviser, and even if Drinna comes forward . . . I don't know if that will help you if you kill him."

"I have agreed *not* to take his life," Tarren answered. "You are correct in believing the prince would be displeased, and although the madness is gone, his commission remains. Knowing Topis will be exposed in a short while satisfies me for the moment, so you may set your mind at ease. As for the rest of you, seeing to it is *my* task."

He picked me up then and kissed me, and I kissed him back with all my strength. I still couldn't quite believe that my dreams had come true, but the reservation was very small and very far away. It had made me reluctant to even hug Tarren, as if my happiness would end if I did, but now that he held me in his arms I saw it for the silliness it was. The book had ended and he still loved me, and no one in the entire universe had ever been happier than me to be wrong.

We went to his bed and made love, and although the passion and excitement were all there, I had the strangest impression that Tarren was . . . distracted, I suppose you would call it. He enjoyed himself as much as ever, but we'd made love often enough for me to notice the difference. Tarren wanted to make love to me and he did, but there was still something on his mind.

Tarren napped for a while afterward, understandable since he hadn't slept the night before, but I didn't join him. I was almost as tired, but a small nagging worry kept me awake. I sat in the reception room and drank coffee, watching through the windows as day became evening and then full night. A servant came in to light a fire in the giant hearth, and after she left Tarren came out of the bedroom.

"I had expected you to sleep beside me," he said, sounding almost diffident. "Has hunger returned to you? We lunched late, I know, but—"

"Tarren, I'm not hungry," I interrupted, feeling a chill coming from somewhere. "Will you tell me what's wrong? And why are you putting your sword-belt back on? Are you going somewhere?"

"Yes, I must go out for a short while," he answered after letting out a deep breath. "And the time has come for us to discuss how I found you."

I suddenly remembered he hadn't told me that, and just as suddenly something said I'd be better off not knowing. But I really hate not knowing things, so I simply shifted in my chair by the window and waited for him to get on with it.

"That house Agnal Topis used had not been bought in his name," Tarren continued after a brief hesitation, not quite looking at me. "There are those in this city who know all things including the truth of such an ownership, but I have no acquaintanceship with them, nor do they know me. Questions coming directly from me would have gone unanswered, therefore did I ask another the favor of putting the questions *for* me."

"Another," I echoed, by that time having figured it out. "You mean you asked Mavial."

"And she was able to accomplish it," he replied with a nod. "Many know her as a true member of the assassins' guild . . . I hesitated to mention this before, as I have reason to believe that you are—unsure—about my being in her company. Will you take my word that I go now merely to thank her for her assistance, and that *you* remain my one and only love?"

I hesitated just for an instant, *hating* the idea that he was going to see her, but the problem was one *I'd* started. He might not be forced to follow the book any longer, but he did still have to finish the prince's commission.

"I'll take your word for anything," I told him then, leaving my chair to be near him. "I love you, Tarren the ordinary citizen, and that means I also trust you. Go and do whatever you need to do. I'll be here waiting when you get back."

"Beloved," he breathed, then touched my face very gently as a smile wiped away all his worry. "I would take you in my arms and kiss you for being as wonderful as you are, but such an action would delay my departure and my return as well. As I wish no delays—most especially of my return—I will take no more than a small kiss to warm me on my way."

He bestowed a soft, lingering kiss on my lips, and then he was on his way out of the apartment. That was what had been bothering him, then, the need to tell me about Mavial. I'd been worrying for nothing . . . I went over and retrieved my coffee, then worked at trying to make myself believe that.

Tarren didn't get back until late, and on the assumption that he would eat with Mavial, I'd had a light snack delivered for me alone. I had also realized that she was the one he'd given the promise to about not killing Topis, and for some reason that bothered me. Not jealous-bothered but logic-bothered, as though something important wasn't making sense. I didn't know what that something was, and *that* was what bothered me.

"You *are* still here," Tarren said when he saw me, pretending to be surprised. "Perhaps the gods do smile on me at last, and my woman no longer needs to be kept under lock and key."

"The last time wasn't entirely my fault, so you can't blame me for it," I told him firmly as I went and let him put his arms around me. "So how did it go with Mavial? You haven't told me yet what you think of her."

"I find her a very attractive woman," he answered, looking down at me without trying to avoid my gaze. "Not as attractive as that other finds her and not as attractive as *you,* but still of considerable interest. It was for that reason we talked longer than I had intended, and I would know what you think of my response."

"I think I enjoy being told the truth," I answered with a smile as I toyed with the material of his tunic. "You have my thanks for thinking enough of me to do that, and now I'd like to know if you've eaten. If you have, there's a certain job waiting for you to attend to."

"Another task awaiting me," he said with a very phony sigh, pretending he had no idea what I meant. "What a curse it is to be known as a man who never shirks his duty, no matter how distasteful that duty may be. Very well, you may lead me to this onerous task."

"Onerous, my eye," I said, punching him in the short ribs. "If you're out of juice already, I don't think I'll marry you after all. Having to look around for lovers is *such* a pain."

"And you know, I think, where the pain would be applied," he said, now bending a very stern look on me after having ignored the punch. "Should I find you even *thinking* of taking a lover, I promise you no understanding or sympathy whatsoever. Tomorrow, immediately after lunch, we will sit down together and plan the details of our wedding. Is that clear, woman?"

"Yes, Tarren," I said meekly, trying to look chastened rather than delighted. "Whatever you say, my husband-to-be."

"Then I say bedtime has arrived," he replied with a grin, bending to scoop me up in his arms. "Such complete obedience from you will be as rare as hen's teeth, I know, therefore I mean to take full advantage of *this* time. Are you braced to be taken advantage of, my Wildea?"

"I'm terrified and desperate to escape, but I don't think I can," I answered, wrapping my arms around his neck and starting to kiss his face. "I'll just have to accept the situation as bravely as I can, and think about escaping later. A *lot* later."

He chuckled as he carried me into the bedroom, possibly because I was now nibbling at his ear. We bathed before going to bed, which was fun in itself, and then we made glorious love. I would have enjoyed having it go on for the rest of the night, but I was just too tired. After the first time—with the bed a raging sea and the curtains a rainbow-filled sky—I fell asleep. When I awoke for a moment during the night, Tarren was asleep beside me—with his arm curled protectively around me. I went back to sleep after seeing that, and dreamed some marvelous dreams.

Breakfast was waiting for me when I awoke the next morning, but Tarren wasn't. His absence gave me time to think. Tarren had wanted to talk about the wedding after lunch and I was perfectly willing, but I couldn't forget the fact that I had a family back in my own world. Even if I wanted to forget about the rest of my personal affairs and property, I couldn't leave my father and brothers wondering for the rest of their lives about what had become of me. I had to let them know I was all right and happy and that I would probably never be back again, but I didn't know just how to accomplish that.

And then there was the question of what to do with *my* time while Tarren was busy putting together the life he'd always wanted. I'd go crazy playing the domestic female, but I couldn't very well continue to write. I'd need something to hold my interest, and it had come to me that studying magic would be just the thing. I'd not only learn to control what I did, but I might even learn how *not* to do it when I didn't want to. That would let me write again, and maybe even finish the story of Tarren the Barbarian. I owed it to my publisher and readers to at least try—assuming I could get the manuscript back to my own world.

The possibilities and ramifications were endless, even if there turned out to be a problem about going back and forth a few times. There had to be *some* limit on world-commuting, otherwise people would be doing it already. That was only the first of the things I needed to find out, and a lot of time disappeared while I thought of, considered, and listed some others.

I knew I hadn't awakened that morning particularly early, but when I finally looked at a clock I had a nasty surprise. I'd been so involved in my plans and thinking, that I hadn't noticed lunch time coming and going. It was almost two in the afternoon, about the time Tarren had scheduled for our discussion about the wedding. The time *he* had scheduled, and rather forcefully. If he wasn't here, something had happened to him.

With that thought I was up and running, or at least moving fairly fast. My first objective was the hall outside the apartment, and just as I'd hoped there were four fighters on guard. The last time I'd pretended they weren't there and then had lost them, but this time I went straight up to the nearest one.

"Where's Tarren?" I asked the woman, trying not to bark the question. "Do you know where he's *supposed* to be?"

"Tarren went to work with others of our company earlier," the woman answered, still flinching a little. "There is much for the leader of a company to do, after all . . ."

"I'm sure you're right," I agreed, just to keep from starting an argument. "Take me to where you think he went."

By then the other three bodyguards had joined us, and they exchanged glances, shrugged, then did as I'd asked. If they hadn't, I would have gone searching on my own, and I'm sure they knew that. Taking me straight to where I wanted to go saved *them* the effort of having to tag along all over the landscape.

There was a yard behind the stables nearest to the palace entrance Tarren had all but been given as his own, and that was where the bodyguard contingent led me. There were quite a few members of the company there including Kergil and the boy Lamor, but Tarren was nowhere to be seen.

"Kergil, what's happened to Tarren?" I demanded. "I was expecting him back for lunch. Has he been hurt?"

"Calm yourself, Wildea," Kergil soothed, coming over to put a hand to my shoulder. "Tarren was perfectly fine when he left here, a thing I saw with my own eyes. Likely he has been delayed by some matter of business, for he still labors in the service of the prince."

"But there's nothing he has to do *now*," I protested, noticing Kergil's odd expression and not understanding it. "He knows everything he needs to already, so without the book forcing him to its own pace he can bypass all the danger and trouble and simply skip to the revelations when the times for them come. If he left here, when and where did he go?"

"I believe it was shortly before lunch that he went," Kergil said, now looking downright uncomfortable. "As to *where* he went . . . that you will need to ask him when he returns. I would suggest—"

"But Kergil, you know as well as I where Tarren went," the boy Lamor interrupted with a frown, stepping a bit closer. "Why do you say you do not?"

"Lamor . . ." Kergil began warningly, something like panic coming into his light eyes, but I wasn't about to let him interrupt.

"Why don't *you* tell me where that is, Lamor," I suggested, rolling over whatever else Kergil might have said. "If you really do know, that is."

"I most certainly *do* know," the boy returned stiffly, responding to the doubt I'd deliberately put into my request. "He began the morning describing what occurred in the guildhall of the assassins. More than once he told us of the woman he had met, and how strongly she had impressed him. Somewhat later he mentioned his time with her yesterday morning, and how she had discovered the magic user who had put the spell on him. She had spoken to the magic user and had had the spell removed, and had only told him of it so that he would no longer worry. A bit later than that he said he had been thinking all morning of the time they had spent together last night, and how he would enjoy having her company again today. Just after he made that observation he left, obviously to be with a woman he *cares* for."

"*That* is an unwarranted assumption!" Kergil snapped, glaring at the boy, then he turned again to me. "Wildea, Tarren has said that it is *you* whom he loves, and that you cannot doubt. For both your sakes, I ask that you wait until he returns and can discuss the matter with you. Will you do that?"

I nodded after a moment and turned away from his searching gaze, needing to be alone to think. What I'd just learned—it changed everything, and I needed to see just exactly how. Lamor had stood there looking defiant, his attitude saying he had protected Tarren from the dangerous foreign sorceress despite Kergil, and he wasn't sorry he'd done it. Whether or not he'd also accidentally protected *me* was something I'd have to decide.

I returned to the apartment and paced the entertaining room long enough to get the possibilities straight in my mind. There were two lines of thought involved, and when I had them clearly defined I went to pour myself a cup of coffee.

The two possibilities were that the book—or madness—was really over, or that it wasn't. Tarren had all but sworn that it was, but that could have been wishful thinking, an honest mistake, or an outright lie. Whichever, he'd been so desperate to keep me from leaving, he hadn't mentioned that Mavial had had the spell removed from him. My suggesting a meal presided over by four servants had told him I'd forgotten *when* Mavial did that in the book, so he hadn't reminded me. He'd simply let the "test" take place, knowing all along that he would pass.

But that had only taken care of last night. By this morning nothing was the same, and that went for both possibilities. If it was true that the book had run its course, he had already begun to lose interest in me just as I'd said he would. Mavial, a woman of his own world whom he found attractive, was drawing him away from someone he had nothing in common with, not even a world.

And if the book *wasn't* over, then it would only be a matter of time before he did lose interest. If only I'd remembered Drinna's painting of us, with absolutely no background. But I hadn't wanted to remember, not when it would have meant the end of my happiness. I loved him so *much,* but I never should have said it out loud. Too often, talking about something jinxes it, and that must go double for a world with working magic.

I carried my coffee cup to a chair and sat, seeing Tarren's laughing face, feeling his arms around me, remembering our shared passion. Chances were I'd never see or feel any of that again, and the thing that hurt most was that he'd forget me. In just a little while I'd fade out of his memory completely, and not even my ghost would remain. I'd love him forever, but for him I'd be someone who had never been.

"But it *is* better that way," I whispered to the empty room as quiet tears rolled down my cheeks. "If he didn't forget you he might miss you, and that would be horrible. Spending the rest of your life missing someone you'll never see again . . ."

I moved my head to look out the window on the far side of the room, seeing the bright sunshine dim a little as clouds passed across the sky. I was very tired, more tired than any night's sleep would ever ease, and I suddenly wanted very badly to go home. It hurt too much to stay in that world, but I owed Tarren the chance to say goodbye. It would be *my* goodbye, of course, since he would forget it, but he did deserve the chance to say it.

I waited through the rest of that day until darkness descended, and then I ordered dinner. I wasn't particularly hungry even after missing lunch, but I needed the sustenance for the trip ahead of me. I ate slowly and as much as I could, but finally it was too late to wait any longer. I sat down at the desk, got out my pen and ink, and wrote, "The horse was saddled and waiting right outside when she left the palace, and none of the guards in the corridor saw her go. She had no trouble leaving the city, and the trip to the wizard's house was uneventful. The wizard was at home when she knocked, and

I tried to write more, but as soon as I'd gotten to the word "wizard," I'd felt a resistance of some sort building up. It had to have something to do with magic, and that wizards were better at magic than everyone else. Oh, well, it didn't really matter. I'd put in everything else I needed, and would deal with the wizard—Massaelae, Tarren had called him—when I reached him.

I sanded the ink and let it dry, then finally picked up the piece of paper and took it with me. It really was too late to wait any longer . . . after all, it was only a last goodbye I'd been waiting for, and no one really *needs* one of those . . . What they do need is to remember that dreams always end, and then there's nothing but reality left. The only goodbye was the one I said to foolish dreams, and then reality and I rode away together.

The ride was long, dull, and exhausting, but I reached the wizard's house the next morning shortly after the sun had risen. I tied my horse at the front and went to knock on the door, and a few minutes later it was opened by an ordinary-looking man. He inspected me with a frown for a moment, and then his expression cleared.

"Of course!" he said with revelation dawning on his face. "Our sorceress from distant realms. Do come in, young lady. I have questions I would like to put to you."

"How did you know who I am?" I asked, stepping inside as he gestured for me to enter. The outside of the house had looked rather grim, but inside it was surprisingly neat, cozy, and homey.

"How could I not know?" he countered, soft brown eyes warm with amusement as he closed the door. "Am I not the one who established the doorway through to your world for Tarren? When you returned with him I was aware of it, and had you not come to pay this courtesy call, I would have eventually visited *you*. I would know something of the world you came from."

"If that's your price for sending me home, you've

got it," I said, using one hand to push my tangled hair back. "I'll answer any question I can, as long as I can leave some time today."

"My dear, what troubles you?" he asked, suddenly serious. "Come, let me offer a place to sit and some refreshment. It has only just come to me that you were many hours arriving here. Surely you did not come alone . . . but then, of course you did. I must have misplaced my mind today."

He bustled me out of the entrance area and along a hall, and then into a room with chairs and a fire and a desk and books. He got me settled in a chair near the fire and hurried out again, only to return in a couple of minutes with pitchers of coffee and chai and two mugs on a tray. I'd been so cold for most of the ride that the fire felt heavenly, and when a mug of coffee was added to that, some of the ice began to melt off my bones.

"Now you must tell me what befell you since you came through the doorway," Massaelae said after I refused his offer of food, settling into the chair opposite mine. "And also, of course, what purpose you had in coming to this world."

"I didn't really have a choice," I answered after sipping the hot coffee. "Tarren simply appeared in my office and dragged me back here with him."

"Yes, Tarren did strike me as a man of abrupt decision," Massaelae said with a sigh and a nod. "So you did not come through of your own volition. And what occurred when you arrived?"

"Tarren convinced me that his life was being affected by my writing," I said. "I set about taking steps to inform him of what he'd be facing. And then I made a promise not to write about him again. Now I'm ready to go home."

"A succinct description of events," Massaelae commented after sipping at his own coffee. "And nothing else occurred?"

"What else *could* have happened?" I countered, looking at him directly. "So . . . what questions do you have about the world I come from?"

He stared at me uncertainly for a moment before getting to his questions. I couldn't tell him anything about magic, but I have a fairly good layman's grasp of science and technology. I kept to the basics, for the most part, but after a couple of hours Massaelae held his hands up.

"Enough for the moment," he said, looking as if he'd been digging ditches all morning. "My mind reels with what you have told me, and yet there is clearly so much more. What must it be like, to live with those devices called automobile, computer, telephone, television, jet plane, *space ship!* And a microscope! What I would not give to own a microscope!"

"I'll find out if UPS delivers here," I said, rubbing my eyes wearily. "And speaking of deliveries . . ."

"Yes, you wish to go home," he said. "And so you shall, but not until we have lunched. It requires strength to open a doorway to another world, and mine needs to be replenished with food. Ah . . . what was that you referred to, the youpeeess? Is that some component of a spell?"

I explained what UPS was while he showed me to the dining room, and once he understood he chuckled at the joke. Lunch was waiting for us on the table, the first indication of magic I'd seen since arriving there. We were alone in the house, I was sure of that, but a tasty lunch was ready and waiting. That was one trick a lot of people would have enjoyed learning—if they could have lived with the relocation problem.

The food *was* tasty, but I couldn't eat more than politeness required. Massaelae kept the conversation going mostly by himself, and he seemed to be sticking to nothing but chitchat. I also noticed that he didn't seem to be quite as hungry as he'd claimed, and finally he gave it up.

"Well, the time seems to have come to send you home," he said after putting his linen napkin back on the table, the lightness of his tone sounding somewhat forced. "Deanne, my dear, are you certain that this is what you wish?"

"I'm certain that this is the only thing I'm entitled to wish," I answered, having gone over that point many times during the night's ride. If I'd sat down and written that Tarren really did love me after all, there was a good chance it would have come true like all the rest. But I didn't want to *force* him to love me, not when he'd already been forced through so much. I wanted his love only if it came freely, of his own accord, and that wasn't going to happen.

"What a pity," Massaelae sighed as he stood. "Self-discipline is the most difficult thing for a magic user to learn, and you have mastered it only to leave . . . Well, the worlds spin without asking our permission. My workshop is this way."

I followed him up a couple of flights of steps, to a

room that looked like a scientific lab. It didn't have Bunsen burners or computer terminals, but those seemed to be the only things missing. He opened a book and then began to take bottles from their shelves, and once he had them in reach he turned to me with a smile.

"The *method* of opening doorways is really quite simple," he said, as if he were sharing information with a colleague. "The strength required, however, is substantial. There are no more than two others in the world besides myself capable of doing this, and those two are engaged in other pursuits. Ignore the circuit diagram, we will not be requiring it."

"Circuit diagram?" I echoed, looking up from the floor. "I thought that was your ordinary, everyday pentacle. It's also a circuit diagram?"

"Under most conditions," he agreed with a smile. "But explaining further would take a good deal of time. If you would care to accept my hospitality, I would be glad to share the details."

Just for an instant I was tempted, but then I shook my head.

"I appreciate the offer, but I really do want to get home," I said with as much of a smile as I could manage. "Pressing engagements and all that . . . I'm sure you understand."

His smile faded, and he simply nodded in understanding before turning back to his book and bottles. He opened the bottles and took a pinch of things from each of them to hold in one hand, looked into the book for a moment, then turned away from the lab bench to speak some words I didn't understand. After speaking the words, he threw the handful of pinches into the air, and if I hadn't seen it myself I never would have believed it. The handful of whatever turned instantly into a large, billowing cloud, which after a moment settled down into a familiar doorway of mist.

"Thank you," I said to Massaelae, but the words insisted on coming out a whisper. "Thank you for everything, but especially for being so nice. Do I just . . . walk through and I'll be home?"

He nodded again with a sad smile, and I turned and walked toward the doorway of mist. I didn't say goodbye. I'd given up on goodbyes. The doorway was in front of me and I stepped through . . .

. . . right into my office, which looked exactly the way I'd left it more than a week earlier. I took another couple of steps and then turned, just in time to see the doorway begin to fade away. It grew fainter and fainter, and then there was nothing but the bookshelves it had appeared in front of. That other world was gone, forever closed to me and those in my world.

Twenty-one

I felt numb and exhausted, but wasn't in the least interested in the idea of lying down. Instead I went toward my desk chair, but was diverted by the sight of two self-stick notes attached to the bottom of my computer's keyboard. I changed direction and went to the notes instead, and the first one was from my editor, Erin Wayse.

"Dee," it read. "Thanks for the ms. Sorry you didn't get back in time for us to visit, but we can do that *after* I finish reading. I'll call when I do. Love, Erin."

The second note was from Jessie, my part-time housekeeper-assistant, who could always be relied on to do what was needed.

"Dee," her note said. "Finished putting away the groceries before refilling the paper in your printer, but it couldn't have been off more than half an hour or so. Tomorrow's school, so I'll see you the day after."

So the printer had stopped for a while, and that was why Tarren had thought the madness was over. He'd really believed it, but then it had taken him again without warning. What I *couldn't* understand was that comment from Jessie about the printer being off for only half an hour or so. It had been more than a day for Tarren, not just a matter of minutes.

Which brought me to the question of why everything looked so normal in my office. For the length of time I'd been gone, there should have been evidence of missing-person police sifting through everything for a clue to my whereabouts. I couldn't imagine Jessie, Erin, or my father not calling the police, but everything looked untouched.

And suddenly I felt as if I were starving to death. Since I *had* eaten in Massaelae's house less than half an hour ago that didn't seem possible, but I couldn't ignore the hunger. It was intense to the point of pain, so I hurried into the kitchen and began to stuff my face with whatever came to my hand. Four pieces of bread and a quarter pound of sliced turkey breast later I felt better, but only for a minute. Then the hunger was back again, and I was back in the refrigerator.

That insanity lasted for about an hour, and then it was gone as abruptly and unexplainably as it had come. After leaving the bathroom I sat at the kitchen table for a while to be sure, but then it came to me to wonder why I didn't feel bloated. I'd eaten enough to keep a normal person fed for days, but— I'd also had enough in the refrigerator, freezer, and pantry to do that feeding. After more than a week there shouldn't have *been* that much food, not when Jessie took her meals at my place five days out of seven. And with me among the missing, the cupboard should have been almost bare.

There was definitely something strange going on, and after a few minutes of intense thinking I came up with an equally strange idea. I couldn't really believe it, it would be much too weird, but there was an easy way to check it. I went first to my computer and turned it on, stared disbelievingly for a minute, then went to the television and turned on the Weather Channel. Both things showed the full date and time, and both things said the same exact thing.

I'd only been gone about a day and a half.

I turned off the set and stumbled to a chair to sit down. I'd lived in Tarren's world for more than a week, but in my own world only a little more than a day had passed. It wasn't possible, it *couldn't* be possible—but it had happened.

After a while things began to fall into place, making sense now where they hadn't earlier. The length of time Tarren had believed the madness was over, compared to the brief time the printer had been off. The fact that no one had reported me missing, and the presence of a houseful of food. Since Jessie had shopped only yesterday and wouldn't be back until tomorrow, the conclusion was obvious.

And now I even understood the strangeness about my eating habits—my lack of hunger and being ravenous now. Somehow time moved faster there, and I'd actually digested everything I'd eaten in that hour.

I leaned back in the chair, now feeling horribly disappointed. I'd had the vague intention of doing something like rewriting the book to make completely sure that Tarren survived, but by now most of the real trouble was already over in his world. He'd survived or not on his own, and I'd never know which had happened. My time there was already beginning to feel like a dream . . . a sad, *lost* dream . . .

And somehow, somewhere, I'd have to find the will to go on alone. On to where I had no idea, and didn't have much interest in finding out. And tomorrow afternoon was the barbecue, the one I'd been so happy to have missed. I hadn't missed it, it was still ahead of me, but I no longer cared. There was only one thing I cared about, and that was gone forever. A smile, a gentle touch . . . the tears began again, and I ran to my bedroom to hide from the bright, happy world outside my windows.

Tarren lowered his sword when the last fight was finally done. The fool Rimin of House Gisten had hired fighters in anticipation of the downfall of Prince Drant. When the prince found his missing ring and there was no longer a chance of his making a wrong decision, the man Rimin had sent those fighters to attack Tarren and his people in an attempt to turn the tide back again. That, too, had failed, and only Fael and Kergil and others of Tarren's people still remained on their feet. And Mavial, of course, the marvelous woman he had spent so much time with since they had first met. He had returned to his apartment at the palace just once in the past days, and then only to get some of his belongings. The apartment had seemed strangely empty, but he had not had the time to puzzle the matter out.

"And now the fool who hired these men will have to face the prince once His Highness has coped with his wife's betrayal," Fael said from Tarren's side, looking about in disgust. "So many dead or dying, and all because a fool coveted the prince's place. And the prince's wife, which proves the man a double fool. Who in his right mind would want a woman who was willing to aid in the destruction of her husband?"

"A man with more gold than sense," Tarren said, answering the rhetorical question Fael had put before turning to Mavial. "And you, woman? Now that this matter is nearly over, have you thought upon the offer I made? You should find my fighting company a good deal more hospitable than the guild of assassins."

"It seems certain that that would prove true," she replied in that smooth and sultry voice he found so exciting, a smile accompanying the words. "But I will need to think a bit longer on the matter before I give you my answer."

Tarren felt disappointment, but only briefly, followed by confusion, followed by relief and an inexplicable elation.

"Free again," he muttered after taking a deep breath and relaxing from the very straight posture of the other. "And this time for good, I think. Rather than half done, the adventure is completely over."

"Perhaps not as completely as you think," Kergil said, surprising Tarren by having heard what he had said. "Nor are you done with disappointment. There is a thing you must know, Tarren, but we none of us have the heart to speak of it. Perhaps if you spend a moment remembering the real world . . ."

Remembering. Horror and fear flashed through Tarren with that word, for he had already begun to remember Wildea. She was in the first thought to return to him, and his fondness for Mavial was like a candle to the raging inferno of his love for Wildea. But something had happened to her, and Tarren was almost too afraid to put his question.

"She could not have been harmed," he said to Kergil in a voice choked with dread. "She would not have put herself in danger again and she was to have been guarded, so she cannot be—"

"No," Fael interrupted quickly, knowing him far better than the others. "As far as we know she still lives, Tarren, and is unharmed."

"Then what do we discuss here?" Tarren demanded, fear turning to anger. "I had thought her lost to me forever, and—Fael, why did you say 'as far as we know?' How could you not know?"

"The woman is no longer residing at the palace," Fael answered heavily, the words slow and reluctant. "She came seeking you the day the madness reasserted itself, and was told . . . where you had gone. Kergil was present and begged her to wait until you returned to speak to her, but that night she disappeared. None saw her leave, and no one has seen her since."

By then Tarren had remembered a good deal more, including the fact that they were to have made their wedding plans that day. Instead he had ridden off to find and share the company of another woman . . . That thought made Tarren ill, but then he recalled that Wildea would know the decision had not been his. It was the madness . . .

"But I told her the madness was done with," he

whispered, now remembering that as well. "I gave her proof she would believe, although I knew the proof to be false. Belief . . ."

And now her beliefs returned to him, centering about the madness and his love for her. She had believed his love would be no more once the madness was done, and he had attempted to prove otherwise. How had she felt when she realized he had proven nothing, and had even failed to return to speak with her? He ached to imagine her pain then, pain caused by the man who claimed to love her.

"I must find out where she has gone," Tarren said. "She may well have returned to her own world, but first I must be certain she has not been taken captive again. Agnal Topis is no longer a consideration, but there could well be others."

"Perhaps I had best offer my assistance again," Mavial said as his fighters began to prepare to leave. "As it seems likely that I will eventually join your company, I may as well begin working with you now."

"Is that your only intention?" Tarren asked her after a brief hesitation. "My behavior these past days and the time we spent together—you may well have been given a false impression . . ."

"Not at all," the woman replied with a wry smile. "Perhaps you fail to remember, but the one time we shared a bed, we shared no more than a kiss. You fell immediately asleep, and after calling me Wildea. It was impossible to know what drove you to behave as though you had feelings for me, but it was clear you did not. Which bettered the matter in my eyes. It pleases me to see a man remain true to the woman he has pledged his love to."

"Nothing occurred between us that night?" Tarren said with raised brows, and then he laughed. "Of course, I should have known. Never have I been allowed to do more than kiss a female during these instances, and most often I am immediately asleep thereafter—or riding off to battle. I know not why bloody battle is permissible in Wildea's writings while the sharing of love is not, but for the first time I find myself delighted that it is so. At least I shall not have *that* to apologize for as well. Now we must learn where she has gone."

Tarren and his men returned to the palace to begin their search, and Mavial took herself off to speak with certain denizens of the dark side of the city. Happily for Tarren's patience, the prince was seeing no one and attending to nothing but matters of state. Tarren felt pity for the prince, for the man had discovered that the woman he loved did not return that love. In point of fact she had wished to see him dead, a position Tarren himself might well stand in with Wildea. He must find her quickly, else she might never return with him.

Fael and Kergil returned to report that a guardsman on duty at the innermost gate that night recalled seeing a woman ride by. Mavial reappeared with the news that *her* informant was a guard on the outermost gate of the city, and she had learned that Wildea had indeed left the city that night, and alone. Mavial's informant had been puzzled, for it was his habit to attempt to extract an "exit toll" from any comely female alone or nearly so. What puzzled him was that he had not even considered the idea until the woman was long gone, which was not at all like him.

"Either the woman used magic, or the gods watched over the man that night," Kergil observed once Mavial had finished her narrative. "Had he attempted to stop her and demand his 'toll,' she would likely have paid in a manner most painful."

"Or, had I learned of it, *I* would have paid *for* her," Tarren growled, then looked at Kergil again. "You mentioned magic. I had been told she could not *use* magic here, and yet some of the things done by her can be explained in no other way. I hesitate to doubt the word of a wizard like Massaelae, but . . ."

"But there can be no other explanation," Kergil said. "Perhaps she has an ability Massaelae is unfamiliar with, and it was for that reason that he said what he did. In any event our people saw nothing of her, which should not have been possible *without* the use of magic."

"She and I will discuss the matter when I have returned her to where she belongs," Tarren said, glancing around to see if there was anything else he wished to take with him. "The prince, in his gratitude and generosity, has said my company is welcome to rest here until I return. I expect you all to do exactly that, as I ride directly for the wizard's house. I hope to return in no more than three or four days."

"And if you do not?" Fael asked, speaking the question in all their eyes. "What are we to do then?"

"Whatever you wish," Tarren answered, smiling

mirthlessly. "I shall return with Wildea or not return at all. In any event, I wish you all the best to be had."

He took the saddlebags he had packed and strode toward the door. On opening it, he discovered the princess Drinna standing on the other side, poised to knock.

"Oh, Tarren," she said, startled, and smiled at him. "It seemed likely from what you said earlier that you would soon ride after Deanne—Wildea—in an attempt to return her to us. I have therefore come to tell you that my prayers ride with you. You *must* find her, for she loves you very much."

"As I love her," Tarren replied with a gentle smile. "I shall tell her you asked after her."

"Tell her also that the oddest thing has happened," the princess said with pink now tingeing her cheeks. "I was just told that a prince has arrived from one of our neighboring realms, and wishes my brother's assistance in finding the artist who created a number of paintings he recently acquired. He wishes to tell the artist how much he admires his style of art, and that he would like to purchase additional paintings. My brother is not available at this moment so I have been asked to speak to the prince, and . . . I have the strangest feeling . . . I mean, I have not even met the man as yet, and he believes *me* to be a man . . ."

"I take your meaning, and will certainly tell Wildea," Tarren said to end her floundering, privately amused and delighted. He had grown very fond of the princess during his time at the palace and hoped she found a soulmate in the prince she was about to meet, but he had his own affairs to attend to. He bid her farewell and good luck, and was finally on his way.

The journey brought Tarren to the wizard's house in the dark hours of the night, but the sight of a candle's glow in an upper window encouraged him to knock. He thought he would need to camp for the night after all, when the door opened to show Massaelae accompanied by the glow of a small but very bright fire in the palm of his hand.

"This place is far worse by day than it is by night," Tarren said, suddenly afraid to ask of Wildea. "If I have come at an inconvenient time, I will certainly leave and return at your . . . convenience."

"Not at all, my friend, do come in," Massaelae said pleasantly, stepping back to allow Tarren entrance. "And certainly visiting here at night is less difficult, for the illusions are harder to see. You may be interested to know that your young lady came in the daylight, and yet seemed to see nothing of them. She obviously has great potential as well as great beauty and heart."

"She would not, by any chance, still be here?" Tarren asked at once, hope flaring.

Tarren's words broke off at Massaelae's immediate headshake, and then he sighed. It was certainly too much to hope that she would still be in his world, where he might reach her easily. He now must follow her to her own world, and convince her of his love all over again.

"You seem much changed from when you first visited here," Massaelae observed as he led the way to his sitting room, taking in Tarren's clothing and boots, the swordbelt slung about his hips. "Can this be evidence that your great difficulty is no more?"

"I feel certain that it also will never be again," Tarren confirmed, reluctantly going to the chair the wizard indicated. "Wildea was unaware of the madness her writings caused, and now that she has learned the truth I feel certain it will never happen again. Massaelae, she has returned to her world believing a lie, and I cannot allow that to continue. She is the woman meant to be mine, and I must follow her and make her know this."

"I was certain that that was your intention," the wizard replied with a sigh, looking up at him unhappily. "Please sit down and accept refreshment, for there are important matters we need to discuss."

"Please," Tarren said as he took a step after the smaller man, fear chilling his blood again. "You cannot be saying it will be impossible for me to follow her. My life has no meaning or value without her . . ."

"No, no, the matter is not quite *that* serious," Massaelae assured him at once, glancing up from the decanters he had gone to. "But you also cannot leave on the instant, therefore you may as well seat yourself for the time. As soon as we have glasses in hand, I will explain."

Tarren hesitated a moment, but in truth he had no choice. He turned back to the chair and sat, and when Massaelae came to hand him a glass of wine he accepted it gratefully.

"Somehow I feel I will have need of this refreshment," he said after nodding his thanks and taking a bracing sip. "What new disaster has been thrown in my path?"

"I consider it more a matter of awareness than disaster," the wizard said carefully as he seated himself. "The doorway I created for you to use was a drain on my strength, but that was only to be expected. When your young lady arrived and I created the second doorway, I discovered that even more strength was required. The matter piqued my curiosity—and my concern—as I considered it possible that I had *lost* magical strength with the two efforts. Subsequent investigation, however, has proven that this is not so. My magical strength remains at the level which was previously reached."

"And that indicates what?" Tarren asked, faintly alarmed again. He had been told that he *would* be able to follow Wildea, but . . .

"It indicates, in my opinion, that each time a doorway is opened into that other world, the universe about us resists with greater and greater strength," Massaelae said with worry in his expression. "Doorways between worlds are unnatural, you understand, at least doorways created with magic. Nature apparently strives against such efforts, attempting to keep matters as they are by making those efforts impossible. I theorize that very shortly it will be beyond my strength— or anyone's—to open a doorway to that world again."

"But it still remains possible?" Tarren pressed, desperately needing reassurance. "I have not been separated from Wildea forever?"

"This time, no," Massaelae replied, but his expression had not lightened. "I believe I have strength enough to open the doorway one more time, but this must be carefully explained to your young lady. If she accompanies you back here, it must be with the understanding that she will never be able to return. Are you willing to tell her that?"

"I must," Tarren muttered, staring into his wine without seeing it. "Should I bring her back here with less than the full truth, she will likely lose trust in me for all time. That would surely be the end of our love. I will remain there with her if she refuses to return with me."

"You would do such a thing?" the wizard said with surprise. "She spoke to me for a time of what her world contains, and I tell you that even I would be lost among so much strangeness. How you or any other ordinary individual from our world would fare is not to be contemplated without alarm. Perhaps it would be best if you considered your decision again."

"I have no doubt that such reconsideration would be best," Tarren agreed with a rueful smile. "My difficulty lies in the fact that my choice must be the same no matter how often I reconsider it. May we begin once you have finished your wine?"

"The attempt must wait until morning," Massaelae said with a sympathetic shake of his head. "My strength reaches its peak in the mornings, and in any event you appear to be in need of rest yourself. After breakfast we will send you to your lady love, and what occurs beyond that will depend on your powers of persuasion."

"It will depend more, I think, on her willingness to hear me," Tarren said, his sigh deep as he allowed himself to relax back into the chair. "And to forget that the last time we spoke, I allowed her to believe a thing which was not so. In such an instance, men and women are fully alike. To lie once is to say you may well do so again, and who would wish to rely on one who lies?"

Massaelae said words of sympathy and support, but Tarren was too deeply into his thoughts to hear them in detail. The virtues possessed by the "barbarian" Wildea had written of were certainly those virtues the woman considered to be most important, and the barbarian never lied. This, above all other things, twisted Tarren's insides about, but would not keep him from stepping through the doorway. What awaited him on the other side was another matter, but nothing would keep him from stepping through, nothing!

Twenty-two

I got to bed early and slept deeply, rising early the next morning. I had a lot of things to do today, and the first of them was accomplished at my computer. I owed Drinna a thank you for the part she had played in my rescue from Agnal Topis, and I'd thought of something to do. I'd have to be careful, but it just might work.

So I wrote a short little piece about a young, handsome, and available prince from a neighboring realm, who finds out that the artist of the work he's been collecting lives in Kesterlin. He really loves the paintings, so he decides to visit Kesterlin in order to meet the man. He goes to the palace to ask Prince Drant to help him find the artist, but Drant is still too distressed about his wife's treachery to see him. For that reason Drinna is asked to help the visiting prince, and his thinking that she's a man amuses her. When they meet she gets to tell him the truth, and . . .

And that's where I left it. If they found something real to base a relationship on, *they* would take care of getting together; if it didn't work, they would go their own ways. What I'd provided was the opportunity for something to develop. It had come to me that there had to be a solid basis in reality for what I wrote, otherwise it wouldn't have worked. I'd written into enough dead ends—situations that refused to work—to know that.

As soon as I printed out the piece, I went on to my next chore. It was Saturday and rather early, but my lawyer was a morning person and a friend as well as a business associate. I explained what I wanted and why, and he agreed to have the document ready later that morning. He wasn't happy about doing it, but once he understood that I'd made up my mind, he agreed to do as I asked.

What I'd decided to do was go away, to some place I hadn't yet decided on, probably permanently. I'd asked my lawyer Phil to make up a power of attorney in my father's name. My father could maintain my property and possessions or sell them, and do what he pleased with the money. I didn't care about any of it any longer, and didn't want to stay around here and be pestered about any more books. There would *be* no more books, not about anything.

The bathtub felt cramped when I took a bath before dressing, but I knew why that was so I ignored the impression. By then Jessie had arrived and was bustling around the house, and I got dressed and went out to talk to her. I'd included only one set of instructions with the power of attorney, and that set was about her.

"Hi, Dee," she said with a grin when she saw me. "Up early in anticipation of the great Barbecue Day? Since you haven't headed for the hills, I'm assuming you've decided to go."

"Strangely enough, I'm almost looking forward to it," I answered as I poured myself another cup of coffee. "I really do want to see my father and brothers one last time."

"What do you mean, one last time?" she asked with a frown. "Where are they going?"

"Not them, me," I said. "Jessie, I'm leaving tomorrow. I haven't decided where I'm going yet, but I won't be back. Don't worry—I know this is your last semester before graduation, so the paychecks will keep coming. I've arranged them to continue for six months after you graduate. That should give you enough time to find a real job, and if you find one sooner—which you probably will—just tell my father. He'll be handling everything for me."

"Does *he* know that?" she asked, looking stunned. "But of course he doesn't, otherwise he would be here, camped out in the living room."

"Dee—why are you doing this?"

"It's too long a story to go into right now," I answered with a shrug. "Besides, getting tossed into a padded cell would mess up my travel plans. Just believe that I have my reasons, and don't worry about trying to make sense of them. Nothing about *any* of this makes sense, but I really can't stay. I couldn't stand it, walking into my office every day to see nothing but a set of bookshelves . . ."

A set of bookshelves, where a doorway of mist had once appeared. I told Jessie I'd see her later. I agreed that she could help me pack, but only if she promised not to ask any questions.

Jessie wasn't happy about leaving things as they

stood, but I had to be on my way. Phil was waiting with the completed power of attorney, and then it would be time to go to that barbecue. But not to tell my father about the arrangements I'd made. If he knew I intended leaving he *would* camp out in my living room, and there was no need to create complications for myself. I'd written him a letter this morning, and would have Phil give it to him along with the news that I was gone.

I got into my car and pulled out of the garage, then stopped at the end of the drive to wait for a lull in the traffic. It should have felt better to be in an expensive new car than in an old, bouncing wagon or on horseback, but it didn't. I would have preferred the wagon even if it bounced twice as hard, but I wasn't going to be getting it. Instead I'd get to go some place where I could just sit in peace and solitude, making myself forget about Tarren. Although deep down, I knew I'd never forget him.

And that let me smile a little as I turned right out of the driveway.

Tarren watched as the doorway of mist formed again in Massaelae's workshop, but this time the wizard was less—offhand—about the matter. The doorway had formed more slowly, and during the process Massaelae had looked more intense.

"It was a fortunate thing I chose to wait until this morning before attempting that," the wizard said once it was done, sounding somewhat out of breath. "Keeping the portal open is far easier than forming it, but that is *not* to say it is effortless. I will maintain it for as long as possible, but I urge you to all possible haste, Tarren. Your young lady will be somewhere in the vicinity of the doorway, and that is all I can tell you. Save that time runs more swiftly here than in her world, so waste not a single moment of it. Do whatever you must do before the choice is taken from you."

The warnings chilled Tarren, but he nonetheless moved immediately toward the doorway and then stepped through it, expecting to find himself once again in Wildea's workshop. Instead he was outdoors, behind a small metal building of some sort, and a few feet from a thin stand of trees. Despite the odd appearance of the metal building everything seemed normal, and then his attention was taken by what he was able to see past the stand of trees, beyond a high mesh fence that also seemed to be metal . . .

At first Tarren stared, unable to believe his eyes, and then he was appalled. Brightly colored conveyances of some sort raced past on a road the likes of which Tarren had never imagined. Each side of the road was wide enough for ten men at the very least to ride abreast, and on the far side the stream of conveyances sped by in the opposite direction. And there were *people* within the conveyances, people who seemed unconcerned over the breakneck speed at which they were carried along! Tarren had never seen such powerful magic in operation, magic which apparently left a stench behind in the air, thick enough to make breathing difficult.

And then a roaring boom caused him to look up, which sent him into open-mouthed shock a second time. A thing of metal rode the air as if it were a bird, but no bird had ever had the same look. There was also the impression of great size, although in that Tarren was certain he was mistaken. Nothing of great size would be able to ride the *air*, not even *with* the assistance of magic.

Feeling thoroughly shaken, Tarren took his attention from the discoveries he had made. He was there to find Wildea, not indulge in waking nightmares, and Massaelae had said she would be somewhere about. Rounding the metal building allowed Tarren to see some sort of gathering, the people dressed oddly but otherwise appearing normal. They stood at various places beyond the expanse of neatly trimmed grass between him and them, and some reclined in odd-looking furniture. The smoke of a fire arose from another thing of metal, this one having the appearance of a container on legs. There was also the smell of food cooking, and Tarren felt a sudden, intense hunger.

But satisfying hunger was not the reason he had come here, at least not the hunger of his belly. From somewhere came another roaring sound, as though a dragon consumed rock, but Tarren ignored it. Wildea would surely be among the people in the gathering, and he fully intended to find her. As he began to walk, Tarren wondered what would occur once he did find her, but refused to dwell on the question. Anticipating disaster often brought it instead, and there was enough arrayed against him that seeking more would be the actions of a madman . . .

* * *

My father had a really nice day for his barbecue, just as he usually did. As I walked toward the grill where he cooked hot dogs and hamburgers, I smiled and nodded to the people I knew. They were mostly Dad's friends and coworkers, with some of my brothers' friends thrown in. I usually invited friends of my own, but there was no reason for that this time. I didn't expect to stay more than an hour or so.

"I think I've seen everything now," my father said when he turned to discover me, a grin creasing his face. "My baby has actually gotten here before dark. You have no idea how often I wondered whether or not I'd raised a vampire."

"Night people tend to prefer the dark," I countered, actually finding it possible to return his grin. "That's when we come alive. How are you, Daddy?"

"Better now that I'm seeing *you* again," he answered, examining me in a half-approving, half-critical way. "You look as good as ever, but it would have been nice if you'd worn a skirt. A lot of people don't believe you really have legs."

"Talk about your typical male comments," I countered with a snort. "The only woman here in a skirt has to be sixty if she's a day. Her generation grew up in skirts, Daddy, mine didn't."

"Maybe that's what's wrong with your generation," he replied with a wry smile. "Well, since you seem to have come alone, I'm assuming you haven't found anyone to interest you yet. Have you at least been looking?"

"Hmmm," I said. "I considered one guy who came on to me while I was running the other day. He wasn't bad looking and he does live in my neighborhood, but he didn't seem to like the idea of leather and whips."

"Oh, Dee," he said with a sigh. "Why do you have to act this way? What was wrong with the guy that you didn't even give him a chance?"

"Daddy, all he wanted was to get in my bed. You would want that now, would you?" I asked sweetly. "Don't you want me to look for more substance?"

"You're absolutely right," he interrupted hastily, using one eye to take care of a couple of burgers that needed turning. "I *do* want you to look for more, and I trust you to know when that's all the guy is after. I'm proud of you for getting rid of him."

"Thanks," I responded dryly, relieved that my problem with my father would soon be over. I loved him and knew that he loved me, but we would never come around to the same point of view. Even if I *hadn't* intended to go away . . .

"Hey, Dee, I'm glad you made it early," I heard, and then my brother Ben was beside me, his arm around my shoulders. "This is Art, one of the guys I work with, and this, Art, is my gorgeous sister Deanne. Was I lying when I described her?"

"No, you certainly weren't," the man named Art agreed, speaking softly and looking somewhat embarrassed. He was about my height, kind of thin with regular, ordinary features and brown hair and eyes. He looked like the sort of nice, shy man many women were drawn to, a quietly sincere guy who might not even expect a kiss on the first date. "It's nice to meet you, Ms. Lane," he added with a small, kind smile.

"Oh, call her Deanne," Ben told him heartily,

squeezing my shoulders again. "We're among friends, aren't we? Art writes in his spare time, Dee. You two have a lot in common. You said you do essays, didn't you, Art?"

"Ben, may I speak with you privately for a moment?" I said, pulling my brother aside. "If you think I won't make a scene because there are strangers around, guess again," I said through clenched teeth.

"Why do you have to be such a brat?" Ben whispered harshly. "Art is a perfectly nice guy, which you'd find out if you took the trouble to get to know him. Are you going to blow the chance just because *I* introduced you two?"

"That has nothing to do with it and you know it," I countered, beginning to wish I hadn't come to the barbecue after all. "I'm sure Art is a wonderful man. I just don't—"

"Hey, Dee, look who's here," another voice interrupted, this time belonging to my brother Steve. He came up to us with someone who looked vaguely familiar, a dark-haired man who was just as big as my father and brothers. "You remember Mike, don't you?" Steve went on, gesturing toward his companion with a grin. "Mike uses the same gym we do, and he sure remembers *you*. Why don't—"

"No," I interrupted flatly, unable to restrain myself. "Yes, I do remember Mike, and no, I'm not interested. What I'm going to do is get out of here, before Bob and Ronny drag *their* offerings over. You all have a hell of a lot of nerve trying to tell me how to live. Just get out of my way."

"Dee, no one is trying to tell you how to live," my

father objected as my brothers both started their own arguments. "We *care* about you, and we just want to see you happy. That's what the father and brothers of girls *do.*"

"Oh, spare me," I said, finding it impossible to control myself now. "I know you all love me, but you *don't* care. If you did you would never try forcing me into *your* version of what's right. Have I ever asked *any* of you to matchmake? Ever?"

That quieted them for a minute, which should have been long enough to let me walk away. It *would* have been long enough, if Steve's friend Mike hadn't gotten in my way.

"Come on, Deanne, no harm intended," he said, shifting his weight to keep me from passing him. "All women need somebody to look after them, someone big and strong who can't be pushed around. You won't be able to push *me* around, you have my word on that, so what do you say? How about giving it a try?"

"What I say is *no,*" I answered, pronouncing the words slowly and clearly. "I also say you'd better move aside right now, before I prove you very, very wrong."

"Behave yourself, Deanne," my father said, and "Don't start what you can't finish," Steve advised, and "Stop being a dumb brat, Dee," Ben put in, all of them absolutely certain that no girl would ever be able to stand up to a man like Mike. And Mike agreed with them, something his confident stance and cocky smile made clear.

"I don't think I need to worry, Deanne," he said, then reached out a hand and wrapped it around my right arm. "Let's take a little walk to let you cool down, shall we? And then we can decide where we'll go on our first date. How about—"

But that was as far as he got. I'd really had it with all of them, and my patience didn't seem to be what it once was. I got my arm free by using that easiest of hold-breakers, then leaned back and side-kicked Mike right in his well-muscled middle. It was perfectly clear that simply getting his hand off my arm wouldn't have done anything to get him out of my way. His attitude reminded me quite a lot of that fighter back in the other world, the one who had stopped me while I was running, and my reaction was almost automatic. Mike staggered back a step and went to one knee, clutching his stomach, and my male relatives were finally shocked into silence.

"I think I've had enough family fun for the day. I'll be leaving now."

I managed to take one step in my newest effort to get out of there, and then Mike was suddenly in my way again. The grin was now gone from his face, and seething anger had taken its place.

"You had no right to do that to me," he growled, still rubbing his middle. "You made me look like a fool, and *nobody* does that to me."

"You're right," I agreed, already halfway into assuming a fighting stance. "Nobody needs to. You do that perfectly well all by yourself."

"You know what you need?" he snarled. "You need a good beating, babe. And I've a mind to give it to you."

My father and brothers all began to move towards

the confrontation. Mike, obviously a southpaw, started to launch his fist at me, and then—

—and then suddenly out of nowhere an even bigger fist shot out, stopping him in mid-punch. Mike's blow wasn't deflected, it was stopped cold, and everyone including me turned in shock to the giant who'd done it.

"A man who attempts to strike a woman in such a manner is no man at all," Tarren growled, his expression turning Mike pale. "If you seek to fight with someone, bring your fight to *me.*"

Mike was all but trembling as he looked up at Tarren, and I knew just how he felt. Everyone around us was dumbstruck, and then Mike began to shake his head. There was no doubt he rejected Tarren's invitation to a fight, and as soon as Tarren let him go he effected a hurried strategic withdrawal.

"Was he able to harm you, Wildea?" Tarren said, and I turned to face the man I thought I'd never see again. "If he was, I will follow after him and cut his heart out."

"What are you doing here?" I demanded breathlessly, still too numb with shock to know what I was saying. "Why aren't you back where you belong, with—"

"With Mavial?" he asked, speaking the name when I couldn't. "I have no reason to be with Mavial, for even she knows the one to whom my heart belongs. *You* are that one, Wildea, and I have come to ask you to return with me."

Return with him. The shock turned to fear at that, and I couldn't even look into those very blue eyes staring down at me.

"I can't go back there," I whispered miserably. "You may still believe you love me, but once the madness has been over long enough you'll change your mind. Even if it hasn't happened yet I know it *will,* so how can I—"

"Wildea, listen to yourself!" he said harshly, putting a hand under my chin to raise my face to him. "When first you mentioned this, I was to have ceased loving you as soon as the madness was finally done. Now that days have passed and I still feel no differently, you say it will happen *eventually. I* say it will not happen at all, and you simply seek to throw away the life we might have together. I shall not allow that, so if you refuse to return with me, I will remain here with *you."*

"You'd stay *here?"* I echoed, having trouble with what I was hearing. If days had passed, then he should have already forgotten me . . . "But you *know* there's nothing here for you, and you had so many plans. How can you abandon them so casually?"

"What are plans and hopes without the one who makes all effort worthwhile?" he countered. "I would sooner have no life at all, than—" His words broke off as pain flashed across his face.

"Deanna, who is this man?" my father demanded.

"He's the man I love," I answered shortly.

My brothers gasped and Tarren's eyes lit up. "You have admitted for the second time that you love me," he said. "That alone was worth the madness I see all around me here, and should you choose to remain it will make worthwhile my remaining here as well. Is this man your father?" he asked then.

"Yes, I'm her father," my father said when I hesitated. "And these men are her brothers, Ben and Steve. You seem familiar to me for some reason, but I can't remember when we met."

"We have *not* met," Tarren answered. "I am Tarren do Hannin, third son of Duke Samil do Hannin, captain of a large and experienced company, and very much a man of means. I say to you now that I would take · your daughter to wife, and therefore ask your blessing and permission. I will see that she wants for nothing, most especially not love."

"You're actually asking my permission?" my father said, surprised but obviously pleased. "I didn't think young men did that any more, but I have a question. What if I say no?"

Tarren didn't answer him, but he didn't have to answer. My father took one look at those ice-blue eyes, then hastily backtracked.

"I withdraw the question," he said at once, the expressions on my brothers' faces saying they thought that was very wise of him. "Besides, I wouldn't dare say no. If that wasn't the answer my daughter wanted, she might show us again what she learned from all those classes. So what do *you* say, Dee? Are you going to marry the man?"

I hesitated again, trying to decide what to do.

"She hesitates for the reason that she knows not whether she might trust my word," he said, only those eyes showing pain-filled shame. "But listen to your heart and trust I will love you until the end of time, my Wildea."

My father and brothers shuffled around in discomfort behind me, clearing their throats but not finding anything to say.

After looking into his eyes, I realized I did love him. I'd always love him and I would follow him to the end of the world. "I trust you." I admitted.

Tarren himself was all but grinning, and he put a gentle hand to my face. "If that means you have chosen to trust in my love and return with me, I am more delighted than it would be possible to say. But if you have not made the decision yet, take what time you require. Massaelae urged me to hurry before his strength fails and the doorway collapses, but I have been here for less than a quarter of an hour. Surely that will not—"

"Wait a minute," I interrupted, suddenly feeling the ghost of a chill. "Why would you have to hurry? If the doorway happens to collapse, he can just open it again as soon as he's rested."

"Massaelae feels he will never find it possible to open the doorway again," Tarren replied with a headshake. "After this time it will require more strength than he possesses, but as I said there is little to fear. I have been here for only a short time—"

"But, Tarren, the time passes differently here," I interrupted again, now thoroughly frightened. "By now Massaelae's been holding that doorway open for about half a day—if he still *is* holding it open. And I do want to go back with you because I feel at home there, and because it's *your* place."

"Then we had best go at once," he said, his eyes mirroring the worry that must have been in mine. "Say farewell to your father and brothers, my Wildea, but say it *swiftly.*"

He hadn't had to tell me *that* twice, so I turned to my father. Poor Dad was looking as bewildered as my brothers, but he still returned my hug.

"I don't have the time to explain, Daddy, but I love you and the boys and I don't want you to worry about me," I said as quickly as possible. "I'm afraid you won't ever see me again, but you have to believe that I'll be where I want to be, and that I'm happy. Talk to Phil, because everything's been taken care of. Goodbye, Daddy, goodbye, you guys."

My father and brothers tried to stop me and demand explanations, but I took Tarren's hand and let him lead me at a run toward the back of the yard. We were heading for the storage shed that held the lawn mower and other assorted tools, and I couldn't help praying harder than I ever had before. Tarren would hate living in my world and might even end up hating *me,* and that would surely kill me. Adopting *his* world as my own—a world I already felt *was* my own—was a much better idea—if the doorway was still open . . .

I could hear people running and shouting behind us, which made me glad Tarren had left his sword in his own world. An unarmed man, even one Tarren's size, didn't generate the same fear and suspicion that an armed one did. Someone might have had a gun, and if anyone had shot the man I loved—I couldn't think about it, and I couldn't think about the doorway being closed, and I didn't know what we would do if it was—

"By all the gods!" Tarren gasped, then pointed to

a place at the back of the shed. "The doorway should be there, but——"

"It *is* there!" I cut in. "It's hard to see because of the sunlight and shadow, but there's *something* still there. Let's try it *now!*"

Rather than wasting any more time guessing, he squeezed my hand and began to run with me again. The doorway was as faint as dying mist, and seemed to be getting even fainter as we watched. We ran for it with every ounce of speed we had, at the last instant jumping at it——

And landed in Massaelae's workshop together just as the last of the mist completely disappeared. The wizard himself was stretched out unconscious on the floor beside a chair he must have been sitting in, and Tarren and I hurried over to him.

"He's still alive," I said after checking the pulse in the wizard's throat. "Oh, Tarren, if he had died to give us the chance to come back——"

"But he lives, and has also earned our endless gratitude," Tarren said, hugging me briefly before bending to Massaelae. "We must find his bedchamber and place him comfortably in bed, so that he may sleep his weariness away. Another would have let the doorway fail, most especially as he knew not whether we would return."

"You mean you told him you might stay?" I asked, and when he nodded I didn't know *how* to feel. Massaelae could have assumed at any time that Tarren would not be coming back, and if he had we would have been trapped in my world.

I moved ahead of Tarren, checking behind doors on

the floor below while he carried the unconscious wizard. There were a number of bedrooms, but the largest showed personal touches that the others didn't have. It was a safe guess that that one belonged to Massaelae, so I waited outside while Tarren put him to bed. I spent the time touching things, like the hand-carving on the bedroom doors and a small statue on a hall table, just to convince myself that we'd really made it. It had been so *close* . . .

"He sleeps comfortably now," Tarren told me, closing the door behind him as he left the room. "Come downstairs with me, Wildea, for I feel there are things left unsaid between us."

I followed him down to the cozy room with a fire where the wizard and I had talked, and then accepted one of the glasses of wine Tarren poured. He sat in one of the two chairs nearest the fire—which was still crackling merrily—because the house was somewhat on the cool side, then he took me onto his lap so that we could hold each other.

"I still feel a certain reserve within you, my love," he said, holding me with one arm while his other hand held the wine glass. "Tell me what troubles you, and perhaps we will find it possible to see to the matter together."

"I'm still afraid," I admitted, taking a small sip of the wine to fortify me. "I love you so very much, but I'm still afraid that my writing is the reason *you* love *me,* and in a little while the tie will fade. The way that doorway of mist faded, disappearing forever into nothing."

"And yet you returned to my world with me," he

pointed out, pressing his lips briefly to my hair. "If Massaelae was correct, you will never find it possible to go home again. Was this done for *me?*"

"You would have hated my world," I answered with a shrug, resting my head against his shoulder. "It's easier to do without things than to learn a worldful of new ones, and you also would have felt useless. I couldn't let that happen to you, even if the time comes that you do forget about me."

"Why are you so convinced that such a thing will happen?" he asked, and I could hear the restrained annoyance and frustration in his voice. "As I have already pointed out, the madness is now done for good and my feelings remain the same. What leads you to believe that this state will not continue?"

"Unfortunately, there are a couple of things," I responded with a sigh, feeling as if I never wanted to move away from him again. "The first is that name you call me, Wildea. I told you that *I* invented that name, the name of the barbarian's one true love, and even though I never wrote it down anywhere it was still my invention. And then there's the matter of a painting Drinna did as a wedding gift for us. It shows the two of us together, but nothing of a background. She told me she'd *wanted* to do a background, but something wasn't letting her. That has to mean there isn't anywhere the two of us belong *together.*"

"On the face of it, your reasons seem valid," he granted as he reached over to put his wine glass on a nearby table. "I, however, see the first of these matters a bit differently. You cannot deny that I know the feeling of being forced to something by your writings, and I give you my word that there is nothing of the sort connected with the name Wildea. It is *your* name, and another thought occurs to me. As so much of this world appears in your writings, you cannot deny that there has been a link between you and it, bringing you knowledge of it."

"Okay, I can buy that," I granted slowly when he paused to let me answer. "I noticed that I *used* the reality here rather than creating it, but I don't see your point. What has that got to do with the name Wildea?"

"It has this to do with it," he said, using both arms to hold me close. "Wildea is the name of *my* dream beloved, and I believe it came to you *from* me. You admit you have never used it in your writings, therefore my theory is more likely than yours. If you had created the name rather than simply receiving it from me, would you not have used it?"

His question was a good one, and even made sense. I wasn't in the habit of thinking up names for the fun of it, not when each character I wrote about usually had a name of his or her own when I first thought about them. That was one of the harder points to explain to nonwriters, that we don't "think up" names for our characters. Those names come naturally, and we usually have little say over it.

"And as for your second point, I have news that could not have reached you," he went on when I remained silent. "When the madness was over and I began to search for you, I needed to know that you *had* returned to your world and had not simply been kidnapped again. While the others spoke to gate guards and such, I myself went to Drinna. She told me she knew nothing of your whereabouts, then spoke of the painting she had done of us. I paused briefly to see the painting, and she told me how pleased she was to have finally put a background to it."

"What?" I yelped, sitting up straight. "Tarren, are you telling me the truth? What did the background look like?"

"It looked like an expensively appointed room in any large house," he answered, taking my wine glass and placing it beside his. "It was no place I had ever seen before, but somehow it still seemed familiar. As though I *would* know it, at some time in the future. But as I had no knowledge of what rooms in *your* world were like, it could well have represented a place *there*. I knew then that we would be together, but not which world would see it so."

I stared at him silently while I thought furiously, and when the thinking was done, I smiled and put my hands to his face.

"I'm tempted to point out that your objections could be nothing but wishful thinking, but the truth is I don't care. I'm tired of being practical and facing reality, especially a reality that might never come to be. I love you more than life itself, so what have I got to lose by taking a chance? If you ever decide you don't really want me after all, you won't have to ask me to leave. But until that happens I'll be right here, driving you crazy with everything I say and do."

"Then you will be driving me mad forever," he said with a grin, beginning to pull me even closer. "As I will never wish to be rid of you, the time will never end. And it will be a time of joy rather than madness, this I pledge to both of us. I love you, my Wildea, and shall do so till the day I die—and beyond."

We kissed then, frantically trying to make up for all the time we'd lost, and a couple of minutes later we were heading for one of the empty bedrooms on the second floor. I had no reservations left at all, and for the second time was looking forward to making a life in that world. I would marry Tarren and study magic, and anything else that happened would be something we faced together.

As Tarren hurried with Wildea to a place where they might share their love in comfort, he found his peace of mind to be incredibly complete. He and his beloved would marry, and then she would stand beside him while he built a life for them free of want and filled with satisfaction. Tarren could hardly wait to begin, but they must first be certain of Massaelae's well-being before embarking upon their new life together.

And then there would be nothing but love between them, and they need never concern themselves with High Magic again . . .